PROLOGUE
SOUTH CHINA SEA

He is shouting now. Shouting to be heard above the noise of the wind and the hammering of the rain on the tin roof. My name. He is calling my name. Ducking my head, I pull my knees towards me, making myself as small as possible. Why? He cannot see me. No one can. I can ignore him, but he will not give up. He knows I am here, knows that I am trapped as he is trapped, as we all are trapped. He will call my name until I reply and if I do not reply ...

If I do not reply, he will come find me. He will not care about the pitch darkness, the constantly shifting deck, or the risks to himself and others. He will not give up. It is not in his nature. I call out. He does not respond but I know that he has heard me. I peer into the darkness, but it is pointless; I feel my head wrapped in black velvet. I wait, seated, back pushed against the steel wall, knees bent, rubber-soled boots pressed to the floor, hands covering my mouth and nose. The smell is overpowering. At first, it was only the foul air of men living for a week in a confined space, the stink of body odour, rotting food and fumes from the chemical lavatory. Then, it was the stench of sweating men, night clothes soaked, crammed into a steel box. Now, it's the smell of fear, the fear of confined men, praying for a salvation that they suspect may never come.

A movement close to me. A man cries out in pain. Another swears. A hand grips my shoulder. 'Aleksis?'

'Yes.'

I sense him slide down the wall until he is sitting next to me. I cannot see him but am aware of his bulk and the smell of stale whisky.

'Where did they find you?' he asks. It is an odd question, suggesting that he already knows that I wasn't in my cabin.

'On the way to the bridge,' I reply, careful to offer nothing that might fuel his suspicions.

'Why the bridge? You weren't on watch.'

'I couldn't sleep,' I say, knowing that it is a poor excuse.

He doesn't reply but reaches forward to touch my feet, checking to see if I'm wearing boots.

'Where exactly?' he asks.

'Does it matter?'

He doesn't reply and I answer anyway.

'By the entrance to the bridge. At the top of the companionway. I walked straight into them.'

He thought for a moment. 'How many were there?'

'Three. One of them brought me here and there was a fourth man guarding the door to the container.'

'Nationality?'

'I couldn't tell.'

'What language were they speaking?'

'English,' I say, hoping to throw him off the trail. 'Didn't they speak English to you?'

'They did. But it's not their first language. The leader's fluent but he's not English or American.' He paused, deciding whether to share his suspicions with me. 'If I had to guess, I'd say they're Russians or Ukrainians,' he said finally.

The floor moves upwards, slowly at first but gathering speed as it climbs. A sudden halt and for a second, nothing, until my stomach rises as the rest of my body begins to fall. Eyes closed, I try to control my breathing, reminding myself of the laws of physics, of

CONSEQUENTIAL
LOSS

CONSEQUENTIAL LOSS

A THRILLER

Luna de Casanova & Robin Mackie

First published in 2025 by
Luna de Casanova and Robin Mackie,
in partnership with Whitefox Publishing Limited

www.wearewhitefox.com

EU GPSR Authorised Representative
LOGOS EUROPE, 9 rue Nicolas Poussin, 17000, LA ROCHELLE, France
E-mail: Contact@logoseurope.eu

ISBN 978-1-9175237-5-2
Also available as an eBook
ISBN 978-1-9175237-6-9

Edited by Louise Tucker
Designed and typeset by seagulls.net
Cover design by Dominic Forbes
Project management by Whitefox Publishing Limited

In Memoriam
Bill McGhee
1953 - 2020

To Bertie and George
My constant companions in whatever I'm doing
L de C

the tropical storms I have navigated without incident, of the money that awaits me if I can only keep my head. It doesn't work. Why would it? Nothing I have seen from a ship's bridge, or from the comfort of a sunlit shore, could prepare me for this medieval hell.

A sudden lurch. Several men cry out. I push my back flat to the wall, praying that nobody is crazy enough to try to stand. The Captain elbows me in the ribs to get my attention. 'Did you feel that? They've changed course. Either that or the storm's getting worse. What do you think?'

I hesitate, reluctant to speculate when I already know the answer. 'It's the storm,' I say. 'It must be the storm. Why would they change course now? Better to wait until the storm abates.'

'You would think so. But I'm not so sure. These people have a plan and a timetable. I'm sure of it. Otherwise, why wait a week in a stinking container before taking over the ship?' He pauses. 'So, you think there are only four. Only four men to take a ship like this?'

'I didn't say that I thought there were only four. I said that I had only *seen* four. There may be others. I have no idea.'

'Four is not enough. There must be more of them. I was woken by two of them, one of whom was the leader. Was the leader in the group that picked you up?'

'I don't know. How would I tell? They were all dressed the same. Blue boiler suits and black balaclavas.'

'The leader is shorter, stocky, confident. Uses hand signals as if he is military or ex-military. Was he in the group that picked you up?'

'I couldn't tell. What difference does it make?'

'Did they know your name?'

'My name?'

'Did they know who you were?'

'I don't know,' I lie. 'Possibly.'

'You don't seem very sure.'

'It was so quick. It was almost as if they knew I was coming. One minute, I was heading into the bridge. The next, I was being marched across the deck at gunpoint.'

'They knew who you were. They know the names of all the officers and crew.'

'How can you be so sure?'

The older man pauses. 'They knew my wife's name. They knew where we live. They knew the names of my children and where they live. Do I have to spell it out?'

'I'm sorry,' I say, and mean it.

The older man changes tack. 'What do you suppose they'll do with us?'

I wait before answering, choosing my words carefully. 'Let us go as soon as they can. Wait for the storm to die down, load us onto a lifeboat and send us packing.'

'And run the risk that we're picked up almost immediately? I don't think so. Not if they've got any sense and this lot don't look like amateurs to me.'

'But why go to the trouble of keeping us when they already have the ship and cargo?'

'What trouble? What possible threat are we while we're in here? If I was them, I would keep us locked up until they're close to their destination and then let us loose. Anything else would be too risky. No, I think we might be in here for weeks.'

I know he is wrong, but his argument unnerves me. 'I don't think so,' I say. 'The longer they keep us, the greater the chance that we'll be able to recognise them again.'

'How? They're wearing balaclavas now and I don't imagine they're going to take them off when they feed us. Once this is over, we're never going to see them again - and they know it. I would like to think you're right, Aleksis, but I can't see it. They're going to keep us locked up and - if we're really unlucky - make the company pay twice - once for the cargo and once for us. I think we're going to be in this container for a long time.'

There is a sound of machinery from outside, audible only for a moment or two before it is drowned out by the whistling of the wind through the stacked containers. The Captain falls silent and we listen intently. The sound returns, only louder.

'You know what that is?' he asks.

I don't reply. It doesn't make any sense. Nothing makes any sense. The crew is silent. All of them are listening now. Even the most passive understands that something is wrong. The noise grows louder as the operator increases the power. The Captain voices what we are all thinking.

'A crane? In this storm? They're insane. We'll capsize.'

I search for alternative explanations but find none. Infuriated by my naïvety, I grab the Captain by the arm and pull him to his feet. He, in turn, kicks the men next to him. 'Get up,' he shouts. 'Get up, damn you.'

Holding the older man by his sleeve, I stumble towards the door of the container. The noise of the crane is growing louder. All around us, even though I can see nothing, I sense men rising like wraiths from the steel floor. Grabbing the nearest, I drag them towards the doors of the container and try as best I can to move them into position. I lean forward, shoulder against the door, my cheek brushing its cold steel. 'Push,' I shout. 'Push, for fuck's sake.' I feel but cannot see the force increase as more men join. The steel doors shift under our weight but do not buckle. We need more men.

Stretching out my hands into the darkness, I find one man and then another. I drag them into our small group. 'Again. Let's do it again. Come on. Shove.' The impact of the additional men is immediate. The rivets that secure the locking mechanism begin to pop and the doors begin to shift an inch or two. A thump on the roof is ignored. The breaking down of the doors is all that matters. The men at the front, caught between the heavy steel and the combined weight of the others behind them, cry out in pain, their bruised bodies jammed against the doors. More men join, driving forward in blind panic, crushing us against the steel. Any semblance of organisation or rank has disappeared. Any pretence of civilisation has gone. There are only two divisions now – the living and the dying. The newcomers redouble their efforts as the doors begin to creak under the renewed attack. I cannot cheer them on because I cannot breathe. My arms pinned to my side, my ribs buckling under the pressure, I grow faint and know that I will lose consciousness in seconds. If the doors do not break open soon, it will be too late for me and most of the others around me.

I awake, lying prone on the steel floor, confused. I look around in the dark, trying to work out whether we succeeded in breaking out, hoping to catch a glimpse of the deck lights or feel the rain and wind gusting through the fetid container. But I see and feel nothing. Has the ship rolled? I sit up, trying to find my bearings, but am immediately thrown to one side. The engine of the crane, operating outside its tested tolerances, emits a metallic shrieking. The floor is sloping as the container is lifted from the ship's deck and tilts upwards. I try to stand but the angle of the floor makes it impossible. Starting to slide, I spreadeagle myself on my back, my knees bent, my rubber soles flat to the floor, seeking whatever traction I can find. There is none. The pitch increases. I spread my arms wide, looking for a handhold, something, anything, that will slow my descent. I accelerate, slipping helplessly, my nails scratching hopelessly at the steel floor. My feet hit something, somebody, who cries out in pain, releases his grip, and begins to slip away from me, screaming in desperation as he tumbles into the dark. I seize his handhold, a tethering loop welded to the wall, and cling to it with both hands.

A second later, somebody slides into me, but he is smaller and lighter and hasn't the weight to dislodge me. He hangs from one of my upstretched arms as the floor tilts nearer the vertical and I know at once that unless I dislodge him, he will drag me down with him. I try to drive my knees into his chest, but he is too close and realises what I intend. Before I can shift position, the palm of one of his hands catches me under the chin, pushing my head back with such force that my neck must surely break. Holding on with one hand, I push my fingers deep into his eye sockets. He does not cry out or release his grip on my face as if he has determined that we must die together. I find the fingers of the hand that is holding my arm and begin to break them, one by one. When he falls into the void, I feel nothing.

The floor is now vertical, the container slowly spinning. A new sound emerges, a metallic growl, growing louder by the second. The joints of the metal frame are weakening with every turn. Suspended at only one end, and hanging vertically, the container is being torn apart by its own weight. The metallic growl ceases and there is a sense of falling as the container is released. I tighten my grip on the ring, but it is pointless. Ripped from my handhold, I fall through the dark into a writhing knot of bodies, faceless, nameless men expending their remaining strength in a desperate attempt to claw themselves clear. I free my arms, pushing down against the struggling bodies, to drag my legs from this human quicksand. Blood trickles into my eyes, my ribs are cracked, my legs kicked and bruised. A surge of adrenalin and I break free, and crawl through the darkness. The injured men, trapped under a pile of bodies, scream like animals caught in a trap.

I struggle to my feet and find myself in water up to my thighs. It is coming in fast. How long do I have before the container fills? The screams and shouts of the trapped and dying men subside as the water rises. Now, there is only the noise of the wind and the rain. My panic has gone, and I am calm. The water is at my chest. I start to tread water. The container is sinking far faster than it should. It can only mean that the impact has torn holes in the metal skin.

If just one of those holes is large enough to swim through, then I am free. Alone and adrift, but in one of the busiest shipping lanes in the world. I will be lucky to survive but if I do, I will have my revenge on these people, you can count on it. Reaching above me, I touch the steel roof of the container. It's time. There is only enough air left for a couple of attempts at finding the holes. Trying not to think about the dead men beneath me, I fill my lungs and dive into the dark waters.

CHAPTER ONE

When Farquharson arrived, Chadwick knew it was over. They only ever sent Farquharson to funerals.

'Let's take a walk,' said Farquharson. The others started to stand but he shook his head. He held the door open and pointed to the beach. Chadwick fell in beside him.

They walked in silence along the path which led out of the forest and through the dunes. The tide was out and the wet sand seemed to stretch to the horizon. Chadwick followed the sweep of the bay. There was not a soul to be seen. No sign of human activity or habitation. They might have been the last two men on earth.

He had only ever seen Farquharson in the Office, and from a distance. Close up, every part of him seemed oversized. Several inches taller than Chadwick, he was twice as broad. His skin, habitually white, had turned pink in the wind. His eyes, the palest of blues, had shrunk so that they looked too small for his face. His head tilted to one side, as if he had grown weary of supporting its weight. A ring of curly grey hair clung to it like a wreath on the bust of a Roman emperor, who had seen too much and forgotten too little.

He noticed that underneath his waterproof jacket, Farquharson had on the same dark-grey chalk-stripe suit and black semi-brogues he wore in the Office. His shoes and the cuffs of his trousers were soaked but he seemed not to care as he strode towards the approaching tide. The fact that he hadn't changed suggested that his journey was either impromptu or unofficial. Neither conclusion was encouraging.

'Haven't been up here for years,' Farquharson said. 'Doesn't change much, does it? Still looks like it was abandoned a decade ago. Same bloody awful huts. Same rusty wire. Heating still broken?'

'I don't know. I didn't pay too much attention.'

Farquharson stopped and turned. 'Sleeping all right?' he asked. Chadwick shrugged. Farquharson nodded towards the camp. 'These clowns, they treat you okay?'

'How were they supposed to treat me?'

'They ask you anything?'

'No.'

'Tell you anything?'

'Nothing I didn't already know.'

'I wouldn't worry about it,' Farquharson said. 'They don't know much. But they know enough not to ask. That's why they were picked. Careerists have a highly developed sense of survival.'

'So,' Chadwick said, 'who does know?'

'Does it matter?'

'It matters to me.'

'Then it shouldn't.'

Farquharson, his eyes half-closed against the wind, looked at Chadwick for a moment or two as if seeing him for the first time. He was, thought Chadwick, like a buyer at an auction, trying to determine authenticity and price. Eventually, Farquharson turned back towards the sea. 'Forget,' he said. 'That's the best advice I can give you. Forget about all of it. Forget about it, as if it never happened.'

'It's not that easy,' Chadwick replied.

'Then you need to practise. Forgetting's a skill. An important one if you want to survive in this business.'

'If that's all I'm supposed to do, why bring me here? Why not let me do my forgetting on my own time?'

Farquharson ignored him and continued walking. 'Why do you think you're here?' he asked.

'For an inquest. An inquiry into what went wrong.'

Farquharson stopped, surprised. 'An inquest? Why? What would be the point?'

Chadwick hesitated, conscious of Farquharson's scrutiny, as if he had been leading him to this point. He knew better than to reveal his anger, but his weariness got the better of him. 'To stop it happening again.'

Farquharson tugged down the sleeves of his waterproof jacket until only the tops of his fingers were visible. 'But it *will* happen again,' he said. 'You can count on it. It's about the only thing you can count on in this trade. You need to understand. Ours is a business of failures. Of betrayals. Of disappointments. A stream of defeats punctuated by the occasional success so that we can pretend to ourselves – and to our betters – and to a fickle public – that what we're doing is worth the candle. What would be the point of an inquiry? What would it tell us that we don't already know?'

He resumed walking before changing tack. 'Why do *you* want an inquest? You were there. You know what happened and why it happened better than any of us. What would be the point of an inquest? What makes you think this fuck-up was any different from any other? What do you think an inquest will achieve? Exoneration? It won't happen. Nobody's sins are expiated. They just keep accumulating until either you or the Office decides that you've become a professional liability. I thought you would have learned that by now.'

Farquharson emphasised the 'you' and Chadwick hesitated. The discussion was very different from the one he had intended. Farquharson was too well-prepared and too experienced to be pinned down by an angry field agent. Every time Chadwick tried to press his point, there was nothing to press against. It was an odd sensation, like falling from a great height in the dark. He tried again.

'People died,' he said.

Farquharson was unimpressed. His mood had changed, his tone harsher. 'So what? People die every day. With or without our involvement. The Group believed in a different future and tried to make it happen. They failed. Maybe the others that follow will be more successful. Who knows? All I can tell you is that they knew the risks and would have taken them, with or without our funding. Our money didn't change their fate. Sooner or later, they were going to spin the cylinder and come up against a loaded chamber. It was just a matter of time. In this business, it nearly always is. How they died is not your concern. You didn't call time on them. They called it on themselves. Forget about it. It's over.'

Chadwick considered whether he was being provoked into saying too much. Afterwards, once he had replayed the conversation in his head, he wondered instead if Farquharson had been deliberately clumsy as a way of warning him to be careful. 'I know that,' he said. 'I'm not naïve. But in this case, we owed these people, and when they came looking to collect, we weren't there.' Chadwick despised himself for saying 'these people' but he didn't trust himself to say their names, not so soon, and not to Farquharson.

Farquharson said nothing. He was probably waiting for Chadwick to hang himself. They walked in silence while Chadwick tried to gather his thoughts. 'They worked for us,' he said. 'Gave us what we wanted and then we dumped them.'

'Did we?' Farquharson stopped and prodded a half-buried branch with his toecap. 'Aren't you forgetting something? They approached us. We didn't approach them. They knew how it might end. They didn't come because they were our friends. They came because they wanted our help. Our help and our money. And they got both. That was the deal. That was the contract between us. And we honoured it. We gave them what they wanted, and we got what we wanted.'

'And when we got what we wanted, we left.'

'You left,' Farquharson said. 'And you were right to leave. If you had hung around any longer, you would have been rounded up with the rest of them and be in prison or dead. You were lucky. Or smart. Or well informed. Which was it, I wonder?'

'I was lucky,' Chadwick said.

'So it would seem.'

He knows, Chadwick thought. *He knows, but he doesn't want to press it.*

'Tell me, is there anything, anything at all, that might connect you with them?' Farquharson said.

Chadwick shook his head.

Farquharson persevered. 'Are you sure?'

'I'm sure.'

But Farquharson had no intention of letting him off so easily.

'What about Samira?'

'What about her?'

'You didn't get too close?'

'No.'

'You're sure? You spent a lot of time with her.'

'No more than the job required. I was to develop her as a conduit to the rest of the group - or had you forgotten?'

'She was attractive. You wouldn't be the first field officer to succumb to temptation. It's not a crime. It's barely a misdemeanour.'

'Nothing happened between us. Even if I had been interested, she wouldn't have let it happen.'

Farquharson turned. 'You seem very sure of that,' he said, and Chadwick cursed himself for volunteering additional details that Farquharson hadn't asked for.

'I am sure of it,' he replied.

'When did you last see her?'

Chadwick saw now how clever Farquharson had been. Lucky, smart or well informed: Farquharson had offered him three choices but only the last mattered. Farquharson dangled the latter like a piece of bait to see how Chadwick would react. He needed Chadwick to deny that she had warned him to be confident that Chadwick would continue to lie about his relationship with her.

'When I delivered the last payment.'

'And not afterwards?'

'No. Why would I see her afterwards?'

Farquharson didn't reply. He had achieved what he wanted and seemed for a moment or two to have lost interest in the discussion. Finally, he said, 'Good. I'm glad we were able to clear that up.'

There was no longer any pretence that it was a conversation. It was an interrogation. An interrogation designed not to find out what Chadwick knew, but what he might do.

They walked on in silence. Eventually, Chadwick asked, 'What happens next?'

Farquharson stopped, apparently surprised by the question. 'Next? There is no next,' he said. 'I told you. My job is to make this operation disappear. To erase it from institutional memory, as if it never happened.' He pointed towards the Atlantic. 'I'm to take it out there and sink it so deep that nobody will ever find it.'

'Why bother? It seems like a lot of trouble to avoid any embarrassment.'

'Embarrassment? It's not about embarrassment. We can live with embarrassment. But if we are seen to be incompetent, we're finished.'

That's what you've been doing for the last week, Chadwick thought. *Checking file servers and opening personal safes. And now that every piece of paper has been shredded and the last digital fingerprint wiped, you've come to deal with me.*

He felt light-headed. It was like standing outside the headmaster's study, knowing that your fate had already been decided and there would be no court of appeal. He decided not to make it easy for him and changed direction, walking towards the far side of the beach. It took Farquharson a moment or two to catch up with him, and when he did, he placed his huge hand on Chadwick's shoulder. He did it very gently, as if worried that Chadwick might overreact. The two men stopped and faced each other.

Farquharson said, 'Look, I'm sure you're not expecting good news. Which is fine, because I don't have any. My instructions are clear. I'm to clean the house. I'm to make sure that there is nothing left that could connect us with this operation ...'

He paused.

'Or with you.'

Farquharson stopped, waiting for Chadwick to speak. But Chadwick said nothing. There was no point. He might as well let Farquharson finish. Nothing he said now would make any difference to the outcome.

The older man inspected the horizon for a moment or two. Was he steeling himself for the task ahead? It seemed unlikely. Farquharson's career had been built on delivering messages that nobody else wanted to contemplate, let alone deliver.

'You're out,' he said, without looking at Chadwick. 'Your relationship with us is over. When you leave this camp, you're on your own. Completely on your own. If somebody comes looking for you, you'll have to deal with them as best you can. Don't expect us to protect you or even help you. As far as the Office is concerned, you're a leper.'

Farquharson turned towards Chadwick, his eyes as cold as the winter sky. 'It might not be forever. Perhaps one day, we'll come looking for you but, personally, I wouldn't count on it. If I were you, I would forget about the Office, forget about what happened, and go build a life somewhere far away.'

Chadwick grimaced. He had known that he might face a reprimand or even a demotion on his return, but no amount of anticipation could have prepared him for the sense of loss he felt on receiving this news. For all its faults, the Office had been his life for almost a decade.

His shock must have shown, because Farquharson changed tack, moving closer, his large hands thrust deep into the pockets of his waterproof jacket. 'There's more, I'm afraid,' he said. 'The Office doesn't want you back in this country, at least not for a year or two.

Currently, nobody suspects that we had any part in what happened and that's how it must stay. We want you out of here, far away from any prying journalists. You need to keep your head down and out of sight. We'll get you to the Continent, but you need to stay there until we tell you that you can come back.'

'And what if I do come back?' Chadwick asked. 'What will you do then?'

'I wouldn't expect you to be so impetuous but if you insisted on it, you'll wish you had stayed abroad. Is that clear enough?'

'And what am I supposed to tell people?'

'What people? The only people you know are here or in the Middle East and you won't be in either place. Nobody knows that you are back in Europe, and you need to keep it that way. Don't contact anybody. Family, friends, colleagues. No one. And when you're back across the Channel, best stay away from people. Find somewhere to hide out for a while. We don't mind where it is, but we would prefer to see you as far from the madding crowd as you can possibly manage. Seclusion is not only good for the soul, it's sometimes better for your health too.'

Chadwick scarcely registered Farquharson's orders, wondering instead why he hadn't seen this coming, why he had been so sure of an investigation, and whether the Office knew more than it was letting on. He had expected it to be bad, a rebuke, a posting to some backwater, but not this. This was unprecedented.

He turned towards Farquharson and started to speak, but Farquharson cut him off as if he had read his mind. 'No exceptions,' he said, 'Including your parents. As far as everybody is concerned, you're abroad and you're staying there.'

Now that Farquharson had said what he had been told to say, his tone softened. 'A word to the wise. Don't get confused. If you keep your head down, and your mouth shut, you'll be fine. Quite possibly we will come looking for you. But in the meantime, forget about us. Forget about what happened and forget about how unfair it feels. The Office looks after itself. Always has done. That's why it has survived. The Office doesn't do apologies or pardons. If it's absolution you need, you must find a church.'

Farquharson stopped, reached into the pocket of his jacket and pulled out a set of car keys. He held them out for Chadwick to take. Chadwick hesitated.

'Take them. You are not going back to the camp. If you keep walking straight, you'll find a path. Follow it. It leads to a farm road. The car's there. There's a map in the glove compartment. The route's been marked. You need to start now if you're to be there at dusk. It's not much of a boat, but it'll get you there. You need to go tonight, before the weather deteriorates. When you've finished with the boat, get rid of it.'

He handed Chadwick a sealed envelope. 'I'm sorry. There's not much more I can do for you. But this should help a bit.'

Chadwick felt a key inside. 'What is it?'

'Safety deposit box,' Farquharson said. 'Not a pension, exactly, but it'll keep you for a while.' He pulled back his sleeve and checked his watch. 'It's time you were going.'

Farquharson didn't offer his hand. He simply turned, hunched his shoulders against the wind, and started back across the bay. In a few minutes, he was swallowed by the gloom.

When dawn broke the following day, Chadwick, standing thigh-deep in the chilly Northern Irish surf, pointed the small cabin cruiser towards Kintyre, opened its seacocks and watched it disappear beneath the swell. Catching a bus to Belfast and a train to Dublin, he flew to Porto, crossing the border into Spain on foot. From there, he drove to Barcelona and took the ferry to Genoa. Three days after leaving Kintyre, he walked out of a Milan bank with €100,000 in cash and nowhere to go.

CHAPTER TWO

The front room of the café was almost empty. There was only one occupied table. A group of men was seated in a semicircle listening to a large man, who had his back to her. The speaker had reversed his chair and was resting his arms on its back, his legs planted on either side of it. She could tell that several of the men were looking at her, but she avoided eye contact. The large man, irritated at the interruption, stopped talking, but didn't turn. She waited for a waitress while he continued.

'*Every* morning. *Early.* Early for me, *very* early for you. And always, at exactly the same time.'

'Where does he run?'

'The coast path. Always the coast path.'

'But it's been closed for days because of the storms.'

'Maybe it has. But not as far as he's concerned. He ignores the barriers. Just jumps over them. I know. I've watched him doing it.'

'Perhaps he doesn't speak French?'

The large man shook his head. 'No. He speaks excellent French.' He paused. 'But he is not French.'

'Not French. What is he then?'

'I don't know. His French is *too* good. He has no accent and perfect grammar. He speaks it like he was reading the news.'

A waitress appeared in front of her. 'How many?' she asked. The question seemed superfluous, but she answered it anyway.

'One. A table for one.' She paused. 'By the window.'

The waitress shook her head. 'Those tables are reserved,' she said.

She looked around. There was nothing to indicate that the tables were reserved.

'All of them?' she asked.

The older woman looked her over. It wasn't clear if she liked what she saw.

'All of them,' she repeated. 'Follow me.'

She fell in behind the older woman who walked towards the back room of the café. As they passed the table of men, there was a second break in the discussion as they watched her pass. She scarcely registered the hiatus. She was used to it.

In contrast to the front room, the back room was almost full. There was an empty seat at a table of four. The first two chairs were occupied by an elderly couple, the third by an older man. She sat down. The couple ignored her. They had lived too long in a resort to invest time in a stranger. The man looked up from the menu and smiled. She smiled back and looked for the waitress, but she had disappeared. She turned her attention to the man opposite.

He was a grey-haired man in his late fifties or early sixties, smartly dressed, in a sports jacket, twill trousers and tie. His face was angular, with a sharply defined nose and chin, grey hair cut short, and penetrating blue eyes. He appeared embarrassed to have found himself sitting opposite an attractive younger woman. He patted the side pockets of his jacket and retrieved a worn leather case that had seen better days. Placing it on the table in front of him, he opened it slowly as if uncertain about what he might find inside. His spectacles belied the appearance of the case. They were contemporary, with transparent frames, and seemed more suited to a younger man, an architect or a designer. He appeared to sense her surprise, smiled by way of apology, and turned his attention to the menu.

She considered him for a moment. *This is how old age begins*, she thought. Surreptitiously, like ivy at the bottom of a tree. Actions that were once unconscious become mannered, preparation for the day when they will become difficult or impossible. She watched him read the menu, line by line. He must have been a handsome man when he was younger. He still carried himself well. He had his hair, his skin was pink and looked healthy, his clothes old but clean and well cut. He took care in his appearance. She liked that. He looked up – his blue eyes magnified in the lenses of his glasses. For a second, she thought she saw something in his eyes, a sudden hardness, but, when she looked again, it was gone.

He returned to reading the menu and she was surprised to find herself disappointed. She was used to men approaching her. There was a childish inevitability about it which both pleased and irritated her. Now, she was frustrated that he hadn't, despite an obvious opening. Never mind. There was still time. She needed to make friends quickly here if she was to succeed.

The waitress reappeared and took their orders. The man surrendered the menu reluctantly, as if he realised that he had nothing else to divert his attention. He looked around the room with great care as if it was his last visit and he wanted to memorise every detail.

The waitress returned with the orders and left. The man reached for the sugar. He stopped, confused. She held out her spoon. He looked at her outstretched hand and then at her.

'Thank you,' he said.

'I think they need to work on their service,' she said.

He thought about this for a second or two as if she had said something much more profound. He looked at the spoon and began to stir his coffee with the same sense of mechanical perfection he seemed to bring to all his movements. He stopped stirring and watched the coffee until the swirl faded. He looked directly at her, as if her suspicion of his shyness was misplaced.

'They do. Have you not been here before?'

She shook her head.

'It's a strange place,' he continued. 'It has its own rules. Did you see the owner when you came in? Biggish man, long hair, slicked back?'

'Sitting at a table of men?'

'Holding court? That would be him. He only leaves his *Nice-Matin* or his place behind the bar when he has some interesting gossip. Otherwise, he has very little time for his customers.'

'I don't understand why we have to sit in the back room when the front room is empty,' she said.

'It is his way. Everybody sits in the back room until Leclerc decides otherwise. It can be quick or it can take forever. It's up to him. Apparently, it helps if you are female and good-looking.' He stopped and coloured slightly as if he felt he had overstepped some boundary.

She took pity on him. 'Have you lived here a long time?' she asked.

'No. I only just arrived,' he said. 'I came from Paris.' He looked at her and smiled. He seemed to think that this explained everything. She persevered.

'It is early for a holiday.'

He considered this. 'It is. But I am not on holiday.'

'You are working?'

'No.'

'You don't work?' His reluctance to tell her anything was clear and she began to wonder how she would extract herself from what was becoming an awkward and one-sided exchange. He appeared to sense her unease.

'I am retired,' he said. 'I've moved here. I came for the sun and, so far, the weather hasn't been very encouraging. But it will change. It is still winter. And still better than Paris.'

'What was wrong with Paris?'

He grimaced. 'How well do you know Paris?'

'Quite well.'

'Have you lived there?'

'No. But I have been there many times.'

'It is different as a visitor. Different to living there. Living there is more difficult.'

'What is wrong with it?'

He thought for a moment. His eyes fixed on hers. 'Everything, I suppose. I just grew tired of it. As one grows older, one tires of a great many things.' It was the first time he had referred to his age and it made him seem somehow vulnerable. She felt herself relax without knowing why.

'And you? Why are you here?'

His eyes were softer now, kinder, concerned. Let me bathe your cut knee and tie my clean white handkerchief around it. I will look after you. From now on, you'll see that everything will be fine. For a second or two, she allowed herself to wallow in the warmth of his gaze. It seemed a small luxury to allow herself. But she already knew that she was not going to tell him why she was there. Not yet. It was too soon to confide in anybody. She must take her time. She must be careful.

'I came for a break,' she said.

'Will you be here long?'

It was an obvious question, and she was annoyed with herself for not anticipating it.

She stalled. 'I don't know,' she said. 'It depends.'

He waited for her to explain but she said nothing. Eventually, he said, 'So, I am not the only one who is too early for the sun.'

'No.'

'You should have kept flying south. Another two hours and you could have been in Morocco.'

'I am not very interested in the sun. If I was, there are many other places I would choose before Morocco.'

Her voice had an edge to it that she didn't like.

'I am not surprised,' he said. 'North Africa has little to recommend it. Personally, I hate the place.'

'You seem to dislike a great many places.'

He smiled slowly. 'You must think me an old fool. I suppose I am. That is the problem with age. You begin to realise that you have spent too much time with people you don't like in places you detest.'

'Why did you do it then?'

He sat back and considered the question. He shrugged.

'For money. The same reason that everybody does anything. For money. They paid me and I went. And for a while, it was okay but then it wasn't. Like every job.'

The older couple paid their bill and started to get up. She said, 'I must go too. I hope I will see you again.' She signalled the waitress. He shook his head.

'I will get this. It will be my pleasure.'

'You are very kind.' She stood up and she saw that he was admiring her figure. He stood too. He held out his hand.

'Until the next time,' he said.

'Until then,' she said and started to walk towards the entrance to the front room. Before she reached it, she turned as if something had struck her. 'By the way, what did you do in Paris?'

'In Paris? I was a policeman.'

CHAPTER THREE

It is always the same dream. His face burns from the heat of the desert sun that is directly overhead. He walks towards the edge of the flat roof and leans over the waist-high wall. Below him is the market square: in the distance, her apartment building. She appears below him but does not see him. She is moving away from him, heading for home and safety, picking her way through the crowded aisles of the market as best she can.

She walks fast without checking behind her and, as always, he grows anxious. Reaching the end of the stalls, she starts to cross the road in front of her building. *If it is going to happen, then it will be now*, he thinks. *They will have no better opportunity*. He looks to his left and right but can see nothing unusual. Halfway across the street, she stops to allow several cars to pass. He feels nauseous. *Keep moving, keep moving*. There is a break in the traffic and she walks into the building.

She is behind schedule but has enough time if she hurries. One to two minutes waiting for the lift. One minute to reach the seventh floor. One minute in the apartment. One to two minutes to get out. Maximum six minutes. He checks his watch. One minute has already passed since she went inside. He notices that his hands are shaking and grips the top of the wall as if he was about to climb over it.

He hears them before he sees them. The repeated bursts on the car horn rise above the cacophony of sounds that dominate the market square. Below him, people turn to find the source of the noise. A merchant is dismantling his stall and blocking the street.

The driver leans out of his window and shouts at the stall holder, who ignores him. The back doors of the car open and two men get out. The first man puts one hand on the merchant's shoulder and pulls him around so that he is facing him. With his other hand, he holds up an identification card. It is impossible to hear what he says but the expression on the stall holder's face changes. He shouts to a co-worker and together, they start to drag the partially disassembled stall from the street. The car noses past but makes slow progress along the crowded street.

You have just enough time, he thinks, *if you get out now. Their view of the door to the building is still blocked by the market. If you get out now, you can be gone before they arrive.* He checks his watch. Six minutes is up. He scans the entrance of the apartment building but there is no one there.

Where are you? You need to get out now. His heart is racing but he can do nothing. He can only watch. The car draws up in front of the building, three men get out, and start to run towards the entrance. He surveys the sixth floor and sees a movement behind the windows. The door to the balcony opens. She comes out and he sees who is with her. He shouts although he knows she cannot hear him. Light-headed, he leans out further and falls …

Chadwick opened his eyes. The room was pitch-black and cold compared to the warmth of the bed. He lay still for a moment or two, listening to the sea and the sound of the rain clattering against the windows. He decided to get up and go running. He had no idea what time it was. Not that it made any difference since time had long since lost any meaning.

He crossed the small park in front of the casino. The police had placed barriers across the entrance to the coast path and made a half-hearted effort to bind them together with red and white tape. A sign warned of the dangers of a *coup de mer*. He vaulted the barrier and ran past a pink house clinging to the coast like a wedding cake left in the rain. It was closed for the winter, its small stone dock deserted, its lanterns covered, its shutters and doors sealed against the relentless pounding of the sea.

St Jean was in darkness, the boats rigged for winter, wrapped in tarpaulins, their hatches padlocked. He passed through it like a ghost. He had a choice of routes. He could bypass the cape and head directly for the lighthouse. The concrete pathway, flat and protected by a broad strip of rocks that held the sea at bay, was the safer option. He might be soaked by the spray but was unlikely to be knocked over and dragged into the sea. The path around the cape was a different prospect. It was scarcely a path at all. On one side, it was hedged by a high stone wall that was designed to deter the sea and intruders in equal measure. On the other, there was a drop to the rocks below. The path was narrow, constructed of large stones set in cement, and in poor repair. At its low points, it lay just above the high-water mark, too exposed to be properly maintained.

He headed towards the cape and the path deteriorated almost immediately, with ankle-deep holes where large stones had been dislodged. In other places, the cement at the edge of the path had broken off and fallen into the sea. He slowed, picking his way carefully, keeping a wary eye on the sea. Stopping to watch a wave sweep over the bottom of a dip in the path, he waited for the next wave to strike before he set off, hitting the lowest point just as the last of the sea water was draining from the path.

He made the point of the cape easily and grew more confident. He sensed the wind changing direction as he reached the point but thought little of it. It was only when he was knee-deep in water that he realised the danger. Looking right, he saw a wave almost upon him, and accelerated. But he was too late. The wave caught him just below his waist, lifting him off his feet, and flinging him at the wall. Winded, he fell and felt the retreating wave drag him towards the edge of the path and sea below. Arms and legs outstretched, he scrabbled for a hand or foothold, any small gap in the cement, which would allow him the few seconds he needed to allow the torrent of water to subside. There was nothing. First one, and then the other foot, slipped off the path and hung in the air. Just as he was bracing for a fall onto the rocks, the fingers of his left hand found a hard edge and fastened to it. He held himself for a moment or two as the water flowed over him. As it began to ease, he pulled himself back onto the path, checked the sea and ran up the short incline. He stopped at the top, turned to look back, and saw immediately what he had overlooked. On this side of the cape, the waves moved in a different pattern, occasionally combining to create a larger wave. It was one of these that had knocked him over. He should have paid more attention to the wind.

He crossed the small cast-iron bridge that connected the path to the stony beach and came down the steps by the side of the wooden café. The café looked derelict in the grey light. Its windows were boarded-up and its green-and-white paint was peeling. It reminded him of a cricket pavilion that had long since fallen out of use. In front of it, a worn strip of rope matting, intended to help the café's customers traverse the heavily pebbled beach, lay sodden and rotting.

A man was sitting on the bench which ran the length of the café's verandah. He had grey hair, closely cut, and was wearing a long, green coat. His trousers were neatly folded into a pair of boots. He was looking at Chadwick.

Chadwick remembered what Farquharson had told him, that one day, they might come for him. He jogged towards the café and stopped just short of the verandah. The man stood up and came towards him. He leaned on the balustrade. His face was lined from the sun, and he had very blue eyes.

'Not a very good day for running,' he said.

'Perhaps not,' said Chadwick. 'What's your excuse for being out so early?'

The man thought for a moment or two. 'I couldn't sleep,' he said.

'Perhaps you have a guilty conscience?' said Chadwick. It sounded more aggressive than he intended.

The man considered this for a moment or two. 'Or no conscience at all. Sometimes, it's hard to tell the difference.'

Chadwick examined him more closely. He was in his late fifties or early sixties. He carried himself well and looked fit for his age. Chadwick glanced down at the boots. They were old but had been well maintained by a man who knew the importance of a good pair of boots.

The man changed tack. 'I'm surprised you made it around the cape. It's a big sea.'

Chadwick wondered whether he had seen him fall.

'It had its moments,' he said. The man nodded.

'Are you a local?' asked Chadwick.

'I am now, I suppose. Moved here. A couple of weeks ago. From Paris.'

'For the weather?'

The man smiled. 'I should ask for my money back. And you?'

'I came for a break.'

'A holiday?'

'Something like that.'

The man picked up on Chadwick's reticence. He looked at his watch. 'Time for my breakfast,' he said.

'You might have to wait awhile,' said Chadwick, pointing towards the shuttered café.

The man smiled. 'Not here. At the Sebastopol. Always at the Sebastopol. It opens early,' he added, by way of explanation. 'Do you know the Sebastopol?' he asked. Chadwick shook his head. 'You should try it.'

Chadwick was about to explain that he didn't go out but thought better of it. 'I'll think about it,' he said.

The man straightened. 'Until then,' he said, and returned to his bench. Chadwick turned and ran towards the stairs leading to the road.

CHAPTER FOUR

Chadwick conceded defeat, closed his book, and examined the three people at the next table. There were two girls, almost certainly sisters, and a tall, thin boy. All were in their early twenties. He looked around the terrace of the Nice café. The only other occupants were an American family wearing matching rain jackets.

'Does anybody work here, or have they all drowned?' asked the elder of the two girls. 'Johnny, please go find somebody who might, just might, be persuaded to bring us a coffee.' Johnny, his face flushed with annoyance, unwound his long legs and stood. The elder girl pointed towards the space heaters. 'And ask them to turn those on too. I don't want to get hypothermia.'

Johnny disappeared inside the café.

'Sylvia, what are you going to do about him?'

Sylvia looked at her sister and shrugged.

'Give him away, I suppose. It's all been a huge mistake. I should never have invited him.'

Sylvia reached below the table for her handbag and placed it on the table. She began to rummage in it, eventually pulling out a packet of cigarettes. It was empty. Her sister pulled a packet from her jacket pocket and offered her one. Sylvia accepted a light and turned her chair to get a better view of the port.

The weather was improving. On the far side of the road that separated the café from the port basin, there was a row of large motor yachts, moored side by side, their sterns abutting the port wall. Most remained closed, but others showed signs of life. Young deckhands, tanned from the Caribbean winter, began to swab the decks and clean the windows, confident that the rain had passed. The little sun that made its way through the shifting clouds was sufficient to encourage small groups to walk the quayside, inspecting and comparing the different boats. Scooters reappeared, weaving through the late-afternoon traffic, their exhaust leaving a smell of petrol hanging over the street. Johnny returned with a waiter in tow.

'Finally,' said Sylvia. 'I thought you had run away.'

'I thought about it.'

'I doubt it. Where would you find another one like me?'

Johnny ignored her. 'What would you like? He is waiting.'

'Isn't that his job description? Or doesn't that apply in France?'

The waiter stood impassively while Sylvia ordered. Johnny sat down at the table morosely, his chair turned slightly outwards, one leg crossed over the other. Sylvia ignored him and spoke only to her sister. Johnny turned his attention to the boats and began to review them, trying to decide on a favourite.

Chadwick returned to his book, but his interest had waned. The American family had gone, leaving only Chadwick and the English group. He watched Sylvia talk to her sister. She was trouble, he thought. Johnny would learn the hard way. He examined the younger woman but learned nothing. Nobody paid him any attention.

He heard a rapid beeping and looked towards the knots of people gathered around the yachts. He watched as several onlookers jumped clear of a speeding scooter which carved its way through the crowd and accelerated as it found open space. It raced down the street towards the café. He saw what was going to happen and knew that he could prevent it. All it needed was for him to take several strides towards the English group and take the handbag from the table. Then it would have been over before it had even begun. But he didn't take the several strides. He didn't move. He didn't do anything except tell himself not to get involved.

The scooter drove along the side of the terrace. It slowed as it approached Sylvia and her sister. Johnny, slow to realise the danger, was halfway out of his chair when the driver's foot caught him in the ribs. Falling backwards, he lay helpless as the pillion passenger grabbed the handbag from the table. It was over in an instant.

Chadwick watched the thieves accelerate down the street. The scooter was almost out of sight when he noticed somebody running towards it. At first, it looked as if the scooter would hit him but, at the last second, it slowed, and the pedestrian grabbed the handbag from the pillion passenger. The scooter skidded, its rear wheel slipping to one side, almost tipping the riders into the street. Both the driver and the passenger turned their helmeted heads towards the third man. *Now we will have a fight,* thought Chadwick. But the robbers didn't move, perhaps realising that additional passers-by would be sure to intervene. The driver opened the throttle and the scooter disappeared into the afternoon traffic.

Chadwick looked over at Johnny, who was still on the ground, his right arm wrapped across his body, his face white. He walked over and knelt beside him.

'Ribs?' asked Chadwick.

Johnny tried to sit but the pain sent him back onto one of his elbows. 'Yes,' he said.

Chadwick got behind him and gripped him under the arms. 'Let's get you up,' he said.

'I am not sure. It hurts like hell.'

'It will. But you'll feel better sitting in a chair.'

Sylvia moved next to the unlucky Johnny. 'He's hurt,' she said. 'I don't think you should move him until a doctor looks at him.'

'Don't you?' said Chadwick.

'He could be seriously injured. He shouldn't be moved at all. Darling, you must stay still until we find you a doctor.'

'He's been kicked in the ribs. The only thing that has been hurt is his pride.'

'How can you say that? Look at him. He can hardly move.'

'It was a nasty kick, but it isn't going to kill him. He probably has a couple of cracked ribs.'

'You're a doctor, are you?' she said.

By this time, several of the staff had appeared from the restaurant. They stood quietly, watching the argument between Chadwick and the English girl, glad of a break in the afternoon routine.

Chadwick tried again. 'Are you ready to move?' he asked Johnny.

Johnny looked at his girlfriend, hoping that she would acquiesce. She didn't.

'Johnny, stay where you are.' She turned towards Chadwick. 'You are *not* to move him.'

Chadwick released his grip on Johnny and stood up. 'Well, Johnny, I wish you luck. You'll need it.'

'What do you mean by that?' Sylvia's cheeks had coloured, but her voice was calm. *You are used to this*, he thought. *Used to bullying people into submission.*

For a moment, he thought she might strike him but before she could move, her sister grabbed her arm and said, 'Sylvia, your bag.'

They all turned to look. Standing on the road, next to the restaurant's terrace, was a man holding Sylvia's handbag. He was in his mid-twenties, his black hair heavily gelled and brushed back so that it swept over his head like a breaking wave. Dark-skinned even for the South of France, his eyes were deep-set and sleepy, his lips too full for his face. He wore an expensive black leather jacket and a well-ironed pair of jeans.

Fixing his attention on Sylvia, he said, 'Your bag,' and held it aloft like a sporting trophy. 'I got it back for you,' he said, offering her the bag.

Sylvia took it with a smile. 'Thank you *so, so* much,' she said. 'I thought I had lost it for good. If it hadn't been for *you*, I would have done.'

The newcomer returned her smile. His teeth were white and even. 'I was lucky this time,' he said. 'It often happens here. You must be more careful.'

Sylvia took hold of his arm and pulled him towards the table. She had lost all interest in the others. 'Come and join us.'

The man continued to smile. 'It would be my pleasure,' he said. 'I am Adil.' He sat and seemed to notice Johnny for the first time. 'Is he badly hurt?' he asked.

'No, he's fine,' said Sylvia, and sat next to Adil. Her sister, unsure of what to do next, sat opposite her.

Chadwick bent down behind Johnny, and said, 'One, two, three, *up.*' Johnny moaned as he came upright and pressed his right hand against his ribcage. He looked gloomily at Adil and Sylvia, both of whom ignored him, as he settled in the last of the chairs, next to Sylvia's sister. By this time, the manager and the staff had dispersed, leaving only the original waiter standing as impassively as ever. 'Is Monsieur joining?' he asked.

'No, Monsieur is not,' said Sylvia, giving the man a thin smile. 'Monsieur is not with us.'

Chadwick looked at her, his face expressionless. It had been a mistake. He should have known better than get involved. He shifted his gaze to Adil, who looked through him as if he didn't exist. He had seen that look before and it made him uneasy. He made his way back to his table. The waiter followed him, waiting until he sat down.

'Does Monsieur want anything else?'

'No, just the bill. Tell me, is bag-snatching a problem here?'

'Here? In Nice? Or here, here?'

'Both.'

'There are always some thefts, sometimes from scooters, but not usually so early in the season. It is normally the Romanians, but they don't usually arrive till June.'

'Have you ever had a bag-snatching in this restaurant?'

'No. Not while I have been here, and I have been here very many years.'

Chadwick handed him a €20 note. It was too much but Chadwick waved away the change.

'And have you ever heard of somebody grabbing a bag back from a scooter after it was stolen?'

The waiter gave him an old-fashioned look. 'No. But then there is always a first time, no?'

'Is that what you think?'

The waiter raised his eyebrows but said nothing.

'And our young hero, have you seen him before?'

'No, Monsieur, he is new to me. He is not from here. Of that, I am sure.'

'Not French?'

'No. Moroccan or Algerian. But not *French*.'

'Still, lucky he was around at *just* the right time and in *just* the right place.'

The waiter smiled. 'We should give thanks,' he said sarcastically, 'for your friends' good luck.'

'We should but I am afraid my friends' good luck may be about to change.'

CHAPTER FIVE

The rain was getting worse. Seeking shelter, Chadwick stepped under the awning of a café and stood for a moment watching the weight of rainwater on the canvas increase until it fell like a waterfall on the pavement below. On either side of him were piles of folded tables and chairs secured by a chain. He tried to look through the café window, but the combination of condensation and grime made it impossible. He hesitated. Should he go in? His last attempt at going out hadn't ended well. But that was in Nice, and this was a lot closer to home. He looked at the sky. The rain was falling in sheets. If he walked back to the hotel, he would be drenched in seconds.

'I see you have decided to try the Sebastopol.'

He turned. The grey-haired man from the beach was standing behind him, wearing the same long, green riding coat. His hair was wet, his face pink from the cold rain, his eyes the same penetrating blue.

'I'll try anything once,' said Chadwick.

'Good. Then we'll have breakfast together.' It was a statement, not a question.

Chadwick pushed open the door and went inside. He was about to sit at a table when the older man took him by the arm.

'This is not for us,' he said. 'We are relegated to the back room.'

'Why?'

The man shrugged. 'Who knows? It is one of the owner's little foibles. Nobody is allowed a table in the front room until he decides that they can have one. But don't worry, the back room is fine.'

They found a table for four, and sat down, side by side, facing the door, their backs against the wall. A waitress came and they ordered. The grey-haired man took a newspaper from his coat pocket. Chadwick noticed that it was a local newspaper, several days old.

'Isn't your paper a bit out of date?'

The grey-haired man turned towards him.

'I'm not sure it matters. There is not much news here. I would lend it to you, but I don't think you'll find it very interesting. I've read it twice. I can tell you everything from the finalists in the local schools' football league to the price of a plumber. I can also point you towards several escort services, a tattooing parlour and a fortune teller.'

'It's hard to know where to start. I didn't know the town had so many attractions.'

The older man offered it to Chadwick. 'Would you like it?'

'Not right now. I am not sure I'm ready to have my fortune told.'

'Really? You should try it. I thought you said that you would try anything once.'

'Perhaps not the tattooing parlour.'

'Why not?'

The older man stretched out his left arm, the palm of his hand facing upwards, and with his right hand, he pulled back his jacket and shirt sleeves. Just above the wrist was a faded blue symbol that Chadwick thought he recognised as the sign of the French airborne division.

'That wasn't done yesterday.'

'No, it wasn't. It was done a very long time ago. But I won't be getting another one. I'm too old for tattoos. Tattoos are for the young.'

Chadwick turned to get a better look at his neighbour. It was difficult as they were sitting shoulder to shoulder. At first glance, there was little to distinguish him from the other occupants of the back room. He sat erect, his back against the wall, his head inclined slightly towards Chadwick, a minor blemish in an otherwise perfect posture. His hair was thick, and he wore a dark-green tweed sports jacket, a blue shirt and a tightly knotted tie. The clothes were of a good quality and had been well maintained. The man's hands were clasped together on the table. They were strong but beginning to show signs of age. Chadwick noticed that one of the buttons on the sleeve of the jacket was slightly out of line with the others and knew immediately that the man had done the repair himself. The stranger gave a half-smile. He seemed to know that he was being inspected.

'Why did you leave Paris?'

The grey-haired man hesitated. Perhaps he had forgotten telling Chadwick where he was from or was surprised by the directness of the question.

'I decided to retire in the South. I thought it would be better to grow old in the sun. But so far, I have seen very little sun and a great deal of rain. And you, how did you end up here?'

The question fell awkwardly between them, and the older man changed tack. 'I am sorry. It is none of my business. I live alone and when one lives alone, one becomes insensitive. Forgive me.'

Chadwick, annoyed at himself for overreacting and making the question seem more important than it was, said, 'I needed to get away. To somewhere quiet. For a break. I thought this place would be quiet out of season. So, I came here.'

He stopped, afraid that he might say too much. They fell into silence. The older man extended his hand and said, 'Charles Verlaine.'

Chadwick shook his hand. 'Chadwick,' he said.

'Will you stay long?' asked Verlaine.

Chadwick, surprised at the question, tried not to show it. He said, 'I have no idea. I don't think I've ever thought about it.'

Verlaine was silent. Chadwick turned towards him and saw that he was looking towards the entrance to the back room. He was not alone. Most of the people in the room were looking in the same direction. She wore a long, white raincoat that she was unbuttoning as she crossed the floor. As it opened, it revealed the boots, the tight, black leather leggings and the black sweater she wore underneath. Chadwick felt a sense of guilt sweep over him as if he had seen something he shouldn't. He tried to avoid her eye, but she was looking straight at him. She walked towards the table, shaking the water from her raincoat until, at the last moment, she veered to her left, and stood opposite Verlaine.

'Hello,' she said. 'May I join you?'

Verlaine stood up. 'I would be delighted.' He gestured towards the empty chair. She leaned forward and kissed him on both cheeks. He remembered Chadwick and turned towards him. He was about to introduce the newcomer when it became clear that he didn't know her name. Embarrassed, he reversed the process.

'This is Mr Chadwick,' he said. Chadwick tried to push the table away but the chair opposite him caught on the floor and began to tilt. He stopped pushing and tried to stand. It was impossible. He slid back into his seat, feeling foolish.

The woman seemed amused by his clumsiness. 'Hello,' she said, 'I'm Julija,' and sat down opposite Verlaine.

'What would you like, Julija?' said Verlaine, one arm held high above his head to attract a waitress. *Like a drowning man*, thought Chadwick.

'A café crème.'

The waitress took the order and disappeared. The woman waited for Verlaine to speak.

'This is unexpected,' he said. 'I didn't think I would see you again so soon. You surely aren't here for the food or the service.'

She began to pull off her black gloves. 'I came back for the company,' she said.

Verlaine smiled with pleasure and seemed suddenly younger. 'You are too kind,' he said. 'You flatter me. Not that I mind. At my advancing age, every compliment is gratefully received. Did you get very wet in the rain?'

'Yes, but it doesn't matter. It rains a lot at home, so I am used to it.'

'Where is home?' asked Chadwick.

She turned to look at him. Her blonde hair was swept back from her face in a ponytail. He noticed that she had beautiful skin. Her eyes were green. She held his gaze.

'Latvia. I am from Latvia,' she said, repeating the words as if she could not quite believe them herself.

'I have never been,' said Chadwick.

'You should go. But go in the summer. The summer is much better than the winter. I would not go in winter. The winters are very wet. Have you been?' She directed the question to Verlaine.

'Yes. A long time ago, mind you, but I have been.'

'Summer or winter?' asked Chadwick.

'Winter. I remember that it seemed to be dark all the time. Dark and cold. With snow. A lot of snow.'

'What were you doing there?' asked Julija.

Verlaine thought for a moment. 'Waiting.'

'Waiting?' said Julija

'Waiting.'

'And was it worth it?' asked Chadwick.

Verlaine shook his head. 'No. No, it certainly wasn't. I spent a week waiting for somebody who never came.'

'Who were you waiting for?' asked Julija.

Verlaine shrugged. 'Who knows? Somebody who was important at the time and now isn't important at all. A nobody. More wasted time.'

'Was it police work?' asked Julija.

'I suppose so,' he said. 'I can't think why else I would have been there.'

Interesting, thought Chadwick. *I wouldn't have guessed you were a policeman. Ex-military, yes, but not a policeman.* He made a note to ask

Verlaine about it another time. He watched as Julija continued to question Verlaine. He wanted to ask her why she had left Latvia and come here but thought better of it. Partly, because it was none of his business, and partly, because she would undoubtedly have asked him the same question. *Forget about her,* he thought. *Go back to the hotel.*

'Were you waiting for him or looking for him?' asked Julija.

Verlaine thought about her question for a moment or two. 'Who knows? As I said, it was a long time ago, and he never turned up. That's all I *can* remember,' said Verlaine without conviction.

'At least you got to see the sights,' said Chadwick.

Before Verlaine could reply, Julija said, 'There are no sights. No sights worth seeing. Two weeks in Riga is like two months anywhere else. Riga's visitors come for two things: cheap alcohol and strip clubs.'

'You don't sound very patriotic,' said Chadwick.

She seemed surprised by his remark, unsure about its intent, and coloured slightly. 'I love Latvia, but I love the old Latvia,' she said. 'I liked it the way it was. I don't like what it has become.'

'You preferred the Russians?' asked Verlaine.

'Of course. Who wouldn't prefer the Russians to what we have now: a sleazy playground for any idiot with enough money for a cheap airfare and a weekend of drinking.'

Verlaine smiled as if to warn that he was teasing, 'And the Russians didn't drink?'

'Yes, of course. The Russians *always* drink. But they wouldn't have tolerated what the city has become. They wouldn't have allowed it to become so sleazy.'

'I visited Russia several times before the Wall came down,' said Verlaine, 'And you're right - it wasn't sleazy. Grim, depressing and bureaucratic - but not sleazy.'

'Another useless wait?' asked Chadwick, intrigued by Verlaine's past, and wondering why a French policeman would have been the wrong side of the Iron Curtain.

Verlaine seemed to sense that he had said too much. He shrugged. 'Maybe. You must think me very dull. Travelling around waiting for people.'

'Not at all. I like that you wait for people. Perhaps you will do the same for me?'

'You are leaving?' asked Julija.

Chadwick watched her carefully but didn't learn anything.

'I am.'

'You should stay. Or perhaps you don't like people who like the Russians?'

Chadwick held her cool gaze. For a moment or two, he regretted his decision to return to the hotel. But he needed to be disciplined. It would be better in the long run.

'I have nothing against the Russians, or the people who like them,' he said. 'But I have to go.'

Verlaine considered him for a moment and turned towards Julija.

'You know, my dear, I have always been jealous of the British. We French want to charm but we try too hard. We want to be Laurence Olivier and end up as Maurice Chevalier. You need to be careful. The British have a natural charm that makes you want to forgive them everything. That is why they are so dangerous.'

Chadwick smiled. 'I must leave this master class on cultural archetypes', he explained, 'before he has more fun at my expense. But I am sure I will see you again. Will you be here for long?'

She took a second or two to answer. 'I don't know. It depends.'

Chadwick slid out from behind the table. He considered for a moment asking what it depended upon but thought better of it. Seconds later, they heard the door open and then close.

CHAPTER SIX

It's always the same, thought Chadwick. *The most dangerous lies are the ones you tell yourself. You saw her and followed her because she's attractive. That's all. There was no other reason. Don't pretend. Just accept it.*

He watched as she climbed the steps of the casino and went inside. He was loath to follow her through the main entrance. If she was still in the lobby, it would be clear that he had been tailing her. Walking around the building, he came to a second set of steps, partially hidden by the green shrubbery that ringed the casino. At the top of the steps was a pair of doors, each one an ornate patchwork of individual panes of glass, a reminder of the casino's late-nineteenth-century roots.

He climbed the steps and looked inside. He could see a corridor, its walls draped in dark-green fabric, the floor covered with an ornate burgundy and gold carpet. There was no indication that it was an entrance of any kind. It was more likely a fire escape. He was about to give up when a woman appeared, carrying a tray with a bottle of champagne in a bucket of ice. Tapping lightly on the window, she saw him and smiled. He gestured towards the door, but she shook her head. He shrugged, his hands raised in front of him as if to ask why. She smiled again and put down the tray.

She was attractive, a slim brunette who wouldn't see thirty again but looked like she had the good sense not to care. She put her hands on her hips and cocked her head to one side as if gently admonishing him. He tried again, simulating the turning of a handle. She signalled him to wait and disappeared down the corridor. Reappearing almost immediately, she inserted a card into a box on one side of the glass door. Satisfied, she reached for the handle of the door and pulled it open.

'Be quick,' she said. He stepped inside while she closed the door, removed the card from the box, and tucked it into a pocket on the front of her uniform.

'That was exciting,' he said.

'If you had taken much longer, it would have been more exciting.'

'Why?'

'Security don't like this door being opened. The rules say that everybody must enter and exit via the main entrance.'

'But you don't agree with the rules?'

'Not always - and anyway, this door is always being used - they just pretend it's not.'

'Why pretend?'

She looked at him suspiciously, 'You ask a lot of questions,' she said.

'I do. Is that bad?'

'Sometimes.' She gestured towards the ceiling and the corridor. 'What do you see?'

He looked carefully. 'No cameras,' he said.

'Smart boy. Maybe I should have left you outside.'

She picked up the tray, handed it to him and slipped her arm through his. He could feel the warmth of her body through her thin uniform. She smelled clean, as if she had just come out of the shower.

'Do you always make others do your work?'

She ignored him and he tried again. 'What's your name?'

'Pay attention.'

She stopped just before the end of the corridor in front of a door on the right. He watched her as she typed 1789 into a keypad. The door opened, and they found themselves at the top of a set of concrete steps that led into a workroom. The lighting was harsh and fluorescent, the walls painted a dull grey. On three sides of the room were rows of similarly grey metal cabinets. The fourth wall had a work bench with a vice and a second door.

'Off you go.'

'You are not coming?'

'You are suspicious!' She smiled. 'Look,' she said, and went down the steps and across the room. She opened the door so that he could hear the noise of the casino in the distance.

'It opens up into a small hall behind the main salon. From there, you can go anywhere in the building.'

'Are you always this helpful to men trying to get into the casino through the side door?'

'Not always.'

'I must have an honest face.'

'I hope not. I never trust an honest face. You never know what it is hiding.'

'What's your name?'

'Why do you keep asking? You don't need my name. If you want to see me again, you know where I work. If you don't, then my name isn't important.'

'Practical girl.'

'Very. Now go before I do get into trouble.'

Chadwick handed her the tray. The first door was still ajar. She pushed her heel into the gap, pulled it open with her leg, spun around it with her tray and was gone. The door closed behind her with a metallic click.

Chadwick stood for a moment. He reached for the handle of the door and turned it. It opened easily. There was clearly no need for a code from this side. He looked up and down the corridor. It was as empty as before.

He went down the concrete steps and crossed the workroom.

Opening the door on the opposite side of the room a fraction, he looked through the gap. Everything the girl had said was correct. The door led to a large hall. At one end, a set of marble steps, split by a heavily ornate brass rail, led to what he assumed was the main floor of the casino.

A minute later, he found Julija sitting at the bar at the far end of the main salon. A man approached her and offered his hand. It was a formal gesture without warmth, suggesting that they were meeting for the first time. The newcomer sat down next to her, facing the bar.

Chadwick decided to move closer. There were several empty seats at the other end of the bar. He sat down and ordered. Julija and her new friend were deep in conversation. Between them lay a large, flat envelope. It was open. Several photographs protruded a few centimetres.

The man was sitting square to the bar, his forearms resting on its marble top. He was below average height but stocky. His complexion was ruddy. *Outdoors with the elements or indoors with a bottle,* thought Chadwick. The only effort he made towards the woman was to incline and turn his head from time to time whilst he was speaking. Otherwise, he faced the bar. He seemed like a man more used to sitting with men. He shrugged, lifting his palms from the bar. *They are talking about money,* thought Chadwick. That kind of conversation can never be hidden. He has suggested some number and she doesn't like it. Not for the first time, he wondered whether his initial intuition about her had been correct. She looked as if she was waiting for the man to concede.

While he continued to stare ahead of him, she turned her head and noticed Chadwick sitting at the end of the bar. She smiled and gave him a wave that reminded him that she had once been a child. He walked around to where she was sitting. She turned on her bar stool and got to her feet. He kissed her on both cheeks. Her companion barely moved, twisting his head to look at Chadwick.

'I didn't think of you as a gambler,' she said.

'I'm not. But I am an occasional tourist. It's quite impressive.'

'You mean compared to our little café.'

If Chadwick liked the reference to *'our little café'*, the Latvian's companion didn't, and Chadwick wondered if she had done it on purpose. The man stood, his chest expanded, his arms by his sides. His fists, Chadwick noticed, were closed.

'Who is this?' he asked Julija. She ignored him and continued to talk to Chadwick.

'Have you been here long?'

'No. I just arrived. I was passing and thought I should look inside.' He stopped, conscious that he was offering more than had been asked, his volubility betraying his sense of guilt. He turned it around.

'And you, did you just arrive?'

'We have a meeting.' The stranger's tone made it clear that he was annoyed about the interruption. He turned to Julija. 'Let's continue,' he said. He turned his back to Chadwick, blocking him from Julija. Julija moved to one side.

'We should meet,' she said.

'We should.'

'Where can I reach you?' She reached for her bag that was hanging on a hook below the bar.

'You can leave a message at the hotel. Just pin it to the side door. The one in the lane.'

'Wouldn't it be easier to give me your phone number?'

He smiled. 'I don't think so. I don't have a phone.'

She looked surprised, so he continued. 'I don't need one,' he said, as if that was a satisfactory explanation.

Ignoring Chadwick, the stranger said, 'Do you want to continue this or not?'

Julija's face betrayed her annoyance, but she said, 'Of course.'

Her back to the stranger, she made a face at Chadwick and smiled. He smiled back. She mouthed, 'I'll leave you a message.'

He nodded. The stranger, who had returned to his stool at the bar, turned to stare at Chadwick as if to ask why he was still there. Chadwick let him stare, making no effort to move. Julija tried to defuse the tension by asking her companion if he would like another drink. He didn't answer but made a show of turning very slowly back to the bar.

Chadwick felt deflated and decided to leave. It had been a mistake to approach Julija, just as it had been a mistake to follow her in the first place. Why allow himself to be annoyed by some French prick? Her business was not his business. Her reasons for coming to France were not his concern. He had himself to worry about. Tomorrow, he would be more disciplined.

CHAPTER SEVEN

He ignored the first 'Hello.' The second registered more strongly, causing him to turn, curious to know who was calling whom in English. He saw nobody, but a second later, felt a tug on the sleeve of his jacket.

'Do you remember me?'

'Of course. How are the ribs?'

Johnny was taller than he remembered, with one of those English frames that looked as if it was about to fill out, but never did. He wore an old double-breasted blue blazer. The buttons were from a cavalry regiment. His father's, Chadwick assumed. Under it he wore a pale-blue shirt, frayed at the collar, a pair of fire-engine-red trousers, and beach shoes. Behind him, peering over his shoulder, was another English face, ruddy with blue eyes and a broken nose that had been poorly set.

'Not great. They hurt like you said they would. I can't sleep very well, no matter how I try.' He looked forlorn before he remembered his manners.

'This is Philip,' he said.

'I am surprised to find you here. I would have thought there were more entertaining places along the coast. You must be dedicated gamblers.'

Johnny looked embarrassed. 'We're not. Not at all. At least, we weren't until today. We were invited.' He looked around and bent forward, lowering his voice. 'By our new best friend. He knows the people here. I would invite you over but ...'

'Don't worry, Johnny, I understand. Your girlfriend and I didn't exactly hit it off.'

Johnny looked embarrassed. 'Oh, it's not that. It's just … It's just that we're invited, you see, so it's not exactly my shout. I wish it was. If it was up to me …' He stopped, finding himself in a verbal cul-de-sac.

Chadwick took pity on him. He meant well. 'It doesn't matter, Johnny. I was on my way home anyway. Have a good time. Don't gamble away the estate.'

Johnny looked perplexed. 'I'm not gambling,' he said. 'I couldn't afford it.'

'So, who is?'

'Sylvia.'

'And her sister?'

'No. Just Sylvia.'

'Why?'

There must have been something in Chadwick's expression that alarmed both boys. Neither spoke for a second and then Johnny said, 'Adil has staked her.'

'How much?'

Johnny told him. It was too large a sum. Chadwick wasn't sure how much more he wanted to know but he persevered. 'That seems like an awful lot of money to be given to you by a man you didn't know two days ago.'

The boys exchanged looks. Johnny tried first, 'His family is rich. He said that it was nothing for him. Apparently, he won here last week.'

'I'm sure he did,' said Chadwick. 'I am sure he wins here all the time.'

'It is okay, though?' Philip was clearly less comfortable with the arrangement than Johnny. 'It's not illegal to give somebody money to gamble, is it?'

'Not that I'm aware of,' said Chadwick, who decided to change tack. If there was something going on, it was probably better that Johnny and Philip remained ignorant. Once again, it was none of his business and he might well be overreacting. He should return to the hotel and go to bed.

'Who chose the table?' he asked. The two boys looked surprised, as if they had not understood the question. Chadwick tried again.

'Nobody, really. They opened one for us,' said Johnny.

'Were the others full?'

Johnny looked confused. 'No, not completely full. Adil thought it might be better to go to a new table so that we would have room to sit together. Why? Does it matter?'

Chadwick shrugged. What could he say? 'No. I was just curious, that's all. Is Sylvia winning?'

Johnny knitted his brows as if there might be greater meaning in the question than first seemed apparent.

'Oh, yes,' he said, 'she doesn't stop winning. Adil says that she is brilliant. That he has never seen anybody play as well as she does.' He stopped, embarrassed at having to acknowledge his rival's charm.

'How much?'

'How much has she won?' Johnny looked over his shoulder to see who might be listening, forgetting that it was obvious to everybody at Sylvia's table. He lowered his voice and leaned towards Chadwick. He seemed unsure of the exact amount but even if his estimate was close, it was a significant sum.

'Has anybody else shown up at the table from the casino?' Johnny looked blank, so he tried again. 'Has there been anybody at the table who works for the casino? Somebody in management. Has anybody spoken to the croupier, for example?'

'No, I don't think so. But I wasn't really looking.' Johnny shook his head and looked apologetic, sorry to disappoint.

'Why doesn't Sylvia stop now that she is so far ahead?'

'She wants to, but Adil won't let her. He says that it is only fair to give the casino a chance to win back some of their money. I don't see why.'

'I don't see why either, Johnny, because my guess is that she is going to continue winning.'

Johnny looked surprised. 'How can you know that?' he said.

'Celtic intuition.'

'Really?'

'No. Not really. Now, tell me, how did you get here this evening?'

'We were invited by Adil.'

'No, Johnny. Did you come by car?'

'Yes. Two cars. Ours and Adil's.'

'Where did you park?'

Johnny was about to say and then thought better of it. 'Look, what's this all about? Why do you need to know where we parked?'

'Because some of the car parks close early here and you might not be able to get your cars out.'

Johnny swallowed it. He seemed relieved that his doubts about Chadwick were so easily dispelled.

'Just in front and to the right. A small car park next the sea. I don't even think there is a barrier,' he added.

Chadwick knew it. It was a few hundred metres from the front of the casino. From the main entrance, they would need to walk down to the boulevard that followed the sweep of the bay. The way was well lit with plenty of passing cars. But the car park was small and probably held no more than twenty cars. At that time of night, it would be deserted.

'Good,' he said. 'You won't have any problem getting out of there.'

Johnny nodded for rather too long as he tried to think of something to say.

Chadwick gripped him by the shoulder. 'Have fun,' he said.

Johnny looked doubtful but smiled.

'Perhaps we will run into you again?'

'Perhaps.' Chadwick decided to cut the conversation short. 'Don't tell the others that you saw me. It will only annoy Sylvia.' Johnny nodded. 'You should go now otherwise they will wonder where you are.'

'I doubt it,' said Johnny with feeling, setting off across the salon floor with Philip close behind.

Chadwick watched them go. If he was correct, it was unlikely they would be hurt. Someone had been smart enough to pick a group that was unlikely to resist. With a bit of luck, it would be over before it began. But what if it wasn't?

He needed the friendly waitress. She was looking at him from the other side of the floor as if she had been expecting a signal.

'Did you forget my tip?' The half-smile was back; her eyes were bright with laughter.

'Perhaps. Or perhaps I just wanted your name.'

She raised an eyebrow.

'I thought we covered names in one of the previous lessons. You can't have been listening.'

'I am a poor student. I'm easily distracted.'

She shifted her weight from one leg to the other so that the light material of her dress clung more tightly to the body. Her head tilted to one side and she looked at him, her gaze moving slowly from his face to his feet and back again.

'So, it would seem. A man of your age should be settling down,' she said.

'I'm trying … but none of the nice girls will give me their names.'

'I'm not a nice girl. Nice girls don't work in casinos. You really don't pay attention, do you? But you do want something. You want to leave. The same way you came in.'

'You must have been the smartest girl in the class.'

'I wasn't. I was the best-looking though and that helps you look smart.'

'Doesn't it just?'

'Well, you know how to get to the corridor. Why don't I see you by the door in two minutes?'

'Too short. Could you make it ten minutes?'

She looked at him sceptically. 'If I was smart, I might ask why you needed an extra eight minutes. Should I ask? What would you say?'

'Not much. Maybe it's better that you don't know.'

She looked at him for a second or two, while she thought about this. Chadwick felt a cold chill go through him.

'Tell me, what do nice girls do in these situations?'

'Nice girls don't find themselves in these situations,' said Chadwick.

She stood looking at him as if she couldn't decide. He said nothing. She wasn't going to be swayed by anything he said. She would choose.

'In ten minutes, then.'

'Thank you.'

She turned and went up the steps.

Chadwick went through the door that led to the workroom. Finding what he needed in one of the larger metal cabinets, he took it to the work bench and put it in the vice. Then he searched the smaller cabinets. Satisfied, he returned to the work bench. By the time he had finished, he had only a couple of minutes left. He opened the door to the corridor a fraction and looked through.

The waitress was standing in the corridor looking towards the door, but she was not alone. Standing between her and the door were two men in suits with ear pieces. Chadwick looked at their shoes and satisfied himself - they were security, not management. He couldn't hear what they were saying but the woman looked relaxed. He closed the door softly. If she had betrayed him, he would already be in the casino basement. Security must patrol all the time. He would just need to wait until they went.

Five minutes passed before the door opened. It was the waitress.

'Let's go,' she said. He watched as she inserted the card in a box and waited for a second or two until she was satisfied that the alarm was off. She opened the door and stood to one side. Neither spoke. He went through the door and down the steps without stopping or looking back.

CHAPTER EIGHT

It was a longer wait than he had anticipated. An hour passed. And then another. The boulevard and the park were deserted. Perhaps they had gone home by taxi, leaving the cars to be picked up tomorrow? He could feel the cold damp from the ground beginning to grip him and pull him close. It began to rain. He moved as far under one of the bushes as he could. The grey estate and the black 4x4 were the only cars in the car park. Pulling his cap low, he wrapped his scarf around his face. It wasn't perfect, but in this light, it would suffice. Several cars passed on the road. He listened but all he could hear was the sound of the waves behind him. Rainwater trickled down his face and his doubts returned.

It was nothing at first, just a fragment of laughter carried in the wind. He listened hard. It came again. He looked towards the road, but it was empty. Then, he heard the laughter again. He strained his eyes but could see nothing. Now, he could hear voices. Looking away from the casino, towards the park, he saw them at once. They were five of them, walking on the grass next to the sea. The tallest, Johnny, was holding a champagne bottle and as Chadwick watched, he raised it and took a swig, before turning and offering it to Philip, who was trailing behind him like a faithful terrier. The other three figures became clearer. The two girls were in the middle, with Johnny and Philip on one side, and Adil, on the other. It hadn't occurred to Chadwick that anybody would choose to walk across the wet grass as opposed to the road. But then, he thought bitterly, it never occurred to you that they might stop and celebrate their win.

Or that the casino might encourage them to do it. And celebrate they clearly had.

He forced himself to concentrate. The two girls were carrying a bag between them, each holding a handle. They were swinging it and laughing. Adil had his arm around Sylvia's waist. Chadwick's anxiety returned. He looked away from the group, his gaze moving methodically along the road from right to left. There was nothing. No pedestrians. No cars. Nothing.

By now, he could hear them. Sylvia was scolding Johnny.

'Johnny, stop drinking. You are supposed to be driving. You may feel like launching yourself off the Grande Corniche, but we would prefer it if you did it alone.'

Johnny stopped sharply as if he had walked into a tree. 'I have not been drinking so much, and even if I had, I can handle it.' A further thought struck him. 'And, even if I couldn't handle it, the drink-driving limits in France are very different to England. They don't mind. They all drive drunk.'

'Johnny, France has the same rules as England. And, it's not the French police I'm worried about. I'm more worried about spending six months in a French infirmary.'

Johnny was now some way behind the others, swaying to and fro like a palm tree in a gale.

'Are you ill?' he said.

'Philip, can you drive please?' asked Sylvia.

'Yes. Yes, I can,' said Philip uncertainly. He looked back towards Johnny. Johnny reached into his blazer pocket and pulled out a set of car keys that he tossed towards Philip. It was a poor throw, but Philip showed a surprising athleticism, reaching low to his left, and catching them deftly, one-handed. Philip clicked and the doors to the grey car opened.

Chadwick looked across to Adil. He still had his arm around Sylvia, but his other hand was reaching for something in his pocket.

Pulling out a mobile phone, he entered the access code with his free hand. Satisfied that it was open, he wrapped it in his hand and tucked it behind his back. *Too soon*, thought Chadwick. *You need them in the car.*

Sylvia turned to face Adil, his arm still wrapped around her waist. 'Philip will drive the others and I will go with you,' she said.

Adil stroked her cheek with the hand that held the mobile. 'That sounds wonderful,' he said. 'But I told you, I have to pick something up on the way and I think it's better you go with the others.'

Sylvia was not used to being told no. She tried again. 'I don't mind your picking something up. I really don't.'

Adil pulled her closer. 'Of course, you don't, darling, but I don't think it would be a very good idea. This place ... The place I'm going - it's not very nice. It is not a place for you, trust me. It is better I go alone.'

She looked at him and started to speak but he pressed his finger to her lips.

'No. It is better I go there alone. You are better with the others. I won't be long.'

Nicely done, thought Chadwick. *A verray parfit gentil knight. So, do you leave first?*

The others were already in the grey car. Philip was driving, with Johnny beside him and the younger sister in the back. Adil guided Sylvia towards the rear passenger door. Pausing, before getting in, she put her arms around Adil. 'Be careful,' she said and kissed him. As Adil closed her door, Chadwick saw his mobile light up. He had dialled a number.

Adil walked around to the other side of the estate. He tapped on the driver's window. It slid down. 'You know the way?' he asked.

'Of course.' Philip looked surprised by the question. He should have been. Adil was only killing time and blocking Philip's view of the entrance to the car park.

They came in a black van with no lights. It came fast and quietly. It braked to a halt directly in front of the two cars, blocking any chance they might have had of getting away. The rear doors opened, and a man jumped out. He had on a black balaclava and carried a baseball bat. He went straight for Adil. A second man, similarly dressed, jumped down from the driver's seat.

Adil rushed the first man. The man stopped and let him come. He transferred the baseball bat to his left hand. Adil made a grab for the bat. The man stepped to one side and hit him with a short, black cosh. Adil went down like a coat falling from a peg.

Chadwick had seen enough. He started moving through the shrubs out of sight. He needed to check the van and get behind the two men. The second man ignored the first man's encounter with Adil. He had no doubt about the outcome. Now he stood on one side of the grey car, facing the rear, leaning against the front passenger door. His colleague moved to the other side. They held their baseball bats above their heads to ensure that they wouldn't be missed. They weren't. Chadwick got a glimpse of Johnny staring out the window, his face ashen. The baseball bats were an irrelevance at this point. Philip and Johnny could have tried for an hour and not moved those doors more than an inch or two. The entire operation was conducted in silence. Nobody had spoken. They might have been in a library.

Chadwick came out of the shrubs on the far side of the van. The driver's door was open and the engine running. He couldn't see what was happening on the other side of the van but could well imagine it. The attackers wouldn't speak but simply point to the bag. The car's occupants would be given a second or two to gather their thoughts; maybe even the opportunity to confer. If nothing happened, then they would start with the windows. When he heard breaking glass, he reached into the van, turned off the engine and removed the keys.

He moved round to the back of the van. The doors were open and he could look through the gap above the hinges. The driver's and passenger's windows of the car were already gone. Chadwick could see Johnny and Philip bent over towards each other, their hands above their heads, trying to protect themselves. He couldn't see the two girls and assumed they must be lying in the rear-seat wells. The first balaclava was instructing the second via hand signals and was pointing to the rear windows. Chadwick moved away from the van and walked towards the first man. It was now or never.

There was a loud crash as one of the rear windows went. The first man raised his baseball bat to smash the last remaining window. Chadwick reached behind him, pulled something from his belt, and stepped forward. The only sound was the wooden clatter of the baseball bat falling to the tarmac. The man reached for his shattered right arm with his left. He was too shocked to realise what had happened to him. Chadwick's front kick hit him at chest height and knocked him to the ground. He screamed in pain as he fell on his badly broken arm. Chadwick was about to kick him again but had a more pressing issue to deal with.

The second balaclava saw Chadwick appear out of nowhere and his partner drop. His confusion lasted only a second or two before he moved around the front of the car and towards Chadwick. He was in a fighting crouch, the bat held in a one-handed grip, two-thirds along the handle. His other hand was stretched out in front of him. He was perfectly balanced, moving in quick short steps like a professional fighter. Chadwick didn't like the way this one handled the bat. He didn't like it at all. He thanked God for the wrench he had taken from the casino work room. He only wished he hadn't been so altruistic as to wrap it in cloth and tape. Right now, his desire to avoid killing somebody seemed to belong to another century. Right now, all he wanted was to land even a glancing blow on this thug – the weight of the wrench would do the rest. But the element of surprise was long gone and his opponent only too aware of the danger. He kept coming, his outstretched left hand weaving in the air. Chadwick knew that if he let him grab his right arm, the one with the wrench, the fight would be over, the baseball bat would see to that.

Chadwick feinted forward, the wrench whipping towards the man's outstretched arm. The man reacted instantly, executing a block that would have pushed Chadwick's right arm clear and opened his body. Chadwick brought the swinging wrench to a sharp halt and stepped back. Sensing opportunity, the opponent stepped forward, reaching for the wrench, but his attempted grab left him momentarily off-balance. Realising the danger, the man tried to pull his arm back, but it was too late. Chadwick's roundhouse kick caught him just above the knee. He cried out in pain, buckled, and went down on one knee, swaying for a second or two before Chadwick knocked him cold with a kick to the head.

The pain that flooded through Chadwick's body took his breath away. His legs wobbled. He dropped the wrench and fell to his knees. It felt like his back was broken. But he knew what it was, and it was that, and that alone, which saved him. The hit to the kidney hurt like hell but he knew he would recover. What he needed was time. He had to stop Adil - it had to be Adil - getting to one of the bats. He turned his head. Adil was standing behind him. He was already too late. Adil reached down and picked up one of the bats. Chadwick looked across at the first man, who was pushing himself to his feet with the aid of the second bat.

Adil looked as if all his dreams had come true at once.

Chadwick ignored him. He rocked back and forwards, half-turning, his arms wrapped around him, moaning. If Adil had been less delighted and more observant, he would have noticed that Chadwick was no longer on his knees. Now, cross-legged, his legs folded beneath him, Chadwick knew that he was out of time. Ignoring the pain, he concentrated on Adil, suspecting that Adil wouldn't hit him while he wasn't looking at him. For Adil, there would be no fun unless Chadwick could see it coming. Sensing Adil moving in front of him, he levered himself to his feet from his cross-legged position and saw the shock in Adil's eyes as Adil swung the bat. Chadwick stepped inside the arc and hit him with a low upper cut to the groin that would have got him banned from boxing for life. Adil wasn't in a state to argue. He collapsed at Chadwick's feet.

Chadwick turned to look for the first man, who was advancing slowly but menacingly towards Chadwick, his bat gripped in his left hand, his shattered right arm hanging uselessly by his side.

Chadwick looked down for his wrench. He couldn't see it in the dark car park. He looked for Adil's bat. It too was gone. He looked up. The first man was badly injured - that was clear - but he could still move, albeit slowly - with a grim determination that boded ill. Chadwick looked over at Adil. His fighting was over for the night. He was curled up on the tarmac, retching. Chadwick looked back at the first man, who was only a stride or two away, his bat swinging ominously.

'Hello.'

A figure appeared behind the first man. It was difficult to tell who was more surprised, Chadwick or his opponent. The first man turned. It was the last thing he did. Philip might not have been a great boxer. Perhaps he couldn't have cut it in Stepney. But somebody, somewhere, some unsung hero of the gym, had spent hour upon hour, year after year ensuring that whatever his talent, Philip's technique would be second to none. It was a textbook right cross and the first man's head whipped backwards like a crash dummy's. There was no count.

Johnny appeared. He gave the prostrate and groaning Adil a wide berth as if he might be infectious. He seemed in no hurry to enquire after his health. Philip was also moaning, clutching his broken right hand in his left.

Chadwick took charge.

'Philip, your hand? Can you drive?'

'I think so. It hurts but I think it will be okay.'

'Get in the car and make sure the girls stay there. Johnny, come here.'

Johnny looked hesitant.

'Give me a hand. Get his feet.'

Chadwick moved towards the first man, pulled off his balaclava and took his phone. Then he grabbed him under the arms and together, they lifted him into the back of the van. They repeated the manoeuvre with the second man before Chadwick reversed the van into a parking space. The two men were alive, but any thought of resistance had long since vanished. Chadwick threw the two balaclavas into the back of the van and locked the doors. It would be some time before either of them felt strong enough to look for help.

He turned to look for Adil. Adil was not alone. He was lying face down, moaning. Sylvia was kneeling next to him, touching him, but too frightened or inexperienced to try to turn him over.

'Adil. *Adil*, can you hear me?'

She saw Chadwick and stood up. 'You bastard, look what you've done to him.'

Chadwick held back. She appeared not to have recognised him in the dark.

'Move away from him and get in the car. Now!'

Sylvia didn't move. 'I want to know who you are. Do you work for my father?'

Johnny said, 'You know who he is. He is —'

'Johnny, shut up. No more talking,' said Chadwick. Sylvia turned to Johnny, her face flushed with anger.

'Johnny, who is he? Tell me right now.'

Johnny said nothing but stared at her, imploring her not to ask, shaking his head.

'Who the hell are you? You do work for my father, don't you?' Without any warning, Sylvia strode towards Chadwick. The look of recognition in her eyes was immediate.

'You are from the —'

Chadwick didn't let her finish. He stepped towards Adil and kicked him in the head. Adil's head sagged to the ground.

Johnny made a half-hearted attempt to grab Sylvia, but he was too slow - Chadwick was better prepared. Just as she reached him, he slapped her across the face. She stumbled and almost fell. She recovered and came at him again. Chadwick slapped her face again, but this time, he spun her around and held her arms behind her back. She started to struggle but it was hopeless. Before she could speak, Chadwick said, 'Listen to me and listen well if you ever want to go home again. You are in one big fuck-up and *you* keep making it worse. Not Johnny, not Philip, not your sister, *you*.'

He let go of one of her arms and spun her around. Her face was red with anger and there were tears of frustration in her eyes. He caught her free hand before she got any ideas of what she might do with it.

'You've been set up from the beginning, do you understand? From the time your bag was "stolen" and returned. They needed a mark and you were tailor-made. You didn't find Adil - he found you. You need to do a better job of picking your friends.'

She stared at him, furious.

'You didn't need to kick him in the head when he was already hurt. You didn't need to do that. Did you like it? Is that it? Is that how you get off? Fuck, I hate all you bastards.'

Chadwick made a point of speaking softly. He needed to take some of the heat out of the situation. 'I didn't need to kick him in the head. But after you started to tell him who I was, I had only two choices - either I put him out or I smacked you. I chose him.'

Sylvia glared at him but said nothing.

'Adil is a piece of shit. Everything about him stinks of the street but you thought he was Alain Delon. He found you, he set you up in the casino, and he brought you here. Tell me it wasn't his decision to park here? He even volunteered to take the first blow - like hell he did - he just wanted out of the way while his pals convinced you to hand over the money. And very convincing they were. But not as convincing as the ones who will come calling tomorrow. I know what this lot looks like - I won't recognise the next ones - and, trust me, they won't be as sloppy as this bunch - their boss will see to that.'

'What are we going to do?' Her voice was calmer, her eyes steady. She wasn't happy, but she was focused and determined.

'Get in the car, in the back.'

She got in beside her sister. Philip was already behind the wheel, nursing his hand. Johnny stood by the open passenger door.

'You need to get out of here now. Did you all bring your passports to the casino?'

The sister reached into her bag and produced four passports.

'Credit cards?'

'Yes.'

'This is what you do, and you do it without any deviations, diversions or changes of plan. You head to Lyons. Under no circumstances do you try to fly out of Nice or even Marseille. You go straight to Lyons airport and book your flight from your phones on the way. You catch the first flight you can to any sensible destination - preferably the UK - but if not, then Amsterdam, Copenhagen, Brussels - anywhere as long as it is outside France. Is that clear?'

They nodded, looking increasingly apprehensive.

'You are *not* to return to your villa, no matter what. You leave your luggage behind. You park the rental car in an airport car park and take the bus to the terminal. You sit in two pairs on the bus as far apart as you can and don't communicate. You go through passport control as quickly as you can. Once you are there, you stay together at all times - don't let any one of you get separated.'

'What about the money?' asked Sylvia.

'The money? Forget about the money. It's not yours. It was never meant to be yours. You were just the means to an end. The men in the van were sent to collect it and when they don't show up with it, their boss is going to be very upset. Right now, that bag is radioactive.'

'So, you are going to leave it here?' Sylvia wasn't going to concede her windfall so easily.

'No. I'm not. I am going to take it and try to return it in the hope that matters will rest there, and nobody will come looking for you in England.'

'How are you going to do that …'

'Without my lifeless body being dumped in the sea? I have no idea. But it's not your problem - you have a plane to catch. You need to get moving. Philip, don't break any speed limits. While you are on the road, you are perfectly safe.'

Sylvia put her hand on Philip's shoulder to stop him driving off. 'What shall we do when we get back to England?' she asked.

'Nothing. Just forget it ever happened. By tomorrow night, you'll have convinced yourself it never did.'

'If you don't work for my father,' she said, 'who do you work for?'

'Providence. Now move.'

Chadwick watched the tail lights of the car until it disappeared. Wearily, he turned his attention to Adil, who was showing some signs of life. He took his mobile and, picking him up under the arms, dragged him to the back of the van and left him lying behind it, out of sight of the road. He could have unlocked the doors and put him with the others but there was always the chance that one or more had revived sufficiently to cause a problem. And the last thing he needed was another problem.

It could only be a matter of time before somebody came to find out what had happened. He picked up the bag of money and threw the mobile phones on top. Perhaps he should have taken Johnny's or Philip's numbers? It was too late now. Dog-tired, he started over the grass to the promenade that led towards the town and his hotel. He stopped only once - to throw the mobiles into the sea.

CHAPTER NINE

'Is there a good part to your plan? Because we don't seem to have reached that part yet. Are you saving the best for last?'

Verlaine looked unhappy. 'I don't see any other option,' he said.

'You don't? What's wrong with the obvious one?'

'She won't go to the police.'

'Why not? She should go to the police. That's what they are there for.'

'She doesn't think they'll believe her. She thinks they'll side with him. And I think she's right.'

'Why?'

'He was with the local police. He was a detective. Not in Nice or Cannes but, *here*, in town. He only left a year ago. You know how these things work. Here, she is a nobody. A good-looking Latvian who showed up with no obvious means of support. Of course, the police will be suspicious.'

'Maybe they're right to be suspicious. Let's face it, you've only just met her. How much do you *really* know about her beyond what she has told you?'

Verlaine shifted uncomfortably. 'Enough. I've seen enough victims of violent men to know that she was beaten up. You can't fake that. Her bruises and split lip are real enough. And why should she lie about employing a private detective?'

'Who knows? People make up stories all the time. Maybe it was another kind of business that got out of hand and she doesn't want to tell you? But, if I were you, and I had no idea who she is and why she is here in the first place, I would be *very, very* careful until I knew a bit more.'

'I know enough. I know that I am taking a risk, but I cannot sit and do nothing.'

Chadwick leaned back in his chair and studied Verlaine, who sat upright, as if he were already in court. *We are all so easily manipulated,* thought Chadwick. *Verlaine knows better than to accept Julija's explanation at face value, but he doesn't care. He has fallen for her and wants to help her regardless of his intuition, experience or reason. This will end badly,* he thought.

Chadwick motioned at the empty cups and Verlaine nodded. Chadwick signalled to the waitress and thought about what he should say next but before he could speak, Verlaine said, 'It would be better if we went together. He is less likely to be difficult if there are two of us.'

Chadwick felt suddenly weary. He had always suspected where the conversation was heading despite his best efforts to redirect it.

'If *we* go together? When did I become part of the plan?'

Verlaine looked embarrassed and Chadwick changed tack. He wanted to avoid what they both knew - that Verlaine's days of confronting thugs were behind him.

'Leave it for a day or two. Let's talk about it again in a few days when you haven't been up all night and the events are a little clearer.' As soon as he said it, Chadwick regretted it. He saw the older man colour, and knew that he had touched a nerve.

'The events *are* clear. They could not be clearer. The only thing that is *unclear* is whether you want to help me do something about it.'

'I am sorry, but they are *not* as clear as you think. They never are. You know how this goes. There is her story, there is his story, but there is no truth. You have no idea what happened between them. You only know what she told you.'

'I know enough. She wants back what she gave him, and I will get it for her.'

Chadwick waited while the waitress served them and took his time preparing his coffee. He wanted to give Verlaine the opportunity to calm down. He needed to be careful or there was a danger that the Frenchman would just get up and leave.

'What do you know about this guy?'

'Here.' Verlaine brought out a photograph. He handed it to Chadwick. It was a poor-quality print, but Chadwick recognised him immediately. He gave it back to Verlaine without saying anything, sat back and folded his arms. Verlaine stared at him. Neither man spoke for some time.

'You know him?'

'I don't know him. I've met him.'

'Where?'

'Last night at the casino. He was with Julija at the bar.'

'What did you make of him?'

'Not much. Unpleasant. Didn't seem very happy that I showed up. Did his best to encourage me to leave. But then he was a policeman; you know what they are like.'

Verlaine didn't smile but he nodded in acknowledgment. 'I know. They have poor manners. But mine are quite a lot better than his.'

'What's his name?'

'Jean-Michel Arcier.'

'And he's a private detective?'

'Yes.'

'What was he doing for her?'

Verlaine hesitated. 'I can't tell you.'

'Can't or won't?'

'I was told in confidence. I haven't said to her that I was going to talk to you. Perhaps I shouldn't have told you this much.'

Perhaps not, thought Chadwick. *Only a romantic would trade a lifetime of experience for a confidence from a pretty girl.*

'What does he have that she wants back?'

'A small file,' he said. 'Some press clippings and a photograph.'

'A photograph of what?'

'A man. Early thirties.'

'Who is he?'

'I don't think I can tell you that. I think it's for Julija to tell you if she chooses to.' He let the last part of the sentence fall away as if he doubted whether she would confide in him. Chadwick didn't react.

'And the press clippings?'

'They're about ships. That's all I know.' He shrugged by way of apology.

Chadwick suspected that it was the same brown envelope that he had seen lying on the casino bar, but he decided against telling Verlaine. It would only make him more certain that everything Julija had told him was true.

'Hardly seems worth the trouble. Tell me, where is Arcier?'

'He has an office. I have the address.'

'Good. So, we show up, ask him very nicely to return this file, thank him, and leave. Is that the plan?'

'Yes,' said Verlaine, but without conviction.

'And if he says he doesn't have it, what do we do then?'

'He has it.'

'How do you know?'

Verlaine flushed. 'You know how I know,' he said.

'And what happens if what she has told you isn't true, and he doesn't have anything of hers? Or worse, it belongs to him.'

'It belongs to her. I am sure of it.'

Chadwick wondered what Julija had told Verlaine that made the older man so certain.

'And if Arcier disagrees, what then?'

'Are you worried that I will not be able to control myself?'

'Possibly.'

'Possibly is a polite way of saying, "Yes" in English?'

Chadwick thought of saying, 'Possibly' again but one look at Verlaine persuaded him otherwise.

'Yes, I'm concerned. If you lose your temper with him, you will be in trouble. I've met him. He will be a handful if he gets riled. And in his office, you can count on his having some weapon to hand. And if he pulls a gun, your cosh isn't going to be much good.'

Verlaine looked surprised. 'What makes you think that I have a cosh?'

'Because you are too experienced to fall back on charm and good looks. Where is it?'

Verlaine reached into his jacket pocket. Keeping it below the table and hidden from the other occupants of the café, he showed Chadwick the top half of a black, leather-bound cosh. The distressed leather betrayed its age.

'Looks like it has also seen some active service.'

'It has. I picked it up in North Africa.'

'Not everybody's idea of a holiday gift. Anything else?'

Verlaine said nothing.

'Knife? Gun?'

Verlaine looked shocked. 'Of course not. I may be foolish, but I am not a fool.'

Chadwick smiled at the Frenchman's choice of words. 'So, we see him in his office, you ask for whatever you are asking for, and if he says no?'

'Then we'll leave.'

'And then what?'

'Look, I don't know what I will do next. I hope he will see sense and cooperate. Otherwise, I will tell him that she will go to the police.'

'And if he cooperates, you will forget all about his beating her up?'

'Yes.'

'And walk away?'

'Yes.'

'I am glad to hear it. This file, is it really so important?'

Verlaine shrugged. 'She says so.'

'Let's run through this again. We go to Arcier's office, tell him that if he gives back the file, Julija will forget about the assault. He gives us the file, we wish him good day, and we leave. Is that the plan?'

'Yes.'

'Good. Then you don't need me, and you certainly don't need that cosh. It's only going to get you in trouble. Why don't you give it to me, and I will keep it here until you get back?'

Verlaine's face flushed. It was clear he was annoyed at allowing himself to be so easily backed into a corner by the younger man.

'You are right. I shouldn't have bothered you with this. It's not your business. That's clear. And maybe it shouldn't be my business either. But at this point, it really doesn't matter.'

Verlaine stood up and reached across for Chadwick's hand. Chadwick hesitated. There was a finality to the gesture which unnerved him. Verlaine gripped his hand firmly and shook it for slightly longer than was usual.

'Charles, give me the cosh?'

Verlaine shook his head. 'I don't think so. If Arcier is as you describe him, I must have at least one friend with me.'

He turned and made for the door. Chadwick slumped into his seat. A wave of tiredness swept over him. He watched Verlaine's back disappear through the door. *It is about time*, he thought, *that I made a good decision. I have already gone to war with the wrong people. I have a bag of their money which they will come looking for. And my only friend here is about to put himself in hospital or worse. The best decision I can make now is to order another coffee.* He signalled to the waitress. She ignored him. He stood up. She continued to ignore him. He threw a €20 note on the table and left in search of Verlaine.

CHAPTER TEN

He almost missed him. He had assumed that he would be walking but when he emerged from the café, he couldn't see him. Scanning the cars, only one was occupied. An old Renault that had seen better days. Walking towards it, he opened the passenger door and climbed in.

'I should have known that you would have one of these.'

'Why is that? Is it because we both take a little time to get started?'

'No. It is just something about being French.'

'So now you like the French?'

'I wouldn't want to go quite that far.'

Verlaine didn't seem surprised by Chadwick's change of heart. Perhaps he had always counted on it. Maybe he had read Chadwick better than Chadwick could read himself. It was impossible to say.

They drove to Arcier's office in silence and parked outside. The building sat grey and disappointed in the middle of a pot-holed car park. The only cars visible were old and neglected. The other occupants were an overflowing skip, a rusted bicycle rack and a decaying cabin cruiser on a trailer, several windows broken, its paintwork streaked with dirt.

The bottom floor of the building had been built to house shops, but few remained open. The windows of the empty shops were boarded. The first floor, immediately above the shops, was offices. Some had signs in the windows; others, rusting air-conditioner units. There were occasional indications of life: a fat man leaning out of a window smoking; a woman's head moving in time with her typing.

Chadwick looked at Verlaine. 'The block that time forgot,' he said.

Verlaine grimaced. 'Even the graffiti looks worn out.'

'Do you know where the office is?'

'No. I assume it must be on the first floor with the others but exactly where, I don't know.'

'Number?'

'107.'

Chadwick pointed to the double glass doors in the centre of the façade.

'Is that the entrance to the offices as well as the apartments?'

'I assume so. Wait.'

Verlaine reached into the glove compartment and pulled out an expensive-looking pair of German binoculars. He handed them to Chadwick. Chadwick looked first at the binoculars and then at Verlaine. 'You a bird watcher?'

Verlaine smiled but didn't reply.

Chadwick scanned the lobby behind the glass doors. One of the walls was covered with pigeon holes, overflowing with unwanted fliers. In front of it, there was a desk and a chair. It was unoccupied. He handed the binoculars to Verlaine.

'Tell me, what's happening at reception?' said Chadwick.

Verlaine studied the building. 'Nothing. It's still empty.'

'Let's go,' said Chadwick.

They walked into the building's lobby and headed straight for the stairs, ignoring the lifts.

The first floor was just as Chadwick had imagined it. A narrow, linoleum-tiled, ill-lit canyon that ran the length of the building with the two lifts and the stairs at its midpoint. There was nobody to be seen, only the occasional sound of a telephone ringing or voices filtering through the ranks of closed doors. Above each door, there was a small window but most of the occupants had placed a sign in it, so that very little external light made it to the corridor. The walls and ceiling were painted, but what the colour had been, or was now, was almost impossible to tell in the half-light. Chadwick looked for a board that might list the offices but there was none. He asked Verlaine. 'Left or right?'

'Left.'

The two men started down the corridor, inspecting each door in turn. Most of the occupants, if they hadn't put a sign in the window above the door, had at least attached one to the door itself. There were about ten doors to the end of the corridor, and it wasn't until they reached the seventh door that they found one without any sign.

'Wait here,' said Chadwick. He walked quickly to the end of the corridor. The other three doors were all signed.

He returned to where Verlaine was waiting outside the seventh door and paused. Should he check the other leg of the corridor first or should he try this one? He looked at Verlaine, who seemed to understand. He knocked twice on the door and waited. Both men listened but all they could hear was noise from the other offices. Chadwick knocked again. There was no sound of movement from behind the door. Behind them, there was the sound of voices from the stairwell. Chadwick twisted the handle and opened the door in one movement. Both men stepped inside, pulling the door closed behind them.

Chadwick immediately wished he hadn't. He wished he had stayed in the hotel. He wished he had listened to his better judgment and told Verlaine to forget it or go alone. He forced himself to breathe regularly. He needed to focus on the here and now. Everything else could wait. But the here and now was what was causing his heart to race. He looked at Verlaine and was surprised to see him unperturbed by what lay around them, standing with his arms folded, reviewing what was left of Arcier's office.

From what remained, it was difficult to tell that it had ever been an office. No one piece of furniture had been left intact. There appeared to have been two desks, both wooden. Each had been dismembered piece by piece, every drawer broken in parts, every leg inspected for hollow hiding places. The desk chairs had been torn apart, their cushions cut into orderly ribbons. The carpet tiles had been lifted one by one; the walls drilled for possible hidden cupboards or safes; several photograph frames lay in pieces, their photos confiscated. The filing cabinets had been emptied methodically, their paper contents lying in piles across the floor. The window air-conditioning unit had been unbolted and dismantled on the office floor. Whoever had led the search had been professional and thorough, and given that no one piece of the office remained intact, Chadwick could only assume that the search had been unsuccessful.

The search was unexpected and unnerving – but the search he could handle. What he found more difficult was the splattered blood that was sprayed across the rear wall of the office like so many red feathers.

'Not good,' he said to Verlaine.

Verlaine looked at him and grimaced. 'What do you think?' he said.

'This wasn't amateur hour. Whoever did this, knew what they were doing.'

'I agree. Look at this place. They didn't rush. They took it apart piece by piece. This took time. And nerve. These people weren't worried about being disturbed.'

'Do you think they found what they were looking for?'

'No, I don't,' said Verlaine. 'And you?'

'I agree. If they had found it, they would have stopped long before they destroyed the office. And, if they had found it, they wouldn't have needed to smack Arcier – if it was Arcier – around.'

Verlaine said, 'What next?'

'Next, we get out. Hopefully without anybody seeing us. We could spend two days in here and still not find anything helpful.'

'I agree. Poor Arcier. I hope he had the good sense to give these people what they wanted.'

'I doubt it. He was a bully, but he didn't look like a pushover. Let's worry about his health somewhere else. If we are found here, you'll be back with the police, but I don't think it'll be quite the same as before.'

Chadwick walked towards the door while Verlaine took one last look at the room as if reluctant to leave. Chadwick took out a handkerchief, wiped, and then turned the door handle. Opening the door a fraction, he waited to see if the corridor was empty. It was. Ushering Verlaine out, he closed the door and wiped the external handle. Pocketing the handkerchief, he walked towards the stairs with Verlaine just behind him. When they reached the stairs, he turned to Verlaine and pointed upwards. It was the correct call. As they turned the corner of the stairs, he heard one of the lift doors open but by then, they were out of view.

When Chadwick reached the fourth floor, he waited for Verlaine, who was right behind him. The older man was fitter than he had imagined. The dimly lit corridor was empty but this time, there were no offices or the sound of people working. He pressed the button for the lift. They were in luck. When the lift door opened at the ground floor, the lobby was empty. They walked straight out and crossed the road to the car.

'Where to now?' asked Verlaine.

'Anywhere but here would be good for me. Why don't you head out of town? Just drive along the coast for a while.'

'You think we might be followed?'

'It's unlikely but I'd rather know about it if it happens, wouldn't you?'

'I suppose so. But why would they wait to see who showed up?'

'Charles, I have no idea. But then I had no idea about what we were looking for in the first place.'

Chadwick paused while Verlaine checked the mirror. 'See anything?'

Verlaine shook his head. Chadwick turned and inspected the road behind them. It looked clear but what did he expect? If these people were as professional as he thought, they wouldn't be caught so easily.

'Well?' said Verlaine.

'Well what?'

'What should we do next?'

'That's easy. We should go home and focus on forgetting. Forget about Arcier and forget we ever went to his office. And when we have finished trying to forget, we should start praying that the people who went looking for him, don't ever come looking for us.'

'Not good, eh?'

'Not good.'

'And Julija? What shall I tell her?'

'Tell her the truth. And tell her to get out of town.'

Verlaine looked surprised. 'Out of town? Aren't you overreacting? This incident may be nothing to do with Julija's business with Arcier.'

Chadwick explained. 'It may not, but I'm not sure it matters any more. It certainly won't matter to the police. Look at it from their perspective. She hired Arcier. He beats her up. His office is ransacked and his blood splashed halfway up the wall. He disappears. You try telling them Arcier's disappearance may have nothing to do with Julija. You're the former policeman. Do they care?' He paused, looking at Verlaine. 'I thought not.'

'So, what do I tell her?'

'Just what I said.'

'You are taking this very seriously.'

'I am. I am taking this very seriously indeed.' He turned towards Verlaine and smiled. 'But then, I did come here for my health.'

CHAPTER ELEVEN

Chadwick barely registered that he had been shown to a table in the front room. He was too preoccupied with his failure to stick to his plan. He couldn't fault the plan. The town and the hotel were perfect, providing the isolation and anonymity he craved. It was his lack of self-discipline, his inability to stay detached, that had let him down. He had been foolish to save the English group. He hadn't achieved anything, except to ensure that whoever was behind the staged robbery would come looking for him. It would take time. They would start with the local suspects, but once the locals had been cleared, they would look for recent arrivals. It wouldn't be a long list and he was sure to be on it.

As if that weren't enough, he had allowed himself to accompany Verlaine to Arcier's office even though he had known that it wouldn't end well. He should have been tougher on the older man. He should have told Verlaine to grow up, get over his crush on the Latvian, and tell her to sort out her own mess. Instead, he had put himself at risk of another visit, this time from the police. Sooner or later, somebody would go to that office, and if it *was* Arcier's blood on his office wall, the police would take it very seriously. Policemen, in his experience, looked after their own.

And, if the police did manage to track him down, at best, they would want to know what he was doing in Arcier's office; at worst, they might feel like persuading him that he had a hand in in Arcier's disappearance. Neither was an attractive prospect. But it was what happened to Arcier after the beating that worried him most.

His only consolation was that it was unlikely that Arcier's captors were looking for Julija's papers. What possible interest could they have in them? From what Verlaine had told him, they were of little importance. Some press clippings and some photos. No, the chances were that they had tripped over somebody else's unfinished business and the sooner he could distance himself from it, the better. If they were lucky, Arcier would eventually reappear, but he wasn't optimistic.

Right now, his priority was to return the bag of cash to the casino as quickly as he could. But returning it was the easy part; ensuring that the incident was closed would be much more difficult.

'May I join you?'

He looked up. Leclerc needed no other invitation. He pulled out the chair opposite Chadwick and sat down. He was a big man who seemed too large for the flimsy wooden chair. He had long, dark-brown hair, brushed straight back behind his ears, and held in place with heavily-applied hair gel. He was pale, as if he rarely ventured outside, with the result that his olive skin looked almost yellow in the artificial light. His eyes were brown and amused. He looked more like a lorry driver than a café owner.

'I was surprised by my promotion to the front room,' said Chadwick.

Leclerc said nothing but shifted uncomfortably in his seat, apparently embarrassed.

'I am not sure I deserve it,' Chadwick continued.

'You deserve it,' said Leclerc, turning in his chair to look for a waitress. 'You are a local celebrity.'

'You must be very short of candidates if I am considered a celebrity.'

'We are. But a man who appears from nowhere and stays in a deserted hotel in the middle of winter has a good chance.'

Chadwick came close to explaining where he had come from

but thought better of it and let Leclerc finish. 'Besides, we are old friends,' said Leclerc.

'We are?'

'I see you every morning on my way here. You once asked me directions.'

'I remember. You get up early.'

Leclerc shrugged. 'It's not so very early. It is only early for people who don't know how to work. I am always early. I open early. You should come then - it is very quiet - a man has time to think.'

'When you live in a deserted hotel, there is already too much time to think. Besides, I have to run first thing.'

'I noticed. You run every day? Even in this filthy weather?'

'I like to run in the rain.'

Leclerc sighed and shook his head as if Chadwick had just confirmed the futility of human endeavour. Turning his head, he finally caught the eye of a waitress and ordered Chadwick a second coffee.

'I'm sorry you have not had better weather since you arrived. It's a pretty town when the sun is shining. We even have our own casino.'

'I know,' said Chadwick, 'I went last night.'

'You have been to our casino?'

'I have.'

'And what did you think?'

Chadwick saw his opening and began to steer the conversation.

'I was impressed. I had no idea that the town could support a casino of that size.'

'It can't. At least, not out of season. It is more popular in the summer. It has a good restaurant, but you wouldn't have seen it - it's closed in the winter. When the restaurant is open, it attracts people from all along the coast. And, of course, in the summer, you have the tourists. Without them, it would never make money.'

'It's very well kept. I am surprised that the Municipality can afford to keep it in such good condition.'

'The Municipality?' said Leclerc. 'It doesn't belong to the Municipality.'

'Then who does own it?'

'A local businessman.'

'He has done well.'

Leclerc blew some air out of the side of his mouth in a show of indifference. 'Perhaps. Perhaps not. Who knows? Things are not always what they seem here.'

'Meaning?'

Leclerc scratched the top of his head and thought for a moment. 'Meaning nothing.'

Chadwick tried another tack. 'You don't like him?'

'No, I like him. He's all right.'

'You know him well?'

Leclerc laughed. 'I would hope so. We were in the same class at school.'

'So, he has done well.'

'He was always going to do well. All he ever thought about was money.'

'So do lots of people. They don't all succeed. How did he do it?'

'Property. He started buying apartments in rough areas and renting them out to people on welfare, immigrants mostly.'

'And where did the money come from?'

Leclerc shook his head. 'Ah, that is a good question. But maybe not for around here. People don't always want you to know where their money came from, and sometimes, when they succeed, they often forget its source. Augustin could always find money - he was a moneymaker. Always ahead of the latest trend or fad, even at school. When the rest of us were broke, he would lend us money. At a price, though. He was never big on charity. And, when we had money, he would take it and do something with it.'

'And pay you?'

'Most of the time. Sometimes, things didn't work out as he planned. But then, he was learning. He was always learning.'

'Why buy the casino?'

Leclerc shrugged. 'Everybody wants to buy the house on the hill, no? When he bought it, the casino was bankrupt. It had been run down for years by the previous owners. He bought it cheap and then invested a fortune in it. Now it's a palace.'

'But still not very profitable?'

'I doubt it. Maybe it washes its face. Probably not.'

'Does it wash anything else?'

Leclerc looked surprised. 'No, I don't think so. He has had some tough partners over the years and I don't say that he's totally clean, but money laundering, no, that's not him.'

'Does he have a record?'

'A police record. No. He was always too clever for that. Besides, if he did, he wouldn't be allowed to operate a casino.'

'Possibly, but maybe once you can afford a casino, you can afford more influential friends?'

'Of course. Around here, it is easy to find friends if you are rich.'

'And if you're not?'

'Then you better get a library ticket.'

Chadwick picked up his book and waved it at Leclerc. 'You see. No friends for me.'

Leclerc shook his head. 'You don't seem to have a problem with making friends.'

'You mean Verlaine?'

'Is that his name? Who is he?'

'He is a retired policeman. From Paris.'

'He must have been a very senior policeman.'

'Why?'

'Because most Paris policemen cannot afford to retire here. Not on their pension.'

'Perhaps he was a good saver?'

'Not with the company he keeps now. With that sort of woman, there is no saving, trust me, I know.'

It was clear that Leclerc had more interest in Julija than he did in Verlaine. 'I wouldn't know,' Chadwick said.

'But you know her,' insisted Leclerc.

'I have met her – I could hardly claim to know her.'

'Your friend, Verlaine, knows her. What does he say about her?'

Chadwick began to feel uncomfortable with Leclerc's persistence and decided the less he said, the better. 'Not much. She's Latvian. She came here for a break.'

'A break?' Leclerc looked scornful. 'A break? I don't think so.'

'You seem very sure.'

'I am. Latvian girls that look like that don't come for a break. At least not without some guy to pay the bills. And besides … I hear things.'

'What sort of things?'

Leclerc leaned closer, delighted to have some new information to impart. 'She is looking for somebody.'

'Aren't we all?'

Leclerc shook his head. 'Not that kind of somebody. Somebody specific.'

Chadwick said nothing.

'She has been asking questions.'

'About what?'

Leclerc leaned back and tapped the side of his nose. Chadwick decided not to push him. He sensed that Leclerc would be unable to keep it to himself. 'You know everything. There can't be anything that happens in this town that you don't hear about.'

'Not much,' Leclerc agreed.

'She should have come to you first.'

Leclerc shrugged. 'Perhaps. At the very least, it would have saved her some money and trouble.'

'Trouble?'

Leclerc leaned across the table as if worried that somebody might overhear. 'She didn't make a very good job of finding help. She would have done better with me. Certainly, better than with the prick she ended up with.'

'Who is that?'

'A local man. A nobody. A former policeman who was thrown out for stealing too much and smacking the wrong people. A drunk and a crook. An imbecile.'

'Why him?' asked Chadwick.

'God knows. He advertises himself as a *private detective*,' Leclerc said scornfully. 'She should have had more sense. Who can make money as a private detective here? Who did she think she was getting? Sam Spade?'

'Doesn't sound like a great choice.'

'No. No, it wasn't. It was about the worst choice she could have made. She should have asked your friend Verlaine for help. Or you.' Leclerc thought for a moment. 'Did she? Did she ask you to help her?'

Chadwick laughed. 'Me? How could I help her? I have only arrived here myself. I know two people, three if may include you?' Leclerc bowed his head graciously. 'I can just about find my way to the coast path and to this café. If she needed me to help her, she must be desperate.'

Leclerc considered this. 'Perhaps she is. Anyway, I hear that her new employee decided to get a bit rough. He thought that his new role should come with some additional benefits.'

'And she didn't?'

'Apparently not. Or maybe that is the way she likes it. There are a lot of strange people in this world, my friend. Far too many to count. And I am good at counting.'

'I'll bear it in mind.'

The waitress appeared behind Leclerc. 'There is a phone call,' she said.

'Tell them I will call them back,' said Leclerc.

'It's not for you. It is for him.' She nodded at Chadwick.

Chadwick walked over to the bar and picked up the receiver.

'Hello, is this Chadwick?' He knew immediately who it was.

'It is.' He stopped, deciding that it would be better if she spoke. She paused.

'I am sorry about what happened.'

Verlaine must have told her. It was inevitable he supposed but for some reason, Chadwick would have preferred Verlaine to have told her as little as possible. He said nothing.

'Are you there?'

'I am.'

'I said I am sorry about what happened.'

'I am too. Is there anything else?'

She paused, taken aback by his abruptness. 'I need to talk to you.'

Chadwick looked around. Leclerc was approaching the end of the bar. He went behind it and resumed his normal position over the *Nice-Matin* only a few feet from Chadwick. He sensed Chadwick looking at him and gave a knowing smile.

'When can I see you?' repeated Julija. There was a harsh awkwardness to her voice that he had forgotten.

'I don't think that would be a good idea.' Chadwick could sense Leclerc straining to hear the other side of the conversation and tried to keep his words to a minimum.

'But I have to explain …'

'You don't. And it is better …' He was about to say, *that we don't meet* but conscious of Leclerc, he said, 'that way'.

'What is wrong?'

'Nothing. Nothing at all. Be sure to say hello to Charles.'

'I'll come to see you there.'

'I don't think that would be a good idea either. Goodbye.' He didn't let her reply before he replaced the phone.

Leclerc looked at him expectantly. 'I hope you invited her here. We could do with some beauty.'

Chadwick smiled. 'I am sure she will turn up. Maybe you can help her?'

Leclerc waved one hand airily. 'Of course, I would be delighted, provided you or Monsieur Verlaine were not offended.'

'I cannot speak for Verlaine but as far as I am concerned, you can help her to your heart's content. All I need is the bill.'

'There is no bill.' Leclerc looked insulted at the very idea. He held out his hand for Chadwick to shake. 'So, you are returning to your hotel?'

'I am. Like Garbo, I want to be alone.'

Leclerc shrugged. 'As you wish. I am not sure that you will succeed any more than Garbo did.'

'Perhaps not.'

CHAPTER TWELVE

When he reached the door, Chadwick began to regret his decision to leave. The rain, that had threatened all morning, had arrived with a vengeance. Despite the time, it was almost dark, and the street was awash with water. Chadwick could sense Leclerc watching him, wondering whether he would change his mind. But Chadwick had no desire to stay, knowing that he would only face further questions and the possible arrival of Julija.

On balance, the rain looked like the more attractive option. He pulled open the door, paused briefly under the canopy, and stepped out into its full force. At first, he hunched his shoulders and lowered his head, but it was hopeless. In a few seconds, there was no part of him that was dry. His jacket wrapped his shoulders in a cold compress while the chill water ran down his neck. He conceded defeat, put his head back and dragged his leaden shoes through the river of water that was running down the pavement.

He made for the staff entrance of the hotel. It was at the end of a narrow lane between the hotel and the next building. He searched for his keys - he needed two: one for the gate at the entrance to the lane, and the other to enter the hotel itself. He found the first and opened the gate. Stepping inside, he was about to close the gate, when he heard his name. Looking up, he saw Julija running towards him. He pushed the gate closed but didn't lock it.

She must have anticipated his leaving the café and come straight to the hotel as soon as he hung up. She had no coat, only a short waterproof jacket that she was holding above her head. It offered little protection from the rain. Her jersey, jeans and boots were soaked. She grasped the railings of the gate, her knuckles showing white against her tan skin. Chadwick placed his foot against the bottom of the gate to stop it opening.

'I need to see you,' she said.

'Why?' It sounded harsher than he intended despite his determination to avoid becoming more involved.

She hesitated. 'I need to tell you about Arcier. About Arcier and me. I need to explain what happened.'

'Why? It's pretty clear what happened. I'm sorry about it but I don't think there is much to explain.'

'Nothing to explain? You don't want to know what he was doing for me?' She looked incredulous.

'No. I only became involved because Charles asked me to come with him to Arcier's office. Which I did. Reluctantly and against my better judgment.'

'And now you want to forget about it?'

'Yes. I do. And I'd advise you to do the same. Except, in your case, I would recommend doing your forgetting somewhere outside France.'

She looked at him carefully as if she was unsure what to say next. Finally, she said, 'You need to know about Arcier.'

'No, I don't. I barely met him and what I saw, I didn't like. I already know more about Arcier than is good for my health.'

'What do you think happened to him?'

'I told you. I don't care what happened to him.'

'But I didn't ask you whether you cared. I asked you what you thought happened to him. It's not the same.'

The direction of the argument was familiar. Only the subjects changed. He remembered when he had last argued like this, and with whom, and grew anxious.

He tried again, softening his tone. 'Julija, none of this is anything to do with me. You asked Charles to help you and he asked *me* to help *him*. I went with him to Arcier's office but shouldn't have done. It was a mistake. I'm sorry but I *can't* become involved.'

She ignored him and repeated the question. 'What do you think happened to Arcier?'

Chadwick spoke slowly, emphasising each word. 'Julija, I don't want to talk about Arcier anymore. Is that clear? It isn't my business, and I don't intend to make it my business. I don't care what happened to Arcier.'

She turned her face away from him for a moment or two. When she turned back, her face was flushed with anger. She reached over the gate and gripped Chadwick's arm.

'Why won't you listen? Do you think this is because I care about Arcier? You think I care about that disgusting pig? I am asking you what you think happened to him. I need to know.'

Chadwick watched her in silence. Her reference to Arcier in the past tense only intensified the fear that had been gnawing at him. He watched her as she talked. She had had given up any pretence of using the waterproof jacket as a makeshift umbrella and the rain had plastered her blonde hair to her scalp as if she had just stepped out of the shower. Her face was wet, accentuating the smoothness of her skin and the near perfection of her features. She wore no make-up that he could see. The shadow around her deep-set, green eyes was natural; her lips, moistened by the rain, were full and pink.

'Why does it matter?'

'Isn't it obvious?' She closed her eyes for a second or two before she continued. 'How could you ever think that I cared about Arcier? I care about what happened to him because I think it is connected to what I asked him to do and I'm worried that the people who went after Arcier are going to come after me.'

She turned away again but this time, Chadwick put his hand under her chin and tried to turn her head towards him. At first, she resisted. When she relented, he saw that she was crying, and he felt ashamed. He let his hand fall and she turned away from him, embarrassed or angry that he should see her tears. Taking his foot off the gate, he pulled it open, and taking her arm, led her down the lane to the side entrance of the hotel. He unlocked the door and guided her through it. Inside was a large room with no windows. The walls were painted in a light-green gloss paint that matched the worn, green linoleum. There was a strong smell of detergent or floor polish.

Julija wrapped her arms around herself and Chadwick realised she was cold. 'Come on, let's not stay here. The owner is not very generous with the heating. There is some but only on the first floor.'

She swept her left hand around her head and pushed her wet hair back from where it had fallen across her face. She seemed lost in her own thoughts and oddly disengaged from her surroundings. Chadwick closed the outside door and the sudden reduction in light seemed to startle her. She looked around, searching for the exit. Chadwick took her by the elbow and pointed her towards the corridor that ran into the heart of the hotel. Her jersey was sodden so that even the slightest touch produced water. He looked down at their feet where a dark stain was spreading across the green floor. 'Let's go,' he said.

She walked ahead of him. The corridor was almost as dark as the entrance hall but she moved confidently. Chadwick watched her outline from behind and was struck by how little noise her boots made on the hard linoleum. She padded silently and easily through the gloom, apparently indifferent to her environment.

She pushed open the door at the end of the corridor. Beyond it, she could see a line of windows that stretched from floor to ceiling and looked out over a terrace to the sea. The room was almost empty. At one end, its furniture had been piled together and covered with white dust sheets. The only other feature was an ornately carved bar with a marble top.

At the end of the bar, there was a set of steps. Chadwick watched her as she climbed them. She had gathered her wet hair and pushed it back so that it fell like a rope down her back. Her close-fitting jeans were soaked but she appeared not to notice, walking up the steps without any apparent effort, her hips square to the ground, her upper body quite still while her long legs took the steps two at a time. She reached the top and continued for a few paces before stopping. The light from the bar was fading and the upper level was gloomy.

'Where am I going?' she asked.

'Keep walking. The stairs are to your right before we reach the reception.'

She waited while her eyes readjusted to the dark. Ahead, she could see the main door of the hotel. The revolving door had been folded closed and a series of wooden shutters fixed across the doorway and the two side entrances. The only light entering the reception area was from the gaps in the shutters. She found the staircase and began to climb.

She reached the first floor and turned around. 'When does the hotel reopen?'

'The beginning of May. You want to make a booking?'

'No. I hope to be finished here a long time before May.'

'We'll miss you.'

'Will you? I wonder. Wouldn't you prefer me to go home to Latvia and leave you alone?'

Chadwick didn't reply and she pointed to an armchair that had been positioned next to a table. There was a pile of books to the side of the chair and another on the table. 'You read here.' It was unclear whether it was a statement or a question and Chadwick let it pass. She walked towards the table and picked up the top book. She glanced at the title and replaced it. 'Where is your room?' she said.

'Keep going and then take the corridor to the right.'

She walked ahead of him, her head held high, her back straight.

Her mood seemed to have changed. Her frustration had disappeared and been replaced by a new confidence. He admired her slimness as she strode silently down the carpeted hallway.

The shutters were closed and his room was dark. She hesitated in the doorway, looking for a light, and he squeezed past her, brushing against her wet jeans and jersey. He turned on the lamp by the side of the bed. The light from the top and bottom of the lamp threw a yellow shadow across one side of the room in the shape of a spinning top. The remainder of the room remained the gloomy grey that pervaded the hotel. Julija hadn't moved. She leaned against the doorjamb and examined the room. There was a double bed, well-made, the dark-blue silk cover pulled tight over the pillows. On either side of the bed, there was a night table. Opposite the bed was a reproduction-style chest of drawers. Next to the chest, there was a chintz-covered armchair. In front of the shuttered window, she could make out a chair and a *bureau plat*. The room looked as if the maid had just left.

'You seem disappointed,' he said. 'What were you expecting?'

'I thought they would have given you a larger room.'

'You think I should have taken a suite?'

She shrugged. 'Why not? They're all empty.'

'I like this room. It's small. But I like it. It suits me.'

'It suits you.' She thought for a moment. 'You are so British. You like small and confined. Does it make you feel safe?'

Chadwick hesitated. 'No. No more than any other room.'

'I don't think so. I think it makes you feel safe.'

Chadwick tried to smile. 'Safe from what?'

'Safe from the outside world. Safe from me. Safe from whatever brought you here in the first place. Who knows? Bring me a towel.'

He was surprised by her assertive tone. It was a marked change from before, almost as if the walk through the darkened hotel had emboldened her in some way that he didn't understand. He waited for a moment or two to see if she would continue but she stayed where she was, leaning against the doorframe, watching him as he walked into the bathroom. He reappeared and held out a towel. She took it and sat down in the armchair while Chadwick sat opposite her on the end of the bed. She looked down at the towel in her lap as if she had forgotten it was there. They sat in silence for some time before she raised her head.

'Why won't you help me?' she asked.

Chadwick held her gaze. The tears had disappeared and been replaced by a fragile defiance. He couldn't tell whether she was still angry with him or with the situation she found herself in. He tried to choose his words carefully.

'I *have* tried to help you. As we both know, it wasn't a great success.'

She shook her head. 'You haven't. You really haven't. You went to Arcier's office but you didn't go there *for me*. You went there because you were afraid for Charles if he went on his own. Why don't you just admit it? It's okay. I understand. And I don't care. I really don't. Just be honest with me. I don't want to be lied to.'

Chadwick thought that the more she talked, the less sure of herself she became. What had looked like defiance, now seemed more like bravado. He leaned forward, his forearms resting on his thighs. He was uncertain how to begin.

'I've always been honest with you.' He stopped. Already he sounded false. He tried again. 'Yes, I went because I was afraid for Charles. And, you should probably know that I did everything I could to persuade him not to go. I thought it was a bad idea and told him so. But, since he was so determined, I decided to go with him.'

'You know that I didn't ask him to go.'

'I didn't. But I'm not sure it would have made any difference. He was determined to confront Arcier about what he did to you and that's what worried me.'

'If I had asked you, instead of Charles, would you have helped me?'

'Maybe.'

'Maybe? And will you help me now?' She was daring him to break eye contact.

Chadwick didn't reply and she tried again. 'Will you help me or not?'

'It would be good if I knew what I was supposed to be helping you with?'

'Are you going to help me?'

Chadwick shrugged. 'Do I have a choice?'

'No. I don't think so.'

'So, what am I helping you with?'

Julija bent her head forward between her knees so that her wet hair fell to the floor. In one movement, she straightened in the chair and flicked her head up. Her hair flew backwards in an arc, splashing droplets of water up the wall behind the chair. For a second or two, Chadwick was reminded of Arcier's office.

She looked at him and grinned. 'Right now, my boots.' She straightened her right leg so that it was horizontal to the floor. Chadwick stood up and walked towards her. He caught the heel of her boot in his hand and pulled. It didn't move. It might as well have been welded to her foot.

'Do you know *how* to take off a boot? Have you *ever* taken off a boot? You can't do it like that. Get lower.'

Chadwick knelt in front of the chair and tried again. This time, the boot slipped off her foot. She leaned forward and rolled down a knee-length sock. Chadwick caught it at the end and pulled it off. She had pretty feet. Her toenails were manicured and painted scarlet. There was a red band around the middle of her foot where the boots had been too tight. He felt the damp socks. He was surprised to find they were cashmere. He reached across and repeated the performance with the left leg. He looked up but Julija ignored him.

Crossing her arms in front of her body, she gripped the bottom of her sweater. She took it off in one movement. She had nothing on under it. He wondered whether he was expected to look away. He watched as she took the towel and wrapped it around her wet hair. It was as if he wasn't there.

She finished arranging her turban and began to unfasten her jeans. She pulled them down over her bottom and looked at him. 'Will you help me?'

He pulled first one leg and then the other of the skinny blue jeans. She wore no underwear. She was quite naked and made no effort to cover herself. She sat on the chair as if she was still fully clothed. Her body was as he had imagined it. She carried no excess weight. Her stomach was perfectly flat, and her collarbone was pronounced. He was surprised by how tanned she was.

She stood and walked towards the bed. Taking hold of the top of cover, she pulled it back as far as it would go. She went to the end of the bed and untucked the sheets. Satisfied, she got into bed, pulled the sheets over her, and turned onto her right side.

'Will you switch out the light?' she said.

He switched out the light.

CHAPTER THIRTEEN

He stopped running and looked around. It was early and the coast path was deserted. The wind was strong and the sea rough. Perhaps he had imagined it? He examined the rusting fence which ran the length of the coast path and marked the boundaries of the large villas on the hill above. Noticing that the nearest gate was open, he traced the path back up the hill until he saw her. She was standing at the top of a set of decaying concrete steps.

'Are you Chadwick?' she repeated, louder this time, concerned that her voice had not carried over the noise of the wind and the sea. Chadwick went through the gate and climbed the steps to where she stood. She had her back to the sea to shelter from the wind and rain and wore a man's raincoat with the belt knotted tightly around her middle. Her hair was tucked into a baseball cap.

'I'm Chadwick,' he said.

She examined him, her head tilted to one side. She was young. No more than eighteen or nineteen. And although there was a clear resemblance to her two sisters, she was better looking than either. Pushing her hands even deeper into the pockets of the oversized coat, she said, 'My father would like to invite you to breakfast.'

'Your father?'

'My father.'

'Wants to invite me for breakfast?'

She smiled. It was a nice smile. 'He does. Would you rather finish your run first?'

A gust of wind partially dislodged her cap so that part of her hair blew across her face. Her hair was dark brown and long. She caught it and pushed it back under her cap. He noticed that her eyes were blue. She waited patiently for his answer.

'I am hardly dressed for breakfast.'

She laughed. 'Me neither. I'm still in my pyjamas. Are you coming?' She turned away from him and began to climb the steps. He watched her for a moment before falling in behind. She climbed quickly, her hands in her pockets.

'What's your father called?'

She didn't stop climbing or turn around.

'David.'

'That's all? Doesn't he have some other names?'

'He does. I call him Daddy but that might not work for you.'

'Probably not. What do other people call him.'

'People who like him?'

'Are there people who dislike him?'

'Plenty.'

'What do the people who like him call him?'

'They call him the Chairman.'

'Why? What is he the Chairman of?'

This time, she stopped and turned, one hand holding down her cap in the strengthening wind. She looked at him with her big, blue eyes. 'I have no idea, the Company, I suppose.' She resumed the climb, as if this explained everything.

By now, he could see more of the house. It was a contemporary villa, built into the side of the hill. On either side of the terrace that ran the width of the house, the architect had designed triangular white panels that began at the terrace and tapered inwards to an apex on the third floor. There was a narrower terrace on the first floor and a balcony on the third. Both stretched the width of the house. The front of the villa was all glass. The terraces were designed to look like decks, and the triangular panels like sails, so that the overall impression was of a ship.

The girl, indifferent to the villa's charms, reached the bottom of a staircase directly under the main terrace, and began to go up. She seemed to have no interest in Chadwick at all. It was as if she already knew everything that she needed to know. They emerged from the stairs in the middle of the terrace that was completely empty. The wind was stronger than at sea level, but the view of the sea and the cape was impressive, even on such a foul day.

Pulling open a sliding glass door, she ushered him inside and closed the door. Immediately, the sound of the wind and the sea disappeared as if the view of the coast, the distant town and the mountains had been projected onto the glass. He stared at it for a second or two to see if he could see anything moving. But nothing did. The striking of a clock interrupted his reverie and he looked around.

It was a large room that stretched from one side of the villa to the other. At one end, there was a fireplace with a stone-built external chimney. In front of it, and arranged around a low table, were three large, white sofas. On top of the table were piles of books. Two marble-topped bureau commodes stood at the back of the room, on either side of a pair of doors that looked as if they had been bought from a derelict chateau. The tops of the commodes were covered with framed photos. Around the walls, there were several large canvases. At the other end of the room, there was a contemporary dining table with twelve chairs. It had been set for two.

He looked for the girl, but she had disappeared. Returning to the window, he looked down towards the cape. The coast path was clearly visible. Anybody with binoculars would have seen him from the moment he reached the head of the cape and known exactly how long it would take him to reach the gate below.

'Sixteen minutes. You were quicker yesterday, but then you had the wind behind you.'

Chadwick hadn't been aware of anybody entering the room, and for a second, he wondered whether he had been there all along.

'I'm David Spencer.'

Spencer was in his late fifties or very early sixties. Tall, almost as tall as Chadwick, he stood with his back unnaturally straight. He had lost most of his hair but what remained was brown and neither his hair nor eyebrows showed any trace of grey. Chadwick thought that he had probably looked the same way for twenty years and might easily look the same for another twenty. He wore a well-cut, light-blue shirt that showed the folds from the laundry and looked as if he had put it on only moments before. His soft-grey flannel trousers had an equally sharp crease. On his feet, he wore a highly polished pair of brown loafers.

He gestured towards the table. 'Why don't we sit down? Would you prefer coffee or tea?' Chadwick watched as the Chairman poured him a cup of coffee from a silver thermos before offering him a small jug that contained hot milk.

'I'm glad we were able to meet. I wanted to thank you for what you did. I am very grateful and I'm sorry if Sylvia hadn't the good sense to thank you herself. I have a pretty good idea of the trouble she was in even if she doesn't. And they were in trouble, were they not?'

Chadwick thought about how much he should say but decided that it was best to be direct.

'They were.'

'Set up by the Frenchman?'

'Yes.'

'In the café or before?'

'Almost certainly before but I don't know where.'

'Will he cause problems?'

Chadwick shook his head. 'I don't think so. He had no real interest in your daughters. They were just marks. Besides, I think he will have other issues to occupy him.'

'Such as?'

'Satisfying his employer that he didn't set him up.'

The Chairman thought for a moment. 'Anybody approach you?'

'Not yet. But there hasn't been much time. I expect they are still running through the more obvious suspects. I need to return the money before its owner comes calling.'

'Who does it belong to?'

'Ultimately? I have no idea, but the casino owner seems like a good place to start. The sooner I return it, the happier I'll be.'

'Even if you do give it back to him, what makes you think he'll overlook your involvement? After all, you beat up a couple of his men.'

'I don't know if they were his men. They may have been collecting for somebody else. They may just have been local muscle for hire. From what I hear about the casino owner, he isn't as pure as the driven snow, but he doesn't sound like a gangster either.'

The Chairman looked unconvinced. 'Why don't you return the money anonymously?'

Chadwick shook his head. 'What would be the point? They are going to keep looking for whomever took the money regardless of whether it is returned or not. And this is a small town.'

'So how *are* you going to do it?'

'Go to the casino tonight and ask to see him.'

'And, if he agrees to see you, what then?'

'I am not sure. I'll play it by ear. It depends on whose money it was, and how annoyed *they* are. If it was his, and it was just local heavies, then quite possibly he doesn't care. He'll have the money back and nobody will be any the wiser. Besides, I hardly think he'll want me to go to the police.'

The Chairman agreed. 'It's a little late for that. Besides, I would be surprised if he didn't have the locals in his pocket. You might even have met some of them moonlighting the other night.'

'You *do* have a cynical view of the local policing.'

'I have a cynical view of the South of France. There is nothing that will surprise me about this place. And, if the money doesn't belong to him but to somebody else, then what?'

Chadwick sighed. 'Then it becomes more difficult. Then, I probably need to get out.'

'You might not be given the option.'

'I think I'll be okay. He is unlikely to try anything at the casino. After all, he has no idea who I might have told about the money.'

The Chairman was sceptical. 'I wouldn't count on that too much if I were you. He may be happy to call your bluff. These people often are. In their view of the world, it is better to call *every* bluff. If they are wrong, then they deal with the consequences. Have you told anybody else about the fight?'

Chadwick thought for a moment, unsure what to tell a man that he had only just met. The Chairman seemed to sense his unease.

'It doesn't matter to me,' he said, 'but there is a risk that they will try to find them too. You need to be prepared for that.'

Chadwick already knew this possibility, which was why he hadn't told anybody. But the knowledge didn't make him feel any more comfortable. Quite the contrary. 'Nobody else knows,' he said.

'Would it surprise you that none of the local hospitals treated any fractures that night? I think you should be careful not to underestimate this man.'

Chadwick wondered at the Chairman's ability to check the admission records of the local hospitals but let it pass.

The Chairman continued. 'Mr Augustin has been busy. He has been asking a great many questions and has made the connection between my daughters and me. It's not surprising, I suppose. They needed to show their passports to gamble, and it wouldn't have taken very long to establish the link. Now that he has made it, perhaps it would be better if you told him that you were working for me all along?'

'Why?'

'I have a certain reputation and the firm is known to undertake sensitive work internationally. We try to keep a low profile but anybody who deals with Lloyd's would know who we are.'

'What sort of work do you do?'

The Chairman reached across and offered Chadwick a plate of pastries. He replaced the plate and poured himself another coffee before he answered.

'Investigations mostly.'

'Like a loss adjuster?'

The Chairman shook his head. 'Not really. Most of our work is rather specialised.'

Chadwick waited for an explanation, but the Chairman seemed to think that he had said enough. He poured some hot milk into the coffee and stirred it with a higher level of concentration than was warranted. 'In any case, if Augustin has done his research properly, he would probably conclude that I wouldn't let my daughters wander the world …' he searched for the appropriate word, *'unsupervised.* It's up to you, of course, but it might be better if you were to suggest to Augustin that you work for me, and I asked you to return the money.'

'And the fight in the car park?'

'You weren't there. You were asleep. The only people there were the team I had looking after the girls.'

Chadwick said nothing. The idea was sound and a great improvement on Chadwick trying to bluff his way through a difficult encounter. Besides, he was warming to the idea of having somebody like the Chairman on his side. Whoever he was, he was well informed. Chadwick hadn't mentioned the name of the casino owner. But it hadn't mattered. The Chairman had done his own research and it had been thorough. He wondered what sort of grilling the daughters had received on their return home and how much more the Chairman knew about the situation, and more important-ly, about Chadwick, that he wasn't disclosing.

'So now I am supposed to work for you?'

'Why not?'

'I always thought insurance work was dull.'

The Chairman shrugged. 'It's supposed to be but when it isn't, it can get interesting quite quickly. Perhaps I didn't do the best job of selling the firm. I think you might make rather a good investigator. Why don't you think about it?'

'Thank you for the offer but I'm not looking for work. I'm here for a rest.'

The Chairman gesticulated with his coffee cup. 'It doesn't seem to have been very restful so far.'

'No. Possibly not. But that may change. In any case, I might claim to be employed by you if that's okay?'

The Chairman sat back in his chair. 'That's fine. I'll let the office know in case anybody checks. If asked, we'll say that you joined us a month ago. Would that work?'

Chadwick was unsettled by the suggested time but was careful not to overreact. He examined the Chairman's face but there was nothing to suggest that the mention of a month was anything other than coincidental. 'Perhaps there is something else you could do for me?' he said, remembering what Julija had told him the night before.

'Of course. What is it?'

'I am looking for some information. About a ship. And given your Lloyd's connections, you might be able to help.'

'Possibly. What is the name of the ship?'

'The *Highland Laddie.*'

The Chairman got up and walked over to the low table. He picked up a leather-bound notebook and a pen. Returning to the dining table, he opened the notebook at a fresh page. At the top, he wrote 'Chadwick' and immediately below, he made a bullet point and wrote '*Highland Laddie*'. 'Who owns it?' he asked.

'Nobody. As far as I know. The insurers, I suppose. It's not around anymore. It sank.'

'How?'

'In a storm, in the South China Sea.'

'Carrying?'

'Carrying?'

'What was its cargo?'

'I have no idea. I know almost nothing about it except that disappeared in heavy seas.'

He watched in silence as the Chairman added bullet points. He noticed that he wrote a question mark after 'disappeared'.

'Crew?'

'They all drowned. There were no survivors.'

The Chairman stopped writing and looked up. 'When was this?'

'About a year ago.'

'They find any wreckage?'

'No idea. I don't know very much about it. Only what I have been told.'

'Why the interest?'

Chadwick hesitated. 'A friend of mine would like to know what happened to the ship.' He knew it sounded weak even as he said it, but he had already decided that he had told Spencer enough.

The Chairman's voice was softer, as if he sensed that Chadwick was holding out on him. 'Is there anything else?'

Chadwick considered it for a moment or two. 'Maybe. The person I'm trying to help knew somebody on the *Highland Laddie*. A man called Aleksis Soldane. He was the Second Mate. A Latvian. Anything that you could find out about him would be useful. I really don't know much more.'

He watched as the Chairman wrote it all down in his leather-bound notebook. He took special care of Aleksis' name, spelling it back to Chadwick to ensure that there would be no mistake. When he finished, he looked up; it seemed as if he was going to ask another question but thought better of it. He closed the notebook and put the pen on the table. 'I'm not sure how much I'll be able to find out but I'll try,' he said.

'Thanks. I would appreciate it,' said Chadwick.

He wondered if the Chairman would have been more confident if he knew that Aleksis Soldane had checked out of a Nice hotel two days before.

CHAPTER FOURTEEN

Augustin's office was on the first floor facing the sea. The windows ran from floor to ceiling and were framed by heavy silk curtains, pulled back and tied with brocaded ropes. The office was unlit so that the impact of the evening sun over the gardens, the white buildings, and the blue sea beyond was magnified in intensity.

The walls were covered in dark-green silk. The furniture was antique. A large nineteenth-century painting of gamblers seated around a card table dominated one of the walls. In front of the fireplace, there were two sofas facing each other, an oriental carpet and a coffee table displaying a variety of *objets d'art*. The room smelled of amber and cigars.

A man was sitting at a *bureau plat* close to the windows. He was only a silhouette against the evening sun. As Chadwick entered, the man stood and walked towards him. As he drew closer, his features became clearer. In his younger days, he would have been stocky, but now, he was running to fat, the price of too much work indoors or too much good living. He wore a blue suit, a cream shirt and a dark-blue silk tie. His cufflinks were gold knots.

The face was tanned and surprisingly unwrinkled, the eyes brown and quiet. His grey hair was straight, combed back from his face, parted on the left and subdued by liberal amounts of hair oil. The face wore a mask of quiet concern, consummate and conscientious, like a surgeon or a banker at the top of his profession.

'Please,' he said, waving Chadwick towards the far sofa. The sofa's cushion had been so heavily plumped that as Chadwick sat, he found himself sinking lower than he had intended. Augustin sat opposite him, one arm extended across the back of the sofa.

He said, 'Would you like something to drink, Mr …?'

'Chadwick.'

Augustin reached across to a side table by the sofa and pressed a button on top of a small wooden box. The door opened almost immediately. The burly bruiser who had escorted Chadwick upstairs came in and stood with his back against the open door and his hands clasped neatly over his groin. He looked at the two men, his face betraying all the emotion of a disused quarry. He said nothing. A second man walked into the room. A waiter. Augustin ordered champagne and returned to his previous pose once the guard and waiter had left.

The two men sat in silence, each wanting the other to speak first.

Finally, Chadwick said, 'I have found some money.'

Augustin gave a half-smile. 'Really? You are a lucky man.'

'Do you think so? I am not so sure. You see, I am not much interested in money. Would you like to know *where* I found it?'

Augustin shrugged. 'Is it relevant?'

'Possibly.'

'Then I'm interested.'

'I found it very close to your casino and thought it might belong to you. Have you lost any money recently?'

Augustin shook his head. 'We rarely lose money, Mr Chadwick, and always to clients. You see, I am a careful man, and unlike you, I have an over-developed affection for money. If we had mislaid even a few euros, I am certain that I would know about it.' Augustin paused. 'May I ask what brought you to the South of France?'

'A rest cure. For my nerves.'

'How unfortunate. It is a very debilitating complaint. You are not, if I may say so, of an obviously nervous disposition.'

The waiter entered with drinks and set them down on the low table. His task completed, he left as silently as before, but not before he had slipped Augustin a folded piece of paper. Augustin opened it, read it, and slipped it into his jacket pocket.

Augustin lifted his glass towards Chadwick. 'To better health,' he said. He took a short sip and set the champagne flute down on the coffee table. He gestured towards the window where the orange light of the setting sun was intensifying the green of the trees that partially hid the view of the sea.

'What do you think of our little town?'

'*Beau de loin mais loin de beau.*'

Augustin looked at him sharply. 'So, you know our sayings: beautiful from afar but far from beautiful - you may be too perceptive for your own good, Mr Chadwick. You must be careful to keep your insights to yourself. This is not a town that is much interested in the truth.'

'What is it interested in?'

Augustin thought for a moment. 'Self-preservation, mostly. Not a very noble sentiment, but if you are going to stay here, you would be well advised to embrace it. Now, what were we talking about?' Augustin looked mildly confused like a genial housemaster caught off guard.

'The money I found,' said Chadwick.

'Ah, yes. The money.'

Augustin let himself slip slightly further down into the sofa, his brown eyes resting casually on Chadwick's face. He took a sip of his champagne and gazed at a painting above the fireplace. He set his glass down carefully and brushed a piece of fluff from his trousers. He looked across at Chadwick.

'What would you like, Mr Chadwick?' Augustin raised his eyebrows to encourage a reply.

'I would like to be left alone.'

'It's a worthy ambition. But an expensive one. You need to be very wealthy to be left alone. Are you very wealthy, Mr Chadwick?'

'No.'

'That's a pity.'

Chadwick tried again. 'You still haven't asked me how much money I was proposing to return? Perhaps you already know?'

Augustin's smile carried all the warmth of an ambitious funeral director soliciting business.

'I am not very interested, Mr Chadwick. As I explained …'

'… You haven't lost any money. I know. But still, you agreed to see me. Do you usually see everybody who asks?'

Augustin shrugged. 'I thought you might appreciate some company.'

Chadwick felt a tightening in his stomach. He smiled and looked at his opponent. Augustin was sitting back in the sofa, one ankle crossed over the other, one hand holding the champagne flute, the other stretched out across the back of the sofa. He looked as relaxed as before.

'Why might you think that?' said Chadwick and immediately regretted it, realising too late that he had taken the conversation in the wrong direction.

Augustin took his time before he answered. 'We always want what we are running away from, Mr Chadwick. That is why we are running away. A man who chooses to live alone always yearns for company.'

Chadwick forced himself to smile. Augustin continued.

'I assume you are alone in your hotel?'

'Is it so easy to tell?'

'I'm afraid so.' Augustin paused. 'So, tell me, why does a man choose to spend the winter in a deserted hotel?'

Chadwick saw now that everything Augustin had said and done since he arrived in his office meant nothing. Augustin, aware that he had been caught off guard, had played for time, time to get as much information as he could on his unexpected visitor. Chadwick would have given a great deal to see what was written on the folded piece of paper that had arrived with the drinks. But it wasn't going to happen. For now, all he could do was wait for Augustin to play his hand.

'There aren't any people,' said Chadwick. 'That's the main attraction. Room service can be a bit frustrating if you want your scrambled eggs before Easter.'

Augustin seemed not to hear. 'For a man who doesn't like people,' he said, 'you seem to make new friends rather easily.'

Chadwick wasn't sure where Augustin was going. 'New friends?' he said.

'The English girl who was in the casino the night before last.'

Chadwick was about to deny that he had been in the casino that night but thought better of it. There was a good chance that Augustin had reviewed the CCTV tapes and Chadwick knew that he must feature somewhere. He took a different tack.

'Which English girl?'

Augustin gave him an arch look.

'The one who had her handbag snatched.'

'You're well informed,' said Chadwick

Augustin smiled patiently. 'I try,' he said. 'You saw it?'

'Saw what?'

'The theft of the handbag.'

'I saw both. The theft *and* its recovery.'

Augustin ran his finger around the top of the glass. 'How interesting,' he said. 'Can I ask you what you were doing there?'

'Reading a book and drinking coffee.'

Augustin raised his eyebrows. 'Was it a complete coincidence that you happened to be sitting in the same café?'

'Yes.'

'But when they came to the casino, you were here too. Is that another coincidence?'

'Complete. How could it be otherwise?'

Augustin didn't answer. Eventually, he said, 'The girl is called Sylvia Spencer. She is … *was* staying locally with her sister and two young men. She was here the other night with her companions and a local boy. Do you remember him?'

'I assume you are talking about North Africa's answer to street crime?'

'I am. You don't like Mr Hamidou?'

'I didn't find too much to like.'

'What do you know about the English girl's father?'

It was a clever question. He considered it for a second or two, and said, 'Only what I have heard. Well-respected businessman. Close to Lloyd's, the London insurer.'

'Would it surprise you to know that he was for many years in the military?'

'I can't say. I've never thought about it.'

'Do you work for him?'

Chadwick had been expecting the question. He could see Augustin watching for his reaction and made sure that all he saw was a touch of annoyance with Augustin's continual questions.

'No. I don't work for him. Although I'm not sure that will help you very much because, even if I did, I would be unlikely to admit it. Anyway, why would you care whether I work for him or not?'

'I don't. I am just intrigued by your being in the same café at the time the handbag was snatched and then being in the casino the same night as the English girl. And, then, of course, there is your good fortune in finding such a large sum of money.'

'Did I say it was large?' said Chadwick.

Augustin ignored him. The direction of Augustin's questioning was becoming clearer, and he had no interest in being diverted.

'What time did you leave the casino?'

'Early. I am not much of a gambler.'

'I wouldn't be so sure about that. Did you go straight back to the hotel?'

'As opposed to what? Enjoying the local flesh pots? And why do you care what I did? Are you planning to stand for mayor?'

Augustin's smile was wintry. 'There was an incident near the casino that night. I thought you might have seen something.'

'Seen, no, but I heard something about it.'

'How?'

'It's a small town. People talk.'

'Did you know that your English friends were involved?'

'I told you. They are not my friends. I barely know them. Hamidou knows them. Why don't you ask him?'

'I have,' said Augustin.

'And?'

Augustin didn't reply. Chadwick, increasingly uncomfortable with how the discussion was developing, changed tack.

'Did they catch the robbers?'

Augustin gazed quietly at his half-empty champagne flute for a moment before lifting his eyes to Chadwick's. 'Robbers? You think there was a robbery?'

Chadwick, realising his mistake, tried to be non-committal. 'That's what I heard.'

Augustin looked disappointed. 'One hears so many things in a small town like this. There are too many people with too much time on their hands. You really must not believe everything you are told, Mr Chadwick.'

You are a talented liar, thought Chadwick. He could imagine Augustin as a courtroom disappointment to any number of prosecutors.

'Even by you?'

'Especially by me.'

'I'm shocked.'

Augustin looked at Chadwick in surprise and then laughed. His laughter seemed out of place with his mannered appearance and the carefully crafted environment. It struck Chadwick as genuine, the one unscripted gesture in a complex piece of theatre. It made Augustin suddenly accessible, friendly, a man with whom one could enjoy spending time. It also, he thought, made him even more dangerous.

'Just so that I am clear, there was no robbery?' asked Chadwick.

'None. There was a misunderstanding. A fracas. A scuffle. The kind of thing that can happen between jealous locals and wealthy and sometimes insensitive tourists. It was no more than that.'

'I thought you warned me a moment ago not to believe everything you said?'

'I did. And it was good advice.'

'If there was no robbery, then presumably the English girl's winnings are safe?'

'I assume so.'

'You know so. I assume that you have searched the bag I left in the cloakroom?'

Augustin smiled. 'Mr Chadwick, do I look like the type of man who goes through people's belongings in my cloakroom?'

'No. But you look like the sort of man that would employ men to do it for you.'

'Mr Chadwick, I am disappointed that you would think so.'

'You don't look very disappointed.'

Augustin sat immobile, his face inscrutable. He looked at Chadwick, his brown eyes resting on Chadwick's face as casually as a fly on a sunlit tabletop. 'Perhaps not. But, tell me, what is to happen to this money?'

It was clear that they had reached a turning point in the conversation. Chadwick paused. 'What money?' he said, and taking the cloakroom ticket from his pocket, he slid it across the table to Augustin, who looked at it for a second, and then palmed it with the dexterity of a stage musician. He looked at Chadwick and raised his eyebrows.

'There have been a lot of things *not* happening around here,' said Chadwick. 'You didn't lose any money from the casino. The English girl didn't win any money at roulette. There was no robbery. There wasn't even a cloakroom ticket.'

'And the English girl and her party?'

'They flew home.'

'Not from Nice.'

'No. I gather they wanted to see Provence before they left.'

Augustin inspected his manicured nails as if he had detected a flaw in their otherwise perfect appearance. 'Lyons.' It was neither a statement nor a question, more an acknowledgment of something that he had considered but dismissed.

Augustin thought for a moment. 'But young people can sometimes be rather naïve in their belief about how the world ought to work?'

'Not these ones. Their naïve days are behind them. I made sure of it.'

CHAPTER FIFTEEN

Augustin's office was bathed in the fading red of the setting sun. It was completely quiet, isolated from the sounds of everyday life. Neither of the two men spoke, each determined to enjoy the silence. When Augustin's office phone rang, it gave Chadwick a start. Augustin looked at it in surprise, before walking to his desk and picking up the receiver. He said, 'Please tell her I will be free in ten minutes and ask her to wait.'

He replaced the receiver and stood by the desk for a moment as if deep in contemplation. He turned and walked towards the windows until all Chadwick could see was his silhouette. From where Chadwick sat, it was impossible to tell if something had caught his eye or he merely wanted to enjoy the sunset. He stood for some moments. Finally, he said, 'I should not like to give this up.'

Chadwick was taken aback and waited for him to continue. But he didn't. He remained by the window lost in his thoughts. It was a statement that emerged from nowhere, unconnected to their previous conversation, or what followed. It made him seem somehow vulnerable, like an aged relative being asked to sell the family home. *'I should not like to give this up.'*

Augustin returned to the sofa and lowered himself gently into it. He remained distant as if his thoughts were elsewhere.

'You have managed this rather well, Chadwick. You have a talent for it. This smoothing of troubled waters. Do you not agree?'

'I can't say that I have ever thought about it.'

'Perhaps you should think about it?'

'Is this a job offer?'

'Perhaps.'

'You don't seem very sure?'

'As I grow older, I am less sure about everything. I envy youth its confidence, but I would rather be less certain and right, than certain and wrong.'

'That's funny. I thought you just told me that this was a town where it is better to keep your perceptions to yourself.'

'I did. And it is still true,' said Augustin, smiling.

'"Self-assertion more often than not is vulgar, but a live and vulgar dog who keeps on barking is better than a dead lion, however dignified."'

Augustin raised his eyebrows. Chadwick said, 'Louis MacNeice.'

'Who is he?' asked Augustin.

'He was a Northern Irish poet. He is a favourite of mine.'

'I don't know him, I'm afraid,' said Augustin. 'I have little time for reading. You must write down his name for me.' Augustin stood, went to his desk and returned with a sheet of cream writing paper and a large enamel and silver fountain pen. He handed them to Chadwick and watched as Chadwick wrote.

'I envy you your education,' he said. 'It's a great privilege.'

Chadwick extended his arm and gestured towards the paintings, the furniture and the window. 'Your lack of knowledge of twentieth-century poetry doesn't seem to have held you back.'

'Perhaps not. But what I have learned along the way, I would have preferred to have learned from books.'

Chadwick finished writing and handed the pen and paper to Augustin, who looked at the paper for a moment or two.

The door to Augustin's office opened. The same granite-faced thug was standing in the open doorway looking at his boss with a mixture of contrition and fear. The source of his concern ignored him as she entered, giving him no more attention than she would have given a doorstop.

For a second, Chadwick thought he saw a cloud pass across Augustin's benign features, but when he looked again, all that was visible was a look of professional delight, the *maître d'hôtel* welcoming a prodigal client.

Augustin stood and walked towards the newcomer. His speed of movement surprised Chadwick, and made it easier to picture a younger, more aggressive man, afraid only of failure. He approached the visitor, his arms outstretched as if trying to recapture a dog that had slipped its collar. He placed himself between Chadwick and the woman. It was almost as if he wanted to hide her. It was an impossible task. She was at least a head taller than Augustin.

'My dear Silje, what an unexpected pleasure! I hadn't realised that you were here.'

The woman, resting her hands on Augustin's shoulders, bent her head to let him kiss her, before she stepped to one side. She was wearing a pair of blue flat shoes with white vinyl leather toecaps, cut low so that you could just see her toes. The feet were narrow and tanned. The white jeans were tight and tapered to a point an inch or two above the ankle. The top of the jeans sat low on her hips where they were nominally kept aloft by a blue crocodile belt. Between the belt and the bottom of an extensively embroidered T-shirt, were several inches of tanned midriff. Her head was tilted back as if the weight of her dark-brown hair was too much for her fragile neck. The face was perfectly still and showed no emotion. It didn't need to. It could have been exhibited in a glass case and there would have been a queue around the block. Chadwick, conscious that his careful inspection might be misunderstood, refocused and was met with a cool stare from a pair of china-blue eyes. They looked at him for a moment, and then, just as suddenly looked through him, as if he had disappeared. The effect was disconcerting.

He waited patiently while she turned her attention to Augustin.

'Your people were rather more unhelpful than usual.'

'I am sorry. It's my fault. I had asked not to be disturbed.'

'Even by me?'

'Of course not, Silje. You are always welcome. You know that.'

'You are a terrible liar, Augustin. They called you from downstairs.' Augustin attempted an explanation, but she cut him off. 'I don't wait. I certainly don't wait downstairs with your teenage hookers and half-witted heavies. Who is this?' Without waiting for his reply, she turned towards Chadwick. 'Who are you?'

Chadwick said nothing. He looked at Augustin for guidance.

She turned towards Augustin and inclining her head to one side as if she were talking to a child, said, 'Doesn't he speak?' Turning back to Chadwick, she said, 'Do you speak?'

Chadwick was surprised by her voice. It was deeper than he expected with each word carefully enunciated as if there were a penalty for mispronunciation. There was no warmth, no trace of emotion, and despite her clear annoyance at being kept waiting, no sign, in her carefully modulated speech, of any irritation. He listened for an accent but found none. She waited, her face perfectly framed by her hair.

'Sometimes. Sparingly. It depends on the company.'

As soon as he spoke, Chadwick was surprised to find himself embarrassed by his words, as if he had failed to impress his elder sister's attractive friend.

'*Sparingly*? You are too well educated to be with our lovely friend. Augustin, I congratulate you. You must be moving in a better crowd. Mr ...?'

'This is Mr Chadwick.' Augustin seemed glad to have been given a chance to speak.

'*Mr Chadwick*.' She thought for a moment and then she said, 'I like your approach, Mr Chadwick. People down here speak a great deal more than is good for them. But, sadly, that does not mean that a man of few words will prosper.'

She passed Chadwick and went to sit on the far end of the sofa diagonally opposite him, as if she had deliberately chosen the farthest point from him. She leaned back on the arm of the sofa, her long legs folded at the ankle, and examined him carefully.

'Mr Chadwick was just leaving, Silje.'

'Was he? Were you, Mr Chadwick?'

'I rather think I was.'

'But you are not certain?'

'I am certain of very little. Augustin has been explaining that it is better to be uncertain than certain and wrong.'

She turned towards Augustin. 'You have hidden depths. You are a philosopher *manqué.* Perhaps that's why we get on so well?'

Augustin shrugged. She turned her attention back to Chadwick.

'Do you speak *sparingly* because you are uncertain? Do you act *sparingly* as well?'

Her face betrayed no emotion until almost imperceptibly, the corners of her mouth drew back in a smile and flashes of brilliance danced across her eyes, disappearing as suddenly as they had appeared. It was the briefest glimpse of a patch of sunlight in a darkened forest. Chadwick felt a chill pass through him. It was a feeling that he couldn't place until he realised that it was fear.

'What are you doing with my lovely friend?'

Chadwick forced himself to focus. 'I think he was offering me a job.'

'A job?' She looked over at Augustin, who was still hovering in front of the sofas. 'You must be raising your standards.' Augustin didn't reply. She turned back to Chadwick. 'And did you accept?'

'No.'

'Why not?'

'I don't need work.'

'What do you want?' This time, she made no attempt to disguise her amusement. She was leaning forward, her elbow on her knee, her chin cupped in her hand.

'What do I want?' Chadwick repeated the question to buy himself some time but to his surprise, Augustin came to his rescue.

'He wants to be left alone. I know. He just told me.'

Silje glanced at Augustin. Perhaps it was to see if he was serious. Her intention was unclear. She resumed her careful consideration of Chadwick.

'I shall leave you alone. But I doubt whether anybody else will. This is not a town that leaves anybody alone. You should go home.'

For a second, the bright-blue eyes re-engaged with Chadwick's and then just as swiftly disengaged, leaving him feeling suddenly giddy. She made a show of uncrossing her legs and self-consciously inspected a possible mark on her white trousers. She smiled.

'I hope you are successful in being left alone. I really do. For your sake.'

She reached forward and picked up one of the books that lay piled on Augustin's coffee table and began to read it. It was clear that her conversation with Chadwick was over. Chadwick stood up and walked towards the door. Augustin came to guide him towards it.

'Goodbye. I hope we meet again soon. It has been a pleasure.'

Chadwick was struck by Augustin's sincerity. Puzzled by Augustin's relationship with the tall Norwegian, he looked back towards where she was sitting. She continued to read as if she were alone in the room. The door was opened by the same heavy-jawed hood, and he walked out. It had been an interesting evening.

CHAPTER SIXTEEN

Chadwick heard the front door open and close. The café grew quiet. Chadwick didn't look up. It had to be an attractive woman. Nothing else drew the attention of the café's regulars. He hoped it wasn't Julija. Conscious of somebody hovering by his table, he looked up. The hoverer needed no second invitation and sat down opposite. It may not have been a woman but he understood the locals' interest.

The newcomer was a little below average height, with a head of thick, brown hair, flecked with grey. The suit could have graced the bar at the Cavalry and Guards Club, but the check would have been more at home on a provincial racecourse. His skin was pale with the pinkness of a man who carries more weight than he should. He sat with his strong-looking hands clasped across his stomach like a successful bishop. His nails, Chadwick noticed, were neatly manicured.

He was hard to place. He could have been a successful bookie or a partner in a City stockbrokerage, a gangster or a well-to-do cattle dealer. Whenever you tried to complete the picture, there were always one or two elements missing, as if the man baulked at any form of categorisation.

Spying one of Leclerc's older and less agreeable waitresses, he waved her over. To Chadwick's surprise, she responded immediately. The newcomer took her by the elbow. Chadwick waited for her to shake off his grip, but she did nothing, apparently pleased to have been brought into the drama. The newcomer looked around at the other tables and didn't like what he saw.

'Darling, do you have *proper* food in that kitchen of yours?' He spoke English with a Glaswegian accent, assuming that the waitress understood everything he said. He pointed at a plate of pastries. 'That stuff's no good to me. I need a *proper* breakfast, with eggs and bacon and sausage, have you anything like that?' Chadwick considered intervening, but each seemed to understand the other perfectly. The waitress had her hand on the man's shoulder while he retained his grip on her elbow.

'And a coffee, *s'il vous plait.* Black.'

She repeated what he had asked for in French. '*Parfait.*' He grinned. '*Tout de suite,* dear,' he said, although he pronounced it 'toot sweet'. He dropped his grip and she left reluctantly.

The newcomer reached into his inside jacket pocket and pulled out a phone. It was vibrating. He held it at arm's-length, gazed at the screen, pushed a button that silenced the vibration, replaced it in his jacket and turned his attention to Chadwick.

'I'm McGhee,' he said, sitting back, grasping the edge of the table as if to steady himself, and letting his chin fall forward on to his chest. 'Decent headquarters,' he added, smiling, as if he had paid Chadwick an important compliment.

'I try,' said Chadwick.

McGhee looked around the café. 'It's good to be back in the South of France,' he said. 'I know it's a rip-off and the French can drive you mental, but I love it. You can take it from me – the South of France is class. Real class. You can't get this kind of class anywhere else. If you just want the sun, Florida's okay but it's full of halfwits. You get a laugh, but you go daft if you stay too long. You can't compare it with here. Here you get proper, proper crooks. Real tricksters, not a bunch of whacked-out losers.'

'You seem to know it well.'

McGhee laughed. 'Oh, yes,' he said, affecting a plummy accent, 'I have had to administer a good thrashing to a scoundrel or two down here. Dirty scallywags that required *a strong talking to*. And a few lashes of the riding crop.'

'Seems rather harsh,' said Chadwick.

McGhee grinned. 'Not really. I think a few of them enjoyed it. You know there are a lot of strange fellows around. Especially here. That's why I love the place. So, thank you.'

'You are thanking *me?*'

'Naturally. I am only here because of you – small Scottish chap bearing message in cleft stick.'

'From the Chairman?'

'From the self-same. Now, any progress on the Breakfast of the Century?' He looked around just as the waitress approached with a black coffee and a plate of toast.

'I didn't hear you order toast,' said Chadwick.

McGhee shrugged. 'I think she knows that I might not be from around here. Thanks, dear.'

The waitress beamed at him before heading back to the kitchen.

'Nice woman,' said McGhee, reaching for a piece of toast. Chadwick watched as he cut it into a triangle. He had the quick, deft, confident movements of a former sportsman. He buttered and sliced each piece in turn, inspected his efforts and then sat back to enjoy his coffee and the first triangle. 'Please, help yourself.' he said, gesturing with the hand that held the toast. He chewed contentedly as if it was the first food he had seen in some time. Chadwick let him eat. He was in no hurry and wanted more time to study McGhee.

'Now, where were we?' said McGhee.

'The Chairman?'

'Aha, yes. The Chairman. Very impressed with you, young Lochinvar. Asked me to check that you're all right.' He stopped and looked up from his food. 'Are you all right?'

'I think so. Did he think I might not be?'

'Well, apparently, there was a small misunderstanding with some of the local ruffians that involved you giving one or two of them a good slap. He thought they or their boss might come looking for you to express their disappointment with your boxing their ears.'

'There wasn't a lot of boxing involved.'

McGhee raised his eyebrows. 'That's a shame, we must do what we can to keep the noble art alive.' He returned to his food.

Finishing, he reached across to take a paper napkin from the dispenser on the table. He wiped his mouth carefully, inspecting the napkin afterwards to satisfy himself that nothing had been left on his face. He crumpled the napkin into a ball, dropped it on the plate, and gave the plate to a passing waitress. He poured himself another coffee, emptied an unhealthy amount of sugar into it, and began to stir. Satisfied with his efforts, he took a sip of the coffee, before setting the cup to one side.

'You asked the boss about Aleksis Soldane.'

'I did. Did he find out anything?'

'Some. Not a very lucky chappie, young Soldane. Not very lucky at all. Second Mate on a container ship called the *Highland Laddie* that went down in the South China Sea in a typhoon. Crew all slept in. No survivors. He'd been Second Mate for a year. Clean record. Good references. Ship's owner was happy with him. Most recent stop was in Singapore where they unloaded part of the cargo before setting out for Dalian in China. Never made it.'

'What was the cargo?'

'Mixed, typical container ship, but mainly machine tools.'

'Was it a normal route for them?'

'Seems to have been. They worked mostly in Asia.'

'What about the crew?'

'Nothing unusual. Captain and officers had been on the ship for some time. Crew was mostly Filipino. It had changed a bit but the officers hadn't.'

'What do you mean?'

McGhee stopped. 'Do you know much about shipping?'

Chadwick shook his head. 'Not much.'

'The Captain and the officers are signed by the ship's owner and typically work nine months with three months off. While they are working, they rarely return home. When these boys go to sea, they stay at sea.'

'But they must go to ports to unload. Surely, they go ashore then?'

'Not always. These are container ships. They are unloaded fast and the crew helps with the unloading and loading. When it's over, and it rarely takes more than a couple of days, they are off again. A ship owner wants his ship working. It's not doing him any good in port.'

'What about Soldane? Did he go ashore in Singapore?'

McGhee winked. 'Aha! Now how did you know that? Young Soldane was the *only* member of the crew who did go ashore. Small tooth problem, apparently.'

'Interesting. And did he make it to a dentist?'

McGhee shrugged. 'Who knows? Impossible to check. The dentists that practise around ports aren't the most diligent at record-keeping – even in Singapore. And even if we could check, and he didn't visit a dentist, so what? He might have had some bird tucked away there. We'll never know.'

'What else can you tell me about the ship or the rest of the officers and crew?'

McGhee shook his head. 'Nothing much. The Chairman checked with the lead insurer at Lloyd's. They took a hard look at the sinking, at the crew, the officers, the ship, the owner but came up with nothing. Absolutely nothing. No, something happened in the South China Sea. Something catastrophic, because they had no time to send a signal. Whatever it was, it occurred fast.'

'No theories on what it might have been?'

'Just the usual speculation. Maybe it was hit by a freak wave, or the cargo broke loose, and the ship overturned. Who knows? You need to remember that ships sink all the time and there are a lot of them. No, it could have been anything. We'll never know.'

'But not piracy? Or a scuttling?'

'Naw. No way. Piracy is all about money. For the ship, the cargo, and the crew. They don't kill the crew. If the *Highland Laddie* had been taken, the owner would have been contacted about a ransom immediately. Lloyd's initially thought it might be piracy, but nobody came asking for cash.'

'Scuttling?'

McGhee paused. 'Possibly, but that's always the owner, and usually if he is in trouble. And this one wasn't. This one was building more ships because he didn't have enough capacity. And the *Highland Laddie* was comparatively new, only four years old, and in good shape. Besides, scuttling is tricky. You need to pay off the crew and hope they don't talk. Which isn't easy. A pay-off and a nearby bar is a lethal combination for the average Filipino.' McGhee sat back and clasped his hands over his stomach, his head dropping onto his chest. He looked at Chadwick to see if he had any other questions.

'Was there a search?'

'Yes. As soon as it went missing, several ships steamed to the last position from the AIS. They searched for a week and found nothing.'

'Isn't that unusual?'

'Not really. If it *was* a freak wave, it could have capsized and gone under in seconds.'

'But wouldn't there be some flotsam, something on the water?'

'There was a tropical storm, remember. And although contain-ers may float for a bit if it's calm, it was anything but calm out there.'

Chadwick thought for a moment or two. 'What's AIS?'

McGhee looked surprised, as if he had expected Chadwick to know more about ships. 'Automated Identification System - sends out signals to other ships or satellites giving the ship's position, speed and course. You can download an app on your phone and check the position of virtually every ship on the planet.'

'So, as far as Lloyd's is concerned, it's over?'

'Pretty much.'

'Pretty much? What does that mean?'

McGhee leaned forward. 'In some cases, like this one, nobody knows what happened. We can speculate but we don't know. Lloyd's insurers like to *know*. They like to know so that they can be sure that the claim was valid and to try to avoid it happening again. So, this file will stay open, in case something emerges that might make them change their mind about what happened.'

Chadwick eyed McGhee carefully. His movements had become deliberate and slow, as if he was holding something back. Chadwick tried another tack. 'Is Lloyd's still investigating the *Highland Laddie* sinking?'

McGhee shrugged. 'Maybe.'

'Maybe? Does that mean yes?'

'It means maybe. I don't know.'

'But you suspect it?'

'Look, I don't know. I *really* don't know. All I know is what the Chairman told me. And he told me that he was surprised that when he went looking for information on the *Highland Laddie*, the senior people he approached all remembered the case a little too well. And were a wee bit too interested in why he was asking. That's all I know. But it could mean nothing. People at Lloyd's have long memories, particularly when they've written a large cheque.'

Chadwick looked for a waitress. As he did so, he spotted Julija and Verlaine walking towards the table. He glanced at McGhee and wondered what, if anything, he should tell him about them. He preferred to keep what little information he had gleaned on the *Highland Laddie* to himself for the moment. He thought of telling McGhee to avoid the subject but decided against it. There was no time and it would only make McGhee suspicious. Better to play it straight. Two friends coming to say hello with no obvious connection to the *Highland Laddie*. He stood. McGhee looked at him in surprise and then turned. He also got to his feet. Verlaine was unusually demonstrative. One hand held Chadwick at the elbow while the other pumped his hand up and down. 'You have been hiding from me,' he said.

'In this café? I might have chosen a better place.'

Chadwick looked at Julija, who was standing slightly apart. Before he could say anything to her, she turned towards McGhee. 'Aren't you going to introduce your friend?' she said.

'This is Mr McGhee,' said Chadwick.

McGhee looked carefully at Julija for a moment before extending his hand. 'Hello, dear,' he said, 'I'm McGhee.'

'And where are you from?' asked Verlaine.

'I'm from Scotland.'

'From the land of the mountain and the flood?' said Verlaine.

'A different part of Scotland. There are no mountains in Maryhill,' replied McGhee.

'Why are you here?' asked Julija. 'How do you know Chadwick?'

'Who is Chadwick?' said McGhee and the joviality of the scene vanished instantly. 'Is that you?' he said, pointing at Chadwick. Before Chadwick could think of what to say, McGhee had burst out laughing. Julija looked annoyed, and Chadwick was struck by her lack of humour. She stood, waiting for McGhee to answer. McGhee sat down, his arms folded across his belly that still moved with the tail end of his laughter. When he realised that she was still waiting for him, he turned to her and said, 'Sit down, dear, and tell me all about yourself. I am sure there is a lot to tell. And as for him,' he said, inclining his head towards Chadwick, 'I should know him well – I've worked for his father for twenty years.'

Chadwick moved behind Julija, encouraged her to sit, and pushed her chair in. He didn't trust his face not to betray the audacity of McGhee's lie. As he was sitting down, Julija continued to push

McGhee. 'So why are you here? Why did you come to see him?' Her tone was pleasant enough but there was an edge to her questioning that Chadwick didn't like.

McGhee on the other hand seemed unperturbed. 'I brought him his books,' he said, as if that answered everything.

'His books?' Verlaine seemed as surprised as Julija. 'What sort of books?' he asked Chadwick.

'The reading kind,' said Chadwick and grinned. 'I can't spend all my time with you, and while I admire French literature, I am not sure I could survive on only Victor Hugo and the *Nice-Matin*.'

'Where are these books?' asked Julija, who was in no mood to let McGhee off so easily.

McGhee reached under the table and produced a parcel wrapped in brown paper and tied with string. He pushed it towards Chadwick, who started to put it on the floor next to his seat, but as he was lifting it, McGhee said, 'Aren't you going to open it?' Chadwick looked at him, but McGhee seemed unconcerned. He reached into his pocket for a penknife, opened it and gave it to Chadwick. Chadwick cut the string and slid the knife along the tape that sealed the parcel. He paused for a moment before pulling back the paper, not quite sure what he would find. Inside, arranged in two piles, were eight or ten books, mostly hardbacks without dust covers. Chadwick recognized them immediately. He picked up the top book and opened it, although he already knew what was written on the inside cover. It was the only way to disguise his surprise.

'May I?'

Chadwick looked up. Verlaine was pointing towards the parcel of books.

'Of course,' he said, and pushed the pile towards him. Verlaine picked a green hardback. He inspected its spine, '*Victory*,' he said, 'by Joseph Conrad.' He opened it and found Chadwick's name written in green ink on the top-right corner of the first page.

'Green ink?' said Verlaine.

'It was a phase I was going through.'

Julija took the book from Verlaine. Satisfied that it was Chadwick's name, she replaced it on the table. Verlaine, embarrassed by her suspicions, started to say something but before he could speak, McGhee said, 'I hate to break up the party, but I have a plane to catch.'

'So soon?' said Verlaine. 'Can't you stay for a while and catch the next plane? There are plenty of planes but not many people who know this man. You are the first we've met.'

'I won't be the last, I'm sure of that,' said McGhee, standing up to draw the discussion to a close. 'Any messages for your parents?' He looked over at Chadwick, who shook his head.

'Tell them I'm fine,' he said, wondering how McGhee had persuaded them to give him the books, or take him to the boxes in the loft above the stables. Or had he even consulted them?

'Bye, dear,' McGhee said to Julija. She didn't bother turning but nodded acknowledgment. He leaned across and shook Verlaine's hand. '*À la prochaine!*' he said and chuckled. He turned and walked towards the door with a quickness and lightness of step that belied his appearance.

Julija turned to Chadwick. 'What does he do for your father?'

'Drives him around. Keeps him amused. Looks after bits and pieces.' Chadwick tried to keep it as vague as possible and was grateful when Verlaine decided to intervene.

Leaning forward, he said, 'We should talk about the hotel in Nice. The trail is getting colder.'

'*If* there is a trail', said Chadwick.

Julija flushed. 'What do you mean - "*If there is a trail?*" We know he was at the hotel.'

Chadwick tried to catch Verlaine's eye, but the older man looked away.

'No, we don't,' said Chadwick. 'We know that Arcier *told you* he was at the hotel. We don't know if it was true or not.'

'But why would he lie about it? Why would he give me the name of the hotel? He must have known I would check.'

'Going to the Hotel Geneva won't help you find your brother. It's a waste of time. I know it, and so does he,' said Chadwick, pointing to Verlaine.

Julija turned towards Verlaine. 'Why is it a waste of time? Why?'

Verlaine looked embarrassed. Before he could speak, Chadwick said, 'I'll tell you why. Even if there is a Hotel Geneva, your brother isn't there. He was probably never there. Given what we now know about Arcier, he was almost certainly setting you up. He didn't believe for a moment that your brother was alive. He saw a good-looking Latvian, on her own, desperate to find her brother. He saw somebody who would pay him to follow up every lead he could produce. He saw a meal ticket, Julija. That's what he saw.'

Julija was angry. 'What is the matter with you? Don't you want to help me find Aleksis?'

'Of course, I want to help you. But I also want you to be realistic. There may be a Hotel Geneva in Nice - I don't know if there is or not - but the chances of your brother having stayed there are *very, very* slim.' Chadwick turned to Verlaine. 'Tell me I'm wrong.'

Verlaine reached for Julija's hand, but she moved it away. He pretended not to notice. 'Chadwick's right. Knowing what we now know about Arcier, it's probably better to believe that everything he told you was suspect. We can check the hotel story, but I wouldn't hold up too much hope that it will turn out to be true.'

Julija stood up.

'Where are you going?' asked Verlaine.

'Where do you think?' she replied.

'I don't think that's a good idea,' said Verlaine.

'I don't care what you think about it. I'm tired of listening to both of you telling me I'm a fool.'

'That's not what we were saying,' said Verlaine. 'We were just suggesting that you shouldn't be too optimistic about what we'll find at the Hotel Geneva.'

'*We* won't find anything at the Hotel Geneva,' said Chadwick. '*If* there is anything to be found, and it is a big *if,* it's a job for one person. If it is a set-up, Arcier will have somebody on the inside, waiting for Julija to show up. That's why you can't go alone. And why there is no point in all of us going. If we go as a group, we'll learn nothing. Do you have another photo?'

Chadwick expected her to keep arguing, but to his surprise, she said nothing, opened her bag and gave him a photo. He glanced at it. It was in black and white and looked as if it had been taken for an official document. The man in the photo looked older than he had imagined, perhaps because he was in a suit and tie. It was difficult to tell whether his hair was blonde or light brown.

'Will that do?' asked Julija. The tone of her voice was less tense. She even managed a wan smile.

'Yes', he said.

'I'll come with you,' said Verlaine and started to rise.

Chadwick rested a hand on his shoulder and pushed him gently down. 'I don't think so. Why don't you stay with Julija? Two is just going to make it more difficult. It is better I do it alone.'

'When will I see you?' said Julija.

'I'll call you when I finish.'

Chadwick shook Verlaine by the hand and kissed Julija. He went towards the door of the café. As he opened it, he could feel the damp freshness of the day. It came as a relief after the overheated atmosphere of the café. He walked into the street and started to look for a taxi.

CHAPTER SEVENTEEN

'Yes?'

The receptionist didn't bother to look up. He was bent over a computer, screwing up his eyes to look at the screen, typing with one finger at a time. His hair was thinning, brushed straight back and plastered to his scalp. His grey roots drew attention to the blackness of the hair dye. Chadwick said nothing.

'You want a room?' The receptionist continued to type without so much as a glance towards Chadwick.

'Not exactly,' said Chadwick.

The receptionist stopped typing and looked up. He had a long, pale face bathed in disappointment. He wore a black suit, shiny with wear, its narrow lapels ten years out of date.

He looked Chadwick over and said sharply, 'What *do* you want?'

'I'd like some help.'

'Are you staying with us?'

Chadwick shook his head. The receptionist seemed pleased. He returned to his typing.

Chadwick waited a moment and said, 'Don't you help non-guests?'

The man carried on typing. Chadwick waited patiently. After a few seconds, the typing stopped and the man examined the screen. 'That depends,' he said.

'Depends on what?'

'Depends on how busy I am. Depends on whether they are nice to me. Depends on whether I like them. I told you, it depends.'

'Are you busy now?'

The man pushed the keyboard away from him and stood. He was thin and a good head shorter than Chadwick. He sighed.

'What sort of help would you like?' he asked.

'The kind that pays well.'

The receptionist examined Chadwick's face carefully as if he might be asked to remember it later. He rested his hands on the top of the reception counter, spreading his thin fingers in two wide fans. There were nicotine stains on the nails and fingers of his right hand and his shirt cuffs were grey with dirt and years of wear. He moved his head closer to Chadwick and said, 'Why didn't you say so earlier? That's the kind of help I like. So, what is it you want?'

He stopped abruptly, looking over Chadwick's shoulder, as his boss approached saying, 'Laurent, haven't you finished yet?'

'Almost.'

'Well, get on with it. I don't know why it always takes you so long. What are you doing now?'

'This gentleman wanted to know about the local bars. I was suggesting Chez Robert.' He turned towards Chadwick and said, 'It gets busy around 7 p.m.'

'I don't know why he always recommends that dump. It's so dirty. There are much better places. If I were you, I would go anywhere but there. Laurent, get on with it. I haven't got all day to wait for you.'

The newcomer moved behind the reception desk and started to look through a pile of papers. He ignored Chadwick. Laurent returned to the computer. After a moment or two, Laurent stopped and looked at Chadwick. 'Well?' he said.

'Thanks for your help,' said Chadwick and walked towards the door.

He was grateful for the rain. The Hotel Geneva had depressed him more than he cared to admit. It was yet another institution with a painted face, denying its years of decline. He glanced at his watch. He had a couple of hours before his 7 p.m. rendezvous with Laurent. He considered showing Aleksis Soldane's photo around the local restaurants but decided against it. Better not to stir up too much interest. Better to wait for Laurent. Whatever Laurent's failings as a receptionist, his commercial acumen seemed sound.

He started walking towards the seafront. It was a grey afternoon that would soon meld into darkness. It was too early for the street lamps and, in their absence, the shop windows cast yellow plumes of light over the wet streets.

A car passed him. There was nothing remarkable about it, or its occupants. Perhaps it was its very ordinariness that triggered his concern? Three passengers, a couple in the front and a single man in the back. All middle-aged. All in hats and coats. It was almost too textbook. Multiple tailing options if they went on foot. Either a single man or a single woman. Working different sides of the street. Or a couple with different coats and hats. But the car was the weak point. If it reappeared with fewer or different occupants, then he would know for certain. He kept moving, unsure about who else might be behind him, and watched the car turn right at the next set of traffic lights.

He pretended to look in a shop window. There was nothing either behind or ahead of him that seemed in any way out of place. Who knew he was here? Only Julija and Verlaine. But they knew where he was going and had no possible reason to have him followed. Was the Hotel Geneva being watched? It seemed unlikely. But if it was, who were they looking for? Aleksis Soldane? Or Chadwick? But why would anybody be interested in him? Just as he was about to dismiss his paranoia, he remembered the spray of blood across Arcier's office wall and decided that, paranoid or not, he should be cautious.

He checked again, using the wing mirror of a parked van. The only pedestrians were running to their cars, to taxis or to shops, trying to avoid getting wet. Nobody showed any interest in Chadwick. He cursed himself. He *was* becoming paranoid. He should just leave. Get as far away from here as quickly as he could.

The rain began to ease and he quickened his pace. He could see the Theatre de Verdure in the distance, blocking his view of the promenade and the seafront. The number of shoppers was increasing. He picked out an expensive store and walked towards it. Once inside, he could see the length of the street, but it was busier than before, making his task more difficult. He started checking faces, looking for anybody that he might have seen since he left the hotel. Different clothes, glasses, no glasses, together, alone. Nobody looked even slightly familiar. The shop door opened and closed.

'What are you buying me?'

He turned. The woman from Augustin's office was standing next to him. He looked through the front doors. A driver with an umbrella was making his way back to a black Mercedes.

'I assume you are buying for me. I would be very disappointed if you were here for somebody else.'

'I am not sure I can afford the prices.'

'I am sure you can't. Neither can I. But it doesn't really matter since neither of us will be paying. Come.'

She took Chadwick by the arm and walked towards the stairs in the centre of the shop. They were halfway up when they were ambushed by several assistants. The other shoppers turned to look as the small group made its way to the rear of the floor, and through a set of double doors into a small sitting room with a sofa, a coffee table and an empty clothes rail. On the wall, directly in front of the sofa, there was a large television playing a video of a fashion show. To the left of the television, there was another door. Chadwick was ushered towards the sofa and offered a glass of champagne.

He looked at Silje, who said, 'Have some. We will be here for a while and you have a lot of work ahead of you.'

'I have to work?'

'You do. But not as hard as me. I must try on the clothes. You only have to tell me if they look good.'

'And what if they all look good?'

'Then either you'll have to try harder or we'll have to buy them all. It doesn't really matter much either way.'

The assistants returned one by one, each bringing a selection of clothes that they hung on a rack.

'This doesn't seem like your first visit,' he said.

'It's not.' She slipped off the short jacket that she was wearing and handed it to Chadwick.

'Now the work begins,' she said and opened the other door that led to a changing room. Stopping on its threshold, she turned towards Chadwick as if about to say something. She stood for a second or two watching him, framed by the doorway, her broad shoulders and narrow waist accentuated by the oversized white shirt and skinny jeans, her heavy brown hair falling loose around her face. He waited for her to speak but she turned and disappeared into the changing room without saying anything. Chadwick felt a disappointment he couldn't explain. In the future, when he thought of her, it would be this scene that he would always think of first. He brought her jacket up to his face. It was warm from her body and smelt of a light floral perfume he couldn't place.

The door to the changing room opened and she came out in a heavily embroidered long coat that flared at the bottom. She spun around so that the coat opened. Underneath, she wore a white shirt with a pleated front, and long, black trousers, cut wide in the leg and high on the waist.

'Do we like?' she said.

'We like,' said Chadwick.

'You might sound more enthusiastic. I used to get paid to do this.'

'And now?'

She pretended to think before she said, 'Now I get paid to do this.'

'Who does the paying?'

She gave him a meaningful look and started back towards the changing room, slipping the coat off her shoulders as she went. She closed the door without answering.

A minute later, she was back, wearing a different outfit.

'Is there anything that doesn't suit you?'

'Poverty. Poverty doesn't suit me at all. Now, pay attention. Don't waste time looking at me. It's the clothes you should be looking at.'

'I thought you might be for sale too?'

She turned to face him, her hands on either hip. 'I am for sale. I am always for sale. I would have thought that was clear. But you can't afford me. Besides, I wouldn't make you happy.'

'You seem pretty sure about that.'

'I am. I don't make anyone happy, not even myself. I don't understand why people obsess about happiness. Happiness requires a blindness I would rather live without. I prefer to see the world as it is and not as I would like it to be. It's not a great trait. And it certainly doesn't make you happy. But it means you don't waste time dreaming of things you can never have. I'm not like you. I know exactly what I can have - and what I will never have.'

'If I can't buy you and I can't afford the clothes, why am I here?'

'To keep me company and to learn.'

'About clothes?'

'About clothes and about other things.'

'You think I need to learn?'

'About clothes, for sure. About everything else? Yes, you need to learn.'

'Are you going to teach me or is that another thing I can't afford?'

'I can teach you. But it's not a question of money. It's whether you want to learn.'

'You make it sound very ominous.'

'Ominous? What does "ominous" mean?'

'It means that something bad is going to happen.'

'It's a good word. I must try to remember it.' She walked back into the changing room. This time, she left the door open.

'Is something bad going to happen?' said Chadwick.

'Of course. Sooner or later, something bad always happens. It's what makes life worth living.'

'You're cheerful,' said Chadwick. She reappeared in a new outfit.

'Cheerful? You forget where I'm from? In the far North, we're never happy. Too much snow, too little sun, too many dark mornings.'

'You forgot the high taxes.'

'They are the price of social cohesion. Apparently. But I can't comment on Norwegian tax.'

'Why not?'

'I have never paid any. I think you ought to pay some taxes before you have the right to complain about them. Otherwise, you are just another hypocrite. I am not much but I am not a hypocrite. At least, not yet. I suppose I will be, in time.'

'Are you always like this?'

She stopped looking at herself in the mirror that took up one side of the room and turned towards him. Once again, the intensity of her blue eyes unnerved him.

'Can I give you some advice?'

'Do I have a choice?'

'No. But you should do what I say. Although I doubt you will.'

'Are you always this negative?'

'I am not negative. I am realistic. Will you take my advice?'

'I am not very good at advice.'

'Giving or receiving?'

'Both, I suppose.'

'I am not surprised. You don't look like somebody who likes taking advice. If you did, you wouldn't be hiding in a deserted hotel.'

'Am I hiding?'

'What would you call it?'

'I thought I was on holiday.'

'It's the wrong time of year, my dear, and I am not sure that you have anything to take a holiday from. Tell me, where will you go back to? To your home? I doubt it. You are like me – you will only ever go home when there's nowhere else to go.'

She disappeared into the changing room and reappeared in a short dress in gold tweed that caught the light as she moved. He admired her tanned legs as she walked slowly towards the mirror. She had taken off her shoes and stood on tiptoe to see how she would look in heels. He noticed that her feet were long and slim with painted nails.

'You haven't asked me if I like this.'

'Why would I bother? You're a man. Of course, you like it. Tell me, are you ready for my advice now?'

'Not really. Must you?'

'I must.'

'Then tell me.'

She walked back towards the rail and ran her hand along the clothes as if looking for a specific outfit. He wondered if it was a ploy to avoid looking at him.

'You should leave here. Immediately. It doesn't matter where you go. That's up to you. But you shouldn't stay here.'

'Why not? Maybe I like it here?'

She turned towards him, her blue eyes betraying only the slightest hint of anger. 'Maybe you do. For now. But you're not going to like it. You're not going to like it at all.'

'You seem very sure about that.'

'I'm very sure about it. This place is not for you. This place is for people like me. And people like Augustin. People who don't believe in anything except themselves.'

'That sounds pretty cynical.'

'Not cynical - realistic. Do you remember in Augustin's office, his telling me that you came here to be alone? Are you alone?'

'What do you mean?'

'Just that. It's not a very difficult question. Are you alone?'

'Well, I'm with you.'

'Hardly. I'm not *with* anyone. But, you, are you *alone*? I don't think so. You are not the type. You can stay in a deserted hotel, but you cannot be alone. If you were alone, you might have a chance here. But I don't think you are. If you had kept to yourself, you wouldn't be sitting in Augustin's office. And Augustin's office is not always a good place to be.'

'You were there.'

'I was. But Augustin and I are alike. We understand each other. That is why we get on. But you shouldn't be there. If you have business with Augustin, you are very far from being alone.'

'Meaning?'

'Nobody ends up in Augustin's office by accident. If you were there, it means your paths have crossed, and if you have crossed paths with Augustin, you have probably crossed paths with some other people who it is best to avoid. That is why you should leave.'

'You seem very well informed.'

'No. I know very little and I don't care to know more. I don't want to know about you and what you are doing. I want you to go while you still can. I told you I had some advice for you. That's it. You can do with it what you like. It doesn't matter to me.'

One of the assistants brought her some more clothes on hangers. She held each up in turn, discarding several pieces and taking the others into the fitting room.

'You really don't like giving advice, do you?'

She replied from within the room. 'No. I don't. But occasionally, one has to make exceptions.'

'Why was I an exception?'

'I have no idea. Poor judgment, I suppose. Or lack of discipline. I am not much given to acts of charity.'

She reappeared in the doorway in a shirt and a dark-blue long skirt. She raised her arms and gripped the top of the doorway on either side so that the full sleeves opened on each side like a fan. 'In any case, it doesn't matter. The advice-giving is over.'

'For today?'

'For ever. If you stay, why would I persist in giving you advice you ignore? And if you leave, you won't need any more of my advice.'

She dropped her arms and walked into the centre of the room. 'Augustin is going to invite you to a lunch.'

'That's kind of him. I didn't know he was so worried about my eating.'

'He's not. He's just doing what he has been told.'

'Who told him to invite me?'

'That's not for me to say.'

She looked momentarily uncomfortable. 'You shouldn't go to the lunch. But you will. So, I think it is better if you and I don't talk about it anymore. Thank you for helping me.'

'I'm not sure I was much help.'

'No. You weren't. I was only being polite. But at least you helped the time pass. And now you should go.'

Chadwick, surprised by her change of mood, pushed himself to his feet and started to walk around the coffee table in front of the sofa. The door to the store opened and the manager appeared.

Silje said, 'Mr Chadwick is just leaving. Would you mind showing him out?' She retreated towards the fitting room as if she wanted to avoid any further contact with him. He thought of following her but decided against it. The manager was already holding open the door.

'Demonstrative people, the Norwegians,' said Chadwick.

Silje wrapped the top part of her body around the doorjamb. 'We are a lot friendlier when people take our advice. Goodbye, Chadwick.' She paused for a second, as if to give him a chance to memorise her face, then disappeared into the changing room and began a conversation with one of the assistants.

Chadwick and the manager walked down the stairs side by side like prisoner and escort. It felt, he thought, as if he had committed some indiscretion and been asked to leave. It was still raining. Chadwick pulled on his jacket and began to retrace his steps towards the Hotel Geneva. The street was gloomy after the bright lights of the store. His encounter with Silje already seemed like a dream. He tried not to think about it, or about her, but only about his meeting with Laurent.

CHAPTER EIGHTEEN

'Do you like this place?'

'Not much. I suppose you will tell me it was popular with Hollywood stars in the nineteen-sixties.'

Laurent shook his head. 'No. This place has never been popular. Not in the sixties. Not at any time. It's a shithole,' he said, as if he had just realised it.

'But you come here. Don't tell me you like the sophisticated crowd?'

Laurent looked around. 'They're okay. They leave you alone. They don't ask any questions. They don't argue and they don't fight. It's not so bad. Sometimes, it's not good when people ask questions.'

He looked at Chadwick as if this was his opening.

Chadwick waited while the waitress left a second double vodka in front of Laurent. He watched Laurent's hand as it reached for the glass. It was a very deliberate movement. Chadwick had seen it before. By the third vodka, it would be unnecessary, as his hand would be steady again. Chadwick was in no hurry to engage. The longer he waited, the more pliable Laurent would become.

'Your boss is a charmer,' he said.

Laurent examined his half-empty glass as if surprised at how little was left in it. He looked Chadwick in the eye in a measured show of defiance. 'He is an asshole.' he said, 'A complete asshole.'

'Friend of the owner?'

Laurent brightened. 'You knew? Or you just guessed?'

'Guessed. It wasn't so hard.'

'He is useless. If anybody wants something in the hotel, they come to me - not to him. *You* came looking for something. What was it again?'

'I didn't tell you. But I'll tell you now. I'm trying to find a friend.'

Laurent lifted his glass to toast Chadwick. 'A *friend?* You should have said so. I can find you a lot of friends. What kind of friends do you like? Blonde or brunette?'

Chadwick wagged his finger at him. 'No, not that kind of friend. A specific friend. Somebody I know who I am trying to find. I think they might have stayed at your hotel.'

'If they stayed there, I would know about it. When was this?'

'Recently. Last week or so.'

'What was her name?'

'Not a her. A him.'

Laurent looked disappointed. 'Name?'

'I doubt he checked in using his real name.'

'What name did he use?'

'I don't know.'

Chadwick watched as Laurent sat back and tried to work out what the information might be worth to Chadwick.

'So, you want to know if this *friend* was at the hotel, but you don't know what name they used. That's a bit *unusual*, no?'

Chadwick didn't reply.

'What does he look like, your *friend?*'

'Height, 1.65 - 1.70, medium weight, thinning blonde hair, blue eyes, late thirties - early forties. Speaks French with an East European accent.'

Laurent pretended to think for a moment or two. 'Difficult. Very difficult,' he said, 'but let's say that I could find out whether he was there or not, why should I help you? Our guests deserve their privacy.'

'Of course, they do. And I'm sure they get it. Except this guest is a friend of mine and I am trying to find him. And if you could help me find him, I would be very grateful. And when I'm grateful, I'm often generous.'

Laurent nodded slowly as if affirming the strength of Chadwick's argument. 'And just how generous might you be?' he asked.

'That would depend on just how helpful you were.'

'Meaning?'

'Meaning that if you were only to confirm that he stayed there, that would be helpful but not *that* helpful. But, if you could tell me when he stayed, in which room, who visited him, who he called – that would be *very* helpful. And if you could let me into the room he stayed in, that would be *exceptionally* helpful. So, you see, there are different degrees of helpfulness and I have this feeling you might prove to be *exceptionally* helpful, in which case, I would be *exceptionally* generous.'

Laurent looked concerned. 'I can't let you into the room. I might be able to do the rest, but I can't let you into the room.'

Chadwick changed tack. 'So, he was staying?'

Laurent realised his error, considered back-tracking, but decided against it.

'Yes, there was somebody like that staying but he checked out a few days ago.'

'What name did he use?'

Laurent smiled. His teeth were surprisingly white and even. 'Aren't you forgetting something, my friend? This is not a cheap town and nothing here is free.'

Chadwick thought for a moment. He had to keep Laurent talking until he had exhausted his knowledge. If he offered too much money, too soon, Laurent would simply shut up once he had enough cash. Laurent was canny enough to hold some information back, hoping for a second bite.

He pulled out a folded bundle of notes and held it with the fold towards Laurent so that he couldn't tell the number of notes in the bundle. He peeled two notes from the bundle and slipped them across the table under his left hand while his right hid the remaining bundle from any onlookers. He moved his left hand away and Laurent covered the two notes with his right hand.

'This does not buy you so very much.'

'It's a down payment. Let's call it a gesture of goodwill. There will be plenty more, provided the information is good.'

'My information is always good. If you don't want my information, that's okay with me. Now, do you want my information or not?'

'I want it.'

'So, how much will you pay for it?'

'It depends what you have. You tell me what you have, and I'll tell you what I'll pay for it.'

Laurent thought for a moment. It wasn't smart to tell Chadwick what he had, but he was struggling to find a way to avoid it. Finally, he said, 'Okay, I have the name and when he checked in and out.'

'That's it?'

Laurent shrugged. 'Maybe he made some calls from the room. If he did, I could get you those.'

Chadwick sat impassively, saying nothing.

Laurent continued. 'What I have is not bad. Maybe it's a lot better than you have right now. Maybe you need to think about it. It doesn't matter to me. I am in no hurry. I can wait.'

Chadwick doubted Laurent was very interested in waiting but he had to be careful in case Laurent simply invented information to satisfy Chadwick's curiosity. He said, 'Did he meet anybody?'

Laurent thought for a second and then shook his head. Chadwick's confidence in Laurent increased. He took the photo from the inside pocket of his jacket and slid it across the table without saying anything.

Laurent picked it up and made a show of examining it.

'Well?' said Chadwick.

'Well, what?'

Chadwick pushed another note across the table. Laurent covered it with his hand and stuffed it into his jacket pocket.

'That's him.'

'Name?'

'I would need to check.'

Chadwick was immediately suspicious. Laurent had played his hand too well to start claiming that he had shown up without a pretty good idea of which guests he might be asked about. 'Then, let's go.'

'Go? Go where?'

'To the hotel.'

'With you?'

'With me. We are old drinking pals, or did you forget?'

Laurent looked doubtful. 'I can't take you to the hotel. It wouldn't be good if we were seen together.'

'Not good for whom? We have been seen together, remember? You suggested this place, we had a few drinks, and you wanted to show me the hotel to persuade me to stay there next time I am in town. Besides, who is going to be around?'

'It would be better if I found out the information and met you again tomorrow evening.'

'I don't think so. We do it now and you double your money. It will only take five minutes.'

Laurent looked concerned. Chadwick ordered him another drink to bolster his courage. Laurent made another attempt to resist. 'My boss will be suspicious when he sees you there while I am at the computer. He is already looking for reasons to get me fired. I won't be able to get you any information. It will be a waste of your time.'

Chadwick said, 'But your boss won't be there, Laurent. He has gone home, hasn't he?'

Laurent said nothing, but Chadwick sensed that he was correct. It was critical to get Laurent moving as soon as possible. He pointed to the newly delivered vodka and said, 'Come on, drink up. We're out of here.'

Laurent looked at him for a second, trying to calculate whether it would be worth arguing, and decided against it. He swallowed the vodka in one go and stood up quickly, his hands resting on the table, steadying himself. Chadwick paid the bill and ushered him towards the door before he could change his mind. During the short walk to the Hotel Geneva, neither man spoke. When they arrived, Laurent stopped outside. 'You should wait here,' he said. 'I will get you what you want and meet you here in ten minutes.'

Chadwick shook his head. He had no intention of letting Laurent out of his sight for even a minute or two. With money in his pocket, Laurent was a liability. 'I don't think so,' he said. 'Let's go.'

Laurent's face acknowledged defeat and they entered the hotel. The lobby looked even shabbier at night. There was nobody in sight. Laurent walked behind the front desk. Chadwick positioned himself in front and to one side where he could see the lift and stairs. Laurent glanced into the room behind reception. It was empty. Laurent sat in front of the computer. Chadwick picked up a brochure from the rack, opened it on the front desk, and began to examine it. He heard somebody enter the room behind reception. He coughed and Laurent looked up, irritated. Chadwick nodded his head towards the room and Laurent understood.

'Beatrice? Are you there?'

A middle-aged woman appeared. She wore a plaid suit that was decades out of date and several sizes too small. Her hair was cut short and streaked. 'Laurent, it's you. What are you doing here?'

'I met this gentleman', he pointed at Chadwick, 'through a friend and he wanted to know if we would have enough rooms for him and his friends next month.'

The woman ignored Chadwick. 'You work too hard, Laurent. You are too good. I wouldn't bother. Of course, there are rooms next month. There are always rooms here. When did we last sell out?'

'I know,' said Laurent, returning to the computer, 'but they want the rooms to be together at the back, away from the street.'

The woman shrugged to show how little she cared. The phone rang on the desk. Laurent, who was closest, picked it up. 'Yes, she is,' he said, and covering the phone with his hand, he said to the woman, 'It's your friend.'

The woman started moving towards the room behind reception. 'I'll take it in here,' she said. As she went through the doorway, she pulled the door closed behind her in order not to be overheard.

Laurent gazed at the closed door for a second or two and then turned towards Chadwick. 'I have it,' he said. He stood up and went to the printer. He waited patiently for it to spring to life, before collecting two pages. He returned to the reception desk and stood opposite Chadwick. 'Now, shall we do some business?'

Chadwick reached into his jacket and drew out the bundle of notes so that Laurent could see how many there were. Laurent looked at it in surprise. Chadwick knew that he was already regretting not asking Chadwick for more. While he was still distracted, Chadwick said, 'I want to see the room.' Laurent seemed shocked, as if he had misheard. 'Show me the room,' said Chadwick.

'I can't do that,' said Laurent. 'I would lose my job.'

'Like hell you can't. You mean it's okay to sell me information on guests but not okay to show me a room. Do I look stupid? Get the key.'

Laurent hesitated. 'It's occupied,' he said.

Chadwick reached across and snatched the two pages from the hapless Laurent. He glanced at them. 'Really? Room 118. Why don't we check?'

Laurent looked shifty and Chadwick knew the room was empty. 'Get the key.' Laurent hesitated. Chadwick reached over the reception desk and took the key from the rack. He grabbed Laurent by the upper arm. Laurent looked down at his arm, startled, but didn't resist as Chadwick guided him from behind reception and towards the stairs. They climbed in silence.

When they reached the first floor, they passed through a glass fire door that led to a small, poorly lit hallway. A corridor stretched in either direction. 'Which way?' said Chadwick. Laurent pushed Chadwick's hand away from his right arm. Chadwick let him. He knew that Laurent was gathering sufficient courage to make another stand but whether it would be to express outrage at Chadwick's behaviour or to demand more money was unclear. Possibly, it would be both. Laurent was beginning to bore him.

Laurent started down the corridor with Chadwick following. The dim lighting was a positive: the shabby wallpaper and worn carpet spoke of years of neglect. Laurent stopped outside a door. 'This is it,' he said. Chadwick gave him the key and nodded towards the door. Holding the door open with one arm, Laurent stood back to allow Chadwick to enter. Chadwick shook his head and pointed to the room. Laurent hesitated and went in. Chadwick followed him.

The room was small. Its only window overlooked the back of the hotel. The bed was too large for a single but too small for a double. Opposite the bed was a chest of drawers. On top was an ancient television. On the far side, a vinyl-covered armchair. Chadwick pulled it towards the bed, pointed to it and told Laurent to sit down. Laurent eased himself into it slowly. The alcohol was wearing off and his unhappiness was manifest. Chadwick sat down on the end of the bed so that he was directly facing Laurent, their knees almost touching. He pulled the two pieces of paper from his pocket and read them while Laurent watched. After a moment or two, he folded them and put them in his jacket.

'Well, you wanted to see the room,' said Laurent. 'This is it.' He made a sarcastic gesture with his hand. 'Now you have seen it, I want the rest of my money. And, I want you to leave.'

Having made his speech, Laurent started to get up. Chadwick let him reach the point of balance, reached forward and gently pushed him back into the chair. He said nothing, his face expressionless.

Laurent, surprised, changed tack. 'We had a deal. You wanted his name and when he stayed. You wanted to see the room. You have everything you wanted. Now, you need to pay me.' He considered trying to get up again but thought better of it. He looked at Chadwick's face for guidance but found none. He tried again.

'Look, I've given you what you asked for. Now you owe me. We had a deal, remember?'

The room was silent. There was no noise from the corridor or from any of the rooms above or to the side. The two men were so close that they were almost touching. Chadwick watched as Laurent turned his head to avoid Chadwick's gaze. Chadwick didn't move. He was in no hurry. He could wait until Laurent's aching neck forced him to face him again. He knew how it worked. Your confidence started high, as you examined each of the options. But as the demons appeared, your confidence fell, and your mind slowed, so that it became impossible to concentrate, impossible to examine any option, impossible to think of anything but the fear that was wrapping itself around you, tighter and tighter, cutting off your ability to move, to think, to breathe.

Laurent was sweating hard, the acrid smell of his body mixing with his cheap cologne and the stale alcohol that was seeping from his pores. There wouldn't be long to wait. He watched Laurent start to shake, imperceptibly at first, and then more obviously. This was the hard part, when they stop pleading and become like an animal awaiting execution. The part when you started to feel sorry for them. But it was important to keep going. To keep them trapped. To use their fear against them. To allow their panic to build until it became unbearable.

Chadwick knew that Laurent's neck ached and that, in the end, the pain would force him to face Chadwick. When it happened, he looked straight at Chadwick, his eyes pleading. There was no response from Chadwick. His eyes were blue-grey stone. Laurent gripped the arms of the chair and tried to hide his shaking. But it was no good. The more his hands gripped the chair, the more his upper body began to twitch in a series of spasms.

Chadwick knew what he was thinking. He had been there himself. He ran through the arguments Laurent would be making to himself. *There's no possible reason for this man to hurt me. I don't even know him. All he wanted was some information and I've given it to him. It will be fine. There is nothing to be afraid of. The man is only playing games with me. Try to be calm. But what if I'm wrong? What if the man has been sent to hurt me? Or worse. What if it is a dreadful mistake and I have been mistaken for somebody else? I must talk to him. To reason with him.*

'Please let me go,' said Laurent. 'I've given you what you wanted. I can't help you anymore.' He paused. 'I don't need the money. You can have back what you paid me. Here.' He reached into his pocket and held the notes out. Chadwick didn't react.

'I won't tell anybody about this. Nobody. I promise. You can rely on me totally.'

Chadwick's expression was carved in granite. It was as if he had heard nothing that Laurent said.

'What do you want? *What do you want?*'

Laurent shrank back in the chair, convinced that Chadwick was about to hit him.

Chadwick reached forward, placed his hands on Laurent's knees and gripped them hard. Laurent felt as if his legs had been put in a vice. 'Tell me everything,' said Chadwick, 'and this time, don't leave anything out. There isn't going to be a second payday for you. Is that clear?'

Laurent managed to nod. He began to talk as if he couldn't wait to divulge what he knew. 'Everything I gave you is correct. He checked in as Aleksis Soldane. Those are the right dates. He made some phone calls. They are on the sheet. You have them. You have everything.'

Chadwick said nothing. He tightened his grip on Laurent's knees and watched Laurent's face. Before, he hadn't been sure, but now he was certain. Laurent was holding something back. He could see the panic in Laurent's eyes and wondered if he should have let him suffer for longer. Laurent had to realise that there would be no future trade. He had to give it up now.

'Tell me,' said Chadwick, 'what happened?'

'He left early. There were other people looking for him. They came to the hotel. But he had already gone.'

'How?'

'He skipped out the back.'

'How many were there?'

'Two men.'

'Describe them.'

'One was short. Broadly built. Blonde hair. The other was bigger and balding.'

'Ages?'

'I don't know. Late thirties, I suppose. The bigger man might have been a bit younger.'

'French?'

'No. Foreign. East European. The shorter one spoke some French. I don't know about the other one.'

'Did they ask for him by name?'

'Yes. They seemed to know that he was here.'

'And then what did they do?'

Laurent looked down towards the ground. Chadwick tightened his grip to remind him that he was still there. 'You gave them the key, didn't you?'

Laurent said nothing.

'Didn't you?'

Laurent nodded.

'So they came to the room? Did you come with them?'

Laurent shook his head.

'And afterwards, what did they do?'

'They came back to reception and returned the key.'

'How long were they in the room?'

'I don't know. Not long.'

'How long?'

'Maybe thirty minutes, maybe forty minutes. I didn't check.'

Chadwick released his grip on Laurent and sat back to think. Whoever they were, they had more than enough time to search the room. If there had been something to find, they would have found it. There was no point in his wasting time searching it.

'When they came back to reception, you gave them the same sheets you gave me, didn't you?'

Laurent said nothing. There was no point. It was clear. Chadwick stood up and looked down at him. He took more money from his pocket, peeled off some notes, and dropped them in Laurent's lap. Laurent didn't look up.

So, Aleksis Soldane *was* alive. Julija would be happy. But whatever Soldane was doing, he had attracted somebody's attention. And Chadwick didn't like the sound of the men who had questioned Laurent. He didn't like the sound of them at all. He opened the door and took one last look at Laurent. He was still sitting in the chair, bent forward, his arms wrapped around his knees. He looked as if he had just been rescued from drowning. *But at least you have survived*, thought Chadwick. The sense of his being pulled down into deep water was overwhelming. He tried to put it out of his mind. He closed the door on Laurent and left him catatonic in his own private hell.

CHAPTER NINETEEN

Chadwick watched the tall-sided yellow ferry leaving Nice for Sardinia. It was the only patch of colour on a shifting grey backdrop. The sea was rough, whipped up by a gusty wind that was blowing towards land, bringing the occasional shower that arrived unannounced and left just as suddenly. The ferry was some miles distant, ploughing its ungainly path through an undulating sea. There were no other boats to be seen. It was not a day for casual sailing. Nor was it a day for the swimming pool of the Grand Hotel, perched above the unfriendly rocks of Cap-Ferrat. But then he hadn't chosen the venue.

Directly in front of him, on the other side of a low stone balustrade, was the swimming pool. Beyond it lay several terraces, a series of cabanas and steps that led to the coast path. On his side of the pool was the main building which housed the kitchens. Between the balustrade and the main building was a covered terrace that ran the length of the pool, its sides open to the sea. At the front of the terrace, there was a curtain of overlapping polythene panels that hung from the roof to the balustrade, providing shelter from the wind. Towards the back of the terrace was a bar and the entrance to the kitchens. The large space, normally filled with tables, was empty, save for a round table set for lunch.

Two waiters stood at the bar, looking incongruous in their uniform shorts. Both had sensibly opted for sweaters over their T-shirts and Chadwick wondered whether they had a spare jersey behind the bar. Beyond them, at the very end of the pool, was the entrance to a funicular lift, a glass box that ran on rails, gliding effortlessly up the steep slope that lay between the swimming pool and the road far above. The pool and its facilities were closed for the winter and Chadwick wondered again at the influence of a man who could have it reopened for a lunch.

Chadwick looked across at Augustin, bent over one of his two phones. He was wearing a blue cashmere coat with a fur collar and a dark-green scarf. He showed no inclination to shed either, suggesting that this wasn't his first visit.

Augustin had invited him to a lunch, just as Silje had predicted. There was no mention of the host, but Chadwick was sure it was the man whose money he had returned to Augustin. He had considered refusing but Silje's warning had only whetted his interest. It was a risk but a small one. If the man hadn't already sent somebody after him, it must be because there was still some doubt in the man's mind, or the man wanted to take a closer look. Well, so did he.

Augustin looked up from his phone, saw that Chadwick was looking at him and shrugged. The host was late. It was to be expected. Chadwick walked towards the table. Augustin put down his phone.

'You should have brought a coat.'

'Thank you. I didn't realise that lunch was eaten *al fresco* regardless of the weather or the season.'

'He doesn't mind the cold. In fact, I think he prefers it.'

'Shouldn't he stay at home then?'

Augustin put his head to one side and gave Chadwick a considered look.

'Are you about to tell me that he isn't Russian?' said Chadwick.

'I wasn't about to tell you anything.'

'I've noticed. I was hoping to borrow one of your phones so that I could have a chat with the speaking clock.'

'A great many people talk too much. I am simply trying to redress the balance.'

'You're doing it well. If I spend too much time with you, I might forget how to talk at all.'

Augustin smiled. 'Our host values his privacy almost as much as he values discretion in his friends.'

'He has friends? I thought friends were an endangered species in these parts.'

'If you have money, you always have friends.'

'But not the other way around?'

Augustin smiled. 'I wouldn't know.'

'Maybe you should experiment?'

'Maybe I should but it is difficult to know where to start. I would not like to sacrifice what I have for the sake of a social experiment.'

Chadwick remembered what Augustin had said in his office. *'I should not like to give this up.'* It had struck him as a strange remark for the casino owner to make. And yet, here was a similar comment. If the self-assured and cynical Augustin was concerned about a threat to his businesses, it was unlikely to be an imaginary one. He became aware that Augustin was looking at him but when he looked him in the eye, Augustin turned back to his phones.

A phone rang behind the bar. One of the waiters reached across to answer it. He stiffened, replaced the receiver, and whispered something to his companion. A woman appeared from the kitchen and took up position behind the bar. The two waiters went to stand on one side of the bar, next to each other, as if on parade. Augustin recognised the signs. He levered himself to his feet, brushing some breadcrumbs from the front of his coat. 'Our host,' he said.

Chadwick looked towards the funicular station. As if on cue, a group appeared and began walking towards the table. At its head was a thin man in his early sixties. He had grey hair that he wore long and brushed straight back. He was wearing a pair of tan-coloured, large-framed glasses and a blue-checked suit without a tie.

Silje was on his right, wearing a long cashmere coat. He noticed that she was not holding his arm. Instead, she seemed to have left a gap between them as if to demonstrate her independence. He told himself to toughen up and stop imagining. Silje was right - it was dangerous to dream of things you could never have, especially in this company.

On the other side of the grey-haired man was a shorter, thickly set man, who walked on his toes like a boxer. He wore a baseball cap pulled low at the front and was younger: mid-to late-thirties at most. Behind them were two middle-aged men running to fat, followed by three good-looking, well-dressed girls some way short of their twentieth birthdays. The others were bodyguards who arranged themselves around the terraces according to some prearranged plan. Chadwick looked at each in turn but recognised nobody. He wasn't surprised.

The thin man was shaking hands with Augustin, who was holding the man's forearm with his left hand to emphasise the warmth of the connection. The thin man stood to one side and examined Chadwick. There was no warmth in the inspection. Silje bent low over Augustin so that he could kiss her on both cheeks. She turned towards Chadwick and nodded. She clearly had no intention of greeting him.

Augustin turned towards Chadwick. 'Chadwick, this is Anton Melnikov.'

Chadwick moved towards the thin man, his hand extended. The thin man didn't reciprocate, at least, not immediately. He waited a second or two before reaching for Chadwick's hand. There was no awkwardness about the gesture. His hand was dry and soft like an old person's. He shook Chadwick's hand briefly and then let his hand fall to his side. Turning to Augustin, he said, 'Shall we sit?'

Chadwick saw that he was not going to be introduced to the rest of the party. The two middle-aged men seemed to know this, either from instinct or experience, it was hard to tell. They moved towards the table and waited for the host. The short man in the baseball cap gestured to the three girls to follow him to the bar while the waiters prepared a second table.

The main group sat. Melnikov took off his glasses and began to clean them with his napkin. Nobody spoke. He looked around the table, his thin face immobile. 'Are we going to eat?' he said. One of the middle-aged men signalled a waiter, who rushed towards Melnikov holding an open menu. Melnikov ignored him. 'Bring us the usual,' he said, and waved him away.

Melnikov turned towards Chadwick. 'I hope it is not too cold for you? I like to be outside. I can see little point in living here if you are always inside.'

'Even in the winter?'

'Especially in the winter. The winter is the best season. It's why people started coming here. You should know as the British were among the first to arrive. Look at the cemeteries. Every second gravestone has an English name.'

'They liked it so much, they never left.'

Melnikov looked at Chadwick carefully. Something that might have been a smile passed his lips. 'I'm afraid they never had a choice. Most were suffering from tuberculosis. They were medical tourists, you see, trying to escape certain death at home. Unfortunately, many of them didn't succeed.'

'That's too bad. What brought *you* here? I hope it wasn't to escape certain death at home?'

Chadwick sensed the rest of the table grow still but Melnikov seemed to welcome the question. 'Nothing so dramatic, I'm afraid. I'm here because I like it here.'

'It's a step up from the Black Sea.'

'I detest the Black Sea. It's a dreadful place. The beaches are so covered in bodies that there is no place to walk. The bars are full as soon as they open and everybody you meet is either drinking or drunk.'

One of the middle-aged Russians, sensing an opening, attempted to defend his homeland, addressing Melnikov with careful respect: 'Anton Alexandrevich, I know what you mean, and some of what you say is true, but there are still towns there that are very nice to visit.'

'Are there? Then why don't you go? Give up your villa for the summer and take your family to the Black Sea. I'll arrange it for you. I'll even pay. It would be my pleasure. You can go for July and August and then we'll see how much you enjoy the smell of sweat and cheap cooking.'

He waited until it was clear to everybody that his guest had no intention of replying before turning back towards Chadwick. 'People talk nonsense about the past, don't you think? Everybody likes to tell you how they could go back tomorrow - *if* they had to. But you can never go back. Isn't that right, Augustin?'

Augustin shrugged. 'I suppose not,' he said. 'It's too difficult to forget what you had.'

'Exactly. It's too difficult to forget what you had. I'll give you an example. My family had a house here, not very far from where we're sitting. My great-grandfather and my grandfather were the last to use it. Before the revolution, of course.'

'What happened to it?' asked Chadwick.

Melnikov shrugged. 'Knocked down and rebuilt. Not just once, but several times. A perfect illustration of why you can never recapture the past. What about your past, Mr Chadwick? Can you go back?'

Despite the cold, Chadwick felt himself begin to sweat. *It's a game*, he told himself. *He doesn't know anything. He is only fishing.* 'I've never thought about it,' he said, 'but I'm not sure I can see any point. There is usually a reason the past is the past. Tell me, what did you do in Russia before you went into business?'

Melnikov smiled as if he had been waiting for the question.

'Me? I was an academic.'

'What was your field?'

'I am a mathematician.'

The use of the present tense was interesting. He was an unlikely academic. His English suggested that he had lived in an English-speaking country for an extended period.

'Where did you learn your English?'

'In Russia.' He paused. 'Before the Wall came down. We were not quite the barbarians you might think.'

'You speak it well for a mathematician.'

Melnikov ignored him. It was clear that he felt he had said enough on the topic.

'Why did *you* come to France, Mr Chadwick?'

'Change of scenery.'

'Where were you before?'

'Here and there. I travelled a great deal.'

'But not anymore?'

'Not for the moment, no.'

'And do you like it here? You don't find it dull.'

'It hasn't been dull so far.'

'Even in an empty hotel?' asked Silje.

'Even in an empty hotel.'

'How do you spend your time?' asked the Russian called Viktor.

'It depends,' said Chadwick. 'I run. I use the gym in the hotel. I read. I go to the local cafés. I even visit Augustin's den of iniquity. The time passes.'

'How are the natives?' asked Silje. Chadwick looked at her. She wore a bored expression that he had come to recognise as one of her masks.

'They're all right. Friendly enough if a little overzealous with their advice.'

'Really,' she said. 'How so?'

'Apparently, I don't belong here, and I should go.'

'That doesn't seem very friendly,' she said. 'Perhaps you have been spending time with the wrong people?'

'I never give advice,' interrupted Melnikov. 'People resent it and rarely accept it. It is a waste of time. It is like telling one of Augustin's clients that he should quit while he is ahead. There is no point. When a man is determined to meet his nemesis head on, there can only be one result. Don't you agree, Augustin?'

Augustin hesitated. 'I suppose so. I've never tried to persuade my clients to leave. I would find it hard to recover my money if they were home in bed.'

'I don't know about that,' said Melnikov. 'There are many ways of recovering money. If somebody refuses to stay at the table, you need to find another way. Wouldn't you agree, Mr Chadwick?'

Chadwick had already seen which way the conversation was headed. 'I suppose so,' he said. 'I'm afraid I don't know much about money - how to make it or how to recover it.'

'But you are living in the most expensive hotel in town,' said Viktor.

Melnikov started to laugh. 'You must excuse these two,' he said, indicating the two Russians. 'I sometimes feel that I have adopted two stray dogs.' Turning towards Viktor, he said, 'The hotel is closed. There is nobody there but Mr Chadwick. Isn't that so, Mr Chadwick?'

Chadwick nodded, increasingly uncomfortable with what Melnikov knew, and the way he was slowly introducing it into the conversation. Melnikov, on the other hand, seemed energized, pleased with the opportunity to humiliate one or other of the Russians.

'Tell me, Viktor, there is something I would like to know. Who is going to charge him in this *expensive* hotel?'

'How do I know, Anton Alexandrevich? Perhaps the owner has …' Viktor stopped, realising that Melnikov was playing with him. Bemused, he looked around the table for support. Nobody spoke.

'Perhaps the owner has done *what*, Viktor Sergeyevich? Is the question too difficult for you? Would you like more time? Or should we ask Ilya Nicolaievich?'

The second Russian shook his head. 'I do not know what the owner might or might not have done. It would be better to ask Mr Chadwick how he came to be living in the hotel.'

'Bravo, Ilya Nicolaievich. I'm impressed. Of course, it would be better to ask Mr Chadwick because Mr Chadwick will surely know the answer. But we don't need to bother Mr Chadwick with the question. Do you know why?'

The Russian stiffened. He knew that he was now the target of Melnikov's sarcasm but could see no easy way to escape. He opted for safety. 'No,' he said.

'Ah, don't disappoint me. If you eat my lunch, you can at least entertain me. Why would we ask Mr Chadwick when the answer is obvious? It is obvious, isn't it, my dear.'

Silje looked at Melnikov without speaking. He held her gaze and waited. 'Yes,' she said. 'It's obvious.'

'Would you like to explain to Viktor and Ilya?'

Silje's face made it clear that she had no interest in explaining anything to the two Russians, but she did it anyway.

'He must know the owner. Otherwise, how could he be staying in a hotel that is closed for the season?'

'Exactly,' said Melnikov. 'And now let us ask Mr Chadwick how he is able to stay there?'

'I know the owner,' Chadwick admitted.

'Thank God,' said Melnikov to Chadwick, 'that those two were born in the right place at the right time. If they hadn't been taught to steal, they would have starved. Maybe they will yet if I am not around to feed them. Who knows? So, you have stayed there before?'

The sudden question surprised Chadwick. His first instinct was to lie but he bought himself some time instead. 'Yes,' was all he said.

'As a child.' Melnikov phrased it as a statement, not a question. Chadwick felt uncomfortable. It was unlikely that Melnikov knew his connection with the hotel. He was more likely testing a hypothesis, pushing whatever he knew as far as he could, in the hope Chadwick confirm it. Chadwick was familiar with the technique.

'Yes,' he said, waiting for Melnikov's next question. But Melnikov seemed to have lost interest.

'Tell me, Augustin, how is the casino business? Are you making any money?'

Augustin seemed surprised by the question. 'Anton, you know these are not the months for making money. I am afraid that while you like the quiet of the winter months, they are not very good for casinos.'

'So, you are losing money?'

Augustin shrugged. 'We always lose money at this time of year. It's a big casino. We need to fill it to make money. There are simply not enough tourists until Easter.'

Melnikov turned to Chadwick. 'I am not like Augustin,' he said. 'I do not like to lose money. Not even for a few days.' Melnikov paused as if to emphasise the point. Chadwick hoped that he looked more relaxed than he felt. Melnikov continued: 'To lose money is to lose blood. When you lose blood, you move from predator to prey. Augustin is lucky. His investors don't seem to mind his losing money. That is the difference between the East and the West. In Russia, if you lose money, you are weak, and somebody will move against you or your backers will replace you. There is no discussion because there is no *need* for discussion. It is accepted. In Russia, you are either in control or controlled. There is no middle ground. This is what every Russian understands. Even Russians like Viktor and Ilya.'

'It sounds a very Russian form of capitalism.'

'It is. State-sponsored capitalism is not so very different to state-sponsored terrorism. It is just another form of fanaticism. It is not capitalism as you understand it. There is no independence for the Russian businessman as there is for the Western businessman. You encouraged Russia to embrace capitalism and it did. Except it was not your version of capitalism. You had no more success exporting your version of capitalism to the world than you did with your version of democracy. Russia hasn't changed in a thousand years. It is a utilitarian autocracy except that in our country, utilitarianism is always the greatest good for the *smallest* number. Until you understand that, you will never understand Russia.'

'I understand very few things,' said Chadwick. 'It sounds as if I will have to add Russia to the list.'

Melnikov laughed and turned towards Viktor and Ilya. 'You should learn from the British. They say they know nothing and yet they know everything. With you two, it is the opposite.'

Melnikov turned back to Chadwick. 'I want you to come with me after lunch,' he said.

'Anywhere in particular?' said Chadwick.

'I want to show you my boat. Do you like boats?'

'I have no strong views. They seem like a good idea for travelling over water. I am not sure I would go much further than that.'

'Good. I dislike people who obsess about boats.'

Melnikov looked at his watch. He signalled to the waiter by drawing the edge of his flattened hand across his throat and stood up. His intention was clear. The lunch was over. He said, 'Mr Chadwick, why don't you come with me?' and began to walk towards the swimming pool. Chadwick looked across at Augustin, who shrugged.

Out in the open, the wind had increased. Chadwick accompanied Melnikov to the top of the steps that led down towards the coast path. Melnikov stopped and pointed. His gesture was redundant. Nobody standing on the coast and looking seawards could have missed the blue-and-white motor yacht that was travelling west across the bay. There may have been larger yachts patrolling the Côte d'Azur but none that looked like this. It had an axe bow and a low, streamlined superstructure, giving it a silhouette more like a frigate than a superyacht. It was hardly moving despite the rough sea, indifferent to the heavy swell. As the two men watched, it started to turn towards the shore. *Another piece of theatre*, thought Chadwick, *but a well-coordinated one.*

The shorter man who had been sent to sit with the girls reappeared. His baseball cap made it difficult to see his face. He was broad-shouldered and moved with an arrogance that seemed out of sorts with his carefully controlled boss. Melnikov spoke to him in Russian. The man said nothing but went back towards the restaurant.

Chadwick looked at the yacht. It had turned into the wind and launched a tender towards the shore. Melnikov turned to Silje. 'Why don't you come with us?' It was, thought Chadwick, more of an order than a request. She avoided his eye and walked past them, standing on the top step with her coat pulled tightly around her.

'I don't envy your ride in the tender,' said Augustin, 'but you'll be fine once you are on board.' It was Augustin's way of telling Chadwick that he wasn't coming but Chadwick had already seen the exchange of looks between Melnikov and the Frenchman.

He waited to see whether the Russians were included but Melnikov made it clear that they were not. 'Go home,' was all he said before he started down the steps.

Augustin tapped Silje on the shoulder. She turned, surprised, and then let him kiss her on both cheeks. She looked across at Chadwick. 'Are you going to let me go down these steps in these heels, alone?'

'My mother would never forgive me,' he said, and offered her his arm. Her grip was stronger than he expected. He glanced back at Augustin, who flipped him a casual salute. He noticed that Viktor and Ilya had already returned to the restaurant. He looked down the steps to where Melnikov, accompanied by two bodyguards, was approaching the metal gate that led directly onto the coast path. One of the security men punched in a code and the other pulled the gate open and went through it. Beyond the gate lay the stones and cement of the coast path, and beyond that, only the rocks and the sea.

CHAPTER TWENTY

As they reached the gate, Chadwick ushered Silje to one side so that the wall broke the force of the wind. Chadwick looked through the open gate. Melnikov was standing on the coast path, a bodyguard on either side, watching the tender battle its way to the shore. The sea was rough. It would be a wet trip, thought Chadwick.

The only possible place for the tender to berth was immediately in front of the gate. A natural channel that ran through the rocks had been broadened and deepened into a rectangular cove. The rocks on either side had been blasted to create just enough space to berth a small boat or allow the residents of the Grand Hotel easier access to the sea.

In the current conditions, neither seemed like a good idea. Those waves that found their way into the channel swept forward into the cove, where, trapped by the sheer sides, they surged higher, until they crashed onto the end of the cove, sending spray far into the air. As each wave retreated in anticipation of the next, the water raced out of the small cove, revealing the full extent of the side walls.

Concerned, Chadwick watched the approaching tender. Boarding wasn't an attractive prospect. The combination of the wind, the waves and the slippery rocks would make even the trip to the side of the cove treacherous. He looked at Silje. She seemed unconcerned.

'Is it normally like this?' he asked.

'Like what?'

'Does he always pick the most difficult piece of coastline to get to his boat? Why doesn't he just drive to St Jean and board from there?'

'He always picks the closest place if that is what you mean. He is more interested in saving time than getting wet.'

'And what about you?'

'I hate to get wet but I'm getting paid for it. And my dry cleaner loves me for it.'

The tender slowed as it neared the entrance to the channel - at times disappearing behind the rocks as it sank lower in the grey swell. The helmsman was waiting for a break in the waves to enter the cove and needed all the power of the large outboard motor to hold the boat in position. Every now and then, when the wind dropped, they could hear the noise of the engine under stress.

A wave exited the cove and the tender accelerated into the narrow channel. A new wave entered the cove. It swept forward, gathering strength but just at the point where it seemed inevitable that it would pick up the tender and fling it onto the shore, the helmsman threw the boat into reverse so that it seemed to climb backwards up the swell, allowing the mass of water to pass safely beneath it. As the wave passed, the water level fell, and the nearest of the crew threw a rope to one of the bodyguards.

Melnikov picked his way carefully across the rocks and was soon on the side of the channel. One of the crew had now moved to the starboard side of the tender and was waiting to catch the passengers as they jumped. Melnikov looked left towards the sea, and, as the next wave entered the channel and the tender swung suddenly upwards, he stepped off the rocks and into the tender. One of the crew caught him and guided him towards the far side of the rib where he sat, staring straight ahead.

Chadwick and Silje started across the rocks. A breaking wave showered them with spray. Silje shook her arm loose. Perhaps she wanted to control her jump herself? Maybe she didn't want Melnikov to see Chadwick helping her? It wasn't clear.

Reaching the side of the channel, Silje stood at its edge, looking towards the entrance of the cove as Melnikov had done. The helmsman, working overtime, gunned the engine, his head swivelling as he manoeuvred the tender. The bodyguard holding the rope, unused to the vagaries of the sea, was watching Silje. One of the crew, spotting the danger, shouted, but was too late. A wave cutting diagonally across the mouth of the channel broke over the bodyguard, who disappeared under a curtain of water. The rope went slack, a gap opened between the tender and the edge of the cove, and Silje, stepping off the rocks, disappeared beneath the surging current. A second later, Chadwick jumped in after her.

Chadwick, shocked by the cold and the strength of the currents, looked up. Above him was the dark silhouette of the tender and the bubbles thrown off by its propeller. He looked down and saw Silje struggling to get out of her long coat, which was dragging her down. One arm was stuck in a sleeve which had reversed. Swimming towards her, he pulled the coat away but as she began to swim upwards, he held her down and pointed above them to the spinning propeller.

As soon as the tender shifted position, Chadwick took her hand and began swimming towards the surface. The surface of the water seemed to recede before them, a mirror-like mirage that was tantalisingly close but always beyond the reach of their outstretched arms until finally they burst through it, their lungs heaving, their bodies focused only on the simple act of survival.

Chadwick looked behind them. The tender was back under control. He kicked hard and pulled Silje towards it. A crewman appeared above her and took hold of her wrists. The tender started to reverse, pulling Silje with it, and as the next wave tipped the stern of the tender down, the bow reared so that Silje was almost clear of the water, with only her legs submerged. As the movement reversed, and the bow fell, the crewman, sitting on the floor, his feet braced against the inside of the rib's hull, pulled her hard and she was half-lifted, half-dragged into the boat.

On the next downward movement, Chadwick managed to get his head and upper body over the side of the rib. The bow of the tender reared upwards and he felt his legs pull free of the water. His strength was disappearing fast. As the bow sank again, he pulled himself into the boat, his face pressed into the floor of the rib. He lay there, unable to move, not caring about what happened to the tender, glad, however briefly, to be alive.

Silje was sitting on the floor of the tender with her back against the far side. Her hair was plastered over her face. Her eye make-up had run. Her head was bowed, and she was breathing heavily. He felt the vibration of the engine increase as the throttle was pushed open. He raised his head and pushed himself into a sitting position. They were out of the channel and heading towards the yacht.

Melnikov hadn't moved. He was sitting on the side of the tender, towards the stern, gazing straight ahead. Chadwick looked across at Silje. Her wet shirt was sticking to her body and she had her knees pulled to her chest with her arms wrapped around them to try to keep warm. He smiled but there was no response. She was too focused on staying warm. He watched her shivering for a moment before moving opposite Melnikov. Melnikov ignored him.

'Are there any blankets?' shouted Chadwick over the noise of the engine. Melnikov seemed surprised, either by the question or by Chadwick's asking it. He shrugged, and Chadwick tried again. He pointed towards Silje. 'She's freezing. We need to wrap her in something or she'll get hypothermia.'

Melnikov turned and looked towards Silje, his face expressionless. He said, 'She'll be fine. We will be at the boat in a couple of minutes.' He paused, then added, 'She's a tough girl. You should remember that.'

CHAPTER TWENTY-ONE

Chadwick and Melnikov turned in tandem. Silje was standing in the doorway, her arms folded, leaning against the doorjamb. She had changed into a pair of taupe, loosely fitting cashmere trousers that were gathered at the ankle and tied at the waist like an old-fashioned tracksuit. The matching top had patch pockets and a brass zipper that was pulled halfway down to show the white T-shirt that she wore underneath. Her feet were bare and looked very brown against the cream carpet. She wore no make-up, and Chadwick thought she looked younger - more vulnerable than before.

'Has he converted you to Russian capitalism?' she asked.

'Not quite yet,' said Chadwick, pointing at the paintings on the walls of the saloon. 'Although it has its good points, particularly if you're an art lover. This is like a floating offshoot of The Met. I don't think I've ever seen three Monets outside a museum. You must love art.'

While he was talking, Silje came towards them and wrapped her arm around Melnikov's shoulders. It was unclear to Chadwick whether it was a sign of affection or of submission. Melnikov said, 'Not especially but it's more mobile than real estate and lighter than gold. Would you like to see the rest of the boat?'

Chadwick looked at Silje, whose arm was still wrapped around Melnikov's neck. Her blue eyes looked through him as if she was inspecting the other side of the world. 'I would,' he said. Melnikov reached up and took Silje's hand as the two of them led the way.

They took the lift one floor up. Melnikov ignored the bridge and pushed open a set of double doors. 'This is my office,' he said. The walls were painted steel and the floor uncovered. In the middle of the room was a metal desk and an office chair. The desk had a computer screen, several mobile phones in chargers and a desk lamp. Two secure filing cabinets stood against a wall. Louvred shutters were fitted to the windows on either side, making the room much darker than the rest of the boat. There were no photographs, no ornaments, no papers or documents, nothing that could identify the owner of the office in any way. It was more like a monk's cell than an office. Chadwick looked at Melnikov to see if he might offer some explanation, but his face was as impassive as ever.

From Melnikov's office, they took the lift down two floors, to the cabin where Chadwick had showered and changed. But, instead of returning to the cabin, Melnikov knocked gently on the only other door. There was a short pause until the door was opened by a short, grey-haired man in his late forties. Dressed all in white including white soft-soled shoes, he stood to one side and said in a soft voice, 'Sasha, your father is here.' Melnikov entered the room with Silje and Chadwick just behind him.

Although identical to the cabin where Chadwick had changed, this one was very different. The first cabin was expensively decorated but bereft of life. This was the opposite. The walls were covered with a child's drawings, done with crayon on paper. None were remarkable. They were the type of picture dutifully affixed to the front of the family fridge, but instead of there being one or two, there were hundreds. They were attached, one on top of another, so that the walls looked like they were adorned with giant petals.

At the far end of the cabin stood a large table covered with paper and crayons. Beside it stood a young man of perhaps seventeen or eighteen. He had his father's thin features but was taller and broader, his hair dark brown and long, falling forward over his face. Pale-skinned, as if he was seldom in the sun, he wore a black T-shirt, black jeans and bare feet. He stared at the group for a second or two as if they had somehow materialised in the room without his noticing. His eyes were dark and his stare sufficiently intense that Chadwick felt uncomfortable.

'Sasha.' It was Melnikov speaking. 'Sasha, why don't you show me what you have been doing?' Melnikov's voice had lost its harshness. The boy turned towards the table and picked up the piece of paper he had been working on. Holding the paper carefully in both hands, he brought it to his father, who took it from him gently, turned it around and examined it. Chadwick could see that it was a childish drawing of a bird and realised that all the drawings in the room were of birds. 'Sasha, it is very beautiful,' said Melnikov, his finger tracing the outline of the bird. 'Is it a seagull?'

Sasha looked directly at Melnikov. '*No*,' he said emphatically. 'No. It's an eagle.' He turned towards Silje. 'It's an *eagle*,' he repeated. Silje stretched out her arms and he moved towards her. She wrapped him in a hug, his head leaning on her shoulder. 'It's an eagle, an eagle.'

'I know,' said Silje. 'Does it fly very high?'

Sasha didn't turn his head. Still resting on Silje's shoulder, he looked away from them, towards the door. 'Yes. *Very* high … So high that you cannot see it from the ground.'

'How wonderful to fly so high. I would love to fly like that, wouldn't you, Sasha?'

Sasha thought for a moment. 'Yes. I would,' he said and lapsed into silence.

'Sasha,' said Melnikov, 'this is Mr Chadwick.'

Silje let her arms fall and Sasha slowly turned towards Chadwick. 'Are you coming to live with us?' he said.

Chadwick was unsure how to respond. 'I don't think so, Sasha. I live somewhere else.'

'Do you live on a boat?'

'No. I live in a hotel.'

'Would you like to live on a boat?'

'I would like that very much, Sasha. You have a wonderful boat. You must be very happy here.'

'I live here with my father,' said Sasha as if that explained everything.

'Sasha, I am showing Mr Chadwick around the *Lara*. Would you like to come with us?'

'Yes.' Sasha paused. 'Will you show Mr Chadwick the engine room?'

'Yes, I suppose so. If Mr Chadwick would like to see it.'

'Would you like to see it?' Sasha turned towards Chadwick. His eyes were very dark, almost black, and were set deep in his face.

'I would, Sasha, I would. Do you like the engine room?'

'It is the beating heart of a ship. The engine room is the beating heart of the ship. Without the engine room, the ship cannot move.'

Sasha looked at his father, who said, 'You are right, Sasha. We will go there after we show Mr Chadwick my cabin.' He held out his hand to his son, who hesitated for a moment and then took it.

This time, they took the stairs that wrapped around the lift shaft. They arrived in front of a set of double doors. Melnikov took a fob from his pocket, waved it in front of one of the wooden panels and pushed the door open.

The cabin was large, occupying most of the main deck, starting amidships and running towards the bow. On one side, there was a pair of sofas and a couple of chairs set around a low table. On the other, an antique desk and chair. Beyond the desk and the sofas, the cabin widened so that its floor plan resembled a fat tee. At the end of the room was a large bed raised on a dais, with doors on either side.

Sasha went to sit on one of the sofas and began to play a game on his phone. Silje moved towards the desk and half-sat, half-leaned against it, while Melnikov moved towards the centre of the room.

Chadwick walked past Melnikov, towards the bed. When he reached the dais, he turned and viewed the room. It would have been impressive in a stately home, let alone a boat.

He wondered why the room should narrow into the tee. As far as he could remember, there was nothing external that would have prevented the cabin being as wide at the far end as it was at this end. The walls that were facing him, either side of the narrow part of the cabin, were panelled in limed oak rather than the green silk which covered the remainder of the room. He became conscious that Melnikov and the others were watching him. He walked towards the walls on his right - a series of panels framed with beading ran from floor to ceiling. Chadwick began to inspect the well-fitted structure more closely, but there were no gaps that he could find.

'Come and watch our friend,' said Melnikov to Sasha and Silje. They appeared to Chadwick's left as he continued to stare at the panels, looking for some clue as to what lay behind them. He ran his hands over the wood, pressing here and there, in the hope of finding a door that would open inwards. But nothing happened. He took a step back and looked at Melnikov, who shrugged.

'He doesn't know how to open it,' said Sasha.

'How does it open, Sasha?' said Chadwick. 'Will you tell me the secret?'

Sasha's face went blank. He turned to look at his father, who nodded. 'Show him,' he said. Sasha walked to the corner of the panelling. He pushed the beading of one of the panels to one side. There was a gentle hum and the panels started to slide to either side. Chadwick watched as another room became visible. It was a dressing room with racks of clothes on either side wall while the rear wall comprised a series of fitted wooden drawers that ran from floor to ceiling. Sasha looked at Chadwick expectantly.

'It's magic,' said Chadwick.

Sasha looked at him with disdain. 'This is not the *magic cave*,' he said gravely. 'You don't know about the magic cave. Nobody knows about the magic cave. Do they?' This question was directed to his father.

Melnikov smiled. 'No, Sasha, nobody knows about the magic cave. Just you and me.'

'And Silje. Silje knows about the magic cave. Don't you?'

This time, it was Silje who looked at Melnikov for guidance, but he made no sign of any kind.

'Silje, you know about it. You do!'

She turned towards Sasha and smiled. 'Of course, I do,' she said. 'I know all about it.'

Sasha relaxed and said to Chadwick as if he hadn't been able to hear, 'Silje knows about the magic cave.'

'Should we show Mr Chadwick the magic cave, Sasha?'

The boy, surprised, looked at his father to see if he had heard correctly. Melnikov repeated the question, which Sasha considered carefully, looking at each of the other three in turn.

Finally, he said, 'Yes, let's show him the magic cave but he must promise to keep it secret.'

Chadwick promised and followed Melnikov into the dressing room. He looked around. He started to walk towards the drawers that covered the rear wall but felt Melnikov's hand on his arm. 'Please, stand where you are.' He looked across at the other two. Silje's face was blank while Sasha's was wholly engaged in whatever was to happen next.

Melnikov said, 'In a moment, the lights will go down but please keep looking at the rear wall.' The doors to the dressing room started to close. When the panelling met in the middle, the lights started to dim, and in a few seconds, the room was completely dark. The four of them stood stock-still, aware of the others only through the sound of their breathing. After a short delay, Chadwick sensed somebody, presumably Melnikov, moving towards the rail of clothes on the left of the room.

The silence was broken by a quiet humming and Chadwick became conscious of objects moving somewhere in front of him. A strip of red appeared, running from the ground to the top of the drawers. He watched as the strip widened, revealing another smaller room, lit with red lighting like the control room of a submarine. Fascinated, he waited while the door opened fully. This new room was very small: no more than a couple of metres in width and three metres in depth. There was no decoration of any kind. The walls were bare and may even have been painted steel – it was hard to tell in the low light. A bench ran around three of the walls. There was no other furniture.

'Why don't you go inside?' asked Melnikov. Chadwick hesitated, uncomfortable about entering the small room alone, while Melnikov remained outside, next to whatever mechanism controlled the doors. Sasha, oblivious to Chadwick's concerns, pushed past him. Only after Sasha had sat on the bench opposite the door, did Chadwick follow him.

The door was steel, and several centimetres thicker than a watertight door. It opened outwards, the drawers sliding to either side by some unseen mechanism. One of the side walls was completely bare, a solid sheet of painted steel. The other had a small shelf at shoulder height. On the shelf were a VHF radio and a second box, which might have been part of the boat's intercom system. By the side of the door was a key pad, which Chadwick assumed controlled the door. Underneath the bench was a water tank with a tap attached to it, and several large packages, almost certainly emergency food.

Melnikov looked as if he was about to enter but thought better of it, preferring to stick his head through the door. 'How do you like Sasha's magic cave?' he asked Chadwick.

'Very practical but it lacks the charm of the rest of your boat. Perhaps your interior decorator ran out of ideas?'

Melnikov shrugged. 'If I ever have to use this place, I won't be worrying about its decor. The most important thing is that it is secure. This door, he struck it with the flat of his hand, 'is specially toughened steel and completely bulletproof. It is as strong as a bank-vault door and as difficult to get through, either with explosives or with an oxyacetylene torch.'

'But what about all the paintings in the saloon?'

'They can have them. The world is full of paintings. Besides, they would have to be very stupid to think that they would ever live to enjoy them. But there are many stupid people in the world, so that however unlikely the scenario, one must protect oneself. Don't you agree?'

'It's a hard point to argue. But it seems a pretty extreme scenario. It would take quite some nerve to board *Lara*.'

'This is the South of France. Villas are robbed all the time. The robbers pretend to be from the gas company, or the security service or the police. They bribe the guards. They poison the guard dogs. They bleed gas into the air-conditioning systems. These are not children, Mr Chadwick. These are thoroughly ruthless professional thieves. I don't think it would be so difficult to take the *Lara*. Far larger vessels are captured every week off the coast of Africa by locals using nothing more than outboards and ladders. The thieves that operate around this coastline do not live in mud huts; they live in the grandest villas and the best apartments. And if they decided to target *Lara*, they would lack neither help nor resources.'

'By help and resources, I assume you mean the authorities?'

'Of course. This is the South of France. Everything is for sale, and everyone. Take you, for example. If I wanted to find out about you, to find out if any of the local authorities had any information on you, how long do you think it would take me? Two days? Three at the outside. No more.'

'And what *did* you find out?'

'Why would I want to find out anything about you, Mr Chadwick? You live in a hotel that is still closed for the winter and you want to be left alone. That is all I need to know about you. I don't need to know more.'

'I'm glad to hear it. You seemed to have grasped my plan better than most. Most people seem to think that I am looking for a job.'

'A job? What kind of job?'

'I have no idea. The kind I don't want, I suppose. The world is full of people trying to sell things to people who don't want to buy.'

'Not me. I am not about to offer you a job.'

Melnikov took a mobile from his pocket and looked at the screen. 'I'm sorry,' he said. 'Unfortunately, there is something I need to attend to, so the engine room must wait for another time. I'll have the tender take you back to your hotel.'

As Chadwick boarded the tender, he looked up and saw that the man in the baseball cap was watching him from the deck of the *Lara*. He smiled at Chadwick, but Chadwick looked away. There was something about the smile that unnerved him and he waited impatiently for the tender to cast off.

After several hours with Melnikov, he was as confused as he had been before. He felt that he knew more about Melnikov after the lunch, but less after the visit to the *Lara*. What was his relationship with Silje? Or with Augustin? Why had he introduced him to Sasha? Why had he shown him the panic room? None of it seemed to make any sense but that meant nothing. If Melnikov had orchestrated it, then it had a logic and a purpose. Of that, he was certain.

The sea was as rough as before but this time, he welcomed it. He looked towards the shore, and away from *Lara*. An uneasiness was creeping over him that rejecting Silje's advice and agreeing to both the lunch and the visit to the boat had been a mistake, but he couldn't work out why. He started to look at the villas high above the shore to see if he could spot the Chairman's.

CHAPTER TWENTY-TWO

'I know you don't like it. And I know *why* you don't like it. I don't like it either. But I can't see what else we can do. Given what we know,' said Verlaine.

'What we know? What *do* we know? I wish you would tell me,' said Chadwick.

'Well, we know that her brother is here. We missed him at the hotel. But he is here.'

'We know he *was* here. There's a big difference.'

'Why would he leave?' asked Verlaine.

'Why would he leave? I have no idea. Perhaps we would be better asking why he came here in the first place? We don't even know that. And that would be worth knowing. If we knew that, then we might, we might, be able to judge whether he's still here, or long gone. But until we know what he came here to do and, more importantly, whether he was able to do it, we really don't have a clue whether he is still here or not.'

Chadwick looked across the café to the bar where Leclerc was reading his newspaper in the hope that he might catch his eye and persuade him to join them. But Leclerc was too absorbed in his reading to notice. The day hadn't started well and looked set to get worse. He searched for a waitress but, as usual, there was none in sight. With no other distractions available, he wearily returned his attention to the conversation.

'But you agree that he must have had a good reason for coming here?' said Verlaine.

'*And* a good reason for leaving. He didn't hang around at the hotel once he knew he had been found.'

'Okay. What about the men at the hotel? Who are they and why are they after him?'

Chadwick knew that he was fighting a rearguard action. Verlaine was not going to give up, not when Julija was sitting next to him. All Chadwick could do was try to steer the conversation as best as he could. He paused for a moment before replying. 'Charles, I have no idea. And neither do you. We must stop speculating. It's pointless and it's not going to get us anywhere.' He turned towards Julija in the hope of getting some support, but she ignored him. Her sympathies lay with Verlaine.

'Exactly. Now, we agree,' said Verlaine. 'There is nothing more that we can do with Soldane for now. That's why we must keep going with Arcier. He is the only lead we have.'

Chadwick sighed inwardly. He was tired. Tired of the argument and tired of the awkward situation in which he found himself. But it was his own fault, and he knew it. It was only by luck that Julija and he hadn't walked into Charles Verlaine on their way into the café. Verlaine might have his suspicions but if he had seen them arrive together, they would have been confirmed. He wished he hadn't let Julija persuade him to sit beside her at the table, the two of them against the wall, facing outwards towards the window. He knew how it would look. Even the taciturn Leclerc had noticed it, smiled to himself, and returned to his reading. Verlaine had shown no surprise, but Chadwick couldn't help but wonder if the vehemence with which Verlaine was pushing the argument that they needed to find Arcier was the result of his finding Chadwick and Julija together so early in the day.

He couldn't blame him. Verlaine wanted to impress Julija with his determination to help her, and he was correct in what he said - there was no obvious way of finding Soldane, now that he had left the hotel. Arcier's connection with the Soldane case, however tenuous, was the only lead that they had. But trying to find Arcier was exactly what Chadwick didn't want to do.

After the Melnikov lunch and his trip to the *Lara*, all he had wanted was some time to himself and a chance to reflect on the day's events. He had assumed that the lunch had been organised to allow Melnikov to meet him and assess whether he was the man who took his money and attacked his men. But there had been no mention, even obliquely, of the car-park incident. If Melnikov was involved, either he cared little for what had happened, or his interest in Chadwick lay elsewhere. And why had Melnikov insisted on his visiting the *Lara*? Why would anybody who so clearly valued his privacy choose to invite a stranger to tour his boat, meet his troubled son and visit his panic room? What sort of man needed a panic room on a boat anyway? Surely not the kind that extends an invitation to a perfect stranger. None of it made any sense. He had needed the solitude of the hotel and a chance to think.

But he didn't get it. Julija was waiting for him by the gate in the lane. He had no idea how she knew when he was returning or whether she had been waiting for hours. In the end, it didn't matter. She wasn't leaving without talking to him. And once she was inside, it became clear to both that she wasn't leaving at all.

It had started harmlessly enough. He had avoided his room and steered her towards the bar where he removed the dustcovers from one of the sofas. He was about to uncover an adjacent chair, but she caught him by the wrist and pulled him down next to her on the sofa. Once they were sitting, she took hold of his hand and squeezed it.

'I've been looking for you all day. Where have you been?'

'I was invited to a lunch by Augustin, the casino owner. At a very grand hotel.'

'All afternoon?'

'Our Russian host wanted me to continue on with him after lunch.'

Julija hesitated. 'A Russian? Who was he?'

'A man called Melnikov. Have you heard of him?'

'I know him.'

'You *know* him. How?'

Julija looked confused for a moment before she corrected herself. 'No. I don't know him. I have never met him. I know …'

'Of him. You know *of* him,' said Chadwick.

'Yes. I know of him. I have never met him,' she repeated. 'Why did you meet him?'

'That is a very good question. I have no idea. Augustin arranged it, presumably at Melnikov's request. Why have you heard of him?'

'People talk about him. He is very powerful here. Very well connected. He has a beautiful boat. It is hard to miss it.'

'I know. I was on it this afternoon.'

'You were on his boat?' For the first time since he had met her, Julija seemed impressed. 'Why were you on his boat?'

'He invited me. He wanted to show me the boat.'

'Was she there?'

Chadwick, surprised that Julija would know about Silje, stalled. 'Who?'

'His girlfriend. He has a girlfriend. She is often with him. She is very tall.' He noticed that she made no reference to Silje's looks and he decided to play down her involvement and not mention that he had met her previously.

'She was. Do you know her?'

'No.' It was emphatic. Her warmth evaporated.

'Then how do you know about her?'

Julija shrugged. 'People talk. And I have seen her in the casino. She walks around as if she owns the place.'

'Maybe she does,' said Chadwick, thinking of Augustin's link with Melnikov. 'Does it matter?'

Julija ignored his question. She said, 'Did you talk to her?'

'Where?'

'At the lunch.' A thought struck her. 'How many of you were invited to his boat?'

'Just me.'

'And she went too?'

'She did.'

'Do you like her?'

He hesitated, surprised about her interest in Silje and unclear about where her questions were heading. 'Like her? What do you mean? I hardly know her.'

'But you have met her. She was at the lunch. She was on the boat.'

'She was.'

'Did you talk to her?'

'Not really. There were others at the lunch. And I wasn't sitting next to her. Why are you so interested in her?'

'She is beautiful. She can get any man she wants.'

'So what? So can you.'

'Not like her. With her, it is different.'

'Different? How is it different?'

She released her grip on his hand. 'Don't treat me like an imbecile. You know how it is different.'

Chadwick retreated. 'I don't understand. You haven't met this woman. You've never mentioned her to me before. Why are you so interested in her now?'

'Isn't it obvious?'

'Not to me, it isn't. Why don't you explain?'

'Explain? Explain what? You have met her. I tell you that she can get any man she wants, and you ask me to explain. You must think that I'm stupid.' She turned away and started to get up.

Chadwick caught her by the waist and pulled her back down. 'Listen,' he said, 'I don't know this woman. I've just met her. I went to see Melnikov. She is with Melnikov so she was there. I have no interest in her. Nor does she have any interest in me.' It unnerved him that lying to Julija about his interest in Silje caused him so little concern while his admission that Silje had no interest in him was painful. He pulled Julija closer to him and said, 'Stop worrying. I have no interest in Melnikov or her. I will probably see neither of them again.'

He could feel her relax. She twisted around to sit on his lap with her legs on either side of him. She gave him a hard stare as if she was testing whether he had told her the truth. Seemingly satisfied, she put her hands on his shoulders and pushed him back against the sofa.

'I don't believe you,' she said, 'but it doesn't matter. Men never tell the truth about women. Besides, if you go near her, he will kill you. And if he doesn't kill you, I will.'

'I don't think I've ever been to a place where so many people are so keen on killing me.'

'Everything has to be a joke with you. But these people are not a joke. You do not know the Russians. Your country has never been part of Russia. You should listen to me and stay away from them. You must help me find Aleksis. You must help me find Arcier. Stop wasting time with the Russians.'

Chadwick took her wrists and pulled her arms downwards. 'Yes, Mother,' he said as he kissed her.

It had been a mistake. His evening of reflection had taken a different turn and left him escorting Julija to breakfast. It was not what he wanted. It was adding further complexity to his already complicated life.

'I know that you don't want to, but we should go back to his office and search it,' said Verlaine.

Chadwick held his temper in check. There was no point. He would only look as if he was on the defensive and encourage Verlaine and Julija.

'Why? What do you expect to find? You saw it. The people who searched it ripped it apart. If there was anything to be found in that office, they found it.'

'But maybe they weren't looking for the same things that we were looking for.'

'What *are* we looking for? I know about the clippings and the photo but *what else?*'

'Something that tells us where Arcier might have gone,' said Julija.

Chadwick resolved to be kind to her. 'And what might that be? There are only two scenarios. The first, and in my view the less likely, is that it wasn't Arcier who was beaten up in that office. If that's right, then it's possible that the people in Arcier's office were searching for something that might lead them to Arcier.

'The second scenario is that it was Arcier who was beaten up in his office and they took him with them when they left. If that's the case, there's unlikely to be anything in that office which will lead us to where they took Arcier.

'It's also very probable that, by now, somebody will have reported Arcier missing. If the police are involved, they will no doubt have reached the same conclusions as we have. What will they do? Go through his files and question the people in the building. Go to his home and search there. And if they don't come up with anything, what next? Come on, Charles, you did this for a living. Why don't you explain to Julija?'

Verlaine sighed. He could sense defeat. Julija looked at him expectantly. 'If they have no other leads, they would stake out the office and home. They would have no choice,' he explained to Julija. 'They would have to be seen to be doing something even if it was a waste of time. It's more complicated because he was a former policeman. Even if they never liked him, he must be a priority – to stop it happening to others.'

'Precisely,' said Chadwick. 'So the real question is do we want to go back to an office or an apartment that is almost certainly under police surveillance to spend several hours sifting through a bonfire of paper that has been searched twice before by professionals - albeit working different sides of the street - on the remote possibility that we might find something that they missed that might, *might*, lead us to Arcier? It doesn't sound very appealing to me.'

Julija ignored Chadwick and stared instead at Verlaine. She said nothing while she thought. She had her blonde hair pulled back and was wearing little make-up. She looked good, thought Chadwick, and turned away towards the bar before she caught him looking at her. Leclerc was in the process of folding his newspaper. Some crisis must have occurred in the kitchen or the back room that required his immediate attention. Before he started moving, he checked the front room. Spotting Chadwick, he smiled. Chadwick waved him over. He took his time, stowing his paper, and admonishing one of the waitresses before he began his stately passage towards where Chadwick and the others were sitting. It was important to demonstrate that he was in thrall to no one, and that in the café, he reigned supreme. To reinforce the point, he sat down and began talking as if he had always been part of the conversation.

'You do not understand how things are done here, my friend,' he said, wagging his finger at Chadwick. 'It is not your fault. It is because you are Anglo Saxon. You cannot help it. You are a cold, uncaring people, uninterested in the lives of others.' Leclerc turned towards Julija. 'Why are you with these monsters, my dear? Can't you find warmer-blooded creatures?'

'They buy me coffees. What can I do?'

'They buy you coffees? *Coffees*. My God! If these were real men, true musketeers, they would buy you all of France. But they are not. They are a pale imitation of men, barely fit to grace my humble establishment. I only let them in because I am ashamed to let them wander the streets. How can you like such watery soup when you are in the land of bouillabaisse?'

Julija smiled and looked years younger. 'I am just a simple girl from the North. I am not used to such rich food,' she teased.

Leclerc reached across and took her hand. 'My dear, you must forget your Northern ways. It is warm here. It is not like the North. You do not spend the winter under the ice, your heart-beat slowing to a standstill. Here, in the South, our hearts are always beating, and our blood is always warm.' He leaned across the table and pressed her hand to his chest. 'Do you see now how different we are from the watery soups?'

'I see very well,' said Julija, smiling at him. 'I can see that I have been very foolish. I must become more Southern.'

'My dear, you won't regret it. Once you have embraced the South, you can never go back North. For you, the North is over. You must stay here with us. The North is only for people like these two. People who like the rain and the snow and the darkness. It is not for us.'

Chadwick watched Verlaine. He was smiling. There was no hint of annoyance at Leclerc's flirting. Perhaps he had been wrong in thinking that Verlaine was interested in Julija or perhaps Verlaine was better at disguising his feelings than Chadwick thought? He had always thought Verlaine an open book, an older man frustrated and embittered by investing his life in a career that hadn't delivered on its early promise, another Riviera retiree looking for rebirth after a lifetime of drudgery. But now he wasn't so sure that he understood Verlaine at all.

'Is this still a café or has it become a tourism office?' asked Chadwick. He pointed to the empty cups.

Leclerc pretended to look annoyed. 'It's the management to blame,' he said. 'The manager loves his country so much, he forgets his duties.'

'Clearly,' said Chadwick. 'A man who loves so much can easily become distracted.'

'You see what I mean? You see how these Northerners are. You cannot spend any more time with them. I forbid it.'

'What? Under the powers vested in you as Head of Tourism for Southern France?' said Chadwick.

Leclerc ignored him and continued speaking to Julija. 'Now we have irritated them. It is all progress. Their cold hearts are melting. Perhaps one day, if we let them live amongst us for long enough, they will learn to love like normal people.'

'I think he is being rude about Parisians,' said Chadwick to Verlaine.

Verlaine shrugged. 'We almost certainly deserve it. As far as I can see, nobody likes Parisians. Even other Parisians. If we are to fight on those grounds, we must surely lose.'

'So, are we fighting or not?' said Chadwick.

Verlaine smiled and said, 'Let's have another coffee and think about it some more.'

Chadwick turned towards Leclerc. 'Apparently, we may fight. My friend has the matter under debate. In the meantime, our thoughtful musketeer would like another coffee. Could the Head of Tourism use his influence to arrange it?'

'It's possible,' said Leclerc, 'but I cannot guarantee it. The staff are under orders not to encourage people from the North to come to the café.'

Or anybody else, thought Chadwick to himself. He waited patiently while Leclerc called one of the waitresses over. She took their orders with the appropriate level of bad grace. She was about to leave when she asked Leclerc, 'Have you given him the letter?'

Leclerc looked surprised. 'No. I thought you must have already done it. Where is it?'

'It's under the till.'

'Bring it!' She disappeared towards the bar at the far end of the room and returned carrying a white envelope. She gave it to Leclerc who tapped it as he spoke, 'You see not only am I responsible for tourism, apparently, I also run a sub-post office for Northern gentlemen who choose not to live in houses or apartments.'

He handed the envelope to Chadwick. His name was on the front. He opened it.

'McGhee here. Some questions still unanswered about the *Highland Laddie*. Possible dirty work at the crossroads. Chairman has asked local quizmaster to meet you at Brasserie La Rotonde, Hotel Negresco, Nice, 13.00 Tuesday. Name of Maclean.'

Chadwick folded the paper. The others were looking at him, waiting for him to tell them what was in the message, but he decided against it. Some instinct told him that this was information he should keep to himself for now. He folded the paper, returned it to the envelope and put the envelope in his pocket.

'It's the name of somebody at Lloyd's who I can speak to about your brother's ship,' he said to Julija. 'They might be able to give me some more information. Information that wasn't in the press at the time or that has emerged subsequently.'

'What sort of information?' asked Julija.

'I've no idea. I won't know until I speak to him. And possibly, not even then. We'll see. It's a long shot but worth trying, no?' He looked towards Verlaine for support. Verlaine nodded and said, 'Why don't you call him from here?'

'Too difficult. He might be busy and want to call back. I can hardly wait around here all day. I'll do it from the hotel. It will be easier. If I do get hold of him quickly, I'll come back and tell you about it. But it might not happen. I don't know who he is but if he is important, I'm unlikely to be very high on his priority list.'

Chadwick stood up. As he did so, Julija started to pull her bag towards her. He placed a hand on her shoulder and pointed to

Verlaine and Leclerc. 'I am sure the other musketeers will be able to keep you amused while I'm gone.'

'Have you not left yet?' said Leclerc, grinning. Verlaine sat back with his arms folded. He seemed content enough. The Arcier issue seemed to have been shelved for now. Julija gave him a searching look which he did his best to ignore. 'Have fun,' he said and left.

CHAPTER TWENTY-THREE

McGhee's note had been delivered late. It was already Tuesday. Contrary to what he had told the others, Chadwick did not return to the hotel but caught the next train to Nice.

Maclean arrived five minutes early. To a man like Maclean, five minutes early was on time. He shook hands carefully as if it was a newly acquired skill and sat down opposite Chadwick. He was older, with the steel-framed oval glasses of an academic. His suit was old-fashioned in cut and his shirt slightly frayed at the collar. Chadwick didn't recognise the tie but felt sure that it had some significance in Maclean's world. He seemed embarrassed, as if he was not quite sure how to deal with the situation, so Chadwick took the initiative.

'It's good of you to see me, Mr Maclean.'

'Please call me Humphrey. My name is Humphrey. My first name, that is.' He gave a small smile as if to excuse his impertinence. 'Here is my card.'

'You are not based here, I take it?'

'No. No, I'm based in Marseilles. That's where our operation is.' He stopped speaking as if he thought he had already said too much.

'And you are a Lloyd's agent?'

'Well, the company is. We've been the Lloyd's agent for Southern France for many years.'

'I'm sorry, Humphrey. I'm afraid I'm very ignorant about Lloyd's. I know it's an insurer, but I don't know what a Lloyd's agent does.'

Maclean looked disappointed. 'Lloyd's is *not* itself an insurer,' he said. 'It's an *insurance market* for syndicates that underwrite insurance. Lloyd's provides the infrastructure, the administration and ultimately the security for the policies but it is not an insurer *per se*. It's a subtle difference but a difference nevertheless.'

'And the agents?'

'The agents are appointed by Lloyd's and are responsible for marine surveying and claims adjusting. In the old days, we used to track ships and notify Lloyd's about wrecks, losses and other cargo issues. Nowadays, technology does that and most of our work is surveying and loss adjusting,' he added.

'Surveying? Does that mean you inspect ships?'

'Yes, amongst other things. We also investigate marine accidents and sometimes appear in court as expert witnesses. Most of the time, we are asked to give our view on damage-repair costs, replacement values, fair-market values. That sort of thing.'

'Were you involved with the *Highland Laddie*?'

Maclean looked apologetic, as if he had proved to be a disappointment. 'I wasn't. You know that it sank in the South China Sea?' Chadwick nodded. 'So, it wouldn't have been my responsibility, but the local Lloyd's agent would have been involved.'

'Involved how?'

Maclean drew a little closer to Chadwick. 'Well, officially they would have to confirm the loss of the ship, its crew and cargo. But it's always difficult when there is no wreck. Or even a clear idea of where the ship went down.'

'Meaning ...'

Maclean looked him over, deciding whether he should say more. 'Modern ships rarely sink, Mr Chadwick. And if they do, it is usually because they run aground or hit some obstacle near land. They typically don't sink in the middle of the ocean. At least, not without some warning. Have you any idea of the electronics on a modern ship?'

Chadwick shook his head.

'Nowadays, ships sail themselves. Of course, they have a crew – and officers on the bridge. And they do need them, mainly to go in and out of port or if something goes wrong. But once on the open sea, the computers run everything. They know where they are going, the sea lanes they must take, where they are, their speed, the weather, the sea conditions. To be honest, the computers are now so advanced, they could move ships around the world by themselves.'

'But you must need some crew on the lookout? What happens if you are heading directly towards another ship?'

Maclean looked bemused. 'AIS,' he said. 'Surely you know about AIS?'

Chadwick shook his head. 'I have heard it mentioned but I have no real idea about what it is.'

'Automated Identification System. Almost all vessels have it now, even very small ones. It is an automatic tracking system used on ships for identifying and locating vessels by electronically exchanging data with other nearby ships, AIS base stations and satellites. Every commercial vessel over a certain tonnage must have one by law, even private yachts.'

'So much for privacy. It must be tough to know that you've spent a fortune on your new boat and any idiot with a smartphone can track you.'

'I suppose so. The security people hate it, but it's the law. Besides, the underwriters wouldn't pay out on a claim if they found out that the AIS had been switched off.'

'They can be turned off?'

Maclean looked unhappy, like a doctor delivering bad news. 'In theory, yes, they can be turned off. But it's not encouraged, as I am sure you can imagine.'

'So, how can you tell whether a ship has sunk or whether somebody simply switched off the AIS?'

'Do you mean the *Highland Laddie?*'

'Yes. How can you tell whether it sank or whether the AIS was switched off?'

Maclean paused. His unhappiness had changed to outright suspicion. He said, 'I am sorry, Mr Chadwick, but I need to understand something. What exactly is your interest in the *Highland Laddie?*'

Chadwick was taken aback by his question. 'I thought you knew,' he said. 'I thought this meeting had been arranged by the Chairman.'

This time, it was Maclean who looked surprised. 'Who is the Chairman?' he asked. Chadwick gave him the Chairman's name.

'Ah,' said Maclean. 'Of course, I know who he is, but I've never met or spoken to him.'

'So, who asked you to meet me?'

'Lloyd's. Or rather my boss at Lloyd's. He's responsible for the agents. He sent through some information and asked that I meet you.'

'What did he send you?'

Maclean coloured slightly. 'I'm sorry,' he said, 'it would be helpful if I knew why you were interested?' Despite the apology, there was a firmness to the question that persuaded Chadwick that he would need to be careful how he handled Maclean. He suspected that the old boy was a lot tougher than his appearance suggested.

'I am helping somebody I know try to find out what happened to her brother. He was on the *Highland Laddie.*' Maclean looked at him sceptically. *He has some justification*, thought Chadwick. *It sounds flimsy to me, and I know it's true.*

'I don't understand,' said Maclean. 'What more is there to know? The *Highland Laddie* sank with all hands. It's terribly sad but it does happen still, even with all the technology that's on a modern ship. It must be very upsetting for her but what can she possibly find out, when even the underwriters couldn't work out what happened?'

Chadwick shrugged his shoulders. 'Who knows? Probably nothing but she wants to try. Apparently, they were close.' Chadwick was conscious that Maclean was looking at him intently, presumably trying to work out just how big a fool he had on his hands. Maclean thought for a moment.

'Why doesn't she hire a detective agency?' he asked. It was a reasonable question, thought Chadwick, particularly as the first question, the one that Maclean had chosen not to ask, would have been: *Why you?*

'She did. She hired a local man.'

'And?'

'It didn't end well.' Maclean raised an eyebrow. 'She gave him some information on the *Highland Laddie* - newspaper clippings, I think - and then he got a bit fresh with her and when she wasn't interested, he slapped her around.'

'Why didn't she go to the police?'

'The private detective is an ex-policeman, a local.'

Maclean took off his glasses and began to clean them with his handkerchief. His blue eyes looked suddenly smaller. 'I see,' he said. 'And did her reluctance to involve the police about the assault mean that she also didn't want them involved in looking for her brother?'

Chadwick could see where Maclean was going and tried to head him off. 'I don't know. I assume so. Anyhow, she asked if I could help.' Chadwick watched as Maclean held his glasses up to the light, moving them this way and then the other, to see if they were clean. Satisfied, he took great care placing them on his nose, hooking the ends over each ear in turn.

'I see,' he said. 'And have you had any success?' Chadwick shook his head slowly to emphasise the point. 'And just how long does this lady intend to carry on this search?'

'I have no idea.'

Both men stopped talking and watched as the waiter served them. After prodding his fish with his fork, Maclean began to eat. He ate in the same careful way that he seemed to approach most things.

'May I ask you a question?' said Chadwick.

Maclean looked up. 'Of course. What would you like to know?'

'Well, anything would be helpful. I know very little about the *Highland Laddie*. I was hoping that you would be able to fill me in.'

'Ah, yes. Of course, you were. I'm sorry. I should have started there. It was, after all, why I was asked to see you. Here, I should give you this.' He reached down to pick up his briefcase. It was an old-fashioned satchel that looked as if he might have owned it since university. He undid the one working buckle, opened the flap and extracted a coloured file. Opening it, he took out some photocopied pages. At the top of the first page were several technical drawings of a ship. Maclean stabbed the pictures with his forefinger. 'This is the *Laddie*,' he said, 'And here are its technical specifications.' He pointed to some tables at the bottom of the page. Chadwick recognised several maritime terms but little else.

'This a bit beyond me,' he said, 'What does it mean?'

Maclean looked surprised. 'Do you know anything about ships? Types? Classifications?'

Chadwick shook his head.

Maclean looked disappointed. 'Well, I suppose I ought to keep it non-technical then. The *Laddie* was a …' He hesitated, trying to think of a non-technical description. 'Medium-sized container ship. But at the smaller end. It was *geared*, meaning that it had its own cranes, but was comparatively small by current standards with a capacity of about 3,000 containers or so.'

'Was it on a regular voyage when it disappeared?'

Maclean nodded. 'Yes, it had been operating in Asia for several years, mostly working between Hong Kong, Shanghai, Singapore, Tokyo and various the regional ports. Its business was pretty typical of any feeder in that region, collecting from the major ports and delivering to the smaller ones.'

'Carrying?'

'Oh, everything. Everything that can be put in a container, that is. And that is pretty much everything apart from dry commodities which would go on a dry-bulk carrier, wet commodities that would go on a tanker and cars that are shipped in specialised roll-on roll-off carriers.'

'What happened to the *Highland Laddie?* Could it have been a fire or an explosion?'

Maclean shook his head. 'It's possible but unlikely. Fires can burn for some time before a crew is forced to abandon ship. If the engine room is on fire, ships have auxiliary power supplies to run the pumps for the firefighting systems. Even an explosion is unlikely to be catastrophic. Most container ships have double hulls so that if the cargo hold was left open to the sea, it's a sealed compartment and unlikely to endanger the ship. The alarms would sound, and the crew would start pumping the water out of the hold. Any explosion would need to blow a very large hole to take down the ship before the Captain was able to send a distress signal.'

'I thought the weather was bad. Wouldn't that have made it more difficult?'

'It's possible but I am sceptical. It was a tropical storm. Unpleasant for anybody not used to that level of sea but not particularly dangerous to a well-maintained vessel and a crew who knew what they were doing. It's true that the combination of an explosion or a fire with bad weather would complicate matters but not to the extent that the ship would disappear without any signal.'

'So, what do you think could have happened?'

'It's very difficult to know and a bit pointless to speculate. If it was an incident, it would need to have been catastrophic and it is very hard to know what that could have been.'

'Something that took out the power system and the radios?'

'No. There are back-up power supplies and emergency radios.'

'Could it have hit something in the water?'

'Like what? It was a long way out at sea. The only candidate would have been another ship and that would require the crews of both ships not to notice each other on radar. Not very likely. And, in any case, if it had been another ship, that also sank, we would surely know about it. No, it didn't collide with another vessel. I think we can be pretty certain about that.'

Maclean looked mildly irritated, like a schoolmaster who felt that his favourite pupil had not been paying attention. He took off his glasses and once again inspected them for cleanliness. Taking out a folded white handkerchief, he began to clean one of the lenses that had failed to pass muster. Without the magnifying effect of his glasses, his eyes shrank and he blinked frequently like a mole emerging into sunlight.

'What do *you* think might have happened to the *Highland Laddie?*'

Maclean looked uncomfortable. 'As I said, I always think that it is unwise to speculate about these things.'

'Why?'

Maclean sighed. He peered around the restaurant as if searching for help and, finding none, returned to cleaning his glasses. 'The *Highland Laddie* disappeared. Literally without trace. That doesn't happen very often. Even in the most catastrophic of events, there is usually some debris, something left behind. But in this case, there was nothing. Nothing at all.'

'Meaning?'

'Meaning nothing. I've looked at many losses on behalf of Lloyd's and the one thing that I've learned is that it is better to keep an open mind for as long as possible. The problem with speculating – which most people can't resist – is that it takes you down a certain path, and when new evidence appears – as it sometimes does – instead of taking it at face value, people are tempted to interpret it in a way that supports their speculation. If that happens, it can be years before the truth emerges, because the original investigators are loath to concede that their original speculation was incorrect. No, it is better not to speculate.'

'What about pirates?'

Maclean gave him a sharp look. 'Did you hear what I said?'

'About speculation? Yes. And I thought it very sensible. I don't want you to speculate. I only want to know what possible causes you might consider *were* you to speculate.'

'And that's not speculation? You should have been a lawyer. You may well be one, for all I know. Piracy would be one option that I would consider but probably not for very long.'

'Why?'

'If I tell you why, wouldn't that be *speculation?*'

'Possibly, but let's overlook it. Why wouldn't piracy make sense?'

'Because pirates are commercial – they want money. The cargo they might be able to use or sell but even if they can't, they can still ask a ransom for the ship and crew.'

'But in the case of the *Highland Laddie,* none of them were ever seen again.'

'Precisely. That's my point.'

'What about sabotage? What if somebody deliberately loaded containers with explosives and ensured that they were placed where they could do the most damage?'

'It's possible, but again, unlikely. There are too many people involved in the loading process for anybody to be sure where the containers would end up. Besides, why would anybody want to blow up a container ship?'

'For the insurance?'

'There are a lot easier ways. You forget that insurance fraud has been around for as long as man has been going to sea. You don't need to blow up the ship. It's too unpredictable. The normal way is to recruit the right crew and scuttle the ship over the deepest part of the ocean that you can find.'

'It's that easy?'

'Pretty much. There are fewer ships with seacocks to open these days but there are other ways of doing it.'

'Like what?'

'You disconnect the pipes leading to the sea chest and the engine room will flood very fast.'

'The sea chest?'

'Most ships of any size have a hole cut into the side of the ship, protected by a grating to avoid debris being sucked into it. The hole is connected via a pipe to the engine room, and allows in sea water to be used for cooling. This is known as a sea chest. Usually, there are valves to shut off the sea chest if required. If you remove the valves, leaving the pipe open to the sea, water will flood through it, particularly if the ship is moving, as the whole point of the sea chest is to force water through the cooling systems while the engines are running.'

Maclean stopped and eyed Chadwick. 'You seem very interested in how to sabotage a ship. Perhaps I should be more careful? My employers wouldn't be very pleased if I spent my time instructing people how to sink ships.'

Chadwick laughed. Maclean was a dry old stick, but he liked him. It was clear that he knew what he was talking about, and he was no fool.

'Don't worry,' he said, 'it's only for research.'

'I am glad to hear it. Now, look, do you want these? Are they useful to you?' Maclean gestured towards the papers that lay on the table.

'I don't know. I'll be glad to take them, but I suspect most of them will be too technical to mean much to me. Were you able to find out what the *Highland Laddie* was carrying?'

'I have the manifest. It runs to quite a few pages, but it may be helpful.' He pushed the papers towards Chadwick. 'I've looked at it, but nothing seems out of place. It's a typical list of shippers – nothing unusual there – and the goods seem to be standard – mostly machinery and machine parts, household effects, electronics, some furniture – the usual stuff you find on a container vessel.'

'Do you have a photograph of the *Highland Laddie?*'

Maclean shook his head. 'No, I asked for one but, for whatever reason, they didn't send one. Why? Do you need one?'

'As you've probably worked out by now, I don't know very much about ships, let alone container ships. A photograph would have given me a bit better idea of how it must have looked.'

'Well, you don't need a photo of the *Highland Laddie* for that.'

'What do you mean?'

'The company that originally ordered the *Highland Laddie* ordered two ships to the same specification. The other was called *Highland Lassie*. Both ships were then sold by the company that ordered them, but they retained their names.'

'So where is the *Highland Lassie?*'

'Right now? I have no idea. But I do know that it is owned by a Nice-based company and that it operates out of Marseille, working between the Baltic and the Mediterranean.'

'Do you have the name of the company?'

Maclean reached down for his briefcase and produce a large, yellow-covered notebook. He leafed through it for a moment or two before he found the correct page. Taking the corner, he tore the page from the notebook and offered it to Chadwick.

Compagnie Loudoun
31 rue Voltaire
Nice 06000

The name and the address meant nothing to him. 'Is it a well-known firm?' he asked.

'Not really. I've heard of it but then I am in the business. I would be surprised if it owns more than two or three ships. But one of them is the *Highland Lassie.* That much I do know.'

'Thank you. You've been very helpful. Have you other business in Nice?'

Maclean thought for a moment. 'Possibly. There is something that I need to check while I am here, but I suspect it is a waste of time. Then, I must head back to Marseille. We have a family trip planned. Do you have a telephone number if for any reason I need to get hold of you?'

'I don't have a mobile. But if you do need to get hold of me, you can leave a message here.' Chadwick took Maclean's pen and wrote the name and number of Leclerc's café in his yellow notebook.

Chadwick shook Maclean's hand. 'It's been a pleasure,' he said, 'I really mean that.'

'It was nothing,' said Maclean, 'I wish you luck although I am not very hopeful that you'll be successful.'

'To be honest, neither am I. In some ways, I wish I had never started.'

Chadwick began walking towards the exit. When he got there, he looked around. Maclean was bent over his notebook, his pen in hand, his tanned brown head tucked into his shoulders like a sleeping bird.

Chadwick began the walk to the train station, reflecting on what he had learned. Something was bothering him, but he couldn't think what it was. It was something that Maclean had said but he couldn't pin it down. It bothered him all evening and it was only when he woke the next day that he realised what it was. It was not something that Maclean had said. It was something that he hadn't said. Or rather something he hadn't asked. Perhaps it had been an oversight, but Chadwick thought it unlikely. Maclean hadn't asked the most obvious question of all. He hadn't asked why Julija Soldane was looking for her brother in Nice. And if he hadn't asked, it was because he already knew something that connected the *Highland Laddie* with Southern France. And that was not a very comforting thought.

CHAPTER TWENTY-FOUR

She was sitting at one end of the bar. There was a man next to her. They were the only two people at the bar. Silje, who saw Chadwick arrive, chose to ignore him. He sat halfway along the bar, close enough to hear the conversation but far enough for them to pay him no attention. He ordered and waited.

The man near Silje was an American who had strayed the wrong side of middle age. His hair was thinning and an unnatural colour of brown. He was running to fat in the American way, the excess weight distributed evenly around the body, so that the overall impression is of a thinner man slightly inflated. It was unclear whether he had sat beside Silje, or she had sat beside him. In any case, it hardly mattered. He was in full pursuit.

'What do you think?' he said.

'About what?'

'About us taking a trip together?'

'To where? Des Moines?'

'No, honey. To Venice. We can go to Venice. There is great shopping in Venice.'

'No, there isn't. Besides, do I really look like I need you to buy me clothes?'

The American thought for a moment. 'Well, how about Milan? There is great shopping in Milan.'

'Does this really work with other women? Are there really women so desperate?'

'Well, how about we take my boat down to Capri? There is great shopping in Capri.'

'Not before Easter, there isn't.'

'Why not?'

'The shops don't open till the hotels open. And the hotels don't open before Easter. How big is your boat?'

'It's big.'

'How big?'

The American hesitated. 'It's fifty metres.'

'No, it's not.'

The American was taken aback. 'What do you mean?'

'I mean you would be the first man in the history of the world who told the truth about the size of his boat to a girl in a bar.'

'It's not really a bar. This is a casino.'

'And your boat is not really fifty metres.'

'Sure it is.'

'Really.' Silje looked unconvinced. 'All right, I bet you €10,000 it isn't.'

The American looked alarmed. '€10,000. That's a lot of money.'

'Not for a man with a fifty-metre boat. We can go measure it now, if you like. Or we can go in the morning. That should give you enough time to find €10,000.'

'What are you saying? That I'm not good for it? Listen to me, I'm good for that and plenty more. *Plenty* more. Now, since we all been so nice and *direct* here, how do I know that you have the €10,000?'

Silje looked at him with disdain.

'Look at how I'm dressed. Almost everything I'm wearing cost more than €10,000 except my underwear. My underwear is not very expensive but since you are never going to see it, I think we can leave it out of the calculation, don't you?' She smiled at him sweetly.

'Now lady, I don't mean to be rude, but I can't see how it makes any difference what you are *wearing*. We are talking here about folding money, and so far, I haven't seen any folding money that I can recognise as such and, believe me, I've seen a lot.'

'How can you say that it doesn't matter what I'm wearing? Look at you. Your shoes are cheap. Your trousers were made in some East Asian sweatshop and tailored by a man who designs circus tents. It's difficult to describe the colour of your polo shirt so I'm not going to try. Your blazer was bought many years ago for the man that you thought you once were. If you paid more than $200 for your entire outfit, then I wish you had a boat. I would enjoy taking it from you.'

The American flushed. 'Jeez, you get pretty personal. Maybe you want to watch that mouth of yours? Remember, I still haven't seen any money. All I've heard is a lot of fancy talk,' he added.

Silje nodded towards Chadwick. 'He has it.'

The American swivelled around on his bar stool and looked Chadwick up and down. 'Hello, friend,' he said.

'He's Russian. He doesn't speak English,' said Silje. The American swivelled back to face her.

'What does he do for you?'

'He's my bodyguard.'

'*Bodyguard*. You have a bodyguard?' The American turned his head to look at Chadwick again. Chadwick gave him what he thought was his best Slavic stare.

'What you need a bodyguard for?' he asked Silje.

'My husband insists on it.'

The American considered this for a moment. 'Your *husband*, what does he *do*?'

'My husband? He is a Russian *businessman*.'

Some of the colour drained from the American's face. 'What kind of business is your husband in?' he asked Silje.

'The wrong sort, mostly.'

The American looked nervously over his shoulder. He reached into his pocket. 'I sure am sorry, but I have to go,' he said.

'Back to your boat?'

'Yes. I mean, no. I mean, I won't be going straight there. I have … I have other things to do first.'

'That's a shame. Maybe we can meet later and see your boat?'

'I … I don't think that will be possible. You see, we're leaving this evening.'

'How disappointing. I was looking forward to taking your €10,000.'

The American raised his arm to signal to the barman for the bill. In two quick strides, Chadwick was by his side. He grabbed the American's wrist and pulled his arm down to the bar. He shook his head, making it clear that the American was not allowed to pay. The American pulled his arm clear and stood up rather shakily. He looked first at Silje, then at Chadwick. He tried to say something, but nothing emerged. He closed his mouth and tried a second time with no greater success. Then half-stumbling, half-running, he made for the exit. Silje and Chadwick watched as he disappeared through the doors and down the main stairs.

'I think he still has some self-respect left. You must be losing your touch,' said Chadwick.

'I'm saving my energy for bigger game.'

'Is there bigger game around?'

'In this town, there is always bigger game around.'

'I should be flattered,' said Chadwick.

'Don't be. You are not the bigger game. Remember, you're only the bodyguard.'

'I thought the bodyguard always got to sleep with the beautiful principal.'

'Only in the movies. And if you haven't worked it out by now, I do my sleeping alone.'

'That's terrible news. There must be a lot of Frenchmen crying themselves to sleep.'

'Not only Frenchmen. I am an internationalist. Just ask our fat friend,' said Silje.

'He's unlikely to forget you in a hurry.'

'Poor man. I rather liked him.'

'*You liked him?*'

'Yes. Why not? He had a go. He was brave.'

'You like heroic failure?'

'No. I don't like failure of any kind. That's why we're so different. You probably came here tonight looking for me. And when you found me, you assumed I must have been waiting for you. You're like our friend, the fat American. You see something and go after it, however hopeless. You think you have more chance with me than he did when in fact, you have less.'

'I might get myself another drink. It looks like it is going to be a tough evening.'

'Then you had better get me one too. I don't want to see you drinking alone.'

'Worried about my drinking already?'

'Not really. I think alcoholism is the least of your worries.'

Chadwick signalled the barman and sat next to her. It was the closest he had ever been to her, and he felt suddenly nervous in a way he hadn't felt for years. It was easier to deal with her when she was at a distance. Up close, he felt inhibited and clumsy, struggling to find something to say that she wouldn't immediately ridicule. He waited for her to speak but she sat silently holding her drink and staring straight ahead, as if she was waiting for him to make a fool of himself.

'How *is* your husband?' he said. 'The Russian *businessman.*'

She turned to look at him to see if he was joking or serious. It would be hard for her to tell, he thought, because he didn't know himself. She turned back towards the bar.

'What's your point? You know he is not my husband. So why are you asking?'

'I'm just curious.'

'Why?'

'You fall in the water and almost drown and when you make it back to the boat, he pays no attention, as if he couldn't have cared less whether you drowned or not.'

'And you think this is interesting?'

'Well, I think it is odd.'

'Then you don't understand Melnikov. You probably never will.'

'What do you mean?'

'If Melnikov had fallen into the water, he wouldn't expect anybody to do or say anything when he got back into the boat. In his world, there is nothing to be done or said. He made a mistake and he fell in the water. That's all. It was his own fault. He wouldn't blame anybody. Why would he treat me any differently to the way he treats himself?'

'It wasn't your fault that you fell in. The bodyguard fell and the rope slipped.'

'So what? Do you think Melnikov would punish him for falling? He might blame himself for miscalculating the number of men needed to hold the boat securely, but he wouldn't blame him for falling. Melnikov takes responsibility for everything he does, whether it succeeds or fails. If he thought he was shifting the blame to somebody else, he would despise himself.'

'How very honourable.'

Silje ignored Chadwick's sarcasm.

'It's not about honour. Do you think Melnikov cares about honour? In Melnikov's world, there is no honour. In Melnikov's world, it's what you can achieve for yourself and the others you work for. It's about getting it and hanging on to it. And for that, he will do whatever is required. For him, it is about success and survival. If he stops taking responsibility for his actions, trying to pretend that it was the fault of others, in his eyes, he is diminished. Not immediately perhaps, but in time. And when the others see that he is weakened, they will come after him.'

'Isn't that a bit extreme?'

'Of course. But you've met him – he is extreme. He doesn't want to be like the others. He doesn't want to fit in. He has no interest in how others judge him because he does not respect their judgment. The only judgment he respects is his own. Right now, the others hate him. You can hardly blame them. He makes no effort to hide the fact that he despises them. But they don't know how to deal with him. And they fear him. In the way that you always fear what you don't understand. But while he continues to deliver, they'll leave him alone.'

'You make it sound like he is some kind of employee.'

'He is.'

'Nice job. Do they give all the employees a boat like *Lara*?'

'Don't be snide. You know very well what I mean. He is independent but only for as long as he does what he is asked to do. As soon as he fails, they'll get rid of him.'

'So how did *you* meet him?'

Silje turned and looked at him. She held his gaze for a moment or two. He wondered what she was thinking. 'It doesn't matter,' she said. 'Forget about me and Melnikov. Don't waste your time. You should work out how you are going to leave that hotel of yours.'

'I can leave any time I want.'

'Really? I wonder. Perhaps you could. If you had somewhere you wanted to go.'

Chadwick watched her carefully but her blue eyes gave nothing away. It was impossible to tell if she was concerned, bored or amused. Maybe it was all three. He thought how he should answer but no words formed. For a second or two, he felt as helpless as the fat American.

'Maybe. Or maybe I just like it here.'

'It's not good for you here. I think we've had this conversation …'

'And you hate to be bored …'

She raised her glass. 'Congratulations. At least you've learned something. Perhaps there is hope.'

'Hope of what?'

'Hope of your being smart enough to leave.'

'Wouldn't you miss me?'

'Every day. But at least there would be someone to miss.'

'That bad?'

'I think so.'

'So why did he invite me to lunch?'

'I don't know. But you can be sure that he had a reason.'

'But why the tour of the *Lara*? Why introduce me to his son?'

Silje shook her head. 'I have no idea. No idea at all. He normally lets me do whatever I want, but in your case, he insisted that I went to the lunch.'

'So, you don't know what it was all about?'

'None. I was as surprised as you. Melnikov never organises lunches or dinners. He has no interest in entertaining. People bore him.'

'But not you?'

'Why would I bore him? I don't bore anybody. I might insult them, but I don't bore them. Do I bore you?'

'No.'

'Maybe I should.'

'Am I about to be told to leave again?'

'Is there really nobody who cares about you?'

'Do I have to answer that?'

'No. You don't have to answer anything. If I don't answer your questions, I don't see why you should answer mine.'

CHAPTER TWENTY-FIVE

The telephone rang behind the bar. The barman, answering it, glanced across to where they were sitting. Silje raised an eyebrow. 'We have been spotted,' she said.

'Wouldn't we have been spotted some time ago?'

'Of course. But now Augustin has a plan.'

'Does it always take time for him to have a plan?'

'Always. He's very cautious. He likes to look at things from every side before he decides anything.'

The barman stood politely while they finished talking. 'Monsieur Augustin sends his compliments to you both and wondered whether Mr Chadwick might be able to join him in his office?'

Chadwick looked at Silje. She shrugged. 'He wants to see you. You should go.'

'And leave you on your own?'

'I won't be on my own for long. I'll try to find one from a different state this time. I need to improve my geography.'

'Will you be here when I get back?'

'Who knows? I certainly don't. Maybe I'll wait to find out what Augustin is up to or maybe I'll be swept off my feet by a tractor salesman from Idaho. Who can tell?'

When Chadwick arrived outside Augustin's office, he was surprised to receive a nod from the granite-faced guard. Augustin was sitting at his desk reading papers. Standing up, he waved Chadwick towards him. 'Come in,' he said. He shook Chadwick's hand and with the other hand on Chadwick's shoulder, guided him towards one of the two chairs on the other side of the *bureau plat*. 'Would you like something? Another glass of champagne, perhaps?'

'Another? I didn't know you were keeping score.'

Augustin smiled. 'We like to look after our clients.'

'Shouldn't that be, "We like to look *at* our clients." Did the cameras manage to get the brand as well?'

Augustin shrugged. 'Possibly but since it will be sent up from the bar, I am sure the barman knows.'

Chadwick settled in his chair and inspected the room. It wasn't any less impressive on a second visit. Augustin watched him without saying anything. His blue suit and cream shirt had been swapped for dark grey and white. Chadwick wondered how Augustin could find a shirt quite so white. Perhaps he only wore them once? Or maybe the shirt only looked so white against the dark-grey suit and Augustin's tan skin. Augustin sensed his interest and turned slightly so that he could inspect himself in one of the long mirrors that ran from floor to ceiling. He reached up and moved the knot of his dark-blue tie slightly to the left. Satisfied, he turned his attention back to Chadwick.

'I haven't seen you since the lunch,' he said. 'How have you been?'

'Never better. My fan club grows daily. I've never been this popular.'

'I've noticed. For a man who wants to be left alone, you attract a lot of attention.'

'Perhaps it's because people down here only want to tell me two things. First, that trying to be alone is impossible and second, that I should leave as quickly as I can.'

'I see. You face rather a dilemma. If everybody is determined to tell you that you should go, they will need to see you to tell you. But if they see you, it will be difficult for you to be alone, no?'

'I didn't say my life was easy.'

'That I can understand. And the lovely Silje, has she told you to go?'

'She is the principal cheerleader.'

'Perhaps you should listen to her. She is remarkably level-headed and doesn't get many things wrong.'

'And you? What do you think?'

Augustin smiled. For some reason, Chadwick's question amused him. 'What do I think? What do you care what I think? Do you care what anybody else thinks? I thought not. You're going to do what you want to do. That much has been plain to me ever since I met you. In any case, if you were going to leave, you've had plenty of opportunities and probably plenty of encouragement. But you haven't. That tells me that you intend to stay. Speaking for myself, I should be disappointed if you left.'

'That's very kind of you.'

Augustin bowed his head graciously. 'Our beautiful little town is a gem on the French Riviera. But it's a dull gem. Since you arrived, life has become much more exciting. Perhaps it's your determination to be left alone?' he said with a smile.

'I'm glad I've become such a tourist attraction. Is that why Melnikov invited me to lunch?'

Augustin's face returned to its normal Buddha-like inscrutability. 'I couldn't say. He doesn't explain why he does anything. I think he regards explanations as a weakness.'

'Apparently, the only thing he fears is weakness. His own weakness.'

Augustin sat back in his chair and looked thoughtfully at the ceiling. 'Interesting. Who told you that?'

'Silje.'

'Did she? Well, she knows him better than the rest of us.'

'What is their relationship?'

Augustin studied Chadwick carefully. 'Do you ask out of curiosity or self-interest?'

'A bit of both, I suppose.'

'Well, I would forget about the self-interest. I simply wouldn't waste your time. Silje isn't available and won't ever be available. As for your curiosity, I can only tell you what I know, which is not much, and what I see, which is not necessarily any more illuminating. They are together but not together. They seem to have reached some form of understanding, almost as if they had been married and divorced. He looks after her and she is available when he wants her to be available. In public, they are unfailingly polite to each other, which is surprising since both can be extraordinarily rude if they choose. He likes her to be well-dressed and since he has the budget and she has the taste, she never disappoints. They don't live together and never have. Perhaps it suits them both better if they don't. It's impossible to tell with those two. Did you meet the son?'

'I did.'

'He's quite a handful. Silje gets on well with him and is one of the few people that Melnikov trusts with him.'

'And Sasha's mother?'

'Who knows? Was there ever a Mrs Melnikov? Melnikov has never mentioned her. There may be an ex-wife somewhere, but whether she lives in Siberia or a penthouse in Monaco, I have no idea.'

'I'm surprised.'

'Why?' A shadow of concern flitted across Augustin's still features.

'Because I thought you were business partners. I thought business partners knew each other a bit better than that.'

Augustin looked at Chadwick for a moment or two before replying. 'Who told you that we were business partners?'

'Nobody. But when he asked you to invite me to lunch, you were pretty quick to respond.'

'Perhaps I was just being polite.'

'I don't think so. I think he asked you and expected you to get it done. To me, that sounds more like a business relationship than politeness.'

'Business relationship, yes. Business partnership, no. I don't think it's wise to be in partnership with Mr Melnikov.'

'Not even in the shipping business?'

Augustin hesitated, surprised by the question. 'No. Not even in the shipping business. What do you know about my shipping business?'

'Not very much. Just that you had one. I don't know much more than that.'

'Why did you assume that Melnikov would be involved in my shipping business as opposed to any of my other businesses?'

'I don't know. It seemed the most logical. I can't see the French authorities being very keen on a Russian owning a casino, and I can't see Melnikov getting very excited about French apartment buildings.'

'And not very good apartment buildings at that. I can see you have done some homework. What else have you found out about me?'

'Not too much. You're a local boy made good.'

Augustin shrugged. 'I am curious. Why were you so interested in finding out about me?'

'I came to see you with a lot of cash. You seemed pretty understanding at the time but you might have changed your mind. I thought I had better find out who I was dealing with.'

'And what did you conclude?'

'That I might get my legs broken but that I was unlikely to end up dead.'

Augustin smiled. 'Well, it's not what I would wish as an epitaph, but I suppose it's true enough.' He paused. 'My shipping business is very modest, you know. Even my mother would find it difficult to describe it as anything else.'

'So why bother with it?'

Augustin shrugged. 'Why bother with anything? I was offered a chance to buy a long-established business where the founder had grown old and the children had no interest in taking over. It wasn't much, three or four small vessels delivering around the coast. I bought a larger ship, which I thought was going to be the first of a fleet, but it never happened. So, now I run what I have. It makes a little money - not much - and it allows my mother to say I am in shipping - which, to her, sounds better than being a casino owner. It's all very harmless. You should visit the office - it's in Nice - but you won't learn much.'

The mention of the office in Nice was enough and he asked as innocently as he could, 'What was the name of the ship you bought?'

It was difficult to tell from Augustin's expression if he suspected anything. He could have been amused or concerned. 'The *Highland Lassie*,' he said. 'If you visit the office, you'll see a wonderful model of her.'

'What does she do?'

'The *Lassie*? She's a container ship. Not very large in container-ship terms but large enough to operate around the globe if needed.'

'And where does she operate?'

'Europe, usually between the Baltic, the North Sea and the Mediterranean. But don't take my word for it. Go see my "shipping division". I don't think you'll be very impressed. Look, I'll make it easy for you.' He took a piece of paper from the desk, wrote on it, and handed it to Chadwick. 'This is the address of the office. It isn't much but you may find it interesting. It opens at 8 a.m. and closes at 5 p.m.'

Chadwick stuffed the piece of paper in his trouser pocket with-out looking at it. He already knew the address. 'Maybe I will,' he said, 'Perhaps it's not too late for me to run away to sea.'

'You would be very disappointed if you ran away on one of our coastal vessels. They are about as exciting as large delivery trucks. But if you yearn for a life at sea, who am I to stand in your way.'

'You are very helpful.'

'Why not? I have nothing to hide. I told you, go there and see for yourself.'

'I might do that.'

Augustin stood. 'Shall we go downstairs? It would be rude of us to leave Silje on her own.'

'I think she can take care of herself.'

Augustin laughed and took Chadwick by the arm. 'Of that, there is no doubt. It's not Silje that I am worried about. It's my customers. Business is not so good early in the season that I can afford to lose too many clients.'

They made their way down the main stairs and into the Grand Salon while Chadwick tried to work out why Augustin had invited him to his office in the first place. What had he wanted? Whatever it was, Chadwick appeared to have given it to him, but Chadwick had no idea what it might have been.

Silje was sitting where he had left her. Nobody had been brave enough to occupy the bar stool next to her. She saw them in the mirror above the bar and watched as they came towards her. When they were next to her, she didn't turn, but addressed them in the mirror. 'So, what did you decide?'

Augustin said, 'Mr Chadwick has developed an interest in shipping. I suggested that he visit my modest office in Nice.'

'I think that's the first time I have ever heard you describe any of your activities as modest.' Silje turned to Chadwick. 'When he is being this self-assuming, you need to be extra careful.' Turning back to Augustin, she asked, 'And when is this excursion?'

'Whenever it is convenient,' said Augustin.

'Then you should do it tomorrow morning,' Silje said to Chadwick, 'and afterwards, I'll pick you up and we'll go for a drive.' Chadwick saw Augustin giving him a strange look, but he ignored him. After Silje had told him where and when she would pick him up, she said, 'Why don't you leave us? I need to talk to Augustin.'

Chadwick kissed her on both cheeks and nodded to Augustin. On his way out, he met his friend, the waitress.

'Leaving so soon,' she said. 'The party's just getting started.'

'That's what I'm afraid of,' he replied, and stepped into the cool air of the night.

CHAPTER TWENTY-SIX

Poor Voltaire. He deserved a better monument than rue Voltaire. It was a narrow canyon of a back street, lined by dustbins and banks of air-conditioning fans. Even the few parked cars looked neglected, their tyres soft, their windscreens smeared with the dusty grime of the inner city. There were no shops because there were no customers. Rue Voltaire's only trade was disappointment and it had long since run out of buyers.

Chadwick missed the entrance to number thirty-one the first time, thinking it could only be a fire exit. There were no signs to indicate that it was anything else. It looked more like a cleft in a concrete cliff than an entrance. There were two steps leading up to a steel door that fitted flush to the wall. Beside it, there was an intercom box. *Compagnie Loudoun* was the fourth name from the bottom. Chadwick pressed the button and waited.

There was no challenge from the intercom. It buzzed, and he pulled the steel door outwards. Stepping into the gloomy interior, he let the steel door close behind him. Directly ahead was a tiny lift. Wrapped around the lift was a narrow concrete staircase. The hallway smelt of dustbins. Chadwick ignored the lift and started climbing.

At first, he had congratulated himself on finding the link between the *Highland Lassie* and Augustin. But Augustin's enthusiasm for the visit had unnerved him more than he cared to admit. Was Augustin deliberately sending him in the wrong direction? Or did he have a more sinister motive? It was impossible to know without visiting the shipping office.

There was only one door on the fourth floor. Affixed to it was a printed card with the name *Compagnie Loudoun* underneath a silhouette of a ship. Chadwick knocked and the door opened immediately. The woman looked him up and down. 'Mr Chadwick?' she asked. He nodded, and she ushered him into the reception area. He must have looked surprised because she said by way of explanation, 'Mr Augustin told us to expect you.'

I'm sure he did, thought Chadwick, *but I didn't tell him when I would call*. Had he been followed from the hotel? He considered it for a moment or two and then dismissed it. He was becoming paranoid. The woman had buzzed him in without checking because her boss had told her to look out for Chadwick. All it proved was that Compagnie Loudoun had few visitors.

The building had been designed as an apartment block. The original sitting room was now the office reception. Opposite the front door was a large metal-framed window with two smaller windows on either side. In front of the window, facing the door, was a desk and a worn red leather swivel chair that had seen better days. On top of the desk was an old computer screen, a keyboard and several empty paper trays.

The woman decided to curtail his inspection. 'I am Madame Dufournier,' she said, and held out her hand. She wore a faded lavender cardigan, a black skirt that was too long and a white shirt that had grown yellow with age. On her feet, she had a pair of carpet slippers. Her eye shadow had been applied unevenly and her lipstick had worn away, leaving only a thin, red line around the outside of her mouth. Her hair, grey and long, was wound into a bun, and secured by what looked like a couple of pencils. If he had been hoping for a master criminal, he was disappointed. Madame Dufournier was more librarian than gangster.

Chadwick turned his attention to the reception. It was unremarkable save for the scale model of the *Highland Lassie*. Chadwick could see why Augustin had mentioned it. It was impressively large. The hull was painted red and the superstructure white. There were two cranes on either side of the deck and a full cargo of containers, painted in different colours.

Madame Dufournier, her hands planted in the pockets of her cardigan, pulled it more tightly around herself, and gave a small cough to indicate that she was impatient to start. 'I manage the business on behalf of Mr Augustin,' she said, emphasising the 'I'. 'He tells me that you would like to know more about what we do so I have arranged to give you a quick tour of our offices and an explanation of our business. It will take about fifteen minutes. Is that satisfactory?' Her manner suggested that deeming it unsatisfactory would be unhelpful. Chadwick nodded.

Dufournier pointed to the largest of several wall maps. 'We have two types of ship,' she said. 'The majority are coastal vessels. They're smaller ships with shallow hulls. This allows them to access ports and cross reefs that are not open to larger, deeper-hulled ships. The coasters operate close to land, moving cargoes from a port like Marseille to smaller ports along the coast.'

'How far do they typically travel?' asked Chadwick.

'Not far. They are not designed to be ocean-going. Normally, they don't go much further than Genoa, not because they couldn't go further, simply because it becomes cheaper to use larger vessels over a certain distance.'

'Are they container ships?' asked Chadwick, keen to hear more about the *Highland Lassie.*

'Oh, no. Container ships tend to be larger. Our coasters are designed for general cargo although they have strengthened hold covers that allow them to carry some containers on deck if they need to. We only have one proper container vessel and that's the *Highland Lassie,*' she said indicating the model. 'The *Highland Lassie* is ocean-going. She can sail anywhere.'

'And does she?'

Madame Dufournier shook her head. 'Not really. She did, at first, when Mr Augustin bought her. She went to America, to Africa, to China and Japan. And once to Australia and New Zealand.'

'But not anymore.'

'No. Not anymore. Now she works mostly in Europe, usually between the Baltic and the Mediterranean.'

'Why the change?'

Madame Dufournier shrugged. 'I don't know. It was Mr Augustin's decision. Perhaps he prefers her here. I don't know.'

'Were you surprised by the change?'

Madame Dufournier looked at him sharply, making him think that he had overstepped some invisible mark. But she relented, saying, 'He was new to the business. I think he liked the idea of his ships travelling the world. But after a while … after a while, he became less interested and realised that it was easier to make money closer to home.'

Chadwick saw his opening. What was it they always said about putting people at ease? *Always ask the question they want you to ask.* 'Have you been with the business for a long time?' he asked.

She hesitated for a moment, as if she was revealing something far more personal. 'All my life,' she said. 'My father too. We worked for the Loudoun family.'

'Here?' said Chadwick, meaning the office.

Dufournier shook her head. 'No. The company had much larger offices then, overlooking the port.' She thought of saying something and then decided against it. Chadwick made a note to ask her about the old offices when he saw the opportunity. 'If you come with me, I'll show you the rest of the office,' she said.

She crossed to the other side of the former sitting room where a corridor led to the other rooms. She showed him each in turn. The first two on the left of the corridor were previously bedrooms that had been pressed into service as offices. Both were occupied by a miscellany of middle-aged office workers who looked as if they had grown old with the company. Nobody paid any attention to Chadwick, either by instruction or indifference. It was hard to tell. The only doorway on the right was open and showed a bathroom converted into two lavatories. The third door on the left was a small room filled with filing cabinets. They were old and ill-assorted. It seemed inconceivable that they were still in use. The only part of the wall that wasn't covered by cabinets was taken up by what Chadwick assumed was the file server for the office's computers. It, too, looked as if it should have been in a museum.

The last room, at the end of the corridor, was larger than the others and had windows on two sides, overlooking a small court-yard. Chadwick walked to the windows. Satisfied, he examined the rest of Madame Dufournier's office. It was dominated by a large mahogany desk, which he assumed had belonged to the founder. The desk was bare of papers. This did not surprise him; Madame Dufournier struck him as an efficient administrator. The walls were decorated with black-and-white photographs.

He made a show of examining the photos on the wall and Madame Dufournier came over to stand beside him. Noticing the same man in several different photos, he pointed towards him and asked, 'Is this the founder?'

'Yes,' she said. 'That's Gilles Loudoun. And these …' she said, pointing to another of the photos, 'were his son and daughter.'

'Did you know all of them?'

Madame Dufournier seemed not to have heard him but just as he was about to repeat the question, she said, 'I worked for the son. By the time I started in the business, the father was already retired. It was a bigger business then, with many more employees.'

'And Mr Augustin bought the business from the son?'

She turned towards him, surprised that he didn't know. 'No. Mr Albert was already dead. He died of a stroke quite young. No, Mr Augustin bought the business from Madame Lily's children.'

'And what happened to the original office?'

Dufournier turned back towards the photos as if she didn't trust her face not to betray her feelings. 'Mr Augustin redeveloped it,' she said. 'As apartments,' she added. Chadwick saw at once what Augustin had done. No doubt he had paid for the acquisition of the family's shipping business by selling its office for apartments. He felt sorry for Dufournier. She had given her life to a family and its business only to see it dismantled and sold. She seemed to sense what he was thinking and decided to bring the office tour to an end.

'Is there anything else I can tell you?'

Her face gave nothing away and Chadwick wondered what Augustin had told her. But it no longer mattered – she had said everything she was prepared to say. As they walked down the corridor, Chadwick pointed towards the bathroom.

He went into the larger of the lavatories and closed the door. There was a WC and a wash-hand basin. Above the basin was a window. It had an opening section, a metal-framed vertical pane that was hinged on one side and opened outwards. It was currently open a few centimetres, held in place by a hinged bar. He examined the swivelling handle that locked the window shut; it was loose. By inserting a thin, L-shaped metal bracket and pushing upwards, the window could be unlocked from the outside. He opened the window and looked out, trying to gauge the distance. It didn't look difficult but then it was mid-morning. Darkness makes even the simplest of obstacles twice as high. He closed the window, flushed the lavatory and ran the water in the basin.

Madame Dufournier was waiting by the front door. He took one last look around to confirm what he already knew before he shook her hand and left. As soon as the door closed behind him, he went in search of the fire exit. It was as he had imagined: a half-glazed door with wire mesh on the exterior. A push on the horizontal metal bar would open the lock and the door. Outside, he could see the courtyard and the fire-escape stairs. He had seen enough. It was time to leave.

CHAPTER TWENTY-SEVEN

'Where did you find this?' he asked.

'The car? In *la France profonde*. In a barn. With some chickens and a cow. Do you like it?'

'Very much. I had no idea they made a convertible.'

'They didn't. Luckily, some others did. This one is by somebody called Henri Chapron, a Parisian coach-maker. He made some other versions, including one for George Pompidou. It was used for the state visit of your queen in 1972.'

'You know a lot about cars.'

'Not all cars. Only this one. I fell in love with it the moment I saw it and waited years to own one. Even now, I can scarcely believe I have it.'

'I hope it is as reliable as it is good-looking.'

'Name me one thing that is. It's even more temperamental than I am. I think that's why we respect each other.'

They were in the hills. Silje seemed to know her way so Chadwick left her to it, happy to have the sun on his face at last. The season was changing. There were leaves on the trees and flowers budding on the grass verges. It had been a while since he had been in the countryside and he realised how much he had missed it.

'Do we have a plan?' he asked.

'I do,' said Silje. 'I can't speak for you.'

'My plans are all short-term.'

'And you think mine aren't? I can get you to lunch. After that, you are on your own.'

Silje slowed the car and turned into a lane. On either side, it was lined with poplars. Beyond the poplars were large, well-tilled fields that stretched into the distance. The lane began to climb but before it reached the crest of the hill, it shifted left and wrapped around it. Now as the landscape opened up, he saw the sea in the distance. They arrived at an ornamental metal gate painted federal blue. It was open. Beyond it, there was an area of gravel centred around a large tree. To the right of the tree, facing south, towards the sea, was a *mas*. As they approached, a dog started barking and seconds later a German Shepherd appeared. When it saw the car, it stopped barking and ran towards it. Silje stopped the car and it jumped up on her door, its head over the window sill. She rubbed its head with both hands. 'Oskar, have you missed me?' she said.

'Oskar? Old lover?' said Chadwick.

She looked at him scornfully. 'No. After Oskar Kokoschka. Do I need to teach you everything?'

'But he was Austrian - not German.'

'So is Oskar. Be careful when you get out. He is not used to strangers.'

'Meaning?'

'Meaning he might bite you.'

Chadwick waited while Silje got out. The dog made a great fuss of her, and even when she had calmed him down, he still rubbed against her, walking first one way and then the other. It was only when he saw Chadwick that his attitude changed. Growling, he backed away from the car on Chadwick's side, his legs bent as if he intended to jump into the car.

'Oskar!' shouted Silje. 'Enough. Sit!' The dog turned to look at Silje. Then he sat. His growl subsided but did not disappear.

'Should I get out?'

'Yes. But do it slowly.' Silje walked over to Oskar and slipped her hand around his collar. Chadwick opened the door gingerly. There was an audible increase in growling, but Oskar stayed where he was. Chadwick put first one leg out and then the other. Oskar's growl was now as loud as at first. Silje slapped his muzzle. Oskar looked at her and then back at Chadwick as he eased himself out of the Citroën and stood up. Silje made a movement with her head and he walked towards her and the dog. As Chadwick approached them, he bent down, stretched out his arm and offered the dog the back of his hand to smell. Oskar duly obliged. He stopped growling and his hackles started to go down. Chadwick waited while the dog grew used to him. Silje let go of his collar and the dog wandered around Chadwick. Satisfied that there was no threat, he lay full-length on the gravel.

'Am I only the second human he has met?'

Silje laughed. 'No. Although he doesn't see many. I have an old couple who live on the property and look after it. He loves them. And the butcher who brings him bones. He isn't very fond of the postman - and that's reciprocated. The postman throws my mail from his van.'

'I don't blame him. Even then, if he isn't careful, he could lose an arm.'

'Don't be mean. Oskar is a sweetheart. He's just very protective.'

'You're not kidding. Is this yours?' They stood for a moment, side by side, looking at the farmhouse.

'Yes. Are you surprised?'

'A bit. I assumed you lived in town.'

'I do but only because Melnikov wants me to be closer to him. Otherwise, I live here.'

Chadwick examined the house. It was a fine example of a *mas* that had been lovingly restored. The walls were newly pointed and the woodwork painted in the same federal blue as the gate. There was a creeper growing around the windows and a border along the front of the house. In a few weeks' time, the house would be a mass of flowers.

He followed Silje through the front door, ducking to avoid the low lintel. The doorway led straight into a reception room. At the far end was a large stone fireplace that seemed too big for the low-ceilinged room. Two antique sofas faced each other in front of it. The floor was covered with worn, red tiles that had faded over the years to a dark pink. The walls were painted a lighter shade of blue than the gate. There were several abstract paintings that Chadwick did not recognise.

She showed him the house. It was decorated with local artefacts. She had a good eye but he noticed there were no personal items, photographs, paintings or objects of any kind linking her with Norway. It was as if her life had only started on her arrival in Southern France. *We are alike*, he thought; *we are both cut off from our homes.*

Once she had shown him the house, she led him outside. An external stone staircase led to a door in the gable wall of an outbuilding. Inside, a large, narrow room ran the length of the barn. The floor comprised the original planks, worn in places, but otherwise unbowed. There was no ceiling, only several solid wooden beams that spanned the width of the room below the underside of the tiled roof. A row of small windows facing the sea flooded the room with light.

Numerous canvases were piled against the back wall, leaning one on top of another. At the far end of the room was a large table marked with paint. Closer to the windows were two easels - one much larger than the other - both held canvases. The only other object in the room was a large space heater.

Chadwick, surprised, looked at Silje for an explanation, but she continued, as if Chadwick should have known that she was an artist.

'What do you think of this?' she asked.

He walked to where she was standing and looked at the canvas that was on the larger of the two easels. It was an abstract painting which he judged was near completion. Predominantly blue and grey, squares and rectangles, it had an Escher-like quality to it. He liked it, but knowing Silje, wondered how best to express it without drawing derision. He missed his opportunity as Silje had already moved to the smaller easel. She turned it towards him. The second painting was similar in design but was painted in greens. He noticed that the squares and rectangles were more detailed than in the larger painting so that the overall effect was quite different.

'Which do you prefer?' she asked.

'I like them both.'

She made a face to express her disapproval. 'That's the answer to a different question,' she said. 'I need you to choose.'

'What will happen to me if I can't choose?'

'You don't want to know. Now, will you choose?'

She was leaning against the wall between two of the windows, her arms crossed. He wondered at himself. Was he really such a fool? Had he learned nothing from recent experience? Was he just going to keep repeating the same mistake? He felt suddenly light-headed, the way he felt in the dream when Samira ran into the apartment building. Dizzy, he grabbed the easel to steady himself and closed his eyes. When he opened them, Silje was staring at him. He straightened, attempting to disguise his near-faint, trying to read the expression on her face. Was it only concern for his health or was it more? *How could she possibly know what had happened in the desert? Nobody knew. Nobody would ever know.* He tried to remember what they had been discussing but his mind was freewheeling. He tightened his grip on the easel until he felt the wooden edge cut into his palm. He forced himself back to the present. He remembered that he had been thinking about her, about how he had learned nothing about the dangers of becoming involved. He had to let her go or he was lost. It was so clear. Nothing could have been clearer. He let his hand drop to his side and smiled at Silje.

'I prefer the smaller piece,' he said.

'Why?' she asked. Her face was blank. Any trace of concern or emotion of any kind had been banished.

'You really want to know?'

'Yes.'

'I think the larger piece is good but derivative. I think the smaller piece was harder for you, required more time and thinking, and was difficult to execute. I think it's a better piece.'

'Would it surprise you if I told you that you are completely wrong? That I did the small piece in a few hours and I've been working on the larger piece for almost a year?'

'It would.'

She smiled. 'But it wouldn't be true. I'm afraid you're right.'

'How annoying for you.'

'It is, but I'm trying to be brave about it.'

Silje pushed herself away from the wall and walked to where the canvasses were stacked. She started to leaf through them until she found a couple that she thought worth pulling out.

'I like both of those,' said Chadwick. 'Do you have a gallery that sells them?'

Silje pushed back a lock of hair that had fallen over her face. 'I do, or rather I did. I sold through a gallery in Nice. But I haven't sent them anything for quite some time.'

'Commission too high?'

She shook her head. 'No. It was when I realised that they were all being bought by the same person that I stopped.'

'Melnikov?'

'Of course.'

'But I didn't see anything that looked like these on his boat.'

Silje laughed. 'And you wouldn't. You still don't understand, do you? He doesn't buy the paintings because he likes them or because he thinks they have artistic merit. He buys them as a way of controlling me. He would never hang these in the boat. Never. He couldn't have my paintings next to his Degas, Renoir or Matisse. He knows they can't compare to his collection. No, he buys them and sends them to a warehouse in Switzerland. I doubt that they will ever re-emerge.'

'He might put them up, just to be supportive.'

'*Supportive?* Melnikov? It would never occur to him and if anybody was brave enough to suggest it, he would laugh at them. Look at Sasha and his drawings. I think they're rather wonderful. I know they all look the same but he tries *so* hard. It's about all the poor kid can do but you will never see any of Sasha's drawings outside his cabin. It's a shame. To be honest, I prefer that he doesn't put my pictures up. I don't want my work on that boat.'

Chadwick had heard enough about Melnikov. He pointed towards the end of the studio.

'What's on the table?'

'A new project. I want to put together a collage of architectural photos and drawings from many different periods. I am not quite sure what I am trying to achieve. I know how I don't want it to be, but I don't know how I want it to be, if that makes any sense?'

'Just about.' He picked up an architectural magazine. 'So, how does it work?'

'I go through the magazines. I find a page I like and I cut out the relevant picture and put it here.'

'You don't seem to have very many.'

'I'm too particular. I have already thrown away hundreds of magazines and I have boxes of pictures in the house. Be very careful with that. It's very sharp.'

'I was going to say. These are dangerous.' Chadwick examined the small knife more carefully. It was very short, with a thin plastic handle and a wicked-looking triangular blade. 'Where do you find them?'

'They are some kind of scalpel. They're not designed for cutting paper, but they do a great job. I buy them from the internet.'

'They make a nasty little weapon.'

'I know. I always carry one.'

'Do you? You are full of surprises. I take it you know just how deadly they are? You cut a major artery with one of these and it's over in minutes.'

Silje shrugged. 'I'm not planning on using one. It's for defensive purposes only. I'm Scandinavian. We don't *do* aggression.'

'Oh really? We should ask the Saxons.'

Silje smiled. 'That was a long time ago. We've become a bit more civilised since then. Come on. We are going for lunch.'

'You're making lunch?'

'I am sparing you that. We are going to one of my favourite places.'

At the end of the lane, Silje turned towards the sea. The road dipped into a small valley which turned first one way, and then the other, before climbing through a wood. There were high banks on either side and the branches of the trees met overhead. Now and again, the sun would emerge, breaking through the canopy and making dappled patches on the road. There was no noise but the sound of the car's engine. Chadwick slipped down in his seat, watching the branches of the trees slip by, some still bare, others green with buds. It reminded him of happier times, and he began to relax, soothed by the smell of the leather, the freshness of the new leaves, and a sense of renewal. He turned his head and watched the definition in Silje's arm as she changed gear. He no longer felt the need to search for something to say. He was happy to be with her. Nothing else mattered for the moment. She, too, seemed content to drive in silence. As they cleared the trees, the road levelled, and the view of the hills was replaced by the sea, blue and endless, cool and unforgiving.

They crossed under a motorway and started to climb again, each side of the road filled with houses and apartment buildings, each one twisting a little this way and a little that way to gain a view of the sea.

Cars were parked on both sides, jammed so closely together that it was hard to imagine any of them could leave. Silje pulled the car into a tiny parking area and turned off the engine. She opened her door and got out without saying anything. Chadwick looked around. There was a large, light-blue-and-white sign by the entrance to the tiny car park. It said 'Franco's'. Underneath the name, there was a painting of an elegant lobster dressed in top hat and tails, waltzing with a fish dressed in a crinoline gown.

'Did you do the sign?' he asked.

'You deserve to be married,' she said.

She walked towards the small restaurant. The front door was propped open and they went inside. It was late afternoon – too late for lunch – and the place was empty. There was a counter at one end of the room. The rest of the room was packed with tables and chairs. A woman in a white apron looked up when they entered. Her face broke into a smile when she saw Silje and she rushed towards her, embracing her as if she was family. Chadwick waited while they exchanged news. Finally, Silje pointed to him and said, 'This is Chadwick. Chadwick, this is Maria. Maria is Franco. Don't ask.' Maria wiped her hand on her apron and shook his hand. She had a strong grip for a slightly built woman. He noticed that after she had shaken his hand, she wiped her hand on her apron.

'We need some lunch,' said Silje. Maria showed them to a table by one of the windows that had a view of the sea and promptly disappeared into the kitchen.

'Is that normal?'

'Completely normal. Don't expect to see a menu. There isn't one. She will decide what we should eat and what we should pay. Just forget about it. Whatever she makes will be delicious.'

'How did you find this place?'

'By complete accident. I was lost and stopped to ask directions. Maria as good as adopted me on the spot.'

'And Franco?'

'I told you not to ask. There is nothing good to say about Franco. Maria threw him out years ago.'

'If there was no Melnikov, would you live at the farm all the time?'

'Of course. If it was up to me, I would never go to town. Maybe, occasionally, to see Augustin but otherwise, I am happier here. But there *is* Melnikov, and while there is Melnikov, I will stay in town.'

'As he wishes.'

Silje sighed. 'He pays my bills, Chadwick. Can *you* pay my bills? I'm a not very successful artist with expensive tastes. I like playing at art and I like living in my beautiful house and wearing wonderful clothes, but it doesn't come free. Nothing comes free.' She paused and looked at him carefully. Perhaps it was a warning to back off. He didn't know her well enough to tell.

'It's a job. A very well-paid job that doesn't require much time or effort. And I am not about to get confused about it. I'm lucky to have it. And if I gave it up, there would be queue of women looking to take my place.'

He started to speak but she ignored him and continued.

'Look at you. You think you are cynical, but you are nowhere near cynical enough. If you had been more cynical, you wouldn't be hiding.'

'You seem to know a lot about me.'

She leaned forward, her folded arms resting on the table, and looked directly at him as if she was issuing a challenge. 'I know all I need to know,' she said. 'I see the world as it is. You would prefer the world to be different. That's *all* I need to know.'

'But most people would prefer the world to be different. Otherwise, why get up in the morning?'

'You get up in the morning to find food and shelter - not to change the world. The world isn't going to change. Not for you and not for anybody else. You have to accept it as it is.'

'But doesn't that depress you?'

'No. Why should it? It *would* depress me if I thought that I could change things, and everything I tried, failed. That would depress me. But I don't try, and I'm not depressed.'

He said, 'You sound like Melnikov. Perhaps you spend *too* much time with him?'

She sat back in her chair, putting some distance between them. 'I spend whatever time he asks for. It's a simple arrangement. And you shouldn't be jealous of Melnikov. I told you. We're together and we are not together. I am with him while he pays my bills. And while that is the case, he doesn't ask me to like him - quite the contrary. Ours is a very straightforward relationship. While I am with him, I can't be with anybody else. And provided I remember that, I can do pretty much what I please.'

She reached across and took him by the arm. 'Get up. You have work to do.'

They walked across to the jukebox. She turned and held out her hand. 'Your money or your life. Coins only.'

'Coins? Is that all my life is worth?'

She smiled. 'Pretty much. You're damaged goods. Now you must choose a song. If you choose the wrong one, I'll tell Maria to throw you out. If you choose the right one, you can have lunch.'

'Isn't that a bit harsh?'

'It's what life is like for those of us who don't hide in a hotel.'

Chadwick examined the songs. 'Is there anything on this jukebox that's not Italian and pre-1965?'

'I hope not. Stop making excuses and choose.'

Chadwick took a coin from his pocket, inserted it, and pressed a button. He turned towards Silje. She looked at the jukebox and then at him. '*Il Mondo*. Good choice,' she said, putting her arm though his, as they returned to their table.

CHAPTER TWENTY-EIGHT

Chadwick grabbed the door just as it was closing, waiting for the woman to leave the hall before stepping inside. He allowed the timed light to go out and stood for several minutes in the dark. *Never be in a hurry going in.* Wasn't that what he had been taught? He could hear a television but couldn't tell whether it was coming from thirty-one rue Voltaire or the building next door. The only other sound was the clunking of the central-heating system.

He took out a penlight and walked towards the fire exit at the back of the building. Shielding the light with his hand, he pushed the horizontal bar. It opened easily and he went out, stopping only to insert a small wooden wedge between the door and the frame. The courtyard wasn't lit but there was sufficient light from the surrounding buildings to make him visible to anybody looking out of their window. He looked up towards the fourth floor. There were no lights in the Compagnie Loudoun offices.

He crossed the courtyard and started checking doors on the far side. Two minutes later, he found what he needed and moved quickly to the street entrance of the building. There was a button on one side of the door. He pressed it. There was a sharp metallic click as the lock released. He opened the door a fraction. So far so good.

Now that he had a second route out, he re-crossed the courtyard to the fire-escape stairway. When he reached the fourth floor, he crouched down next to the wall of the building, and reviewed his next move. He had been right. Things that appear easy by daylight can seem impossible at night, particularly if any mistake results in a four-storey fall onto a concrete yard. He took another look. A small, rusting balcony ran the length of the bathroom window. It had never been intended to be more than a decorative feature or a place for plants. It was just wide enough for a man to stand but far enough away from the fire escape that the only way to reach it was to jump. By moving higher on the fire escape, Chadwick could easily jump the distance. The problem was the landing. Too close to the window, and you risked crashing through it. Too far from it, and you might catch a foot on the short guardrail. As for the balcony collapsing - it was better not to think about it.

Chadwick forced himself to focus. The list of reasons for not breaking into Compagnie Loudoun's offices was long and getting longer. Setting aside the physical perils, had Augustin suggested he visit the offices to show that he had nothing to hide or to encourage Chadwick to return for a second look?

It is always the same at the point of no return. Your thoughts only run one way and the reasons for aborting become overwhelming. Breaking into the shipping office was a pointless exercise that would probably yield nothing except injury or arrest. If he stopped now, nobody would ever know what he had contemplated. This was madness.

It was time to move. He climbed two steps higher, put first one leg and then the other over the metal balustrade that ran around the outside of the escape, and stretched his arms behind him as he gripped the balustrade with both hands. Next, he wriggled his shoulders and body to check that there was nothing that might impede his jump. Satisfied, he concentrated on the narrow balcony that lay a metre below him and just short of two metres ahead of him. The courtyard was too quiet. He needed noise to cover the sound of his landing. He waited until he heard the siren of an ambulance in the distance growing closer and closer. As it passed the building, he launched himself at the balcony.

He landed farther along the balcony than he intended. The balcony creaked on impact but appeared sound. He waited for a few seconds and listened. Nothing moved. He looked across at the fire escape. The return jump would be much easier. Turning his attention to the window, he slipped an angle bracket between the metal window and its frame, released the catch, and pulled the window open.

The interior was completely black. If there was anybody waiting for him, there would be no better time to jump him. He tried not to think about it. He put first one foot and then the other through the window and pulled himself in. He dropped to the floor in a crouch and waited for his eyes to adjust. Moving towards the door, he opened it a fraction and looked through the gap. The rest of the office was even darker than the bathroom.

He took out the penlight. One more check. Pushing the small torch through the gap in the door, he inspected the corridor, wanting to confirm his earlier survey. One infrared sensor covering the reception. None in the corridor or the other rooms. No carpets, so no pressure pads. Provided he avoided the reception, there was no risk of tripping the alarm. He opened the door and started down the corridor towards the room with the filing cabinets.

After forty minutes, he was close to giving up. It was only in last remaining cabinet that he found documents relating to the *Highland Lassie*. The top drawer contained legal agreements concerning the purchase of the ship - the second, third and fourth drawers personnel records. The second-drawer names were Scandinavian or Baltic, while the third and the fourth were mostly Indian or Filipino.

The first file he drew was for a Second Mate called Andrejs Skalbe. There were several official-looking forms, one of which had a photograph of Skalbe attached to the top right-hand corner. He taped a second penlight to the side of a filing cabinet so that it threw a circle of white light on the floor. He placed the Skalbe form in the centre of the circle, took out a small digital camera, and tried a first shot. He checked the result. The focus was fine, but the picture was underexposed. He altered the aperture and tried again. This time, the result was perfect. Replacing the form, he selected the next document, and repeated the process. It was going to be slow work.

He worked methodically, taking great care to place the photographed document back in the file before he took out the next sheet. He wanted to ensure that he left everything as he found it, particularly if he had to leave in a hurry. He was struck by the turnover in officers on the *Highland Lassie* and made a mental note to ask Maclean how long an officer would typically remain with a ship.

He couldn't have told you what he heard. Or why it stood out. Stopping, he listened. Nothing seemed amiss. He waited for a few moments and then reached for another file. He hesitated. He *knew* that something was wrong. Closing the drawer, he carefully removed the penlight and tape from the cabinet. He was now ready. If he was wrong, it would only take him a few moments to resume his work, but if he was correct, every second he saved would be valuable. He waited in the darkness, his eyes slowly adjusting. Nothing. Perhaps he was overwrought? He listened. Still nothing.

He pulled up the hood of his jacket and opened the door of the filing room a crack. At the far end of the corridor, he could see the reception area and the main door to the office, its outline silhouetted by light from the staircase. Somebody had pressed the timer for the staircase lights.

If somebody did come in that way, he risked being trapped in the filing room or Dufournier's office. He started moving as quietly as he could towards the lavatories. The few metres seemed to take forever. He looked at the distant entrance door. Everything was quiet. Maybe the Office had seen what he had been hiding from himself: that his nerves were shot. He took another step and noticed a slight movement across the ring of light that framed the entrance door. He paused. That was a mistake.

There was a metallic thump and the sound of tearing wood as the door flew open. A torch beam cut through the darkness, jumped around for a second or two before settling on Chadwick. The alarm began to beep. Dazzled, Chadwick ran towards the bathroom. The intruder stood still, apparently unsure of what to do next. The triggering of the alarm set off a hidden klaxon that sent a wave of sound through the small office. Neither man hesitated. The intruder ran into the reception just as Chadwick entered the bathroom. By the time the second man reached the locked door of the cubicle, Chadwick was already halfway through the open window. The sound of the door being kicked in was just the encouragement Chadwick required. Several bullets in the back and a fall to the concrete below wasn't an attractive prospect. Pushing himself through the window, he launched himself at the fire escape in one movement.

He misjudged the jump and his body hit the guardrail. It felt like somebody had hit his ribs with a crowbar, his breath forced from his lungs, his upper body dipped in fire. He pulled himself up and over the guardrail and started down the fire escape. With each step, the pain seemed to intensify. He looked up at the lavatory window but there was nobody to be seen.

When he reached the bottom, he was safe. All he had to do was cross the courtyard and exit via the building at the rear. But he didn't. He ran towards number thirty-one. He knew it was a bad idea. The building's inhabitants would now be awake and a police patrol already on its way. He reached the fire-escape door, pulled it open, and headed for the lift. He had to find out who else was breaking into Compagnie Voltaire. It could hardly be Augustin or Melnikov. And if either of those two wanted to catch Chadwick breaking in, they would surely have been waiting for him inside the office. He reached the lift and stopped. There was no sound from the staircase except for the wailing of the siren on the fourth floor and no sign that the front door of the building had been opened. Had the intruder stayed in the office? He paused for a second or two in front of the lift and then turned to look up the stairs.

He managed to pull his head back but was too slow to avoid the kick connecting with his left shoulder. It wasn't the hardest of kicks, but it was more than enough to knock him to the floor. He rolled, jumping to his feet, and dropped into a fighting stance. But he was too late. The door to the building was open and his assailant gone. For a second or two, he considered giving chase but decided against it. There could be few more obvious spectacles in Nice than two men chasing each other through the streets at 2 a.m.

He walked as calmly as he could across the courtyard to the fire-escape door on the far side. Opening it, he pocketed the wedge, and closed it behind him. Making his way to the front of the building, he pressed the exit button. He checked the street. It was larger and busier than rue Voltaire. He started walking, his hands in his pockets, his head down - just another shift worker heading home.

CHAPTER TWENTY-NINE

'We are organising a collection,' said Leclerc.

'What's the occasion?'

'We want to buy you a phone.'

'More messages?'

Leclerc shrugged. 'Only one. You're not so popular as you think. But don't worry about it. It is something that happens to all of us as we grow older. It can't be helped.' He handed Chadwick a folded slip of paper over the bar. Chadwick raised his hand to take it and grimaced in pain.

'You've hurt yourself,' said Leclerc. 'What have you done?'

'It's nothing. I must have slept in the wrong position.'

Leclerc raised his eyebrows and pursed his lips. 'Oh really,' he said, unconvinced. 'Have you been entertaining again?'

Chadwick could see little point in denying it. At least it would move the conversation away from his battered torso. 'You're well informed,' he said.

Leclerc shrugged. 'One tries. You need to be careful with all these exciting new ideas they have about sex. They are best left to the young. You should stick to the traditional ways like the church says. It will be safer for you. Are you joining Verlaine?'

Chadwick looked across to where the older man was sitting with his back to the wall. He beckoned Chadwick to join him.

'I am.'

'Good.' Leclerc took the *Nice-Matin* out from under the bar. 'And now, if you will excuse me, I have to engage with the world for an hour or two.'

'Is the world worth it?' asked Chadwick.

Leclerc shook his head.

Chadwick sat down gingerly, trying to minimise his discomfort. Verlaine watched him. 'What happened?' he asked.

'Everything and nothing. Just like every other day in this town.'

'I assume you didn't hurt yourself in the gym?'

'You assume correctly. Would you mind signalling a waitress? Turning around is not so easy as it was.'

Chadwick ordered breakfast. He was tired. Wanting to avoid taxis, he had walked from Nice and it had been well after 3 a.m. when he had finally made it to bed.

'Well?' said Verlaine.

'Where would you like me to begin?'

'The last time we saw you was two days ago. Julija was worried about you.'

Chadwick was sorry that Verlaine had mentioned Julija. He wasn't sure whether the guilt he felt was about not contacting her or the sense of relief he felt when she was not there to remind him about Arcier and Soldane.

'You were heading back to the hotel,' prompted Verlaine.

'Well, I never got there. I went to Nice to see a man about ships.'

'And?'

'I discovered that I know very little about ships. But, luckily, he knew rather a lot.'

'Who is he?'

'A man called Humphrey Maclean. He works for Lloyd's.'

'Was he able to tell you anything?'

'Not much, unfortunately. The *Highland Laddie* sank. That seems to be about all they or anybody else knows. Although he gave me the impression that Lloyd's hasn't closed the file on it.'

'Meaning …'

'Meaning that they don't seem wholly convinced by the sinking story either.'

'Did you tell him about Soldane?'

'I did. He seemed very sceptical. However, I didn't mention that he might have recently been in Nice.' Verlaine looked surprised. 'I thought better of it. We don't know for sure that it is him. And if I told Lloyd's, I might as well have gone to the police myself.'

Verlaine thought for a moment. 'You're probably right. But at some stage, if we don't make any progress, we may need their help.'

'I will leave that to you. I have no interest in being wrapped up in their investigation.'

'I understand. So, what else did this Maclean tell you?'

'Not very much. I wish it had been more. He gave me some technical specifications for the *Highland Laddie* and its cargo manifest. I am not sure that either will be very helpful. What he did say, though, is that *Highland Laddie* had a sister ship, which was built at the same time. It is called the *Highland Lassie* and it operates between the Mediterranean and the Baltic.'

'Interesting.'

'Not as interesting as the owner. Our good friend, Augustin.'

Verlaine whistled softly. 'The casino owner? That is a coincidence.'

'Isn't it. Just the sort of coincidence you used to stumble across in your former career?'

'Possibly. And then?'

'And then I came back here and had a drink at the casino.'

'Alone?'

'Is this an interrogation?' asked Chadwick, more amused than annoyed.

Verlaine smiled. 'Old habits are harder to shake off than you think. I have had too many years of asking questions to stop now.'

'That's okay. I have no secrets. At least, not from you. I had a drink with Melnikov's girl.'

Verlaine sat up. Now Chadwick had his full attention. His eyes were like blue crystals. 'Was that wise?'

'Probably not, but she was there when I arrived.'

'Another coincidence?' Verlaine looked unconvinced.

'I don't know.'

'She looks tricky, that one. I would be very careful with her. She is too close to both Augustin and Melnikov.'

Chadwick was surprised at Verlaine's knowledge and obvious concern. 'I thought the whole point was to keep your enemies close.'

'Perhaps not quite in the way that *you* intend. But tell me, what did she have to say?'

'Apart from telling me that I should leave town? Nothing. Absolutely nothing. But I didn't speak to her for very long because I was asked to go see Augustin.'

Verlaine thought for a second or two, then said, 'What did *he* want?'

'I am not sure. He gave me some advice about staying away from Silje and being careful with Melnikov.'

'Sounds like good advice.'

Chadwick sat back and folded his arms. 'I asked him about his shipping business and whether Melnikov was his partner in the business.'

'And?'

'He organised for me to visit the offices of his shipping company in Nice. I went yesterday morning.'

'He arranged it?'

'Pretty much. They were expecting me and gave me a tour.'

Verlaine looked perplexed. 'Why would he do that?'

Chadwick shrugged. 'That is the question that I have been asking myself for the last twenty-four hours.'

'Maybe it's his way of trying to show that he has nothing to hide?'

'That's what I thought at first. Or maybe he knew it was a dead end.'

'Was it? A dead end?'

Chadwick thought carefully. Should he tell Verlaine that he had gone back there the previous night? The former policeman might not take kindly to breaking and entering. Could he trust him? He thought so, but he couldn't be certain. He decided to tell a half-truth.

'I am not sure. I went back last night to take another look and caught somebody breaking in.'

'You *have* been busy. Did you get a look at him?'

Chadwick shook his head. 'No. But he didn't get a look at me either. So, that makes us even.'

'Could it have been Soldane?'

'Who knows? It's impossible to say. It could have been anybody. For all I know, it could have been a local burglar, who just happened to pick the wrong night.'

Verlaine shook his head. 'I think that's unlikely. I am not a great believer in coincidences. Particularly when it happens on the very day that Augustin suggests you go visit the office.'

'That thought had occurred to me too. It might have been very convenient for Augustin if I was picked up on a burglary charge.'

Verlaine made a slight motion with his head and Chadwick turned to see Leclerc approaching. Leclerc sat, spreading the *Nice-Matin* across the table. He turned to Chadwick and started talking as if he had always been part of the conversation. 'Do you remember the "private detective" we discussed, the one your friend hired?' Leclerc paused. Chadwick tried to avoid looking at Verlaine.

'Yes, I think so.'

'He just washed up on the beach.'

'Where?'

'Here. Just next to the casino.'

'Drowned?', asked Verlaine.

Leclerc studied Verlaine's face for a moment. 'Not clear. Apparently, his face was so badly damaged that it took some time to identify him. These idiots,' he pointed towards the *Nice-Matin*, 'say it was because the body was battered by the waves against the rocks.'

'But you don't think so?' said Verlaine.

'It would be a first. There are no rocks anywhere near that beach.'

'What have the police said?' asked Verlaine.

'Nothing. They haven't even made a statement for the papers. That tells you everything, doesn't it? You should know. You used to be one.'

Verlaine nodded. He preferred that Leclerc continue.

'There is no way he drowned. No, he was worked over first and then he was dumped. You mark my words. You'll see that it will all come out in the next day or two.' Leclerc paused as he remembered another point that he wanted to make. 'There is something else that these imbeciles didn't spot.'

'What was that?' asked Chadwick.

'It's a big sea out there. If you are halfway competent and you decide to dump a body at the bottom of the sea, you wrap it in chains or attach weights, and it stays there. It doesn't wash up on the town beach.'

'So?' said Chadwick, although he already knew what Leclerc was going to say.

Leclerc bent lower over the table, afraid of being overheard. 'Somebody did it deliberately. Somebody dumped Arcier's body knowing it would wash up on the beach outside the casino. Whoever dumped it wanted it found.' Leclerc sat back to give them time to react to his theory.

Chadwick had already reacted but was trying hard not to show it. He lifted his coffee cup to his lips but thought better of it. Feeling nauseous, he glanced at Verlaine. He looked like a man who had never heard of Arcier, let alone broken into his office.

'Maybe you are jumping to conclusions?' said Verlaine. 'Perhaps, this detective just got drunk and fell in the sea. It happens.'

'It might happen in Nice or Cannes. It doesn't happen around here. Trust me, the police will be all over this. You'll see. They look after each other. It doesn't matter if you've left the police – they'll still look out for you. You must know that?'

'It's true,' said Verlaine. 'Although they generally dislike private detectives.'

'Look,' said Leclerc, 'Arcier was a louse, a drunk and a bully. He had no friends and was about as much use as a private detective as Marie over there. But it won't stop the police making this a priority. Just wait. You'll see that I'm right.'

Leclerc got to his feet. 'And now, gentlemen, you must excuse me. I can't stay talking all day. This café doesn't run itself.' He picked up the newspaper. Chadwick was about to ask him to leave it but thought better of it.

Chadwick waited until Leclerc was well out of earshot and said to Verlaine, 'Not good. Not good at all. Do you see it like Leclerc does?'

Verlaine grimaced. 'I'm afraid I do.'

'If you were investigating this, where would you start?'

Verlaine thought for a moment or two.

'Background checks. How was his business going? Did he have debts? How much did he drink? Was there a girlfriend? Who did he still speak to amongst his old police colleagues? Then, I would try to work out where he was last seen and put together his final movements. *And*, I would go to his office to see if I could find out what cases he had been working on.'

'Exactly. Do you think they've already been there?'

'Probably. If they couldn't find any next of kin, the office or his apartment would be obvious places to start. But I wouldn't worry too much. Our only risk is that somebody saw us entering or leaving the building *and* remembers us sufficiently well to be able to give the police worthwhile descriptions. Frankly, it's unlikely. The police will have to ask about visitors over a period of several days, maybe even a week. Most people can't describe somebody they saw two hours ago. No, I think we're safe as far as his office is concerned. Unfortunately, I am not so sure that I can say the same about Julija.'

'You think they'll find out he was working for her?'

'I think it's likely, don't you?'

'Well, she didn't exactly hide it. I saw them together at the bar in the casino. And you're right. If they go see her, they are bound to ask if anything happened between them, and if she says he beat her up …'

'They won't look too much further probably.' Verlaine ran his hand through his greying hair. 'I'd better go see her.'

'I think so. Some coaching on what not to say during aggressive French police questioning might also be a good idea.'

'Agreed. Do you want to come?'

'No. I think it's better coming from you. Given everything that's happened, I have someone else I need to see.' Verlaine looked as if he was about to ask who it was but thought better of it. If Chadwick had wanted him to know, he would have told him.

CHAPTER THIRTY

Chadwick was growing frustrated. It hadn't occurred to him that it might be difficult to identify the Chairman's villa from the road. He had overlooked the wealthy owners' obsession with privacy and forgotten the tall walls and fences that masked the houses from the street. The Boulevard du Générale de Gaulle was deserted. It always was. Either nobody lived in the villas out of season, or they never ventured out. Conceding defeat, he decided to try the gate on the coast path.

The coastal path was as deserted as the boulevard. There were no anglers, runners or dog walkers. He found the gate easily; it was locked. He looked both ways. There was nobody to be seen. He raised his arms - his ribs ached. Trying to ignore the pain, he jumped, gripped the metal frame at the top of the gate and pulled himself up and over, dropping quietly to the ground on the other side. Standing up, he walked briskly up the steps towards the villa. There were no signs of life but that meant little. The large plate-glass windows reflected the light. There could have been a cocktail party for two hundred inside and he wouldn't have known. He stopped by the bottom of the staircase that led up into the centre of the terrace and looked down towards the sea. The coast path was still empty. He had never seen it so quiet. He walked slowly up the stairs, emerging into the middle of the large terrace. He could hear a lawnmower in the distance. Otherwise, it was perfectly still. Walking towards the large windows, he placed the edge of his hand against the glass to reduce the light and looked inside.

There was nothing there. The large room was completely empty. No chairs, tables, sofas, paintings. Nothing. Shocked, he walked across to the other side of the large window to where he had eaten breakfast with the Chairman. It was just as empty. There was nothing on the floor, not even a discarded box or an old newspaper. He tried to make sense of it. Had he been duped all along? But surely nobody would have staged the original bag theft, the casino success and the car-park robbery simply for Chadwick's benefit? There were simply too many people involved. Could the Chairman be working with Augustin or Melnikov? It seemed unlikely. And what about the daughters? No, there had to be a good reason for the Chairman vacating the house without telling him. He remembered the message that Leclerc had handed him. He hadn't even bothered to look at it. He searched his pocket until he found it. Unfortunately, it wasn't a message from the Chairman or from McGhee:

'Call me on this number. It's important. Humphrey.'

Disappointed, Chadwick stuffed the message back into his pocket, walked around the side of the house, and straight into two men coming the other way.

He had no choice but to brazen it out. Neither of the two men spoke. The taller of the two wore jeans and a leather jacket over a white shirt opened at the neck. He had an ornate belt buckle on an imitation crocodile leather belt and receding black hair, brushed straight back from a sallow face. The second was running to fat and wore a black suit that had seen better days over a faded patterned shirt. Sallow Face gave a thin smile.

'You know this is private property,' he said.

'Is it?' said Chadwick. 'I didn't see any signs.'

Sallow Face turned to his companion and repeated, 'He didn't see any signs.'

Chubby thought about this, playing the straight man as best he could. 'Signs? Why do there have to be signs? Pretty clear it's private.'

'See,' said Sallow Face, '*he* knew it was private. *Without any signs.*'

'Then he must be much smarter than me.' Chadwick took a step backwards. Partly to see around the back of the villa to check that there was nobody sneaking up on him and partly to give himself some room. Neither of the two men looked like fighters but then they hadn't looked surprised to find him there either. And that wasn't a comforting thought.

'No. I don't think so. I think you're a pretty smart guy. Smart enough to know when you're trespassing. And you *are* trespassing. I think we can agree on that.'

'Isn't that up to the owner to decide or can anybody in France determine it?'

Sallow Face looked delighted. He turned to Chubby and said, 'Did you hear that? Not just smart but a smartarse too.' He turned back towards Chadwick and said, 'So let's go ring the bell and ask the owner?'

Chadwick said nothing and Sallow Face continued, 'So how about it?'

'He's not here.'

'He's not here,' Sallow Face repeated to Chubby. 'That's a bit of a problem, isn't it?'

'Is it? Why?'

Sallow Face started to turn to Chubby but was growing tired of the game. He said to Chadwick, 'Who is the owner?'

Chadwick, surprised, said, 'An Englishman called David Spencer.'

'And you know him?'

'Yes.'

'So, if you know him so well, how come you didn't know that he had moved out?'

'What business is it of yours?' said Chadwick, deciding that if this was going to turn rough, it would be better to get started than concede any more information.

Sallow Face started to reach inside his leather jacket. Chadwick stepped forward, lifting his right arm. Sallow Face stopped moving. Keeping the hand that was in his jacket still, he said, 'You're a nervous man for a tourist, Mr Chadwick.'

Chadwick stayed where he was, his weight evenly balanced. He didn't react to them knowing who he was. He had suspected as much. 'It's the locals,' he said, 'they keep telling me that this is a dangerous town.'

'They're right,' said Sallow Face. 'May I?'

'Go ahead.'

Sallow Face pulled out a document in a dirty plastic cover. It had his photograph on it. Chadwick knew what it was but waited until Sallow Face handed it to him. He pretended to examine it before handing it back.

'So, Inspector Prieul, what else can I do for you?'

'What else? So far, Mr Chadwick, you haven't done anything for me except be cheeky and look like you were going to hit me.'

'I meet two strange men on my friend's property. How else would you expect me to react? I don't remember you and your colleague identifying yourselves as policemen or did I miss that part of the vaudeville act?'

Prieul's smirk disappeared. 'You're coming with us,' he said.

'Am I?' said Chadwick. 'Why?'

'Because we found you trespassing on a private property and we want to ask you some questions.'

'Start asking.'

Prieul shook his head slowly, as if saddened by this turn of events. 'I wish we could, Mr Chadwick, but we have to be somewhere else.'

'Then come and see me later. I am sure you know where I live.'

Prieul sounded almost apologetic. 'No, that won't work. That won't work at all. You see, we need to ask you the questions now. I'm afraid you'll need to come with us. Shall we go?'

'Are you arresting me?'

Prieul pretended to look shocked. 'Certainly not. Why would we arrest you? Have you done something wrong?' He paused, watching for Chadwick's reaction. 'No, let's just say that we would like your help. As a concerned citizen, I am sure that you are keen to help.'

Chadwick thought it over. He had no option but to accompany them. It was probably better to engage and give them something than spend the next few days trying to avoid them.

'Okay,' he said, 'let's go.' The trio turned and walked towards the front of the villa. There were four policemen standing in the villa's garden between the house and the boundary wall. As they walked past them, the gates began to open. Beyond the gates were two police cars and an unmarked car. Chadwick said nothing. Now he understood why the coast path had been so quiet and why there had been no traffic of any kind on the Boulevard du Générale de Gaulle. Prieul had sealed the immediate area. He must have been hoping that Chadwick, when confronted, would make a run for it. And he was very nearly correct. *If I had run*, thought Chadwick, *I would now be in handcuffs. I won that round, but this fight isn't going to be over quickly. Prieul is smart. I am going to have to tread very warily with him.*

They arrived at the unmarked car. Prieul gestured to Chadwick to get in the back with him. Chubby sat in the front passenger seat. The driver ignored all of them. He waited until the first squad car pulled away and then fell in behind it. Chadwick glanced out of the rear windscreen. The second squad car was following them.

Prieul wound down the window. He took out a packet of cigarettes and without offering them, lit one. Chadwick noticed that he had nicotine stains on his fingers. He sat back and pretended to watch the houses passing by, wondering how Prieul would begin. He didn't have long to wait.

'When did you arrive here, Mr Chadwick?'

'About ten days ago.'

'And where did you come from?'

Chadwick thought for a moment and decided to tell them the truth. 'Milan,' he said.

'Why did you come here?'

'For a holiday.'

'So early in the year?'

'I don't like crowds.'

'How are you able to stay in a hotel that is closed?'

'The owner is a friend of my family.'

'Really? It's an unusual arrangement.'

'What of it? If he doesn't mind, why should you?'

'There are other hotels nearby that remain open all year. Why pick the one that is closed?'

'I wanted to be alone. Is there something against that in the French criminal code?'

'Not as far as I'm aware. Why are you so keen on being alone? Does it make your life easier?'

'Easier?'

He saw where Prieul's questioning was heading and decided to change tack. He waited for Prieul to explain.

'You can come and go as you please without bothering anybody or without anybody knowing what you are doing.'

'No more than if I rented a villa. Now, do you have some real questions or are we going to continue like this for the next hour?'

'It won't take an hour. We should be there in twenty minutes.'

'Where are we going?'

'You'll see.'

Chadwick looked out his window and realised that the car was heading away from town into the countryside. He said nothing. He was sure it was only another trick of Prieul's to unnerve him. It was hard to know how to handle Prieul. He couldn't tell whether the inspector knew more than he was letting on or was just fishing for information. Had the police managed to connect Arcier with Julija? If so, how? Had he been recognised by somebody who had seen him visit Arcier's office with Verlaine? Perhaps one of the casino bar staff remembered that he had been introduced to Arcier by Julija? It seemed unlikely. There just weren't enough people who knew him in this town.

If he was questioned about whether he knew Arcier, he would ask to see a photo. Then, and only then, would he concede the possibility that it might be the man who had been with somebody he knew at the bar of the casino. He didn't want to involve Julija more than was necessary but if he denied the meeting against the statements of the bar staff, Prieul would surely ask Augustin for the CCTV tapes from the casino. Once he saw those, he could hardly miss the fact that Arcier and Julija had been together at the bar for some time. Better to admit that he had met him briefly than to send Prieul towards the tapes.

'How do you spend your days, Mr Chadwick?' asked Prieul. 'Doesn't it get rather dull in an empty hotel?'

'Not really. I read. I run. I use the gym. I look at the view. Mostly I look at the view.'

'How do you manage for food?'

'I go out. I am not a cook.'

'Where do you go?'

'Various cafés and restaurants.'

'But not one in particular?'

'I probably go to Leclerc's more than the others.'

'The Sebastopol? I'm surprised. Leclerc is famous for being unfriendly to tourists.'

'I didn't think it was only tourists.'

Prieul laughed. 'No, you're right. He doesn't like most people. I am not sure why a misanthrope like him should have chosen the restaurant business.'

'Maybe he couldn't get into the police.'

Prieul turned and looked at him. 'You know, Chadwick, you're lucky that I have a good sense of humour. Some of my colleagues might not appreciate your jokes.' He looked as if he was about to say something else, but his mobile phone rang. While he was answering it, Chadwick thought about their latest exchange. *Misanthrope*: he wondered whether it was a slip or Prieul's way of telling him that he was better educated than he looked. Prieul closed the phone and put it away.

'Your friend,' said Prieul, 'the one that owns the villa. What's his name again?'

'David Spencer.'

'And you've known him a long time?'

'Not very long.'

Keep it as close to the truth as you can, thought Chadwick. *Tell him as little as you can. Keep your options open. Make him work. Slow him down.*

'How did you meet?'

'Through his children.'

'His children? Where? In London?'

'No. Here.'

'Where?'

'In town.'

'Are they still here?'

'No, they went home.'

'And their father owns the villa where we found you?'

'Yes, I believe so.'

'You *believe* so. You should have been a lawyer, Mr Chadwick. Would it surprise you to learn that the villa is owned by a Swede called Erik Jens Fredrickson? He is the registered owner of the property. There is no record of any David Spencer ever having owned it. Indeed, there is no record of David Spencer having owned any property in this part of France.'

'So what?'

'I find you trespassing. I find that you tell me that the villa is owned by your friend, this *David Spencer,* but when I try to verify it, it turns out that nothing you have told me is true.'

'I'm sure there is a very good explanation. Why don't you find this Frederickson and ask him?'

'I don't think that is very fair, do you? Poor Mr Frederickson has done nothing wrong. After all, he is the registered owner of the property. Don't you think it would be better for us to speak to your friend, Mr Spencer? Then we can clear this matter up very quickly. Don't you think so?'

You're clever, thought Chadwick. *Unless I can produce the Chairman, I look like a liar. And while the trespassing is not very serious, it gives you the excuse to turn my life upside down. And if you go down that road, you will find plenty to keep you occupied.* He had no qualms about pointing Prieul towards the Chairman. He was certain that the Chairman was more than a match for the French policeman. But he still had the problem of how to contact him. At least he knew that the Chairman existed. Humphrey Maclean knew him or knew of him. Humphrey would be able to tell him how to contact the Chairman.

'Well?' said Prieul.

'I'll put you in touch with him if that's what you want.'

'That is what I want. If you give me his number, I'll call him now.'

'I don't have his number here. I'll need to get it for you.'

'Ah,' said Prieul, as if this only confirmed his suspicions about the existence of David Spencer. 'You don't have it on your phone?'

'I don't have a mobile phone.'

'That's unusual.'

Chadwick ignored him and looked out of the window.

261

CHAPTER THIRTY-ONE

They were now some ways inland. The manicured coastline had been replaced by a dusty hinterland. The terrain was hilly and the land stony with few attempts to farm it. They could have been in North Africa. Everything was neglected, broken or discarded. The few buildings were mostly built with breeze block and roofed in tin. From time to time, they passed an industrial park, or a low-built factory surrounded by wire. The occasional lorry lumbered past them on the other side of the road. The bleakness of the surroundings seemed to affect the mood of the men in the car. Nobody talked.

The car left the main road and began to climb. They drove past a poorly-painted wall, topped with rusting metal railings. It ran for a couple of hundred metres. Beyond a set of gates, Chadwick could see a two-storey building, surrounded by a large car park. Outside the gates was a bus stop. A large sign on top of the building proclaimed 'Villin - For All Your Precision Engineering Needs!' in a font that had long since fallen out of favour.

Five minutes after the factory, they turned onto a narrow road that started to wind backwards and forwards across the front of a hill. Just below the summit, they turned into a small lane. A police car was parked at the junction. One of two policemen waved them through. The lane led them around the side of the hill into a scruffy wood. The lane was narrow and heavily rutted, more suitable for a tractor than a car. The wood was mostly scrub. The few trees that had taken root were poor specimens, unable to find much water in the stony ground. In the middle of the wood was a small clearing where two cars were parked. One was a police car; the other, a very ordinary-looking family saloon. They stopped and Prieul said, 'We'll walk from here.' Chadwick got out and looked around. He could think of no reason for Prieul to bring him here. If he only wanted to rough him up, there were a thousand places better suited, closer to town, without as many police witnesses.

'Come over here,' said Prieul, who walked towards the family saloon. 'Do you recognise the car?' he asked. Chadwick looked at it carefully. He shook his head. Prieul said, 'Are you sure? It's important.' Chadwick went closer and was about to open one of the doors when Prieul said, 'Please don't open it. We haven't fingerprinted it yet.' Chadwick let his hand drop but looked carefully at the interior. There was very little to be seen. The car's owner was either exceptionally tidy or somebody had cleaned the car thoroughly. He sensed Prieul standing beside him. 'A bit too clean, wouldn't you say?' said Prieul. Chadwick didn't say anything.

Prieul said, 'We can't go any further in the car. Why don't you lead?'

'Where are we going?' said Chadwick.

'You'll see. Just follow the path.'

Chadwick looked ahead. The track petered out beyond the clearing and became a path of sorts. Parts were grown over or covered by fallen branches. He started to pick his way through the wood. After a couple of minutes, the path split into two. One fork led upwards to the right, the other followed the contour of the hill down, to the left. He stopped and turned to Prieul, who was just behind him. 'Which way?' he asked.

'You choose,' said Prieul.

'How can I choose? I've never been here before.'

'Choose,' insisted Prieul.

Chadwick thought for a moment. Now there was only Prieul and Chubby. The other policemen had stayed in the clearing.

Perhaps he had been too quick to rule out Prieul trying something? He chose to go left, taking the fork that led down. Prieul made no comment and followed him. It wasn't long before they emerged from the wood and the topography became clearer. Chadwick looked upwards and to his right, to see where the other path would have taken them. He received a shock. The hill had been cut neatly in two and one half removed. There was no reverse side. There was only a near vertical cliff where the hill had been quarried away. His surprise must have shown. Prieul said, 'You made the correct choice for somebody that hasn't been here before.' Chadwick looked below him. The path they were on zig-zagged down what was left of the shoulder of the hill. The rest of the hill had long since disappeared.

As they made their way towards the bottom of the quarry, Chadwick saw a blue tent just below the quarry face. The tent was closed. There were two policemen positioned at the entrance to the quarry but none around the tent.

Chadwick steeled himself. He knew now what was coming. When they reached the level of the quarry, he let Prieul lead. Prieul walked towards the tent in silence. When they reached it, he turned to Chadwick. 'Do you know what's inside?'

'I have a pretty good idea.'

'Do you know who it is?'

'I have no idea but since you brought me here, I can only assume that it is somebody that you think I know.'

Prieul didn't reply. He went to the side of the tent and lifted a flap. 'It's not pretty,' he said, and went inside. Chadwick followed him. It was warmer in the tent than outside, but the air was thick with the smell of death. Chadwick tried to put it out of his mind and concentrated instead on the light-blue plastic sheets that took up most of the floor area, leaving very little room for the two men to stand. They stood side by side, their feet almost touching, with so little room that Prieul had to warn Chadwick before he leaned down to pull back the plastic sheeting, in case he should knock him over, and they should both fall on the corpse. Prieul looked pale. *You never get used to this*, thought Chadwick, *even as a policeman.*

Prieul hadn't exaggerated. The fall from the top of the quarry made any kind of identification difficult and it took Chadwick a few seconds to realise who it was. But he was less shocked by the disfigurement of the corpse than by the relief he felt when he realised that the victim wasn't who he thought it might have been. Ashamed of himself, he took longer inspecting the corpse than Prieul expected, and it was only when the inspector asked him if he had seen enough, that he nodded and stepped back, watching Prieul bend down and carefully replace the sheets as if straightening the blankets of a sleeping child.

Prieul went outside. By the time Chadwick joined him, he had already lit a cigarette and was inhaling its smoke as if his life depended on it. Chubby stood by expectantly but Prieul was in no hurry. He motioned to Chadwick to join him as he walked away from the tent towards the entrance to the quarry. They walked in silence for a minute or two until they reached the start of the quarry. In front of them was a road, which must once have been the main route in and out of the quarry, but which was now in complete disrepair with weeds growing through the joins of the concrete.

'Well?' said Prieul.

'It's a man called Humphrey Maclean. But then you knew that. Can I ask why you came to collect me to tell you something you already knew?'

Prieul kicked the gravel with the toe of his boot. 'I don't see why not,' he said. 'He had your name and the name of the Sebastopol and its telephone number written on a piece of paper in his pocket.'

'But he must have had many other names and numbers on him or on his phone. Why pick me?'

'Why indeed? That's a very good question, Mr Chadwick. Maybe it's the only question right now. So why don't you start by telling me everything about you and Humphrey Maclean.'

Chadwick knew then that he was in serious trouble. Prieul had played his cards well. He had given nothing away about what he knew about Maclean – Maclean and Chadwick – and the circumstances of Maclean's death. Now Prieul would keep asking questions and give nothing back in return. If it had been hard before, now it was near impossible to avoid telling Prieul about Maclean. The problem was that Maclean potentially led to the Chairman, the two Soldanes, Augustin, Melnikov and Arcier. He thought how best to tackle it.

'Was there a note?' he asked.

Prieul blanked him.

'A suicide note?'

'Should there have been?' asked Prieul.

Chadwick hesitated. It was worse than he thought. 'It wasn't suicide?'

Prieul threw away one cigarette and lit another. 'You tell me, Chadwick. You knew him. I've only just met him and as you can see, he's not saying much. So why don't you tell me how you know him, and we'll go from there.'

'We'll go from there.' Of course, we will, thought Chadwick. *We'll go from there all the way to a French court and a life sentence.*

'I didn't know him, as you put it. I only met him once. Two days ago, in Nice. We had lunch. At his hotel.'

'What hotel?'

'The Negresco.'

'How did you meet him?'

'He left me a note to call him. At the Sebastopol. They'll confirm it.'

'Why did he leave you a note?'

'He had been asked to contact me about some research I was doing.'

'What was the research about?'

266

'Shipping.'

'Shipping?' Prieul paused, considering this. Then he asked, 'What did Maclean do?'

'I'm sure you know what he did.'

Chadwick caught Prieul giving Chubby a look. Chubby said, 'What's the name of his firm, sir?' It took Chadwick a moment or two before he realised. He turned towards Prieul.

'You've no idea who he was, do you?' Prieul looked embarrassed but said nothing. Chadwick continued, 'How can you *not* know who he was?'

Chubby looked at his feet. Prieul said, 'We know enough. We would just like you to fill in some of the details.'

All three knew it was a lie, but Chadwick chose to ignore it.

'I'm sure you would. Okay, I will tell you what I know about Humphrey Maclean but, in return, I want you to tell me what you know and what you don't know.'

Prieul, irritated, stepped closer to Chadwick so that they were only a metre apart, and said, 'This is a police investigation, Chadwick. We don't share information unless it's necessary. And right now, *I* don't think that it's necessary. So why don't you tell us what *you* know about Humphrey Maclean and what research he was help-ing *you* with and then we'll decide if there is something *we* want to share with you.'

'Where is his briefcase?' asked Chadwick. 'Do you have it here? Or is it in the car?'

'We have it,' said Prieul. 'But it's not important right now. Right now, I'm only interested in what you know.'

'Describe it,' said Chadwick, looking at Chubby. Chubby looked uncomfortable. 'What does it look like?' Chadwick repeated. Chubby started to speak but Prieul shook his head. Chadwick turned towards Prieul. 'You haven't a clue, have you? Do you have his phone? Is that his car that is parked up there?'

Prieul smoked the cigarette down to its very end, dropped the butt and ground it into the dirt with his heel. He gazed at the middle distance for inspiration and finding none, conceded defeat. 'You're right,' he said. 'We think that's his car. But there was nothing in it. Nor was there anything on the body. No papers, no wallet, no briefcase, no phone. The only thing that we could find on the body was the piece of paper with your name on it.'

'But why would somebody strip the body of information? Surely, they must have known that you would run the car registration number and know who it was in hours?'

'Hours but not minutes. Maybe these people only needed to ensure that they had sufficient time to get away. Or maybe they wanted to make a point. After all, they went through everything very thoroughly. The only thing that they missed was the piece of paper with your name on it which leaves me wondering …'

'Whether they "missed" it at all?'

'Exactly. How does that make you feel, Mr Chadwick?'

Chadwick didn't reply. He was too busy wondering what sort of people kidnapped a middle-aged man with a family, killed him, and threw the body over a cliff. He felt suddenly cold as another thought occurred to him. He turned and looked up at the cliff. Without turning back towards the other two men, he asked, 'Have you examined the path to the top?'

'Yes,' said Prieul, knowing what Chadwick was about to ask.

Chadwick felt himself begin to shake. He put his hands in his pockets to make it less obvious to the others. He spoke as loudly as he dared trying to hide the tremor in his speech. He began to feel faint but knew that he couldn't sit. He concentrated on a point at the top of the cliff to stop himself swaying and tried to block all thoughts of his dream. It couldn't happen again. It was a coincidence. Just a coincidence. He tried to pull himself together and ignore the sweat that was gathering on his face, concentrating instead on his questions to Prieul. He turned back towards the other two and saw at once the change in their expressions as they saw his face. He persevered.

'Well, did he walk up or was he carried?'

'There are prints of his shoes on the path,' said Prieul, avoiding the question.

'And when they got him to the top, what did they do then?'

Prieul shook his head. 'We don't know.'

'Of course, you know. We all know. We just don't want to admit it. We don't want to believe that Maclean was still alive when they threw him off that cliff. But that's the way you see it, isn't it? *Isn't it?*'

Chadwick wondered at his ability to control his anger. What was the point? Was it self-preservation or just further weakness? What did he care about Prieul and his chubby sidekick? He cared only about the men who had thrown Maclean from the cliff. He cared only about making them pay for Maclean. For Maclean and for the dream that would haunt him forever.

Prieul looked embarrassed. 'It's a possibility, yes. But we don't know for sure.'

'And just as possible that you'll never find out? So, what will you tell Mrs Maclean and the Maclean children when they get around to asking?'

Prieul ignored him. It was clear that he had seen something in Chadwick's expression that had only confirmed his suspicion that Chadwick was capable of violence, and he was in no mood to let his prime suspect bully him.

'Right now, I'm more interested in what *you* talked to Maclean about.'

'Why? Why should what I talked to Maclean about be any more relevant than any of the other work he did?'

Prieul and his sidekick exchanged looks before Prieul continued. 'We don't know what work he did. At least, not yet. So why don't you tell us? And the reason we think *you* are more relevant than most is because whoever led him to the top of the quarry and threw him off didn't leave a note with somebody else's name on it. They left one with your name on it. Is that clear enough for you?' Prieul was angry and didn't mind showing it.

Chadwick decided to relent. 'Okay,' he said. 'He worked for a firm in Marseille that is an insurance agent for Lloyd's, the London insurance market. They do marine work - salvage, loss adjusting, valuations of vessels. That sort of thing. Nothing remotely exciting.'

'How were you put in touch with him?'

'By a friend.'

Prieul shook his head in exasperation. His phone rang. When he saw who was calling, he walked some distance away so that he couldn't be overheard. Chadwick watched as he argued. Prieul was losing the argument. He ended the call and put the phone back in his jacket. He walked back, avoiding eye contact with Chadwick. His mouth had a determined set to it. 'You can go,' he said to Chadwick. 'We'll contact you at the hotel if we need you.' Chubby started to protest but Prieul cut him off. 'Walk him back up to the top. Make sure he doesn't touch anything and have a car run him back into town.' Prieul still couldn't bring himself to look at Chadwick. He walked off in the opposite direction without saying anything else.

Chadwick wondered who had ordered him to leave Chadwick alone. Whoever it was had made an enemy of Prieul. Chadwick felt some sympathy for the French policeman. His instincts in this case were good. If he had carried on questioning Chadwick as he intended, it would have been impossible to stop him learning more than would have been healthy for Chadwick. No wonder he was angry. But not as angry as he would have been, had he realised that a simple search of Chadwick would have produced a note saying:

'Call me on this number. It's important. Humphrey.'

Chadwick fell in behind Chubby who made slow progress on the path up the side of the quarry. He looked over to the top of the cliff and wondered what possible reason there could be for murdering Humphrey Maclean in such a brutal way. And he had worried that the police might be asking him about Arcier? How naïve he had been. He was way out of his depth here. He should have listened to all of them. To Farqharson. To Silje. To Augustin. He should have stuck to the original plan and stayed away from people. If he had done that, Humphrey Maclean would have been home with his family.

It was time to face the facts. He was a liability, to himself and, more importantly, to others. Whatever he did seemed only to make things worse. He was not clever - he was a fool. A fool who was running out of time. A fool who could no longer pretend to be a disinterested bystander - not to himself and certainly not to the police. Whoever had left the note on Maclean's body had made sure of that. Now there could only be one objective - to find out who murdered Humphrey Maclean and why.

CHAPTER THIRTY-TWO

Chadwick watched Julija sleeping. She lay on her side, facing away from him, her hands together and tucked under her face like a painting of a sleeping child. She was still, her animal energy and sexuality dormant. He wondered at her determination, her absolute conviction that her brother was alive despite all the evidence to the contrary. He had never experienced such conviction and it unnerved him. It struck him that hers was another form of fanaticism, well hidden, perhaps, but just as dangerous. He knew that he was using her as she was using him, and he wondered what would happen if there was incontrovertible proof that her brother was dead. Would they stay together? He doubted it. Theirs was a relationship of convenience. Why was he with her? Was it a sense of obligation to help her find her brother? Or, if he was honest with himself, was he trying to fulfil an obligation to another woman, a woman who was dead?

He walked quietly into the bathroom, trying not to wake her. Sensing a movement behind him, he turned. Julija was standing in the doorway to the bathroom. She had pulled on his shirt. It was unbuttoned and falling off her shoulders. It only emphasised her nakedness. Aware of the chill of the bathroom, he remembered her warmth and wanted to go back to bed with her. She looked at him without speaking. *Is it always like this?*, he thought. *If I go to her now and take her back to bed, am I in control?* Or was it her decision? Was it always the woman's decision? He watched her to see what she would do next. He told himself that if she approached him, if she walked just a step or two towards him, he would relent and take her to bed but if she stayed there, if she stayed in the doorway and did nothing, he would tell her to go. She leaned against the doorframe. She pushed her hair back with her hand so that the shirt fell open.

'Why did you get up so early?' she asked.

Chadwick shrugged.

'Come back to bed,' she said. They stood for a moment or two looking at each other. Any sense of intimacy had disappeared.

'I can't,' he said. 'I have things to do.'

'What things?'

Chadwick thought for a moment. He hadn't told her about Maclean's murder. He had avoided it the previous evening, partly because he was too sickened by it to discuss it, and partly not to alarm her. He dreaded telling her. At this point, her only sensible option was to leave town, but he knew she wouldn't do it. Maclean's death would only confirm her suspicions that her brother was caught up in a larger conspiracy and still alive. If he told her now, it would only lead to a row. He decided to discuss it with Verlaine. If the two of them worked together, they might at least be able to persuade her to disappear for a week or two.

'I need to look at some papers,' he said.

She considered this for a moment and said, 'What papers?'

'Just some technical papers,' he said, knowing that if he mentioned their source, she would demand to see them. 'They are probably not useful but I should look at them. Just to be sure.'

'I'll help you.'

He made a point of smiling. 'It's a nice idea. I wish you could help me, but it's more efficient if I read them on my own. You are too much of a distraction,' he added.

She gave him a sulky look. 'I don't think so. If I was such a distraction, you wouldn't send me away. You want to be alone. You always want to be alone.' She turned slightly and looked past him, surveying the empty, grey sea. He knew her well enough by now to know that she wouldn't say any more until he coaxed her. He considered and then thought better of it. He walked towards her but went through the doorway without either speaking or touching her. He knew it would irritate her, but he was too tired to care. They were in trouble, far greater trouble than she realised. He should have followed Farquharson's advice and maintained his isolation. But he hadn't. He had let his guard down again. He had let himself become involved, just as he had before, and if he wasn't very, very careful, he was going to end up dead or spending the next twenty years of his life in a French gaol.

Several hours later, his mood hadn't improved. He had learned little from his morning's work.

The personnel files showed a marked increase in the turnover of officers on the *Highland Lassie* dating from about a year earlier, immediately after the sinking of the *Highland Laddie*. Was it significant? It was difficult to know. At least it was something.

Maclean's technical specifications and manifest had proved disappointing. He had been through both documents twice and seen nothing that looked in any way unusual or suspicious.

He considered whether Maclean might have held back some information but ruled it out. Not only would it have been out of character, but it would have directly contradicted the instructions Maclean had received from Lloyd's, and Maclean didn't strike Chadwick as the kind of man to ignore a request from his employer.

He got up from the table and stood by the tall windows. It had started to rain, making it hard to tell where the grey of the sky and the sea met. There could be no better metaphor for this town, he thought. Maclean had discovered something that prompted him to make an urgent call to Chadwick. He was certain of it. And if it wasn't in the cargo manifest, where was it? He thought back to the lunch. Had Maclean told him something important without either man realising it at the time? What had he missed that Maclean had spotted?

Irritated at wasting his morning, he returned to the table and looked down at the pile of papers. There was too much information and most of it meant nothing to him: meaningless lists of suppliers, shippers and consignees. He considered a third trawl but couldn't see why he would spot something on a third review that he had missed in the previous two. It would only waste more time. What else could he do?

He sat down, and reached for the top sheet, having decided on a different approach. Instead of examining all the information on every sheet, he would focus only on the buyers or consignees. It took him only twenty minutes before he found what Maclean had surely found before him. He took the document over to the window to examine it more carefully and wondered how he could have missed it. By focusing on the buyers, the name had jumped from the page - Villin SA. He remembered passing the factory with Prieul. It was the closest building to the quarry where Maclean had been killed.

When they had parted, Maclean said he had to check something before returning to Marseille but hadn't been more specific. If he had already spotted that Villin was the buyer of some of *Highland Laddie's* cargo, what would he have done next? Would he have confronted Villin based on the cargo manifest alone? It seemed unlikely. Maclean was an engineer, methodical and cautious. What other information would he have wanted before approaching Villin?

Information on the claim, of course. Who made it and when was it paid. If he had the claim file, he could come up with any number of reasons for calling on the company. And if Maclean visited the factory, how did he arrange it? Did he call ahead or turn up unexpectedly? If he called, it would have given whoever killed him plenty time to prepare. If his visit was unannounced, it would have given the killers less time and forced them to improvise. That might explain why they chose the nearby quarry.

He looked through the papers until he found the commercial invoice for the Villin cargo. There was a list of different types of machinery, each of which had a manufacturer's serial number attached. An idea was forming but he was reluctant to push it too far. First, he needed to see the Villin factory and talk to its boss. It would have to be an unexpected visit. Just like Maclean, but hopefully with a different outcome.

It was already early afternoon. He gathered the papers together, took the sheet with Villin's name on it, circled the name, and placed it on the top of the pile. He walked to reception, found a large envelope, placed the papers inside, and wrote McGhee's name on the front. He didn't know whether McGhee or the Chairman were who they claimed, whether he would ever see them again, or whether they would act on the information inside. But he was short of friends, and right now, he would take any help he could find. He looked at the reception clock. It was 3 p.m. He needed time to drop the envelope at the Sebastopol and get to the Villin factory before the end of the day's shift.

CHAPTER THIRTY-THREE

He had the taxi drop him a short distance from the factory so that he could approach on foot. There was a steady stream of cars - all leaving the factory gates. He was late. The shift had finished earlier than he had anticipated and he quickened his pace. By now, he was at the beginning of the wall that surrounded the factory and car park and could see the last of the workers leaving the building. He checked behind him. The road was empty except for a parked car. It was unoccupied.

Two men were walking out of the building. The one on the left was older and shorter. He was wearing a blue blazer, grey trousers and carrying a briefcase. Chadwick lengthened his stride. He was sure that this was the boss. The other man was wearing overalls that looked too small for him. Anything short of a circus tent would have been too small for him. If the first one was the boss, then the second had to be the largest man in the factory. Was it a coincidence or was the boss worried about his safety? The boss lit a cigarette, opened the driver's door of a Peugeot saloon and placed his briefcase on the front passenger seat. He turned to say something to the giant and then got into the car. The giant turned and made his way back into the factory.

Chadwick checked the distance to the factory gates. The Peugeot reversed and turned its nose towards the two brick pillars that guarded the entrance. Chadwick made the first of these just as the Peugeot's nose pushed through the gates and saw that the boss had opened the windows to let the smoke out. As the car stopped to check for traffic, Chadwick reached in, opened the passenger door, and got in.

'Keep driving,' he said.

The boss looked confused. His fear hadn't kicked in yet and Chadwick needed him frightened, the more frightened the better. 'Drive,' he repeated.

The man started to speak.

'MOVE,' shouted Chadwick.

The man accelerated away from the gates, turning left towards Nice. He was driving on the wrong side of the road but seemed not to have noticed. He had turned pale, a film of sweat on his brow, his hands gripping the steering wheel as if his life depended on it, his forgotten cigarette clamped between his fingers.

'You're on the wrong side of the road,' said Chadwick calmly, as if he was instructing a nephew on how to drive. The man didn't look at him. He stared at the road with exaggerated concentration. *Give him time*, thought Chadwick. *Let him think. Let him try to work out who I am. Let him try to work out his options.* In the meantime, he moved the briefcase from the floor where it had fallen and placed it carefully on the rear seat. There was a leather name tag attached to the handle. He read it. Next, he made a point of settling himself in his seat and fastening his seat belt. 'Nice car,' he said.

The man turned his head to look at him and then quickly returned his gaze to the road. Close up, he was considerably older than he looked from a distance. His hair was thinning but carefully brushed to maximise what little hair was left. His brow was suspiciously wrinkle-free and the area around his mouth was pronounced, no doubt the result of cosmetic filler. He looked like a geriatric chimpanzee, thought Chadwick. The man said, 'What do you want?'

Chadwick ignored the question and said, 'Is it expensive - a car like this? Must be, I suppose. It's never the purchase price, is it? It's the fuel and the maintenance. That's where they get you. A car like this - big engine, heavy body - must eat fuel. And then there's the depreciation. Must be quite a dip in value when you come to sell it.'

The man, unsure about whether he was dealing with a simpleton or a lunatic, repeated, 'What do you want?' He spoke loudly but his belligerence was built on fear.

'I want a long and happy life. How about you, Calvet? What do *you* want?'

The use of his name was enough to convince Calvet that this was no random carjacking. He finally noticed the burning cigarette and tossed it out of the window, shaking his hand to try to reduce the pain in his fingers.

They were approaching the main road. Chadwick said, 'Head to Nice.'

Calvet looked at him. 'Where in Nice?' he asked.

'Police headquarters.'

'Police headquarters?' Calvet's face was white.

'Do you know it? If you don't, you soon will. You're going to be spending quite a lot of time there. I want you to meet a friend of mine, an Inspector Prieul. Lovely man. Busy, though. Works on the murder squad.'

Calvet braked and pulled in to the side of the road.

'Did I tell you to stop?' asked Chadwick.

'I'm not going any further.'

'Yes, you are, Calvet. You're going where I tell you to go, and you're going to do what I tell you to do. Don't get confused. It's very simple. If you don't cooperate, I'm going to drag you out of this car and slap you around until you do what I want. And if that doesn't persuade you, I'm going to knock you out, put you in the boot and drive you there myself. Is that clear enough for you?'

'Who are you?'

'Who I am doesn't matter. All you need to know is that I work for the insurers. Remember them?'

Calvet collapsed over the steering wheel, his arms wrapped around it, his head buried in its centre. His shoulders rose and fell as if he were sobbing but no sounds emerged. Chadwick left him alone. The longer he was left to dwell on what might happen to him, the more likely he was to cooperate. *I don't even know your first name*, he thought. *But I don't want to know it. I don't want to know anything about you. I only want to find out who killed Maclean. It wasn't you, that's clear. Firing a delinquent employee is about your limit.*

Finally, Calvet raised his head. He looked at Chadwick with red-rimmed eyes. 'I didn't know,' he said. 'I didn't know that's what they would do.' Chadwick said nothing. 'You have to believe me, I had no idea. No idea at all.'

'Tell me what happened,' said Chadwick. 'From the beginning, from when they offered to sell you the machinery from the *Highland Laddie*.'

'You know about that?'

'I know everything, but I'd like to hear it from you.'

Calvet took a second or two to collect his thoughts. He sat back in the driving seat, turned towards Chadwick and began talking. 'They approached me several weeks after the *Highland Laddie* sank. They knew that I had insured the shipment. I'm not sure how. They said that there had been an oversight, a mistake, and that certain containers, including Villin's, had never been loaded on the *Highland Laddie*. They had tracked down these containers and had negotiated a deal with the people who had them. Since the ship's cargo had been written off by the insurers as a total loss, the insurers had no interest but since my containers were amongst them, would I be interested in buying them at a discounted price?'

Clever, thought Chadwick. The cover story of the containers not being loaded was well pitched. Sufficiently credible that the buyer could persuade himself that he wasn't doing anything illegal and sufficiently suspicious to dissuade him from asking any awkward questions about how his containers didn't make it on board. All the cargo had been sold. He was certain of it. And if the cargo had been sold, then it had to have been unloaded at a port. Had the hijackers then taken the ship out to sea again and scuttled it? It seemed unlikely. But if the *Highland Laddie* had survived, why was Julija's brother the only member of the crew to have made it out?

'Well, what did you say?'

Calvet hesitated. 'I needed the equipment - it's not easy to obtain such tools - the order times are very long.'

'I'm sure,' said Chadwick, unconvinced. 'And they offered you a good deal, so that you could still get the equipment and keep half the insurance money.'

Calvet paused, trying to think how best to explain his actions. 'Why not? It made sense. The insurers didn't want the equipment. It would only have been sold at auction for a knock-down price. Why not buy it? It was a good deal for everybody.'

'Except for the insurers. It was *their* equipment, after all. Or are you unfamiliar with how insurance claims work?'

Calvet shrugged. 'Nobody cares about insurers.'

'Apparently not. Tell me about the people who sold you the equipment. How was it done?'

'I got a phone call one evening at home. He didn't give a name but just said that he knew that my equipment had been lost and would I be interested in replacing it a lower price. I said I would, and he said that that I was one of the very lucky ones, because my containers hadn't been loaded onto the *Highland Laddie* and he could arrange for me to buy them back if I was interested.'

'And you went for it?'

'Not at first. I was suspicious, you see. I thought it might be a scam. We can get your equipment for you but first you must pay us a deposit to secure your interest, that sort of thing. So, I said that I wouldn't pay anything until I had seen the equipment and that it had to be in the condition it left the factory.'

'And what did he say?'

'He laughed. He told me it's good to be suspicious but that I shouldn't worry. They had no intention of asking for money upfront. I could come to see the equipment at any time and if I was satisfied, I could pay them there and then and take possession of it. He was very cool. It was as if he didn't care whether he sold it to me or dumped it. To him, it was all the same.'

'Was he French?'

'No. He spoke French but not very well.'

'What did you do?'

'I made him an offer.'

'There and then? On the phone?'

'Yes,' he said, looking embarrassed. 'You see, I thought if I waited, he might try to sell to somebody else.'

'And the price would go up. Where was the handover?'

'In a warehouse in Nice. I checked everything. It was all correct. They were very honourable.'

'I'm sure. And how did you pay them?'

'Cash. I paid in cash.'

'From where?'

'From my box'

'Safety-deposit box?'

He nodded.

'How many of them did you meet?'

'Just one.'

'Tell me about him. Was it the same man who called you?'

'Yes.'

'Did he give you a name at all?'

'No. He said very little.'

'Describe him.'

'That's not easy. I mean he wasn't tall. Maybe he was a few centimetres shorter than me but broader. Not fat, though. He looked fit. Like he worked out. That kind of fit.'

'Eye colour? Hair colour?'

'I don't remember his eyes. He wore sunglasses. And I never saw his hair. He must cut it short as I couldn't see much of it below his cap.'

'Cap?'

'He wore a baseball cap.'

'And a black leather jacket with a zip and black jeans.'

'You know him?'

'No. But your description fits more than half the men under forty in Nice. And when you handed over the money, what else did he say?'

Chadwick watched him as he shifted uncomfortably in his seat. The sweat had reappeared on his brow. 'Well? He did tell you something, didn't he?'

'Only that it would make sense if I kept the transaction quiet. Just in case the insurers were to hear of it. Not that they would care but if somebody made a point of bringing it to their attention, they might feel the need to do something. So, it would be best for both of us if we were discreet.'

'I'll bet. What else did he say?'

'About what?'

'About anything.'

The man thought for a moment or two. 'He gave me a number. He said that if anybody did ask any questions, I should call him.'

'And that's just what you did, didn't you? After Maclean called you.'

Calvet turned towards him. His eyes were red as if he had been crying but there were no tears. He grabbed Chadwick's sleeve. 'I didn't know. *I swear* I didn't know that they would hurt him. I had no idea. You must believe me. I'm a businessman. I'm not with them. I'm not *like* them. I just did a deal with them, that's all.'

Chadwick pulled his arm away. 'Tell me what happened. How did Maclean contact you?'

Calvet leaned his arms on the wheel, staring into the middle distance. 'He called me.'

'Where and when?'

'At the factory. Two days ago. In the afternoon.'

'What did he say?'

'He said that he represented Lloyd's and that he was meeting people who had lost cargo in the sinking of the *Highland Laddie*. He was in Nice and he wondered if he might be able to meet me later that afternoon.'

'What did you say?'

'I asked him what it was about. And he said that he needed to check some numbers with me. Numbers of machinery.'

'Did you ask him why?'

'No.'

Because you knew why, thought Chadwick. And if Maclean had been a bit more streetwise, and a little less of a gentleman, he would have known as soon as you didn't ask him why, that he was on the right track, and that he shouldn't have gone anywhere near the factory.

'What did you tell him?'

'I told him that I would need to move some things around in my schedule and that I would call him back.'

'And then you called your friends. And from that point onwards, Maclean was as good as dead.'

Chadwick wondered why Calvet had decided to buy back the machinery. Wasn't it enough to cheat on his taxes and embezzle some money from the company? Why did he need more? Was it greed? Or overconfidence? Chadwick would never understand it, just as he would never understand Calvet making the call that sent Maclean to his death. Calvet had killed Maclean. It was as simple as that. Chadwick didn't care whether he had done it consciously or unconsciously. Calvet was as guilty as the men who threw Maclean off the cliff.

'Let's move,' he said.

'Where are we going?'

'To Nice.'

Calvet looked at him in bewilderment, not sure what his words meant.

'Just drive, okay?'

Nervous, Calvet accelerated and pulled away without looking. Chadwick swore and looked behind them. The road was clear except for a parked car several hundred metres away. Chadwick turned to Calvet and said, 'Drive normally, unless you want to be stopped by the police. It doesn't matter to me, but if I were you, I would be more careful.'

He could see little upside in handing over Calvet to Prieul. It would only further complicate things. Prieul had never heard of the *Highland Laddie*, Julija Soldane or her brother, and the longer he remained ignorant, the more time Chadwick had to operate freely. Involving the police now would only lead to more questioning. No, it was better to leave them out of it, even if it did mean releasing Calvet. He had nowhere to go in any case. He was too scared to approach the hijackers. And Prieul wouldn't take long to retrace Maclean's footsteps. If Calvet ran, Prieul would be only too happy to give chase.

He had learned a lot. The *Highland Laddie* hadn't sunk, at least not initially and not in a storm. Its cargo had been hijacked and some of it resold. And not in Asia: here, in Nice. So how did it get here? On the *Highland Laddie*? And was the crew involved?

What else did he know? Was it a coincidence that the officers of the *Highland Lassie* all changed in the months after the *Highland*

Laddie was 'lost' at sea? Why would they all have resigned or been replaced? What was Augustin's involvement and his connection with Melnikov? Why was Augustin so keen that Chadwick should visit the shipping office? And who else would have a reason for breaking into it? He was tired and ached from his encounter with the fire escape. All he wanted was rest but he didn't have time to rest. Of that, he was certain. Whoever killed Maclean was panicked. The murder was rushed. Perhaps it meant that they were beginning to feel the pressure? And if so, why? He didn't flatter himself that it was from his efforts. If they were under pressure, it could only be that they were planning something, something that they couldn't risk being disrupted.

He needed help badly, but from whom? Verlaine was solid but too old. He needed McGhee. McGhee and the Chairman. He would have to take a risk on them despite what had happened at the villa. He needed to check with the café to see if McGhee had returned.

The traffic had slowed to walking pace. They were in a narrow one-way street with traffic lights at the end. He knew it. It led to one of the smaller squares which acted as a large roundabout. In the middle, there was a disused bandstand and a bank of public telephones. He looked over at Calvet, whose mind was elsewhere, no doubt convinced that Chadwick was about to hand him over to the police in a few minutes. Chadwick decided to let him go home. What was the point of hanging onto him for another hour or so? Better to get out, call the café, and find his own way back to the hotel. Besides, Calvet was depressing him.

'Calvet.' He might as well not have spoken. 'Calvet,' he repeated. This time he got a response. Calvet looked at him as if he had just noticed that he was there. 'When you get into the square, get into the inside lane and let me out.'

Calvet didn't understand.

'Did you hear me?'

'Yes. But why are you getting out?'

'Just go home.'

Calvet thought for a second or two. 'What will you do?'

'About you? Nothing. I have no interest in you. The only thing I want from you is to drop me as I asked. Just do it, okay?'

Calvet began to manoeuvre the car towards the first corner of the square. The traffic was at a near standstill, making it difficult to exit the one-way street. The lights changed and changed again but no one paid any attention. Tempers frayed and there was a near-constant blowing of car horns. Calvet steered the car out of the one-way street and into the square, but moving to the inside lane proved harder, and they were only halfway around the first side of the square before Chadwick conceded defeat. 'I'm getting out here,' he said. He opened his door, and ducking low, ran between the cars towards the small park in the centre of the square.

He reached the bank of phones and searched his pockets for some change. As usual, nobody was picking up the phone at the Sebastapol. He knew that when somebody did finally answer, he should expect abuse for phoning at the wrong time. At the Sebastopol, it was always the wrong time. He looked over at the slow-moving vehicles. Calvet had reached the second corner of the square, but the traffic was still backed up. Some drivers were resorting to aggressive tactics, pushing and prodding their way forward, delivering and receiving abuse in equal measure. Chadwick waited for somebody to answer and watched the show.

One of the more aggressive drivers drove onto the pavement at the side of the park to pass some of the cars ahead of him. The car looked familiar. It took him a second or two to remember where he had seen it. And he had seen it twice. Once outside the factory, when he had thought that it was empty. And again, when he had been parked in the Peugeot with Calvet. It had been following them and he had missed it. He had been too preoccupied with getting Calvet to confess.

The car had already passed him, and he started to jog towards the other side of the square. It was only when the car rounded the far end of the square and drove back towards him that he would be able to see its occupants.

Using the deserted bandstand as cover, he checked on the progress of the Peugeot. It was turning into the third side. He looked over at the taxi rank. There was one cab waiting. He looked around. An elderly couple was walking towards it. He had to decide. There was no point in losing the taxi just for the sake of getting a look at the driver. He ran towards the cab rank and could see the old couple looking at him, hoping that he wouldn't be so rude as to take their taxi. But he had no choice. He pulled open the door and got in. The cab driver turned and started to speak. Chadwick knew that it would be about his taking the taxi. He gave him a €100 note. The man looked at him. 'There is a green car passing us. I want you to follow it. If you don't get spotted, I'll give you another €100 and the fare.' Financial advantage overcame the taxi driver's civic fervour. He pulled out into the traffic just as the car passed. Chadwick knew then that he had made the correct decision. He recognised the green car's driver at once. It was Aleksis Soldane.

CHAPTER THIRTY-FOUR

The square was poorly lit. Most of the illumination came from the brasserie where he was sitting. He looked up at the third-floor apartment opposite. The lights were on and the blinds drawn. As he watched, a figure passed across the blind like a traditional shadow play. He relaxed. Time was at last on his side. Soon he would know everything.

The window of the brasserie allowed him a view of the entire square. There was only one access road. Nobody could enter or leave without him seeing them. He examined the buildings on the other side of the street. Most of the houses must originally have been detached, but with increasing demand for space, all the gaps between the houses had been filled and extra floors added. The passage of time, and subsidence, had left several houses so crooked that they could only stand with the help of their neighbours. The houses had been split into apartments, but in most cases there was no front door, only an open entranceway and stairs that led to various landings. One or two buildings had fitted gates across the entrance, but not, Chadwick was pleased to note, the house where Soldane was staying.

He wondered how Julija would react. Should he take Soldane to her immediately or arrange for them to meet the following day? He glanced upwards at the windows of the apartment. The lights remained on but there was no sign of movement inside. The clock above the brasserie counter showed 20.40. He would give Soldane another twenty minutes to get settled.

He asked for the bill, paid and stepped outside. There was no sign of activity from the apartment, nor any other lights in Soldane's building. He surveyed the parked cars. They were all empty. He put on a baseball cap and turned up the collar of his jacket. Without hesitating, or looking to his left or right, he crossed the square and made directly for the entranceway. As soon as he was inside, and hidden from the street, he stopped to listen. He could hear the noise of the brasserie rise and fall as its front door opened and closed but nothing else. The building was silent. He looked up the stairs. They were wooden, uneven and badly lit. He started to climb, testing each tread to avoid making noise. The house was quiet. Any noise, children crying, a television, even a dog barking, would have made it easier.

As he approached the third floor, he looked to his left through a rough wooden balustrade. The landing was poorly lit. Through the gloom, he could make out the door to Soldane's apartment but little else. He waited, giving his eyes time to adjust, before he continued to the top of the stairs. Moving towards the door, he stopped just to the right of it, where he stood with his back to the wall. Stepping on some glass that scrunched beneath his foot, he looked up and saw the remains of a broken bulb. He put his ear to the wall but could hear nothing.

Soldane was a nervous man. He doubted that he would open the door without knowing who was outside. Staying flat against the wall, he stretched out his right arm and knocked twice on the door with the back of his fist, before withdrawing the arm out of any possible danger. He waited and listened. There was no sign of movement from the apartment. A minute went by and then another. He reached across and knocked a second time. The silence in the house had become oppressive.

Wrapping a handkerchief around his hand, he reached for the handle. To his surprise, the door wasn't locked. He pushed it and got ready to jump the balustrade to the stairs below. But nothing moved. There was no gunfire. No rush of feet.

Another minute passed. He called out, 'Soldane.' There was no response, so he repeated it. He pushed open the door of the apartment and risked a quick look. The door opened directly into an empty sitting room. He took a step or two into the room. It was cheaply furnished and unremarkable. There were two doors in the back wall. The one on the right opened into a small kitchen. The door on the left was closed. He walked towards the back of the room and took a quick look at the kitchen. There was no sign that it had ever been used.

He kicked open the bedroom door. The lights were on and the room was knee-deep in discarded clothes that would never be worn again. They had been ripped apart. The mattress, bedframe and various bags had received similar treatment, their seams torn open with a box-cutter knife. The room had been searched and searched fast by people who had come prepared and didn't mind the occupant knowing they had been there. The time for stealth was over. It had ended with Maclean's murder.

There was another door in the room. It had to lead to the bathroom. Chadwick half-waded and half-pushed his way through the debris on the bedroom floor. There was nothing for him here. He was sure of it. The opposition wouldn't have overlooked anything. They were too efficient and too ruthless. It was over. Whatever it was that they wanted from Soldane, they had it.

He pushed the bathroom door. As soon as it opened, he knew. He knew that Aleksis Soldane would never be able to answer his questions. Aleksis Soldane would never be able to answer anybody's questions. There was no more Aleksis Soldane. There was only the sweet, warm smell of blood and death. He leaned against the wall, feeling nauseous, and tried to breathe. He steeled himself to go into the bathroom. He had to do it, if only for Julija's sake.

It was a tiny room with no window, only a small ventilator fan. It was lit by a fluorescent tube which was too large, too powerful, and too industrial for such a small space. The bath, the wash-hand basin, and the tiled walls were all white. There was a shower head fitted to the wall and a rail that followed the outline of the bath. Hanging from the rail was a faded shower curtain, advertising the attractions of nineteen-fifties Portofino. The floor, or what he could see of it, was faded-green linoleum.

He had seen death in its many guises, but nothing had prepared him for what he saw in that bathroom. Afterwards, he would refuse to discuss it, as if it had never happened, another part of his past that was to be forever hidden from the present.

Death had not come easily to Aleksis Soldane. His killers had made sure of it. They had stripped him, stuffed his underwear in his mouth and tied his hands with plasticuffs. Then they had used another zip tie to secure his hands to the shower head, with his back against the wall. Then they had started.

It was impossible to know how long he had lasted. Chadwick tried not to think about it. He focused instead on the nature of Soldane's wounds. At first, it looked as if he had been attacked by a wild animal. Only his face was untouched. The rest of his body, including his arms, was a bloody carcass. He might have been hanging from a meat hook in an abattoir. It could only be the work of a maniac, thought Chadwick, somebody whose vindictiveness, whose frustration at Soldane, had boiled over into a frenzy. But as he looked more closely, he realised that he was wrong. This had been no frenzied attack. The cuts were of a similar size and depth. They were neatly arranged in rows, one above the other, as if the murderer had started at the bottom and worked upwards. The only areas he had avoided were around the major arteries. He must have used a box-cutter on Soldane in the same way that his accomplices were using them on the suitcases in the bedroom. There was only one conclusion – he had intended Soldane to die slowly, in great pain, and to know that he was dying.

Chadwick felt a chill run through him. If he ever fell into this man's hands, he would get the same treatment or worse. He took one last look around to see if there was anything he had missed. There was a bath mat pushed into a corner by the WC. It was covered in blood. They must have used it to wipe the blood from the floor. That explained why there were no footprints.

He retreated to the sitting room. He cursed his earlier exhilaration. His weariness returned, accompanied by an overwhelming sense of guilt. Whoever killed Julija's brother must have entered the apartment just before Chadwick arrived at the brasserie. Otherwise, he would have seen them. If he hadn't waited, if he hadn't been so cautious, Soldane might still be alive. But if he hadn't waited, the chances were that he, too, would be dead.

As far as he could see, there was nothing left that would identify Aleksis Soldane. No passport, wallet, identity card or papers of any kind. Perhaps, if they had had enough time, they would have removed the body too. Otherwise, what reason could they have for leaving it here, when they could have dumped it at sea and nobody would have been any the wiser?

The house seemed quieter than ever. It was time to go. There was nothing else that he was going to learn here. He hesitated. Something didn't feel right. He went to the window, stood to one side, and looked through the gap between the blind and the window frame. The lights were on in the brasserie but there was nobody sitting in the window. All the visible tables were empty. It was too early for it to close. He listened but the distant hubbub of noise that he had heard previously had gone. He looked to the far corner, to the only access road for the square. There was no sign of life. Nobody was coming in or out. He could watch for longer, but he would only be wasting time. The square had been cordoned-off and the people moved back from the brasserie windows. It wasn't the killers. It was the police. He was sure of it. Somebody had tipped them off as soon as he entered the building.

He didn't have much time. The police would move as soon as they had the area secured. How long would that be? Five minutes? Ten at the outside. That was all the time he had to find a way out of the building that didn't go through the square. He could try the back but that didn't look promising. He hadn't seen anything that might have led to the rear of the building when he came up the stairs, and even if there was a rear exit, it would be the first place that the police would go. No, he needed to find another way.

The front door was still open. He took the lock off the latch to make sure the door closed shut behind him as went out to the landing. It wouldn't slow them up much but at this point, every minute might make a difference. Down or up? It had to be up. He couldn't leave by the entranceway or either of the two apartments on the first and second floors. Even if he could drop down from the first floor to the rear of the building, he would only be dropping straight into the arms of the waiting police. There had to be another way. The killers didn't leave via the entranceway. Of that he was certain - he would have seen them. His only worry was that they had left via the rear of the building, long before the police arrived.

He ran up the stairs to the fourth floor. The door to the apartment looked impenetrable. He took out his penlight and shone it into the dark recesses of the landing. Nothing. No fire escape. Only the stairs to the top floor. He went up them two at a time. The fifth-floor landing was wider and longer, and the door to the apartment was set closer to the front wall. The ceiling was lower, and towards the back of the landing, there was a short ladder leading to a skylight. He ran towards it and started to climb. When he was about halfway up, there was a noise from one of the floors below, as if somebody had dropped something on the stairs. He stopped and listened. They were coming. He climbed the last couple of rungs and examined the skylight. It was in a poor state of repair, housed in a rusting metal frame, the hinged part comprising two panes of fire-resistant glass separated by a metal strut. One of the panes had cracked and been repaired with electrical tape. The handle was unlocked and there was a smudge of blood on it. This was how the killers left. Using his handkerchief, he pushed the curved metal bar upwards. It was either very heavy or difficult to move. He tried again. This time, it started to shift upwards. He moved up first one rung and then another. By now, the skylight was approaching the vertical and he feared that if he pushed it too far, it would fall the other way, crashing down on the roof. With his shoulders against the hatch, he reached up with his left hand to grip the skylight. Now that it was almost upright, it was easier to control. His head was now clear of the hatch, and he could look around the roof. Climbing the last couple of rungs, he sat on the edge of the frame and swivelled his feet over the side of the frame and onto the roof. He wiped his prints from the sides of the skylight and lowered it. As it closed, he heard a door being kicked in below.

He turned and looked around him. The square was in the shape of a rectangle. He was in the middle of one of the longer sides, directly opposite the brasserie. The access road was in the far-right-hand corner of the rectangle. The roofs of the houses varied enormously in pitch, style and coverings. Some were steep, others flat, some tiled, others covered with roofing felt.

He had to move. If they trapped him on the roof, it would be over. But which way should he go? He could move right, heading towards the narrow side of the square next the access road and try to get down from there. Or he could go the longer route, turning left, and heading towards the far end of the square, and if he needed to, onto the other long side of the square, above the brasserie. It would take longer but gave him more options. It also made sense because it took him away from, not towards, the waiting police.

He decided against the logical option. He took out his penlight, turned it on, and crossed to the neighbouring roof on the left as if he were following the logical route. When he reached the border between that house and the next, he took the penlight and threw it underhand onto the next house's roof. It hit the roofing felt and rolled towards a gutter, where it stuck, its beam intact. Satisfied, he retraced his steps and began to climb roof after roof on the right. His plan was to reach the narrow side before looking for a way down. The crackle of radios from the square grew closer. He only had three more houses to cross before he reached the corner of the square and the beginning of the narrow side. The first and third had pitched, tiled roofs. The second was flat. He heard a crash behind him. It could only be the skylight smashing down on the roof. He looked back. The skylight was hidden by roofs. But nobody who had seen Soldane's shredded flesh was going through that skylight without first satisfying themselves that it wasn't an ambush. He rushed the next roof, his feet clattering on the slates, conscious that as he passed over the ridge, he would be exposed, not just to anybody at the skylight but anybody watching from the ground. He kept low over the ridge and let himself slide down the other side. He crawled across the flat roof to the third house. Should he go over the next ridge or was he too late? Were the first police now on the roof? This time, he crawled up the roof, pressing his face and body against the tiles. It took longer but left him less exposed. He stopped just short of the ridge. There were shouts from the skylight, and a powerful torch beam touched the ridge of the roof next to where he was about to cross. It hovered for a second and then moved. The torch's owner was at the skylight and too low for him to be able to shine the light into any of the valleys between the pitched roofs. But it would only be a matter of seconds before he climbed higher. Chadwick reached up and pulled himself over the ridge of the third roof and slithered down out of sight.

He was now on the roof of the first house on the narrow side. It had mansard windows and he crawled forward, using one of them to shield him from the man with the torch. From his new position, he could see the front of the roof of Soldane's building. There were now several policemen holding torches, their beams criss-crossing the rooftops. They split into two groups. One moved away from Chadwick; the other started towards him. Suddenly, there was a shout. The first group had found his penlight. The second group turned and came over to them. They stood for a moment or two and then fanned out, their torches moving away from him. He watched for a second or two to be certain, crawled to the back of the roof where he was less likely to be seen and began to move further around the square.

He was three or four houses from the end before he found the half-open skylight. He pulled it open and sat on its edge. Holding the frame with both hands, he let himself drop and found himself on the floor of an attic room. Picking himself up, he looked up at the skylight. It was too far from the floor for him to be able to close it.

He moved to the door and opened it a crack. It was dark. He stepped outside, pulling the door closed behind him. The little light there was came from below via a set of stairs. He went down them two at a time and found himself in a large sitting room. He crossed to the front door and went out and down the communal stairs. He stopped at a large window between the third and fourth floors and looked out. There was another building immediately behind which had to face the street behind the square. Between the two buildings, there was an open space.

Once he was on the ground floor, it was easy to find the back door. He unbolted it and went out. The space he had seen from above was a concrete yard which ran between the two buildings. There was brick wall about two meters high running across it and a heavy galvanised gate at one end. Against the wall, there were several large recycling bins. He went to the gate and looked through. The yard on the other side was identical except for a passageway under the building opposite. The gate was locked so he scaled the wall. Once over, he walked into the passageway. As he neared its end, he stopped.

To his left, he could see the police cars he had seen from the rooftop. There were two policemen behind a tape that stretched across the access road. They were looking into the square and away from him. He turned right, walking slowly like a man deep in thought. He waited for somebody to call out or to tell him to stop but no one did. At the end of the street, he turned away from the square.

For the next ten minutes, he turned left and right, stopped and double-backed until he was certain that he was alone. A nearby clock struck 10 p.m. He was shocked, expecting it to be later. For him, the last hour had seemed like a lifetime. All he cared about was getting out of Nice. The police would check the taxis and the bus was too slow. His best option was the train. The service was frequent and the trains reassuringly anonymous.

He entered the station fifteen minutes later, his head lowered, trying to avoid the cameras. The board told him that there was a train in three minutes. He went to the automated ticket machine and bought his ticket using cash. The platform was on the other side of the station. He walked slowly through the underpass until he heard the rumble of a train overhead. Picking up speed, he ran up the stairs, through the open doors of the waiting train and sat down.

The other occupants of the carriage were a mixture of tourists, families and couples. Most seemed to be returning home from an evening out - so was he. He pulled the cap low over his face and pretended to doze. When the train pulled into his station, he went directly to the exit and headed towards the sea and the hotel. The wind was growing stronger, and it was starting to rain. He knew that he should try to find Julija to tell her about her brother but what was the point? Her brother was dead. Let her sleep. It would wait till tomorrow. And tomorrow, he could enlist the help of Verlaine. He dreaded the thought of doing it alone.

As he approached the hotel, he crossed to the other side of the street. He passed the lane and his normal entrance and kept walking as if heading to the marina. He looked across at the hotel, which was set back from the street. Everything was as it should be. The gates were closed. The circular driveway was empty. There was no movement in the garden. There were no lights on. He kept walking until he had turned the corner by the pizzeria and started downhill. Then he turned, crossed the road and repeated his surveillance. Satisfied, he turned into the lane and let himself into the hotel.

CHAPTER THIRTY-FIVE

He went straight to his room, knowing that he had very little time. As soon as the Russians realised that the police had missed him, they would come for him.

Before he switched on the light, he went to the bathroom window and studied the sea. It was unsettled and increasingly heavy. In the distance, the black of the night met the black of the water. The lights of St Jean and the houses on Cap-Ferrat were intermittently obscured by the falling rain. He noticed a small, dark patch that had appeared in an area of lighter grey. It was hard to distinguish it from the surrounding sea, but it appeared to be moving towards him. It was shaped like a traditional tent, viewed from the front. He closed his eyes. When he reopened them, the tent looked larger. There was no question that it was getting closer. It had to be a boat, probably a small rib, running without lights. The tent wasn't a tent - it was the shape of the men sitting on either side, bending forward to shelter from the rain and wind. They were heading directly towards the hotel but moving slowly. Why? If they accelerated, they would be at the hotel in minutes. What were they waiting for? Then he realised. They were waiting for him. Waiting for him to switch the lights on in his room so that they knew exactly where he was.

He ran to the corridor and into another bedroom. He went to a cupboard, knelt and ripped the carpet from the floor. He picked up a blue ribbon with a clear plastic envelope attached and hung it around his neck, tucking it underneath his shirt. Returning to the corridor, he reversed direction and instead of going to the main stairs, pushed open a panel in the wall that hid the service stairs to the kitchen. He felt his way down without switching on the light. He didn't have much time. The sound of breaking glass somewhere in the hotel only confirmed it.

He moved through the hotel kitchen to a window, unlocked it and slid it upwards. He went through it, pausing only long enough to close it. He fell flat to the ground and moved across the terrace to the swimming pool in a tiger crawl. The lights of the town meant the terrace was better lit than he would have liked, and he needed to be sure that he couldn't be seen by the men in the boat. If he was, his escape route was closed. He was less concerned about the men in the hotel. They would be racing to his room and wouldn't begin searching until they found it empty. But when they did, they would be sure to tell the men in the boat. His best chance was to get beyond the boat before that happened but that wasn't going to be easy.

He rounded the swimming pool. His hands and knees hurt, and he was breathing heavily. He was now only metres from the dock. When he reached its edge, he knew better than to hesitate. The shock was instantaneous. The water was cold, much colder than he had anticipated, and he wondered how long he could survive without hypothermia. Putting the thought out of his mind, he surfaced, keeping as close as he could to the side of the dock nearest to the hotel, out of sight from anybody watching from the hotel windows. As he neared the entrance to the dock, he had a choice. If he turned left and swam around to the neighbouring marina, he could be out of the water and back onshore in minutes. But he would also be next door to the hotel, and he doubted that the Russians would have overlooked such an obvious escape route. Alternatively, if he went right, and swam towards the small beach in front of the casino, he would be visible from the main road. No, if he wanted to be safe, he had to get past the boat, and getting past the boat meant swimming straight for it.

He turned towards the open sea. His plan was to swim as far to the left of the boat as he could manage, and then cut behind it, before swimming right, towards St Jean. But on leaving the dock, he realised that he faced a much tougher challenge than he had anticipated. The wind was blowing towards land, pushing the sea before it. It was impossible to see any distance. Sometimes, when he was on the peak of a wave, he could see a few metres before he was dropped into the next trough; otherwise, he could see nothing but the ice-cold, shifting, black water that seemed intent on driving him towards the shore. From time to time, he caught sight of the lights of St Jean but they were too far away and too intermittent to tell him whether he was making any progress against the opposing wind and sea. He searched for the boat but saw nothing. He was too low in the water. He tried to move to his left, his fingers and feet growing cold, while he concentrated on the oncoming waves. If he was caught unawares, he was picked up and discarded like a piece of flotsam, the breath forced out of his lungs, his mouth filled with briny water. There was no respite. There could be no respite until he was safely onshore.

He heard the rib before he saw it. If it had been hidden in a trough, he wouldn't have seen it until it was too late. If the bow hadn't smashed his skull, then the outboard's propellers would have cut him to ribbons. But the rib wasn't in a trough. The bow appeared on top of a cresting wave and hung ominously above him before crashing down like some great hammer. It gave him just enough time to drive himself into the cresting wave and below the advancing boat, pulling himself further down with every stroke. When his lungs started to burn, he started upwards until he saw the water growing lighter, surfacing to the sound of the outboard fading into the distance. He looked towards the hotel. Every floor was lit. The search was underway. He needed to get moving. He turned towards the lights of St Jean and started swimming hard.

When he reached the entrance to St Jean harbour, he was cold and exhausted. He needed a hot meal, a bed, a warm fire and a bottle of whisky. But none of those were on offer. All he had was the chance to rest his feet on the rungs of a metal ladder set into the wall of the port, his head just above the water. It was still raining.

The St Jean harbour was more marina than harbour. Within it, were a series of aluminium floating docks. On either side of each dock was a miscellany of sailing boats, pleasure cruisers and fishing boats of all different shapes and sizes. Most were covered with tarpaulins or covers, their hatches locked, much of their equipment removed for the winter. It would be Easter before there was much activity in St Jean.

He had rested long enough. He wanted nothing more than to climb the ladder and get out of the water while he still had the strength. But the ladder wasn't an option. The marina was floodlit by the tall lighting standards that stood at the head of each dock. Anybody moving in the early hours could be seen either from the main street or the buildings that overhung the harbour. Cursing, he pushed off the ladder and began the last part of his swim. He didn't have far to go. He swam halfway down one of the docks and towards the stern of one of the larger sailing boats. Above him was a small ladder for swimming. It was hinged and had been pulled clear of the water. A cord was hanging down - he pulled on the cord and the bottom half of the ladder began to lower. When it was in the water, he pulled his feet up so that they rested on the bottom rung and began to pull himself out of the water using the handrails. It was more difficult than he had anticipated. When he finally made the deck, he reached down and pulled up the hinged part of the ladder. This time, he secured it in a knot.

There was a cover stretching most of the length of the boat, secured to the deck. Before he could get to the cockpit or the entry hatch, he would need to lift it. But he had no intention of lifting it.

He ducked behind it so that he couldn't be seen from the road and moved towards the bow. Just past the end of the cover, he stopped by an opaque Perspex hatch, secured by a rusty padlock. He ignored the padlock and went straight to the hinged end of the hatch. With shaking hands, he tried to grip the end of one of the hinge pins. It took him several attempts to get his fingers to work but eventually, he pulled it free. He transferred it to his left hand and moved across to the other pin - this one was easier. When he had both pins in his left hand, he lifted the hatch from the hinged end and slipped his legs through. Then he began to lower himself until his feet landed on a hard surface. Satisfied that his stance was secure, he pulled the hatch cover back down and inserted the hinge pins from the inside. Then, he stepped down from the wooden box that he had left there for just this eventuality.

It was pitch-black inside the boat. He felt his way down a short, narrow corridor, found the correct door and went inside. He didn't use the light in case it was visible through a gap in the curtains that covered the small windows. He stripped and stepped into a small cubicle. The water that came out was just as cold as the water he had just left but it was fresh. He let it run through his hair and over his exhausted body. Once he had finished, he reached for a towel and dried himself as vigorously as he could. His blood was flowing again. The numbing cold was disappearing.

His next priority was food. Wrapping the towel around him, he felt his way to the galley. Here, he opened a cupboard and took out several power bars. Next, he retreated to a cabin next the bathroom where he opened the curtain a fraction. There was a single bunk. He opened a drawer beneath it, took out a set of clean clothes and dressed. By the time he was finished, he was beginning to feel warm again. He ate one of the power bars and left the others on top of the bed. He looked through the gap in the curtain. The port was deserted but he didn't expect it to remain so for long. If he had learned anything about the Russians, it was that they were relentless. Once they were convinced that he wasn't in the hotel, they would start scouring the beach and the marina next to the hotel. After that, they would cast the net wider, which meant that, sooner or later, they would be in St Jean. He picked up the towel and went back to the corridor. Leaving the door to the cabin open, and starting under the hatch, he used what little light there was to dry the floor.

He went back into the cabin and took another look out of the small window. The ground rose steeply at the end of the port. There were steps up to the road and a small, paved area with benches and a maritime statue. To his left was a hotel, sitting some twenty metres or so above the marina. It was closed. To his right, the start of the main street and the buildings that spilled down to the marina itself. There was no sign of life.

He went back to the drawer under the bunk. He sat on the floor, facing the bunk, trying to use what little light there was. He took out a blue money belt designed to be wrapped around the waist. Opening the plastic envelope that he had brought with him from the hotel, he took out a passport, credit cards and a wodge of notes. He put the passport into one of the empty pockets in the belt and the cash in another. The other pockets were full. He put the credit cards into his pocket and tossed the plastic envelope into the drawer. Then he pulled up his shirt and strapped the belt to his waist. He took a jersey and a waterproof jacket from the drawer before closing it and checking the room to ensure that he had left no sign of being there. Only then did he resume his watch at the window.

He knew they would come. It was only a matter of time. From his perspective, the later they arrived, the better. It would be dawn in a few hours and the town and the port would come to life. After that, it would be difficult for them to mount a search of the marina. Now was a different story. The harbour was empty. Anybody within half a kilometre was fast asleep. But what sort of search could they mount in a few hours? There must have been well over 150 boats in the marina. To search them properly would mean breaking in to each one. Even if they had several men, it would still take them more time than they had. Plus, there was always the danger that they would run into a boat that was alarmed. The cape was a narrow peninsula. The only roads connecting it to the mainland had to run past a police station. If there was any trouble, the police could seal the cape in minutes, cutting off any escape. Unless …

He closed the curtain, crossed the corridor and opened the door to the cabin on the other side. He pulled back the curtain a centimetre or two and saw them immediately. Three of them. Standing next to the same ladder where he had rested on first entering the port. They must have left one or maybe two men in the rib. He had to admire them. They didn't miss a trick. Bringing the boat not only meant that they had a route off the cape if they ran into trouble, it also allowed them to inspect the boats in the marina from the water, looking for telltale signs of a break in or any form of disturbance. They were smart. There was no question about it.

But this time, he had an edge. This time, they couldn't be certain that he was there. And they had a big search ahead of them – there were just too many boats. And he was confident that nobody in France knew about his connection with this one. The last time he had been on it was long before he arrived at the hotel. Long before anybody knew or could recognise him. No, if they were going to find him this time, they would need to get lucky. And even if they did break into the boat, it could only be speculative and only after they had broken into countless others. And if they did break in, the first man who came down the companionway wasn't going back up. He would see to it. And if he was armed, so much the better. He could use a gun right now.

The three men were walking along the side of the harbour. In a second or two, he would lose sight of them. The only one he recognised was the one in the middle. It was the short, broadly-built man with the baseball cap who had accompanied Melnikov to the lunch at the Hotel du Cap and then reappeared on the *Lara*. He had always known that the Russians must work for Melnikov, but this was his first tangible proof.

As they disappeared, he closed the curtain and returned to the first cabin. He watched them as they reached the buildings at the end of the harbour, just below the main street. Once they were there, they split up. The short man remained where he was, while the other two stepped onto the first of the aluminium docks. There was a row of boats tethered on either side of the dock, but the two men ignored them for the moment. They walked to the end of the dock and waited. He heard the rib before he saw it. It appeared at the end of the dock next to the two men. There was only one man in it. He stopped and the other two spoke to him. Having received his instructions, he nudged the rib around the end of the dock and began to move slowly down the line of boats.

One of the two men jumped onto the first boat. He switched on a torch and began to inspect the boat for any sign of activity. The other man stayed on the dock. No doubt his job was to prevent Chadwick running. And even if he failed, there was still their boss, the tough-looking Russian to get past. They were professional, this crew, there was no doubt about that. But they had a lot of ground to cover before dawn. He watched as the man checking the boats finished with another and stepped across to the next one.

When they finished the boats on the far side of the first dock, they went back to the end of it and started on the other side. It looked like cold, miserable work but they kept at it. From time to time, he could see, and sometimes hear, a hatch or a small window being broken. If this happened, the man with the torch would push it through the broken window or hatch and peer into the interior. They were moving quickly, knowing they had to complete the search before first light. He was happy to watch them, preferring to know where they were and what they were doing. But once they got closer, he would need to retreat to the corridor.

When they reached the dock next to his, he left the cabin, carefully closing the door behind him. He went towards the main room, the saloon, but stopped just short of it, in front of a locker that was only ever used to store suitcases or hang clothes. Now, it was completely empty. He climbed in. He couldn't stand but otherwise, it was quite roomy. He sat on the floor, his knees bent. There were two brass ventilators let into the door. If anybody did come aboard, he would see them by the light of the torch. There was nothing he could do now but wait. They would come soon enough.

This is how she must have felt, he thought. *Hunted through the streets like an animal, slowly coming to terms with the relentlessness of the pursuit. Knowing that they knew about Chadwick, knowing that it was too late to talk her way out, and knowing that the rendezvous and the planned exfiltration were a dream, a fantasy exchanged between a willing buyer and a willing seller, no more real than the claims of the shopkeepers in the souk. And in the last minutes, in that final stretch, picking your way through the market square, did you remember that I was watching or were you focused only on making it home? When did you concede defeat? When did you decide? Was it only when you arrived in the apartment that you realised what you were going to do?*

He was so quiet that Chadwick almost missed the sound of his footsteps overhead. The man started at the stern and worked his way forward. When he reached the forward hatch, he stopped. A faint light appeared in the corridor. He had to be using his torch to check the padlock. Chadwick was confident about the padlock. It hadn't been opened for a year and it looked it. He was more concerned about the hinges. He waited for the man to move, but he seemed still to be standing by the hatch. He looked through the brass ventilator. The light in the corridor had increased. The man must be trying to shine his torch though the hatch. *Good luck with that,* thought Chadwick. *You will need a very special torch to see anything through tinted, toughened Perspex.* The man must have come to the same conclusion because the light disappeared and the next thing that Chadwick heard was a thumping on the hatch itself, either from a boot or from the end of the torch. *This one knows very little about boats,* thought Chadwick, *if he thinks he is going to break that hatch with anything short of a heavy hammer.* But he was concerned that the man should have decided that it was necessary to check this boat quite so assiduously. He listened as the man walked to the far side. There was the sound of breaking glass. It had to be one of the small windows in a cabin. He could picture the man, lying flat on the deck, his head and shoulders over the side, moving the torch from one side of the cabin to another. He waited. The man got up and walked to the other side where he repeated the exercise. Then, he seemed to spend some time inspecting the cover that ran most of the length of the boat, covering both the cockpit and the saloon, making it impossible to enter either without undoing the padlock that secured it. Surely, he must realise from the position of the padlock that the cover can't be secured from inside? Chadwick waited and listened but heard nothing. Either the man had moved to the next boat or he was standing still, somewhere above him.

Minutes drifted by. Chadwick tried to stretch his legs, but it was impossible in the confined space. He had no choice but to wait. After he judged that about half an hour had passed, he opened the locker door and looked out. The corridor was as black as ever. He untucked his legs and eased his weight onto them. They were stiff from the swimming and his time in the locker, and he lurched rather than walked up the corridor. When he reached the first cabin door, he hesitated. It seemed scarcely credible that the man could still be watching through the broken window. He remonstrated with himself and before he could change his mind, pushed open the cabin door. The curtain from the little window was blowing and there was glass on the floor and on the bunk but there was nobody at the window. He trod carefully, avoiding the broken glass, and looked out. The three men were now two docks away. He saw the rib nosing out from one of the docks and moving to the next.

He went out and shut the cabin door. He checked the one opposite. Its window was also broken but he could see nobody from it. He retreated to the corridor and opened the door at the end of it. It was the master cabin. He got onto the bed and rested his head for a second or two.

CHAPTER THIRTY-SIX

When he awoke, there was a ring of light around the curtains. Sitting up, he pulled the curtains back, and scanned the port. The Russians were gone. There was nobody amongst the boats, but at the end of the docks, next to the town and on the road, there were encouraging signs of activity.

Time to move. He shifted a small box under the hatch and slid out the hinges. Two minutes later, he was climbing the steps out of the harbour, looking as if he didn't have a care in the world. Turning into the main street, he spotted a promising café and looked through the window. A smiling McGhee gestured to him to come in.

'Hello,' said McGhee. 'Take a pew. If I had known you were going to be so prompt, I would have ordered for you.'

McGhee had ditched the suit and was in a zippered suede jacket, grey trousers, a shirt and a dark-blue cashmere sweater. He looked younger and fitter than Chadwick remembered.

'How did you find me?'

McGhee pretended to look peeved. 'Do you expect me to give away all my secrets so early in our acquaintance?'

'Come on,' said Chadwick, pouring himself a coffee.

'I gave up on you at the café and went looking for you at the hotel. Late last night. Unfortunately, it appeared to be closed. For *a private function*. You didn't tell me that you were throwing a party.'

'It wasn't my idea.'

'Ahhh! So, it was a *surprise* party. I thought it might be. They're quite good, your chums, aren't they?'

'They are.'

'Russians?'

'Yes.'

McGhee thought for a moment and stirred his coffee. 'I assumed that if you were trapped in the hotel, you would swim out. You couldn't get very far to the immediate left or right without getting picked up easily. That could only mean that you had swum further. And further, to me, seemed like St Jean. And, soon after I arrived, so did Santa's little helpers.'

'But they searched the whole marina and didn't find anything. What made *you* think I was here?'

McGhee sat back and clasped his hands on his chest. 'They were obviously looking for signs of somebody breaking into a boat and couldn't find any. Therefore, either you didn't come here, you didn't make it or you had access to a boat. I decided it was probably the last. But even if it wasn't, even if it was the first or the second, I still needed my breakfast. Do you want some?'

You are a lot smarter than you make out, thought Chadwick. 'Yes, breakfast sounds like a good idea.'

McGhee waited patiently until Chadwick ordered. 'So?' he said.

'So?'

'Are you going to tell me what's going on or should I just eat my breakfast and shut up?

'I can try. It would help if I knew. But before I start, let me ask you a question. The villa. The villa where I met your boss. Is it his?'

McGhee looked surprised. 'Of course.'

'Then who is Frederickson?'

'Ah, now I understand. You checked on the local register.'

'I didn't. The police did.'

'Did they now? And they told you that you were wrong. It didn't belong to the Chairman, it belonged to Frederickson?'

'Something like that. And it was empty. I went back there to try to find him, and it was empty. Completely empty.'

McGhee shook his head. 'It's not,' he said, 'it just looks that way from the front. There is a problem with some pipes on the first floor and all the furniture had to be moved out of the front rooms. It looks deserted but it's not. We can walk there after breakfast if you like.'

'Who is Frederickson?' continued Chadwick. 'Why does it say that the villa belongs to him?'

'It doesn't. It belongs to the Chairman. But the Chairman doesn't like to hold properties in his name. This way is more discreet. The less people know, particularly down here, the better.'

'So, what would *you* like to know?' Chadwick asked.

'Well, *we* would like to know what happened to Maclean?'

Chadwick felt embarrassed and guilty. It had been the Chairman after all who had arranged for him to meet Maclean. 'All right. But it may not make sense to start there.'

'Start where you like. We've plenty of time.'

'Plenty of time?' I am not sure that you'll think we have plenty time when I finish, thought Chadwick, *but it doesn't matter. You need to know how Maclean died and why.*

'I asked the Chairman to find out about somebody called Aleksis Soldane, the second mate on the *Highland Laddie*, and when we last met, at the café, you gave me what you could find out.'

'The chap with the toothache.'

'It's him I've been trying to find.'

'Find? But he's dead.'

'He is dead. *Now*. He wasn't dead when I started to look for him. And he didn't die on the *Highland Laddie*. In fact, as far as I can tell, the *Highland Laddie* never sank.'

McGhee's coffee cup stopped abruptly, halfway between the table and his lips. He looked concerned. 'So, why are you so sure he is dead now?'

'Because I saw him. Or what was left of him, hanging up like a piece of meat. No, he's dead. There isn't much that I can be certain about in this affair, but I can be certain about that. The Russians caught up with him. Just like they caught up with Arcier and Maclean.'

'Who is Arcier?'

'Arcier is … was … a private detective. He was hired by Julija Soldane to find Aleksis Soldane.'

'And Julija Soldane is Mrs Soldane?'

Chadwick shook his head. 'No. She's his sister. She has been trying to find him ever since the *Highland Laddie* sank. She hired Arcier, and when he disappeared, she asked Verlaine and me to retrieve some papers that he had about the sinking.'

'And did you?'

'We tried. We went to his office, but it had been wrecked. We didn't find the papers, but we did find blood all over the walls.'

'And what about Verlaine? Where does he fit in?'

'He is a retired French cop. From Paris. He moved here when he retired.'

McGhee looked unconvinced. 'What did the police say?' he asked.

'Nothing. We never went to the police. I didn't want to involve them. I thought the whole thing was stupid. We were searching for a man who was already dead - apparently drowned. And Arcier was an unpleasant character who could have been mixed up in any number of shady dealings.'

McGhee raised his eyebrows but didn't comment. 'Did Arcier ever show up?'

'Yes, they pulled him out of the bay.'

'No water wings?'

'Apparently not.'

'Tell me about Maclean.'

'He left a message for me, and I called him. We met for lunch - in Nice. He was a pleasant man. I liked him.'

'I never met him,' said McGhee. 'What did he tell you?'

'Quite a lot about container ships and shipping in general. Plus some technical specifications for the *Highland Laddie* and information on the cargo it was carrying. He also said that the *Highland Laddie* had a sister ship called the *Highland Lassie*, owned by none other than Augustin, the casino owner.'

McGhee sat back for a second or two. 'That's quite a coincidence,' he said.

'Isn't it? Anyway, Maclean gave me the materials and left. He said that he had something that he needed to check. He didn't even say that it was related to the *Highland Laddie*. The last I heard from him was when he left me a message at the café the following day. By the time I received it, he was already dead. I had gone to the villa looking for the Chairman. The police picked me up there and took me to where Maclean was killed.'

'Why you?'

'They found a note on him with my name and instructions to contact me at the Sebastopol.'

'Did they give you a hard time?'

'No. That was what was so odd about the whole thing. The main man, an Inspector Prieul, was just getting into his stride when he was called off by a telephone call.'

'And he hasn't been in touch since?'

'Nope. Maclean was murdered and I was the only lead. But the police dropped me like I was radioactive. Anyway, I eventually worked out what Maclean had found in the cargo documents. There's a local company whose factory is very close to where Maclean was killed. I think he went there because he suspected that the machinery ordered from Asia wasn't at the bottom of the South China Sea. It was in the factory.'

'In the factory?'

'The hijackers contacted the managing director and offered to sell him the machines that he had lost - and that the insurers had paid him for - at a discount.

'He couldn't resist and then Humphrey Maclean approached him, asking if he could come to the factory to check some serial numbers on his machines, and he called the Russians.'

'Who do the Russians work for?'

'A man called Melnikov. He invited me to lunch and then gave me a tour of his boat.'

'So, what is his connection?'

'I suspect that he is in business with Augustin. But exactly how, I don't know.'

McGhee thought for a moment. 'You say that Humphrey Maclean was killed before he could confirm that the numbers on the machines in this factory were the same as the one on the *Highland Laddie*. There is only one problem I see with that. People pull scams like this in shipping all the time - have done forever, it's part of the business. Everybody accepts it. But nobody gets killed.'

'I agree. It's the bit of the puzzle that makes no sense *unless* it was to cover up the fact that the *Highland Laddie* didn't sink, that it's still around, operating under a different name.'

'And the crew?'

Chadwick grimaced. 'If I'm right, and I hope I'm not, the crew are all dead. Otherwise, how can they be sure that nobody will find out that the *Highland Laddie* is still operating? Which brings us back to Aleksis Soldane. He was very much alive. He must have known what happened to the *Highland Laddie* and, if he was the only crew member to survive, what would you expect him to do?'

'Go to the authorities.'

'Exactly. Go tell the police, the insurers, the newspapers. But he didn't, which means that he was either implicated or scared. But if he was scared, what was he doing here? Why didn't he just go hide somewhere in the Pacific? It's a big place. Nobody would bother looking for him. But he didn't. He came here - to Nice. Why would he do that unless he thought that whatever he was looking for was here?'

'Where was he looking?'

'That's just it. I think he was looking in all the same places I was looking. When I broke into the office of Augustin's shipping company —'

'That's a bit strong,' said McGhee, laughing.

'Augustin practically insisted that I visited them. I couldn't understand why at the time. I went, of course. Didn't learn much and decided to go back that evening.'

'And what did you learn then?'

'Not much more, I'm afraid. And when I was there, somebody else tried to break in.'

'And you think it was Soldane?'

'I didn't at the time, but I do now. You see, when I went out to see the factory owner who bought the machinery from the Russians, I was followed - by Soldane. I didn't notice immediately but when I did, I was able to follow him back to his apartment. I waited for a bit and then I went up to see him. That's when I discovered him dead.'

'When was that?'

Chadwick had to think. 'My God, it was only yesterday. It was last night, between 9 and 10 p.m. I had to leave in a hurry. The police arrived.'

'Tipped off?' asked McGhee.

'Almost certainly. Then I came back to the hotel. Well, you know the rest …'

McGhee thought for a moment. 'This Melnikov, what is his background?'

'Oligarch type, pretty well connected politically, I would guess. Highly intelligent, very disciplined. Cynical.'

'Where does Melnikov live?'

'On his boat.'

McGhee looked impressed. 'Proper,' he said, 'proper oligarch. Knows the job.' McGhee thought for a moment. 'Tell me, what do you make of Augustin? Why do you think he sent you to his shipping office? Odd thing to do if he is involved and trying to hide the fact that the *Highland Laddie* is still around.'

'Augustin is a bit of an enigma. He's a successful local businessman who has worked his way up from the wrong part of town. Would he have you roughed up if he caught you cheating at the casino? For sure. But he doesn't strike me as a murderer. I must go see him. I need him to tell me about his connection with Melnikov.'

'You had better be quick.'

'Why?'

McGhee poured himself another cup of coffee. 'You asked the Chairman about him and he did a bit of digging, here, and in Paris. With the wrong kind of people. There is a contract out on your chum - a big one. If I was him, I would fancy a wee break. New Zealand's nice this time of year.'

'Is the Chairman sure about this?'

'As sure as you can ever be about these things. Nobody posts it on Facebook.'

'I'll go see him later today, but I have some things I need to take care of first.'

'Like?'

'Like telling Soldane's sister that this time, her brother really is dead.'

McGhee sat back, his fingers interlaced, his hands resting on his chest. 'Hmmm. Not good. Not good at all. What can I do?'

'Find out what you can about Melnikov, especially any dealings he has with Augustin.'

'By when?'

'By this evening if you can do it. My sense is that we don't have much time,' said Chadwick.

'Why?' asked McGhee.

'Because Melnikov has been very aggressive, even careless. It's out of character. Look at Maclean's murder. It was rushed. Or the search of the marina last night? He's taking a lot of risks, which can only mean that the stakes are high, and time is getting short.

'There is one other thing that I would like you to do. Can you get somebody to look at all the voyages that the *Highland Lassie* has made in the past year, since the disappearance of the *Laddie*? Any information on the ports visited and her cargoes could be helpful. But most important of all – can you find out where she is now and where she is heading?'

'I hate to be the voice of reason – it's not really my *forte* – but is it very smart for you to hang around? We can get you out of France in an hour.'

Chadwick shook his head. 'I can't leave just yet. If I did, it would only confirm the local police's view that I'm guilty. Let's see what I can find out from Augustin and talk about it after that.'

'And the Russians? Won't they be watching this bloke's sister? Won't they be expecting you to try to contact her?'

'Yes. On both counts. And that's why I'm going to need your help. Do you have a car here?'

'Two streets away.'

'Good. Let's get the bill and go.'

CHAPTER THIRTY-SEVEN

Nobody said much. They drove to the cape and parked in a narrow street, close to the lighthouse. McGhee remained in the car while Julija and Chadwick took the steps to the coast path. He held her arm as they went down. The wind was blowing strongly from the sea. She turned towards it and stood for a moment or two without speaking, her face set like a statue, her hair pulled backwards by the constant wind. He suspected that she already knew, that she had known for some time, and that this was a charade, a meaningless piece of stage-craft whose only purpose was to fill the space between acts.

He waited patiently until she said, 'You've found him, haven't you?' He moved towards her and tried to pull her closer, but she resisted. 'He's dead, isn't he?' He loosened his grip and nodded. She pulled her arm free and walked away from him. He followed her until she stopped again. Her back to him, her arms folded, she said, 'Did you see him?'

'Yes'

'How did he die?'

'He was stabbed.'

He knew what was coming and tried to block the image of Soldane's bleeding corpse from his mind.

She thought about this for a moment or two before turning towards him, looking him directly in the eye, daring him to lie.

'How bad was it?'

'Not great. Don't ask me any more questions about it because I'm not going to answer them. There's no point.'

She was facing him but looking at a point in the distance as if he weren't there. He held out his arms, but she wanted no part of him. It was almost as if she blamed him for her brother's death.

She said, 'Do you know who did it?'

'Yes. Maybe not the individuals but I know who ordered it.'

'Who?'

'Melnikov. The Russian.'

She looked puzzled. 'What was my brother doing with him?'

'I don't know.'

'Do you know why Aleksis came here?'

'No. That is still a mystery. I've been trying to find out but it's not easy. I am pretty sure it's something to do with *Highland Laddie* - but I don't know what.'

'What are you going to do next?'

'I'm not sure. Try to get some more information. Try to stay out of the hands of the police. And try not to get killed.'

She looked startled. 'Killed?'

'It's not just your brother they murdered. I'm pretty sure they killed Arcier and a man called Maclean, a man who came to give me some information on the *Highland Laddie.*'

He watched her as she absorbed this. She was tough. Tougher than he had imagined.

'I can't believe it,' she said. 'What was Aleksis doing with these people?' She looked at him as if she was only now beginning to real-ise the danger they were in. 'You need to be careful,' she said.

'We *all* need to be careful. That includes you. I'm afraid you can't go back to your apartment.'

'Why not?'

'Because, sooner or later, they'll come looking for you. We were lucky that they weren't already there. So, no apartment. You need to find Verlaine and get him to take you out of here. It doesn't matter where, as long as nobody knows where you've gone. He'll know what to do.'

She shook her head. 'It won't work.' Her tone was matter of fact. 'Why?'

'Verlaine has disappeared. I haven't been able to contact him for days.'

Disconcerted, Chadwick said, 'When did you last see him?'

'In the café. The day you went to Nice.'

'When I went to see Maclean or when I went to see the shipping office?'

'When you went to see Maclean. I remember because we were all together and you ran off, saying you were going to the hotel.'

'You haven't seen him since then? And he didn't say anything?'

'Nothing. I went looking for him a couple of times. He wasn't in but I didn't think anything of it at the time. But now … now, it looks more serious.' She paused and asked, 'Do you think we can trust him?'

Chadwick grimaced. 'I don't know. I never thought about it before. I suppose so.'

'You don't think he could still be working for the police?'

Her toughness had gone, and she looked anxious. He reached for her, and this time, she accepted. He held her close, although it seemed only to reinforce his guilt. She rested her head on his shoulders and repeated her question.

'I don't think so. I think he is genuinely retired. He is too old to still be with the police. There must be some other explanation.'

'But why leave without telling us that he was going?'

He didn't bother replying. He was tired of trying to find explanations to comfort others that only made him look like a liar or a fool. Verlaine's disappearance worried him, and he had no idea what it might mean. Right now, his only concern was to get Julija to safety, but he needed to find somewhere for her to go.

She read his thoughts. 'Why don't I stay with you?'

'Because I am going into town. And while the Russians might miss me, they're hardly likely to miss both of us, are they?'

'So why don't I stay with McGhee?

'That won't work. I need him to do some things for me today which can't wait.'

'Then I'll stay here. I'll wait for you to finish and then we can go away.'

He thought for a moment. 'Look, I have an idea. There is a place in the countryside. A farm. It belongs to a friend of mine. You can wait there and I will come and pick you up this evening.'

'How will I get there?'

'McGhee will drive you.'

Julija was looking at him suspiciously. 'Who is this friend?' she asked.

'You'll find out when you meet her.'

'Tell me who she is?'

'It doesn't matter.'

She pulled away from him, her face darkening. Any warmth between them had disappeared. 'Yes, it matters,' she said. 'It matters to me. Tell me who she is, or I am not going.'

Chadwick realised he had no option. 'It belongs to a woman called Silje.'

Julija smirked, as if he had only confirmed what she had already suspected. 'I *know* who she is,' she said. 'She is the one with Melnikov. Why would you send me *there*?'

Chadwick struggled not to show his frustration. He needed her to cooperate. He had more important priorities than looking after Julija. He said, 'She is not *with* Melnikov. Not in the way you mean. She's okay. You'll be safe there. She'll look after you and I'll pick you up there this evening.'

'How do you know that I'll be safe there? Why are you so sure that we can trust her?' Chadwick was about to explain and then thought better of it. The less he told Julija about Silje, the better.

'We can trust her. She may not like it much, but she'll look after you.'

Julija looked him in the eye. What was she hoping to find out? That he was lying? That his relationship with Silje was closer than he was letting on? He prepared himself for a lengthy argument but instead, she appeared to concede. *Perhaps she is more frightened than she is letting on*, he thought. Wrapping her arms around him, she said, 'You'll come for me tonight. You're sure?'

'I'll be there. Don't worry.'

'And you'll be careful?'

'I'll be careful. They haven't got me yet.'

'I know but that doesn't mean anything.'

He couldn't disagree with that. He was glad that she hadn't asked him for his plan. Because what there was, wasn't worth discussing. If he couldn't find Augustin, or if he found Augustin and he wouldn't talk, then he had nothing. Nothing at all. He would be no further forward except that he would have to face an angry Silje later that evening. But better an angry Silje than no Silje at all.

They spoke only once on their way back up the steps. She stopped and turned towards him. She hesitated - it was uncharacteristic.

'I want you to find the men who killed Aleksis,' she said. 'And when you find them … when you find them, I want you to kill them.' She stared at him, defying him to argue. He said nothing, but took her by the arm and walked her slowly up the remainder of the steps. He was shaken by her vehemence but tried not to show it. It seemed out of character. But what was her character? How could he claim to know? If character was only revealed in adversity, then this was it. The thought depressed him and left him feeling more isolated than ever.

When he explained his plan to McGhee, he could see that he was sceptical. Chadwick had him call a taxi. There was no point in taking more of McGhee's time by asking for a lift into town. Besides, he was happy to be alone; even though McGhee was easy company, Julija was not.

McGhee waited until Julija was safely in the car with the doors closed.

'Where is the meet tonight?' he asked.

'At the villa. We'll drive to Silje's farm together.'

'Done,' was McGhee's only response. He got into the car and drove away without another word.

CHAPTER THIRTY-EIGHT

Chadwick had the taxi driver drop him some distance from the casino. He found a café opposite the casino and watched the main entrance. He was reluctant to use it - the risks were too high. There were just too many people looking for him.

It took all his self-control not to overreact when he felt the hand on his shoulder. He put down his cup and turned his head. It was the waitress from the casino.

'I see you've added stalking to your other misdemeanours,' she said.

'I needed a hobby and polo was too expensive.'

'What would you like me to do this time?'

'How do you know I'm going to ask you for anything?'

'So far, it's been the foundation of our relationship. It's a bit like being married, but without the security. What is it you want, or is this just a coincidence?'

'Do you believe in coincidences?'

'No.'

'Then I'd better tell you what I want.' He pulled out a chair from the table and she sat down. 'Would you like something?' She pointed to a takeaway coffee that she held in her left hand.

'You are a bit of a disappointment as a stalker. Don't you know my habits by now?'

'I'm still learning how to be a stalker,' said Chadwick. 'It's not as easy as you might think.' He paused. 'I need you to let me into the casino again, through the side door.'

She didn't miss a beat. It was as if she had been expecting it. 'And who are you visiting this time? Mr Augustin? Should I ask whether he is expecting you?'

'You can ask anything you want, and I'll tell you.'

'Is Augustin in trouble?'

Chadwick sat up. 'Why do you ask?'

'More security. Locals. People he knows from the old days.'

'Interesting. Maybe he heard there were too many men trying to chat up his best-looking waitress?'

'He would hardly mind that. That's pretty much in my job description. But I can't help you. At least, not with the side door. Or any door for that matter. One of the reasons the security has been increased is to have two of them on every door.'

'Can you get to Augustin?'

'Of course.'

'I need to see him. Through the side door would be best because I know it.'

'You don't ask for much,' she said sarcastically. She looked at her watch. 'I'm late for my shift. If I do this, am I going to get fired?'

'I don't think so. You're just doing what I asked you to do.'

'Okay. If he asks if you threatened me, I'll tell him you proposed marriage.'

She got up. 'Give me ten minutes, and then go to the side door. If the security guys signal to you, you are in.'

'And if they don't?'

'Start walking home.'

'You still haven't given me your name.'

'You can read it on the marriage certificate.'

The waitress hadn't exaggerated the increase in security. The man with a quarry where his face ought to have been was still there, standing beside the doors to Augustin's office like a souvenir from Petra. But now he had company. Somebody had dragged a heavy mahogany desk across the hallway that led to Augustin's office. It must have taken a bit of dragging, unless you were built like the two men who were sitting behind it. They appeared as hard and competent as any men Chadwick had seen. The drawers of the desk were partially open, and it had been positioned so that it commanded a view over the grand staircase. He didn't speculate about what was in the partially open drawers. If you asked two former legionnaires to guard the entrance to your office, you knew it wouldn't be by charm and good looks. It would be suicide to try to storm Augustin's office using those stairs. All he could hope was that the Russians would give it a try.

Chadwick was surprised by how happy he was to see Augustin again. Augustin, for his part, treated him as an old friend. He took Chadwick by the arm and led him towards the sofas. He noticed that the curtains were drawn and the lights on even though it was still light outside. Augustin's desk had been moved away from the window to the other side of the room. Chadwick pointed towards it. 'Problem with the sun bleaching the wood?'

Augustin smiled. 'Something like that. We must all do what we can to preserve those things we hold most dear.'

'Like life?'

'I see you are, as usual, well informed.'

'Don't say that. I was probably the last to know. I've been rather busy.'

'I've heard. Would you like some tea or would you prefer something stronger?'

'I would prefer something stronger, but I fear that if I started drinking, I wouldn't stop.'

Chadwick waited while Augustin ordered tea. 'Tell me,' he said, 'what have you heard?'

Augustin smiled. He opened the cigar box and selected a cigar. Clipping the end, he lit it with a long match, took a puff or two, and sat back.

'I've heard that you've been irritating our local police.'

'How? By not confessing to murder?'

Augustin smiled. 'Partly. Inspector Prieul is apparently very upset. I don't blame him. By mid-morning, he has a murder to investigate. By mid-afternoon, he has the likely killer, but by early evening, he is told to let him go. The life of a policeman must be very frustrating, don't you think?'

'Does anybody seriously think I killed Maclean?'

Augustin shrugged. 'I doubt it. Maybe Prieul and his brainless sidekick but nobody else. But, from what I understand, they are pretty upset at being told to leave you alone.'

'Will they leave me alone?' asked Chadwick.

Augustin tilted his head and blew smoke towards the ceiling. 'Oh, yes. They will. It has been made very clear to them that if they don't, they'll be checking vehicle registration plates for the rest of their careers.'

'It's you that is well informed. Is Prieul one of yours?'

Augustin looked amused. He carefully tipped some ash into the ash tray. 'My dear Chadwick, what *are* you suggesting? How very shocking. *Of course not.* I would be embarrassed if he were. Prieul has no real power or information. If I only contributed to the welfare plans of men like Prieul, I would be broke, and no wiser. No, if you really want to know what is going on, you must go quite a lot higher than Prieul.'

'Which you did?'

'Which I did. And what I learned was interesting. In your previous life, or lives, you must have made friends with some powerful people in Paris.'

'If I did, I wasn't aware of it,' said Chadwick. 'Why?'

'The order to leave you alone came from very high. Much higher than any of my provincial sources can reach. But that's all I could find out. I'm no wiser about why the authorities wanted you dropped from Prieul's investigation.'

Chadwick was impressed. No wonder Prieul was upset. But why would the French government be interested in him? The tea arrived. Chadwick noticed that one of the guards came into the room and watched the maid arrange it. When she had finished, he followed her out. Augustin caught his eye.

'You think I am being overzealous?'

'With the security?' Chadwick shook his head. 'No, I don't think it's possible to be overzealous with this gang.'

'What gang?' Augustin looked blank.

'Augustin, I am not the police. I have nothing to do with the authorities. Tell me, are we only here to drink tea and tell lies to each other, or are we here to try to fix this?'

Augustin thought for a moment. He said, 'Do you remember what I told you? In this room. When we first met.'

'You told me a lot of things, mainly, as far as I can remember, that the South of France was a tricky place and that I had no chance of being left alone. You were right about that.'

'I wonder. Or did you deliberately get yourself involved? Perhaps if you had stayed in your hotel and read your books, you might be there now, enjoying the solitude?'

'I take your point. I also remember your saying in this room, *"I shouldn't like to give this up."* You don't strike me as somebody who is about to retire. So, who is trying to take it away from you? Melnikov?'

Augustin made a great play of noticing that his cigar was out, leaned forward, took another match from the wooden box on the table, relit his cigar and returned to his previous position, sitting well back in the sofa, watching Chadwick as a child might watch a conjurer. 'You know you have a gift for this,' he said. 'For somebody so apparently innocent, you have a nose for the dirtier aspects of life.'

'Is Melnikov behind the contract?'

Augustin pondered this. 'Not exactly. Or rather, not directly. Of course, it is what he wants. There is absolutely no honour amongst thieves, but it is hard to do any business if you acquire a reputation for killing your partners and stealing their assets.'

'Who is behind it then?'

'Probably the people behind Melnikov. The ones who backed and continue to back him. The ones who helped him get rich, and in return got rich too.'

'Why do they want the casino?'

Augustin laughed out loud. 'I wish they did. Why would they want the casino? It barely breaks even. No, they don't want the casino - they'll take it - just like they'll take the properties - but what they really want is the *Highland Lassie*.'

Chadwick decided to ask the question that had been bothering him from the beginning. He said, 'Why did you decide to team up with Melnikov in the first place?'

Augustin looked rueful. 'It wasn't by choice. I may be ambitious, but I am not so naïve as to ask Melnikov to be my business partner. I needed money to buy and refurbish the casino. So, I borrowed heavily. Not from the nicest people, I admit, but I had borrowed from them before and knew I could handle them. It was all fine, until one day, Melnikov appeared in my office and announced that he was my new banker.'

'He had bought the debts?'

'All of them. And the loans could be called in on demand. I wasn't in a position to refinance them, so he became my new part-ner whether I liked it or not.'

'To get hold of the *Highland Lassie*?'

'Yes.'

'Did he tell you to change the officers?'

Augustin looked at him in admiration. 'How did you find that out?'

'I did some research.'

'In Compagnie Loudoun's offices? I am surprised you had time.

You need to go on some training courses for burglary. There are some people here I could introduce you to.'

'I had plenty time. Since you so kindly arranged for me to visit, I made a point of leaving a window unlocked. It wasn't me who smashed your door.'

Augustin looked surprised. 'What do you mean?'

'There was a second break in,' said Chadwick. 'Or rather, an attempted break in. He ran off when the alarm went off.'

Augustin, concerned at this new development, sat forward. 'Do you know who it was?' he asked.

'I think so,' said Chadwick, 'but I can't know for certain for reasons I'll tell you about in a minute. Let's get back to the officers on the *Highland Lassie*,' he continued. 'Who recommended the new ones? Melnikov?'

'No. They usually came through Kataev.'

'Who is Kataev?'

'He is the short, broadly-built man that you usually see some-where around Melnikov.'

Chadwick knew immediately who he meant. 'Baseball cap?'

'That's him. You would do well to stay away from him.'

'I've been trying. It's not so easy. He's pretty relentless.'

'He's an animal. He thinks and acts like an animal. He is cunning and very dangerous.'

Chadwick wasn't about to disagree. Even discussing Kataev made him feel uneasy. He returned to his original question. 'What was the point of replacing the officers?'

'I'm not sure. I assume they wanted more control. It's not very clear. It's not as if the Captain and crew can decide where the ship goes. It depends on the cargoes and the cargoes depend on the shippers.'

'Where does the *Highland Lassie* typically operate?'

'Almost always in Europe; sometimes as far as North Africa. Between the Baltic and the Mediterranean mostly.'

'And there has been no change of routes since the officers were changed?'

'No. Nothing has changed. That's what makes it so odd.'

'What do you know about the new officers?'

'Not very much. They have mostly worked out of the Russian ports on the Baltic. And that's not necessarily a good recommendation.'

'Why?'

'Those ports are well known for smuggling. The authorities are easily persuaded to look the other way.'

'Interesting. What did Melnikov tell you to do with the *Highland Lassie?*'

'Nothing. Absolutely nothing. He never discussed it and I never brought it up. In fact, he never discussed any aspect of my business with me.'

'Except when he wanted to be paid off?'

Augustin raised his eyebrows, his face a picture of fleshy innocence.

'It was meant for Melnikov,' said Chadwick. 'The money that the English girl won.'

Augustin inspected the ash at the end of his cigar. 'Indirectly, I suppose. But I can't blame Melnikov. I was behind on my payments to him and needed some cash. It seemed harmless enough. I wasn't expecting you to show up. You must try to curb your humanitarian instincts. They'll only get you into trouble.'

'I've noticed. It's not been the most relaxing holiday I've ever had.'

Augustin changed tack. 'Tell me about the murders.'

'There's not too much to say about the first, a man called Arcier. I'm sure you knew of him, even if you didn't know him. His body was washed up on the beach, not far from your window. He was a former policeman turned private detective. He was hired to look for one of the crew of the *Highland Laddie.* I think he found him but decided it would be more profitable to sell his whereabouts to the Russians than report back to his client. Maybe he was stupid enough to try to put the squeeze on them? Whatever he did, he ended up dead.'

'I do remember him from his time in the police,' said Augustin. 'It would have been completely in character. What about the quarry murder? The one that is in the newspapers?'

'That was a man called Humphrey Maclean who was the Lloyd's agent for this part of France. I was put in touch with him and he gave me the technical specifications of the *Highland Laddie* and its cargo manifest. We had lunch, and when I left him, he mentioned that he had one other thing that he needed to follow up locally. I think he discovered that some of the machine tools on the *Highland Laddie* were ordered by a local company, tried to get hold of me and couldn't, so went to see the company on his own. The Russians either waited for him there or intercepted him *en route*, took him to the top of the quarry, and threw him off.'

'Kataev?'

'Probably.'

'What were they so worried about?' Augustin's face had disappeared in a grey cloud of cigar smoke. He waved it away.

'Maclean wanted to check the number on the machine tools from the *Highland Laddie's* manifest with the numbers on the machines in the company's factory.'

'Ah! Now I see. Did *you* manage to check them?'

'No. But the managing director admitted that he had been offered, and bought, the machines that supposedly were at the bottom of the South China Sea.'

Augustin leaned back in the sofa and blew smoke at the ceiling. He thought for a bit and then said, 'So the *Highland Laddie* didn't sink – at least, not when it was supposed to have done?'

'Apparently not.'

'Any more killings?'

'The man that Arcier was supposed to find - and may indeed *have* found. A crew member of the *Highland Laddie*.'

'And what was he doing here?'

'That's a very good question. Latterly, mostly following me. I *think* he was the one who broke into your office. I *know* he followed me when I went to the factory to meet the man who bought the machines from the Russians. That's when I got onto him and tracked him to his apartment. But, by the time I got to him, he was dead. The Russians, almost certainly Kataev, got there before me.' He paused. 'It wasn't a pretty sight.'

'I'm sure. And then?'

'While I was still in the apartment, the police arrived outside, and I got out over the roofs. Then, Kataev and his crew came looking for me at the hotel, and I had to swim for it. I was lucky to get away.'

'You were. I don't think too many people escape Kataev. Tell me, do you think the Russians tipped off the police?'

'Almost certainly. I think they wanted me to be caught in the apartment.'

'They must have been following you too.'

Chadwick was taken aback. 'What do you mean?'

'Perhaps you led the Russians to this man? It can hardly be a coincidence that as soon as you find him, he is killed, and a short time later, the police arrive.'

Chadwick felt suddenly cold. Augustin had to be correct. He *must* have led Kataev to Soldane. There was no other explanation. The Russians must have gone straight to Soldane's apartment and killed him while Chadwick was in the brasserie.

Augustin interrupted his thinking. 'Did you ever find out why this man came here?'

'No. Except that it had to be something to do with the *Highland Lassie* - otherwise why try to break into your shipping office? And, whatever he was looking for, it was important enough for Melnikov to murder three people. I may be wrong, but I don't think Melnikov kills unless it is unavoidable. Murders cause too many ripples and leave too many dangerous loose ends. I can only assume that he had no choice - that whatever he is planning, is very close - and he can't afford the risk of it being uncovered.'

'I agree with you about Melnikov. He moves cautiously and doesn't put himself at risk if he can avoid it. *Either* whatever is planned is very close, *or* so important that a mistake will cost him his head.'

'It could be both,' said Chadwick.

'It could be,' said Augustin, brushing some cigar ash off the leg of his trousers, 'But let's assume, for the moment, that Melnikov has been the architect of everything that has happened - that he has been responsible for everything from the hijacking of the *Highland Laddie* to your involvement.'

'My involvement? How could he possibly be responsible for that?'

Augustin blew out a cloud of cigar smoke. He looked surprised at the question. 'If he has orchestrated everything else, why couldn't he have manipulated you? Remember, he already knew about you before he asked me to invite you to lunch.'

Chadwick thought about it. Augustin pressed the point. 'If we re-examine everything that has happened on the assumption that Melnikov was behind it, how would it change things?'

Chadwick could see the logic. 'All right. So, let's start at the beginning. Why did he pick the *Highland Laddie* out of all the other ships in the world? Let's assume that it was the right type of ship for whatever it was he wanted to do. Now, what else distinguished it?'

'It had a sister ship.'

'Exactly. Not only did it have a sister ship, but the sister ship was owned by an over-extended casino owner who owed money to the wrong type of people. When did he buy the loan notes?'

'Just before the *Highland Laddie* was hijacked. What do you make of that?'

'It makes sense. It would have been foolish to move on the *Highland Laddie* until you could be sure of controlling the *Highland Lassie*.

'The *over-extended* casino owner agrees.'

'Sorry.'

'Why be sorry? It's true. But why would he need both ships?'

'I have a theory. I have no idea whether it will stand up from a technical perspective, but it is the only explanation that I can think of that fits what we know.'

Augustin sat forward on the sofa. He was listening carefully.

'Let's assume that Melnikov or Melnikov's sponsors in Russia want to move some cargo from Russia to, say, North Africa. It doesn't matter what the cargo is, but it's illegal, seriously illegal, and it's worth a great deal of money. Otherwise, why go to the trouble of finding the two ships? But moving anything that is large enough to require a ship is going to attract attention. It's going to be very hard to keep it secret. There will be just too many people involved. Also, ships move slowly. They are at sea for a long time. If anybody suspects that you are shipping something illegal, they can track and board the ship whenever it suits them.

'But Melnikov is smart. He looks at the "problems" and turns them to his advantage. First, he assumes that he will be tracked. That somebody, somewhere, will notice what he is doing and come after him, either to confiscate or steal the cargo - it doesn't matter.

'So, this is what he does. He sends the *Highland Laddie* - now re-named - let's call it *Nemo* - to pick up the illegal cargo in Russia. The cargo is officially listed as something innocuous, and he files that it is heading to an equally mundane port.

'Meanwhile, the *Highland Lassie* is loaded with the same innocuous cargo that *Nemo* claims to be carrying, at a nearby port to the *Nemo,* but files a route to a much more controversial location.

'Both ships leave but the *Nemo* is being tracked by AIS, and possibly for all I know, by satellite. At some point, probably at night or in poor visibility, the ships cross and reprogramme their AIS systems. *Nemo* becomes the *Highland Lassie* and vice-versa. And the crews change the names of the ships - that is the only thing they need to do because otherwise, the ships are identical. Then, the *Nemo* operating as the *Highland Lassie* drops its cargo in the controversial port, while the *Highland Lassie* masquerading as the *Nemo* drops the innocuous cargo in the mundane port under the surveillance of whoever is tracking them. On the way back, the ships cross again and the names are reversed.'

Augustin whistled softly. 'You have to be right. It must be something like this. Otherwise, why do you need two identical ships?'

'Where is the *Highland Lassie* currently?'

'She is in the Baltic, loading timber to go to Algeria.'

'Maybe she is. But if I'm correct, something is going to Algeria and it's not likely to be timber.'

Augustin looked troubled. He got up and walked up and down.

'You don't agree with my hypothesis?' asked Chadwick.

Augustin looked over at him. 'No, I think you're right. It's some of the other pieces that worry me. Tell me again about the third murder. Who was this man?'

'He was called Aleksis Soldane and he was the Second Mate on the *Highland Laddie*.'

'And why were *you* looking for him?'

'Because his sister asked me to help find him.'

Augustin looked perplexed. 'And how did she know that he wasn't dead with the others? Did he contact her?'

'No. She just always thought that he was still alive. That's why, in the beginning, I thought it was a waste of time.'

Augustin was standing still, deep in thought. He appeared to have stopped listening.

'Under what circumstances could this man have survived?' he said. 'Did he hide on the ship and then flee when it reached port? Very unlikely. Melnikov would know the number of crew on board and would surely have found him. The only possible explanation is that he was involved with the hijackers, that he was one of them, but then why show up here?' Augustin shook his head slowly. 'No, I'm afraid that if this operation is as secret and as valuable as we think, then the crew of the *Highland Laddie* are dead – including Mr Soldane.'

'But you are forgetting that I saw him – alive and dead.'

Augustin chose his words carefully. 'I don't doubt that you saw someone – I doubt whether it was Aleksis Soldane. How did you know it was him?'

'From a photograph,' said Chadwick.

'Passport photograph?' asked Augustin.

'No.' Chadwick was beginning to feel uneasy in the face of Augustin's unerring logic.

Augustin thought for a moment or two. 'Who gave you this photograph?'

'His sister.'

'And how did you meet this sister?'

'Through a man called Verlaine, a retired French policeman.'

'From here?'

'From Paris.'

'And where is Verlaine now?'

'I don't know. He seems to have disappeared.'

Augustin gave Chadwick a worried look. It was clear that he was concerned. 'And the sister?'

'The Russians were likely to come after her. I picked her up this morning and sent her somewhere safe.'

'May I ask where?'

Chadwick hesitated. Augustin had good reason to hate Melnikov but that didn't mean he gave a damn about what happened to

Chadwick or anybody else. Augustin sensed that he was uncomfortable and pressed the point. 'I asked you earlier whether you might have been manipulated by Melnikov, and you said not. Are you still as confident as you were?'

Chadwick said, 'I sent her to Silje's place out in the country.'

'Why?' asked Augustin. 'Why would you send her there?'

'Because I thought she would be safe there. And, even if she doesn't like it, Silje will keep her mouth shut. You know her - she won't give her up to Melnikov.'

'That's not what I'm worried about,' said Augustin. He walked towards the desk and picked up the receiver. He studied Chadwick carefully as he listened to it ring. It was impossible to tell what he was thinking. There was no reply. He replaced the receiver and dialled again. After thirty seconds, he put the phone down. 'There is no reply either at the farm or on Silje's mobile.'

Chadwick stood up. Now he was seriously alarmed. 'I'll go out there now. I'm sure there isn't a problem.'

Augustin looked unconvinced. He stood for a moment or two, his fingers tapping the leather top of the *bureau plat*. He looked at Chadwick as if he were about to speak, but instead, he walked towards one of the walls, where he pressed one of the panels. It sprang open to reveal a large safe. Removing a drawer from the safe, and placing it on the table in front of Chadwick, he pulled open the hinged lid. Inside were several pistols and boxes of ammunition.

'Take what you want,' said Augustin. 'I think you might need it.'

Chadwick picked up a Glock, two spare magazines and a box of bullets. Augustin watched him as he walked towards the office door.

'Don't come back without her,' was all he said.

CHAPTER THIRTY-NINE

The house was silhouetted against the sky. The wind had dropped, it had stopped raining and the moon was almost full. There were no lights visible. Chadwick approached the back of the house from the fields, heading towards the far end, and Silje's studio.

He started to cross a makeshift bridge over a drainage ditch. The two rotting planks laid next to each other were dug into the earth on either side. The planks were wet, covered in moss and he crossed cautiously. Looking down, he could see an old sack or a coat lying discarded at the bottom of the trench. Taking out his penlight, he bent down to examine it. He only turned the penlight on for a second, but it seemed like an age. It was Oskar, Silje's dog. They hadn't even bothered to shoot him. Just battered him to death and thrown him in the ditch.

He replayed the conversation with Augustin. He had liked all of it, until the end, until Augustin suggested that if Soldane wasn't Soldane, then, perhaps Julija Soldane might not be his sister. But if she wasn't Soldane's sister, then who was she?

He felt sick, partly from what he had seen and partly for what it meant. There could be no more pretending. The time for pretending was over. Too many people were dead. The Office was right to let him go. He was a liability, a danger to others, responsible for a chain of deaths that led from North Africa to here. Deaths that could have been avoided if only he had listened. And now others might die because of his naïvety. It was time he accepted responsibility for what he had done and time to accept the consequences of what he was about to do. There would be more deaths on his conscience but there could be no turning back. Every decision he had made since North Africa had been inevitable, as if he had been brought to this point by some greater force moving in a pattern that he could not discern. He was surprised to feel no anger. Anger would have sustained him and driven him forward. Anger would have justified what he had to do. But he was denied anger. He had only a weariness that had been growing since Samira's death, and which now threatened to envelop him. It was like a slow-acting poison that he couldn't counter and for which there was no antidote.

He reached for the Glock, checked it, and walked towards the stairs that led to Silje's studio. Ten minutes later, he was back at the taxi. The house was empty. They were gone. Melnikov had them.

It took a considerable sum, and a little less than an hour, to locate the *Lara*. The taxi driver called the dispatcher, who in turn, asked the other drivers. Several confirmed seeing the *Lara* off Cap d'Antibes in the late afternoon and in the early evening. But it was almost 11 p.m. by the time the taxi reached the cape, long past his rendezvous with McGhee.

The driver turned to him with a look of triumph. He pointed towards the sea. 'Look,' he said, 'you can see the lights in the distance, off the end of the cape. We've found her.'

'Not we. You did.' Chadwick paid him generously, too generously, but he wanted to be sure that if he didn't come back, somebody would remember where he went.

'Would you like me to stay? I can wait for you.'

'No. It's fine. Thank you.' Then he had a thought. 'Perhaps there is something that you could do for me? Could you deliver a note to a house in Boulevard du Générale de Gaulle in Cap-Ferrat?'

'Of course.'

'There is a man there called McGhee. Just give him this note. That's all.'

He scribbled a few words explaining where he was and what he was about to do, folded the paper twice, and handed it to the driver. He shivered as he gave it across. He saw the same piece of paper, unfolded and sealed in a clear plastic envelope. Across the top of the envelope, was a typed label.

Exhibit: Note from Chadwick to McGhee

He tried to put it out of his mind. He was only feeling sorry for himself. *Stop feeling maudlin and get moving.*

He waited until the taxi had left the small car park before starting. Immediately in front of him, a low pier stretched out into the sea. It had no practical purpose in the winter. In the summer, it provided additional real estate for sun bathers - their beds rented from the restaurant that lay to his right. Beyond the restaurant was the beginning of Cap d'Antibes.

There were few lights visible on the cape, the houses still closed for the season. To his left, he could see the amber glow that was a distant Nice. He checked the car park and the dock. He hadn't been hopeful, and he wasn't disappointed. There were no boats of any kind. He went to a rubbish bin, detached the plastic bin liner and emptied its contents. Turning it inside out, he put the Glock, the spare magazines, the box of bullets and his clothes inside. He tied it carefully, ensuring that it would be waterproof and buoyant. Then he waded into the water and began swimming.

There were only three possible points of entry to the *Lara*. The first, and easiest, was the platform at the stern. But it was too obvious, too likely to be alarmed, and even if he could get on board without being noticed, he would need to pass the engine room and the crew's quarters. The second, the steps used to land from the tender, were likely guarded, if they hadn't been dismantled and stowed. No, the safest point of entry was inevitably the most difficult.

The water was as cold as before, but the sea was calm. He could see the *Lara* clearly now and was relieved that the lights that lit the hull from underneath were off, and the other lights that floodlit the superstructure were turned down for the night. He swam slowly, checking the decks and the bridge. The bridge was in near darkness.

He swam towards the bow. When he reached the anchor chain, he waited for a minute or two to recover his breath before he stretched for the highest link he could reach and, crossing his feet to trap the chain between them, began to climb. It took him very little time to reach the hawsehole. He squeezed through it and kept crawling across the foredeck until he found some shadow. There, he emptied the contents of the bag, pulled on his clothes and put on his shoes. He stuck the two spare magazines in one pocket and the box of bullets in the other. He was dripping water, leaving a wet trail across the deck, but it couldn't be helped.

He was sure that Melnikov would be holding Silje and Julija away from the crew. The design of the *Lara,* and Melnikov's desire to be apart from the crew, meant they were most likely in the forward part of the ship. The higher decks would bring him closer to the bridge and increase the risk of running into a member of the crew. So, he would start with the lower decks and work upwards.

He stood and walked down the starboard promenade deck. It was well lit and there was no point in trying to hide. If he met somebody, he would need to brazen it out. There was no other option. He reached the door to the hallway, the lift and the stairs. Entering, he closed the door and listened. It was quiet. He started down the stairs, moving silently, the thick carpeting absorbing his footfalls. He reached the next deck and paused outside the double doors leading to Melnikov's cabin. There was no sound from inside.

He continued down the next flight of stairs until he reached the deck with Sasha's cabin and the cabin where he had changed after the tender incident. He stood between the doors to the two cabins, listening for any sounds of life. If they were here, it would be the spare cabin. He held the Glock in his right hand and slowly turned the door handle. He opened the door a fraction. The cabin was dark. He stopped the door from closing with his right foot and reached for his penlight. Using his foot, he opened the door another few centimetres and shone the penlight across the floor towards the bed and the entrance to the bathroom. It only took a second or two before he saw her. She was lying on the floor on her side, facing away from him, her hands and feet tied. He shone the torch into the far corners of the cabin. Satisfied, he went into the cabin, closed the door behind him, and reached for the light switch. As the lights came on, his last memory was of the floor rushing to meet his face. And then it was dark.

He became conscious of two different sensations. The first, and most intense, was a pain in his skull, which radiated down his spine and outwards to his arms and legs. The second was a repeated thumping on his chest which seemed to be pushing him backwards. He was too tired to care. All he wanted was to be left alone. A voice was calling to him. It was very far away. So far away that he wondered why it bothered. He wished it would stop so that he could sleep. But it wouldn't stop. It kept calling his name. The way his mother did when she wanted him to come down from the hills. The thumps to his chest moved lower and he felt himself short of breath as if the air had been sucked out of him. He gasped and inhaled as much air as he could, his eyes now wide open. The cabin was completely black.

'Chadwick!'

He sensed somebody moving close to him and almost immediately, he received another kick.

'Silje?'

'Yes. Listen to me. They will be coming back very soon. Kataev only went to get Melnikov.'

'How long have I been unconscious?'

'Shut up. There is no time. Let me deal with Melnikov, understand? I'll be fine. I can talk my way out of it. Look after yourself and remember what I told you in the studio …' She stopped talking as the door began to open. The lights came on and he closed his eyes.

He heard somebody cry out and realised that it was him. After the initial shock of the pain began to recede, he realised that he had been kicked in the kidneys. Nauseous, he forced himself to concentrate and opened his eyes. Melnikov was sitting on the edge of the bed, his hands tucked under his thighs. Chadwick turned his head. Kataev was standing several paces behind him. Chadwick couldn't think why. He was hardly a threat. His hands and feet were bound with plasticuffs.

Chadwick turned his attention to Melnikov, who looked bored. He signalled to Kataev, who stepped around Chadwick and pulled Silje to a sitting position. She ignored Kataev and stared straight at Melnikov, without speaking. Melnikov jerked his head and Kataev picked up Silje under the arms and began to drag her to the door. Still, she said nothing. Chadwick was about to speak but thought better of it. He was witnessing a private struggle between them about which he knew nothing. She had said that she could deal with him, and he must let her. Besides, there was nothing he could do except shout insults and get kicked as a result. Chadwick heard the cabin door open and close.

Melnikov stared into space, lost in thought, his grim demeanour turned to stone. After some time, he took off his glasses and rubbed his eyes. Replacing his glasses, he looked at Chadwick, as if he had just noticed that he was lying on the floor.

'I should congratulate you. You have been much more successful than I could ever have hoped,' said Melnikov. 'Unfortunately, all success comes with a cost - for you and for me. Tell me, what did you hope to achieve by coming on board?'

Chadwick sensed an opening. If Melnikov was asking questions, it was because he still wasn't entirely sure what Chadwick knew.

'I came to find Julija,' he said, deliberately making no mention of Silje.

'Did you?' said Melnikov. He took off his glasses and held them up to the light to inspect them. 'But instead, you found Silje.'

'Did I? I didn't know who I had found because as soon as I came into the cabin, your boy decided to administer a Russian anaesthetic.'

Melnikov smiled. 'Ah, yes. I'm sorry about that, but you were an intruder. I have to protect myself.'

'Is that what you were doing when you sent Kataev to kill Arcier, Maclean and Soldane?'

Melnikov didn't miss a beat. He replaced his glasses and considered Chadwick for a moment. 'Of course. But what else would you expect me to do? Arcier was a mistake. He should never have been hired. It was Kataev's idea and I should have stopped him. Arcier was dreadful. It is hard to know what he was worst at - detecting or blackmailing. Awful man. Treacherous *and* incompetent. Maclean was different. Maclean should never have happened.'

'Kataev sold some of the goods from the *Highland Laddie* without telling you.'

Melnikov frowned, surprised at Chadwick's knowledge. 'How did you find that out?'

This is an interrogation, thought Chadwick. *It's a subtle one but it's an interrogation, nevertheless. Play your cards slowly and see what they draw in response.*

'I didn't. It just seemed like the logical explanation. I couldn't see you jeopardising the operation for the sake of few hundred thousand euros.'

Melnikov thought for a moment. 'And what is the operation? Did you manage to *guess* that as well?'

'You, or whoever is backing or paying you, is shipping something very sensitive out of Russia. Sufficiently sensitive that if several people get wind of it, the operation will be shut down immediately. Unfortunately, there is a problem. Ships take time to reach their destination and they can be tracked. So, you came up with the idea of finding twin ships – leaving from neighbouring ports with one carrying an innocuous cargo to a controversial location – and the other carrying a dangerous cargo to an innocent location. At some point, the ships cross and exchange AIS signals, with the one with the dangerous cargo then sailing to the controversial destination. On the way back, the ships switch again. That way, if the suspect ship is ever tracked or boarded, the authorities will find nothing.'

'*Bravo*. I'm impressed. I really am. I didn't expect you to get this far, and after all your mistakes, I never imagined that you would finally understand what I was doing.'

'It's all happening now, isn't it? Otherwise, you would never have rushed the Maclean killing.'

'Yes, it's happening now. Maclean was awkward, but there just wasn't enough time. Kataev had to improvise, and he doesn't always improvise well. He is better following orders.'

'So, you told him to kill Maclean?'

'Of course. He doesn't do anything without my telling him.'

'He sold the cargo from the *Highland Laddie* without telling you.'

Melnikov nodded his head. 'Yes, he did. But he won't do it again.' He paused as if he were about to elaborate but decided against it.

Chadwick, anxious to keep Melnikov talking, asked, 'When did you decide to involve me?'

Melnikov seemed surprised by the question but answered it. 'After it became clear that Arcier was more interested in blackmailing us than pocketing his fee. If it hadn't been for his greed and stupidity, we would have had "Soldane" the first time, and we wouldn't have needed you. Instead, all we did was alert him and make him much more careful. I thought he would leave town and we would lose him completely. Perhaps it wouldn't have mattered. But we were lucky. He stayed and you found him.'

'I set him up, didn't I? Kataev was following me when I went to the factory and saw Soldane on my tail. When I finally realised that Soldane was tailing me, I followed him to his apartment. And while I waited, Kataev called you, killed Soldane and tipped off the police. You must have been annoyed when I got away.'

'It was irritating, but we always had a plan to seize you at the hotel. Trying to trap you at Soldane's apartment was opportunistic. Tell me, how did we miss you at the hotel?'

'You barely missed me. Kataev's boat almost split my skull open.'

'And then you swam to St Jean and hid in one of the boats?'

'Yes.'

Melnikov continued in the same measured, unemotional tones. He might have been conducting a tutorial.

'I thought St Jean was the only place that you could have gone. It was frustrating that we didn't have the time nor the manpower to conduct a proper search. But it would have taken too long. Besides, there was always the risk that you didn't need to break into a boat because you had access to one. If that was the case, I always felt that it would be difficult to find you.'

Melnikov stopped. He appeared to be considering something. When he spoke again, his questioning became less professional and more personal. 'Why didn't you leave after St Jean?' he asked. 'You *should* have gone. It must have been clear - even to you - that you had been outmanoeuvred and that you were outnumbered. Why stay? Why board the *Lara?* What could you possibly hope to accomplish?'

It sounded as if Melnikov was genuinely puzzled but Chadwick said nothing. He sensed that it was a trap. Melnikov must know that he had come for Silje but he wanted to hear it from him. Chadwick knew that if he admitted it, Silje was as good as dead.

Melnikov changed tack. 'What stopped you running? Was it only stubbornness? Or was it something else? You could have disappeared. You could have satisfied your conscience by tipping off the authorities. Why didn't you?'

Chadwick, tiring of Melnikov's questions, decided to try to bluff him. 'How do *you* know I haven't called the authorities and told them everything? The only piece of information I was missing was the new name of the *Highland Laddie.*'

Melnikov shrugged. 'Then where are they, Chadwick? Where are these authorities you called?' He let the question hang for a moment or two before he continued. 'You didn't call anybody. If you were so sure that you knew what I was doing, you wouldn't have bothered trying your hypothesis on me. In any case, even if you did contact the right people, who would believe *you*, a man suspected of a double-murder?'

Chadwick ignored Melnikov's question and asked one of his own. 'Tell me,' he said, 'Soldane, the *real* Aleksis Soldane, died on the *Highland Laddie* with the rest of the crew, didn't he?'

'Of course. They all died.'

'How?'

'Kataev herded them into a container and then dropped the container overboard.'

'To drown?'

'I assume so. I certainly hope so. I wouldn't want the embarrassment of any of them showing up. But I shouldn't lose too much sleep over Aleksis Soldane. He was the inside man who smuggled Kataev and his team on board.'

'And what about the others?'

'What about them? They chose to go to sea. It's a dangerous place. More than a quarter of a million people drown every year. Why should a few more or less matter? What difference does it make? To pretend otherwise is just hypocrisy.'

'Who was Soldane?'

Melnikov smiled. 'I am pleased that you never found out. I must count that as a success although I confess that there were times that I thought you would surely see through it. The man you knew as Aleksis Soldane is somebody else entirely. He is, or rather *was*, a Russian journalist called Georgy Alexandrovich Andreyev. He was suspicious about the *Highland Laddie* from the start. I don't know why. Maybe his nose for a story was more highly developed than the other journalists. He specialised in shipping and started researching what happened to the *Highland Laddie*.

'In the beginning, it was fine, even helpful, as he exhausted every lead, every possible explanation of foul play. But he became obsessed. He travelled to Asia and talked to everybody who ever had anything to do with the ship. But found nothing. In the end, his editor ordered him to come back to Moscow. But he refused. He quit, stayed in Asia, began to drink too much and post anonymous pieces on the internet. Even that would have been okay, as nobody took him seriously. Then, he decided to come to Europe, to Nice. And from that point on, he stopped being a harmless crank.'

'Did you know he broke into Augustin's shipping office?'

Melnikov's eyes widened slightly. 'No, I didn't. Augustin didn't tell me that.'

'He was probably confused. I broke into his office on the same night. And in any case, he seems to be preoccupied by the contract that you put out on him. It was you, wasn't it?'

Melnikov's face was expressionless. 'Indirectly,' he said.

'What is the difference between "directly" and "indirectly"? I thought the two of you were business partners?'

'Not really. I bought his debts and from that point, I owned him. I wanted the *Highland Lassie* but never had any interest in the casino or his properties.'

'But if you have the notes and you can call them, you already own the casino. Why kill Augustin?'

'Why not? He is unlikely to go quietly, and he knows more than is good for him. It's tidier this way.'

'I am sure he appreciates your fastidiousness.'

Chadwick heard the door opening. He twisted his head. Kataev came in. He was carrying a bottle and a cloth. He turned back towards Melnikov. 'And Julija, if that is her name, works for you?'

'Of course. She arrived here only a few days before you. And Julija is her real name. Julija Kataev. I believe you've met her husband.'

Chadwick tried not to react. This was Melnikov's way of twisting the knife. He didn't turn. He had no desire to see Kataev's face. He was sure that he would be seeing it soon enough.

Melnikov continued. 'Kataev has a lot to thank you for. Not many men would have endured what you have endured and still rushed back to save the lovely Julija. You see, Kataev, I always told you not to worry, that your wife was in good hands.'

Melnikov stood and walked over to where Chadwick lay. 'You have been very helpful to me, Chadwick. You really have. However, there is one more thing I need you to do for me. I need your help to close the police file on Arcier, Maclean and Andreyev.'

'What do you want? A fake confession that you and your boy here are going to beat out of me?'

'Nothing so melodramatic. Kataev is very jealous and I'm sure would like nothing better. But even the French police might suspect such a tidy solution. No, all I need is a simple drowning. No marks, no bruises, nothing to suggest anything other than suicide. The police will draw their own conclusions. You are lucky. If it was left up to Kataev … Well, you saw Andreyev's body, I'm sure you understand.'

'You know that Silje wasn't involved in any of this.' Chadwick had waited a long time to say it in the hope that it would have more weight, but when he heard himself, he knew it wouldn't be enough. 'She had no idea that I would send Kataev's wife out to her house.'

Melnikov's face hardened and he became sarcastic. 'I'm glad to hear it. I'll be sure to mention it to her now when I go see her. Is this also the time for you to tell me that there was nothing between you? Because I've been waiting for you to say that too and I'm afraid we are almost out of time.'

Chadwick tried to control his voice: to keep it level and strong, to avoid any hint of desperation. 'There *was* nothing between us. She wouldn't have it. She told me to go away. That she was with you.'

'Oh, good. Just as I am sure that you'll be happy to hear that we won't be seeing each other again. It might be difficult for you to sleep, tied up like that, so Kataev has brought something to help you. It's not very nice, I'm afraid, but it does have the advantage of leaving the bloodstream quickly. It requires a very conscientious doctor and a thorough autopsy to find it. I'm afraid I can't see the French state supplying either.'

Melnikov started walking towards the door. Any interest he had in Chadwick was now at an end. He heard the door open and close. He started to turn towards Kataev but was stopped by a foot holding him down.

'Kataev, why don't you just get on with it like your boss told you to do?' said Chadwick.

There was silence. Kataev lifted his foot, walked around Chadwick and stood in front of him. He looked down at Chadwick without speaking, his face expressionless. It was impossible to tell what he was thinking. 'I do what I want,' he said.

Chadwick sensing a possible opening, said, 'Do you? Not anymore. Not according to your boss. He says that it was you who made all the mistakes. That you were responsible for hiring Arcier. That the only reason you had to kill Maclean was that you sold the *Highland Laddie's* cargo behind his back.'

Kataev went down on his haunches directly in front of Chadwick. His face was so close that it seemed unnaturally large. His mouth was pulled back in a cynical smile. His grey eyes were cold.

'You talk too much, English. Tomorrow, you can talk to the fishes. Maybe they listen better than me.'

Chadwick tried again. 'Was it Melnikov's idea to use Julija?'

Kataev thought for a moment, chewing on his bottom lip. Finally, he said, 'What's the matter, English? You upset with her? For what? I'm the one should be upset, English – not you. I'm the one hanging around in the cold, outside your shit hotel, while you're upstairs banging my wife.'

'So, it *was* Melnikov's idea.'

Kataev's face darkened and Chadwick knew that he was on the right path. He had very little time. It was risky but if he could exploit the bad blood between Kataev and Melnikov, he might give himself a chance.

'Your boss doesn't like to get his hands dirty, does he? Not when he can get you to do it.'

Kataev shrugged. 'Who else would do it? He is getting old and losing his grip. You think he can control me? He can't even control his Norwegian bitch. He is losing it. It has been a long time since he did any real work, and he is out of touch. He tells me not to beat you so that your body has no marks on it. He has no idea. I can beat your insides to a pulp, but you'll still look like a prince.' He paused, relishing the thought. 'Would you like that, English?'

Chadwick changed tack, realising the danger. He had no doubt that Kataev could do it, and if he did beat him, any chance of escaping before morning would have gone. He said, 'You know that you can still get out of this if you help me.'

Kataev smiled, enjoying his domination. 'You do like to talk, English,' he said. 'You really do. Maybe you spent too much time alone in that hotel.'

'Do you want to go down with Melnikov or do you want to get away?'

Kataev kept smiling but said, 'Why would I want to get away?'

'The authorities know about the two ships and the switch. They know it's imminent. The only thing they don't know is the new name of the *Highland Laddie*. But they know everything else. Melnikov will never get away with it.'

Kataev thought for a moment or two. 'The authorities know everything, you say. How?'

'I told them. I told them what I knew before I came on board. Right now, they are already searching for the two ships. It's only a matter of time before they come here for Melnikov. *And for you.* But if you were to give them the new name of the *Highland Laddie*, I could cut a deal with them that would allow you to get away.'

'And what would you get out of this?'

'You give me the name, you let me escape with Silje, and I make your deal with the authorities.'

Kataev stood up. 'Interesting idea, English. Do you really think the French would do a deal like that?'

'I'm sure. Why wouldn't they? They want the ships and the cargo - they don't want you.'

'And what am I to say to Melnikov, when he sees me releasing the two of you?'

'Why do you care? He's finished. Do it when he is asleep. By the time he wakes up, it will all be over.'

Kataev rubbed his chin as he considered Chadwick's proposition. It was some time before he spoke.

'You are right, English. In the morning, it *will* all be over. But not in the way you think. The authorities know nothing about what we are doing. Nothing. And you haven't had the chance to tell them shit. And, even if they knew everything, you think they would cut a deal with me after all the people I've killed? You are stupid if you think so, and even more stupid if you think that I would ever believe you. You dream, English. In the morning, I bring you a basin of sea water, and if you don't fight it, it won't take long. And then you can go for a swim. A long swim. And all your problems will be over.'

Kataev stepped around him. Chadwick twisted and rolled so that he could face him. But he was too slow; Kataev was already behind him. He pulled him into a sitting position, and with his left arm holding Chadwick's shoulders, he pressed the wet cloth to Chadwick's nose and mouth with his right hand. He tried not to breathe but knew what would happen next. Kataev's left arm moved away. Chadwick braced himself for the inevitable but when the punch came, it was more powerful than he had anticipated. He tried to stop himself sucking in air but it was already too late. He was being pulled backwards at increasing speed down a dark tunnel. He began to panic but his panic only caused him to start to spin like a Catherine wheel, faster and faster, until finally, he blacked out.

CHAPTER FORTY

From a long way above him, he hears her call his name. He is scared. It is very high and completely dark. He must go back down. He lifts one foot and tries to step backwards, but his foot will only move forwards onto the next step. It is the same with the other foot. He finds himself climbing against his will. With every step, the wind increases until it is difficult to stand. He can barely hear her voice over the noise of the wind. *There must be no walls here*, he thinks. *I am walking up an open staircase in the dark.*

His feet stop. His legs, which have been so tired, are suddenly fresh. He looks around but sees only darkness. 'I'm here,' she says, her mouth close to his ear. 'Give me your hand.' He stretches out his hand and finds hers, which is soft and warm, and he feels ashamed that his are hard and calloused. 'Come with me.' He follows her like a child on his first day at school. They come to a door. 'We are here,' she says. 'Now it is up to you.' She pushes open the door and the wind grows stronger. She stands to one side, and he steps through the doorway.

He is standing on a narrow step, surrounded by chimney stacks and rooftops. Just below him, he sees the edge of the roof, and beyond, nothing but night. He hears children crying. The sound is coming from below him, from somewhere in the darkness, and he knows at once that he has no choice but to go to them.

He steps into the night and feels himself falling. He braces himself for the impact but none comes. He continues to fall through the gloom. Slowly, it grows lighter, and he realises that he is no longer falling but is surrounded by swimming fish. The wind has gone and all he can hear is the sound of dolphins calling to each other. Any sense of danger has gone and been replaced by a feeling of well-being.

The white wall towers over him and stretches into the distance. He walks alongside it until he comes to an opening. Entering, he finds himself in a dark-panelled corridor with doors on either side. He opens the first door. Three men are sitting at a table playing cards. They look up and gesture that he should sit in the fourth chair. He looks at each of them in turn, before retreating, closing the door behind him.

The next cabin is empty. There is an open doorway directly opposite where he was standing. Music is playing. He tries to identify it, but by the time he succeeds, it has become something else. Samira appears in the doorway, wearing a long, red dress. She leans against the door frame and looks at him. Finally, she beckons him with her finger. He walks towards her, but she moves into the other room. He enters. The room is dark. He trips and almost falls. Reaching down, he touches the obstacle. It is warm.

Intrigued, he grips it as best he can and drags it towards the doorway. It is a long object wrapped in cloth. He begins to unwind the material. It becomes clear that there is somebody wrapped inside. He works faster, starting with the feet and moving upwards. He feels the shape of the body and as he reaches the chest and neck, he rips the remainder of the material from the face. It is Silje. Her hair pulled back. Her skin flawless and white. He touches her face. It is ice-cold. He feels her hands, her legs. They are all ice-cold. He hears somebody screaming, buries his head in her chest, and begins to cry. The screaming grows louder until he can stand it no longer. He runs into the corridor and goes up the companionway two steps at a time. When he reaches the door at the top, he pushes it open.

They had left her there deliberately. Her face no more than a few centimetres from his, the beautiful blue eyes set in white marble, with no more life than a medieval tomb. He knew now who was screaming but he couldn't stop himself. He pulled his tethered legs up, twisted and pushed Silje's body with his feet. She fell on her back but at least he could no longer see her face.

He forced himself into a seating position. The lights were on and the furniture was flying, the tables and chairs turning figures of eight above his head. He forced himself to concentrate on a moving chair and tried to fix it to one spot. But it was hopeless. As soon as he succeeded, the rest of the room began to spin.

He remembered Silje and looked across at her body. He began to cry. *Stop it*, he said to himself. *This is not you. This is the drug. It's only the drug. You need to move. You need to work the drug out of your system. Focus. Time. What time is it?* He looked around the cabin but couldn't see a clock. He tried to remember what he had been about to do. Bewildered, he watched the flying furniture until he remembered what he had to do. He forced himself to concentrate, knowing that if he allowed himself to be distracted, even for a second, he would forget again and might never remember.

He rotated himself until his back and tied hands were facing Silje's body. Then, using his legs and upper body, he advanced slowly towards her until he was lying next to her. He started with her feet. He slipped off her shoes and checked both. Nothing. Next, he felt his way up her legs and checked the pockets of her jeans. Nothing. He began to wonder if he had misinterpreted her words, or worse, imagined the whole incident. It was only when he ran his finger around the inside of her belt that he found it. Carefully, by touch, he slid off the cap and reversed the scalpel. The slim scalpel was hard to grip but very sharp. His hands were numb, and he worried about accidentally cutting his wrists. What would have taken him thirty seconds if he could have seen what he was doing, took an age.

He tried to move his arms. They didn't respond but simply flapped by his side. He rolled on the floor until he could feel the blood start flowing. Sitting up, he bent forward and cut the plasticuffs securing his ankles. The furniture was almost stationary. It was now or never. He levered himself up with his arms, but his giddiness worsened as he tried to stand. He manoeuvred himself into a kneeling position and waited for his head to settle.

Time. He needed to know the time. He raised first one leg and then the other. He could stand, but only just. Even in his drugged state, he could tell that he was swaying in every direction. *Walk. You must walk.* He picked a wall and stumbled towards it. He steadied himself by placing one hand on the wall and began to pace up and down. After several minutes, he stopped, unsure whether his head was becoming clearer or he was simply growing used to his drugged condition. He pulled open a window blind a crack. It was pitch-black outside. It must still be at least an hour, maybe two, till dawn.

He leaned against the wall, exhausted. All he wanted was to sleep. But he knew that if he slept, it would be over. Melnikov and Kataev would make sure of it. He forced himself to walk some more, trying not to look at Silje lying on the other side of the room. He couldn't look at her. He knew that if he looked at her, he would be overwhelmed by his failures. He hadn't been able to protect her any more than he had been able to protect Samira before her. He was responsible for Maclean's death. And for Andreyev's. He had made one mistake after another. He had ignored advice and dismissed the many warning signs. What was the matter with him? What point was he trying to prove? Why hadn't he left when he had the chance? Was it just arrogance? Or was Kataev right? He *was* stupid. Worse than stupid, he was naïve.

He could still leave, even now. There would be nobody watching him. He was no longer a threat. He was drugged and awaiting execution. All he had to do was get to the deck, drop into the sea and swim to the shore. He wouldn't be missed until Kataev came for him in the morning, and by then, he would be safely ashore. Once he had told everything to the Chairman or the local authorities, the whole operation was finished. Even if the two ships were already at sea, they couldn't escape detection for very long. Melnikov and Kataev would be arrested and he would have done what he could for Silje, Maclean and Andreyev, the man he had only ever known as Aleksis Soldane.

He might have made mistakes, but nobody would blame him. At least not openly. They would sit him in an overheated room and offer him coffee. Somebody would come to take his statement, ask a few questions and try a few speculations before thanking him for his efforts and wishing him well. He would be *free to go*. The whole experience would be depressingly familiar but at least the whole sorry episode would be over.

Over for him, but what about the murdered crew of the *Highland Laddie*? Innocent men clambering over each other, fighting for their last breath in a container filling with water. Or Silje? What about her? If he hadn't sent Julija to her house, she would be alive. She hadn't helped him. She hadn't been disloyal to Melnikov. But it hadn't mattered. Melnikov had killed her anyway. Just as he had killed anybody who stood between him and the execution of his plan. He was being naïve again. What could the authorities do with Melnikov? Arrest him? For how long? Melnikov's money and influence would ensure that he was released in hours - and that Kataev would never be found.

No, he couldn't leave. It was clear. He had to see this through even if he died in the attempt. It was not just a question of justice. If he didn't do this, he was finished. He realised now what Farquharson had been trying to tell him. He had been exiled, not because of what had happened in North Africa, but because of what had happened to him. He had sinned. Not against the Office, but against himself, against the idea of himself, and as a result, he was damaged goods and couldn't be trusted. The Office was simply protecting itself. It hadn't exiled him; he had exiled himself.

He had debts. Debts that he owed others which if he didn't repay, he would never be whole again. He owed Silje. He owed Maclean. He owed it to the crew of the *Highland Laddie,* to Andreyev and even to Arcier. He knew that the odds were against him. But he knew too, that if he didn't fight, all the deaths would be for nothing.

He walked over towards Silje. He knelt beside her and cradled her head. Very gently, he closed her eyes with the tips of his fingers and said a prayer for her. Then, he kissed her on the forehead and lowered her head to the floor. Her spirit was gone. There was nothing left for him here.

He went into the bathroom, drank water from the tap and stuck his head under the cold water. He searched for any kind of weapon. There was nothing. He would only have the scalpel until he could find something better. Holding it in his right hand, he opened the cabin door a couple of centimetres with his left. The corridor was empty. He headed to the stairs, his tread silenced by the heavy cream carpet. He went straight past the next deck and up to the hall that led to the stateroom. He went out to the promenade deck, checking to see if he could be seen from the bridge – he couldn't. He walked slowly towards the stern, keeping close to the superstructure. The door to the engine room was open. Good. If it was open, it was because somebody was inside. A boat like the *Lara* was unlikely to leave the engine room unoccupied without setting some alarm. It would be easier if somebody was there, provided there wasn't more than one. He took a quick look inside. Stairs led downwards. He stepped inside and started to descend.

The engine room of the *Lara* was unlike any he had seen. The two turbines occupied most of the space, stretching like two large cylinders the length of the room. He could only see the top half of each cylinder; the other half was hidden by the grey metal walkways that extended most of the way around the room. The stairs emerged between the two engines and directly in front, towards the stern, was a man in a white overall, his back to Chadwick, taking readings from a control panel. Chadwick saw what he was looking for. He walked towards an open chest and picked up a wrench. Then he walked towards the man in the overalls and tapped him on the shoulder.

The man turned and looked shocked when he saw who was behind him. *You know, don't you?* thought Chadwick. *Nobody is innocent on this boat.* He said, 'I want you to turn off all the fire, smoke and water alarms. All of them. If you miss one, or you deliberately or even accidentally trigger one, I'll kill you. Do you understand?'

The man nodded. *Watch him,* thought Chadwick. *It must be clear that I am a bit woozy.* The man pointed to a different board. 'They are over there,' he said. Chadwick jerked his head in the direction of the second board and the man set off warily, keeping his head slightly turned so that he could keep Chadwick in his sight. He reached for a set of switches.

'What are those for?'

'Fire and smoke.'

'Turn them off.'

The engineer pointed to another switch. 'This is for water in the engine room,' he said. Chadwick nodded and the man flicked the switch upwards.

'What others are there?'

'That's it. Everything else is related to the engines. Speed, temperature, that sort of thing.'

'Okay. This is what I want you to do next. If you do as you are told, you get to swim to shore. If you don't, you'll be fish food.'

The man nodded. 'I understand,' he said.

'Where are the sea chests?'

The man paled. There could only be one reason for asking the question. He pointed.

'They are down there,' he said.

'Get the right tool to separate the inlet pipe from the valve.'

'Are you sure?' said the nervous engineer.

'Yes. You do this and you can go. If you don't do it, I'll kill you and do it myself. It will take longer but the result will be the same.'

The man indicated a closed metal cupboard on the wall. 'What I need is in there,' he said.

'Open it and then stand back. If you reach in and grab anything, it will be the last thing you do. Understand?'

The man nodded and walked towards the cupboard. He opened the door and stood back. Inside was a series of tools neatly arranged on the wall.

'Which one?' said Chadwick.

The engineer pointed to a large wrench.

'Stand over there.' Once he had moved, Chadwick reached in and took the wrench. It was larger than the one he was holding.

'Let's go,' he said, indicating that the engineer should lead. They moved down another companionway towards the bottom of the hull. The man stopped next to something that resembled a hydrant, with several valves attached to it.

'This is it,' he said.

Chadwick retreated a couple of steps so that he was positioned higher than the engineer. He handed him the wrench. 'Get busy,' he said. 'When you finish that one, you'll need to do the second one.'

The engineer shook his head. 'Impossible,' he said. 'Once this one is open to the sea, there won't be time to open the second one. The water level will be too high.'

'Really? I tell you what, let's open this one first, and then you and I can discuss the second one.'

The engineer climbed over the guardrail and started on the first of the four bolts securing the valve to the pipe. The bolts were stiff, and it took him five minutes before he reached the last. He left two of the bolts half-in to avoid the last bolt being twisted by the force of the water, but by the time he had removed it, there was already a considerable amount of water coming in. When he removed the two securing bolts, the plate flew across the deck, and the sea water came in a torrent. The water spread across the floor of the engine room and started to rise. It became evident that the engineer was correct. It was impossible to work on the second sea chest. Chadwick motioned to the engineer to come up the companionway.

'How long will it take to flood the engine room?'

'You mean so that the engines won't work or to the top?'

'To the top.'

'Ten, maybe fifteen minutes.'

'Put down the wrench.'

He noticed that the engineer hesitated before he let it slip into the water.

'Now follow me up the stairs.'

Chadwick kept several steps above the engineer, so that there was no danger of his making a grab for Chadwick's legs. When they reached the second companionway, leading to the deck, Chadwick again went first. This time, the engineer was slower to follow him. Chadwick was already several steps up when he noticed the engineer glancing to his right, towards a small desk and a chair. Chadwick didn't hesitate. He jumped from the stairs, landing just as the engineer reached the desk. His hand was already in the drawer when Chadwick brought the wrench down on his arm. The man screamed. Chadwick lifted the wrench for a second time. Afterwards, there was no more screaming.

Chadwick picked up the Grach 9-mm automatic from the drawer and stuck it in the back of his trousers. For the moment, the wrench was quieter and just as effective. He started back up the companionway. When he reached the deck, he retraced his steps to the stateroom. The curtains were drawn. He switched on the lights. It took him only a minute or two to find what he needed. He started with the sofas, and then several of the wall panels, before moving to the curtains. By the time he left the room and closed the door, it was already ablaze. He moved to the top of the stairs. Melnikov, on the deck below, was next on his list. He glanced back at the stateroom door to see if there was any sign of the fire burning inside. It was a good decision. It saved his life.

Kataev's hook missed his head by a fraction. Chadwick started to lift the wrench, but he was too late. Kataev's roundhouse kick caught him on the upper arm with tremendous force. He lost his grip on the wrench, which fell to the floor. Kataev moved behind him, grabbing Chadwick's good left arm with his left and wrapping his right arm around Chadwick's neck. He started to strangle him. Chadwick lifted his right arm, gripped Kataev's forearm and tried to pull it free but he had no strength there.

'What's the matter, English? Don't you want to fight? Maybe you are still asleep? Are you still asleep, English?'

Kataev started to increase his stranglehold. He could feel the heat of the other man's body and his hot breath on the back of his neck. Smoke was beginning to pour out from the gaps around the stateroom door, filling the hallway with noxious fumes.

'Come on, English,' said Kataev. 'Is this the best you can do? Even your girlfriend fought better than this.'

Kataev's stranglehold was like a tightening iron ring around his neck. Chadwick was becoming disoriented. Bending his knees, he stepped back so that Kataev's weight shifted above him and he could lift him clear off the floor. Then he took a couple of steps forward as if to ram Kataev's face into the lift door. It was an obvious move, and he didn't think for a second that Kataev would fall for it. Before he reached the lift door, Chadwick stopped and moved backwards, carrying Kataev with him. Accelerating, he slammed Kataev's back into the stateroom door. At the same time, Chadwick jerked his head back as hard and as far as he could and felt the back of his head hit Kataev's mouth and nose. There was a scream of pain and Kataev's grip loosened for a second. Chadwick gulped in a breath, bent his knees and tried to throw Kataev over his right shoulder, but the Russian resisted. He stepped backwards and drove Kataev into the door again, but the Russian had shifted position, protecting himself from a second head butt. The hall was filling with smoke, making it difficult to see or breathe. The hoop around Chadwick's neck was closing. He could feel himself losing strength. Soon, he would have to drop to his knees, and he would be finished. He released his right hand from Kataev's forearm, letting it drop as if he was fading. He reached into his trouser pocket for the scalpel.

Kataev released him and pushed him away almost immediately. He looked down – but it was too late. His trousers were covered in blood from a severed femoral artery. Chadwick, anticipating the release, turned immediately, his right hand jabbing at Kataev's throat. The Russian blocked but before he could lift his right hand, Chadwick hit him with a left hook to the head. It wasn't a strong blow but it was enough to knock Kataev off balance and gave Chadwick time to push kick Kataev towards the stateroom doors. This time, the doors flew open and Kataev went straight through them, falling backwards, disappearing into a wall of smoke and flame. The heat from the fire was intense. Chadwick looked for Kataev but could see nothing. It seemed impossible that anybody could survive more than a second or two in the inferno that had engulfed the stateroom. He could feel his skin burning and his eyes streaming from the smoke. But he had to be vigilant.

Kataev appeared from nowhere, running at Chadwick through a curtain of flames, his face a mess of blood and tissue, his clothes and hair on fire. Chadwick hit him in the face with a left jab but it only stopped Kataev for a second. He advanced again, blocked Chadwick's next left jab and landed a right hook of his own. Chadwick felt his legs buckle. Instinct alone helped him drive his knee upwards into Kataev, who fell to the floor. By now, most of his clothes were gone and his skin was burned everywhere. He tried to get up but couldn't.

Chadwick reached behind him, finally able to draw the automatic. He pointed it at Kataev.

'Please, English, please.'

They both knew that it was a plea for mercy, but Chadwick had no intention of ending Kataev's suffering.

'Welcome to hell,' said Chadwick and kicked him as hard as he could.

He could no longer see the door to the deck but could tell from the movement of the smoke and the surge of the flames that somebody was coming in. He moved to the top of the stairs, lying flat, so that only his head and upper body were visible. There were two of them, wearing smoke hoods and carrying pistols. They stopped by Kataev's burning body and he shot them both without a second thought.

CHAPTER FORTY-ONE

Chadwick made a quick assessment. The fire was now burning out of control. They had sent in two men and lost both. They must suspect that Kataev was dead. He doubted there would be much enthusiasm for a second excursion, but the delay meant that he had very little time to get to Melnikov. He tried his right arm. It was recovering. He felt his face. It was bleeding but he would survive. The emergency lights were on but were of limited use – the smoke was too thick. Chadwick went down the stairs on his belly, trying to keep his nose as close to the clean air as he could. When he reached the landing outside Melnikov's cabin, he checked the automatic, turned the handle and went in.

There were three people standing in the middle of the floor of the cabin: Melnikov, Sasha and Sasha's nurse. The nurse reached into his tunic pocket. He might have been looking for paracetamol. He was going to need it. The impact of the bullets at close range lifted him off his feet and onto his back. He lay still, a crimson rose growing ever larger on his white chest.

'And then there were two,' said Chadwick.

Sasha put his hands to his mouth and started to shout, 'He's dead. He's dead. Sergei is dead.' His father put an arm around his shoulders and pulled him close. He said something to him in Russian. Sasha stopped shouting and began to cry, very quietly, the tears running down his cheeks.

'Was that really necessary?' asked Melnikov.

'I'm sorry. I must be forgetting my manners.'

'There was no need to do it in front of Sasha. He was fond of him.' Melnikov's voice was icy cold.

'He was fond of Silje too. But that didn't stop you. Or, did you forget to tell him that you had Kataev drown her?'

Sasha pulled his face away from his father's shoulder and turned to look at Chadwick.

'Be quiet. Don't talk about this in front of Sasha,' said Melnikov.

'Why not? Doesn't it sit well with your role as a doting father? Tell me, when were you going to tell him? When is the right time to learn that your father is a murderer?'

'Sasha, go open the secret room. I'll join you in a minute or so once I've finished with Mr Chadwick.' The boy hesitated. Melnikov guided him gently towards the closet, kissing him on the top of his head as he passed. 'Go! I'll be there soon.' Sasha walked towards the panelling, pressed the beading and waited while the door to the dressing room opened. He walked inside. Moments later, Chadwick heard the hum of the panic-room door opening. Chadwick moved across the room to have a better view of the dressing room. He didn't think that Sasha would reappear with a gun in his hand, but he was tired of being wrong. Melnikov hadn't moved.

'How much do you want, Chadwick?'

Melnikov showed no outward signs of concern. Chadwick marvelled at his calm.

'Money? Do you have any left? I just set fire to your art collection.'

Melnikov shrugged. 'It doesn't matter. They are all copies. The originals are in a secure warehouse in Geneva. It's an elegant piece of misdirection. Everybody thinks they are real because nobody expects to find a fake on a boat like this. You didn't either, did you?'

'Only the owner.'

'You can be as rude as you like, Chadwick but you are only wasting time. Why don't you tell me how much it is going to take for you to leave and then we can go our separate ways? It's not very complicated.'

'And how can I be sure that I'll live to enjoy it? Everybody else you touch seems to wake up dead.'

Melnikov sighed as if the conversation was beginning to bore him. 'They died because they got in the way. With you, it would be different. I am paying you to stay *out of the way*, to keep quiet. I'm giving you enough money so that you can afford to be alone. Isn't that what you want? Isn't that what you told me you wanted when we first met?'

'How much?' asked Chadwick.

Melnikov thought for a moment and said a number.

Chadwick whistled. 'I'm impressed. Your operation *must* be important.'

Melnikov took a moment or two to reply, giving the impression that he wanted to drag the conversation out for as long as possible. Given his predicament, he had not once looked towards the door to the cabin. *You are expecting reinforcements*, thought Chadwick, *but they are not coming.*

Melnikov said, 'It is. But it's not so important, and my partners and I are not so desperate, that we can be blackmailed. Arcier thought differently and it cost him his life. I am sure you are a great deal smarter than Arcier and won't try anything quite so stupid. Let's just agree the necessary arrangements and go our separate ways.'

'While you wait for Kataev to come to the rescue?'

To his credit, Melnikov didn't react. 'Why would I need to be rescued? We agree this deal and you can go. I'll keep Kataev away from you.'

'I'm sure but you are a little late.'

'What do you mean?'

'His rescuing days are behind him.'

Melnikov didn't reply. The smell of smoke in the room grew stronger and both men looked towards the door. As if on cue, a plume of smoke snaked its way through the gap in the doors.

Melnikov pointed towards the panic room. 'Shall we?' he asked. He might have been suggesting a stroll. He didn't wait for Chadwick's approval. He started walking towards the dressing room. Chadwick moved closer to him, the automatic hanging down by his right side.

Sasha was sitting inside the panic room, bathed in red light. He looked out at them anxiously.

'It's okay, Sasha. I'm here. I'm here now,' said Melnikov, but didn't go in. He stood by the entrance and turned towards Chadwick.

'You still haven't given me an answer about the money, Chadwick. You should take it. You've earned it. Without you, we might never have found Andreyev, possibly the only person who could have put it all together.' Perhaps the deliberate slight was to demonstrate Melnikov's control of the situation, or maybe it was done to bring the situation to a head. Possibly it was a misjudgement. Chadwick would never know.

'You see that's my problem with the money,' said Chadwick. 'I did earn it. I *earned* it through my own *stupidity*. You had me work for you without my realising. Whether I wanted to or not. And consequently, people died. Maybe you would have killed Arcier anyway. I can just about persuade myself that, given time, you would have found Andreyev with or without my help. But not Maclean: Maclean is my responsibility. If I hadn't asked Lloyd's for help with the *Highland Laddie*, Maclean would be alive.'

Melnikov was unimpressed. 'So, give his family some of your money, if it bothers you so much. There is enough there for you to be generous.'

'And what about Silje's family?'

Melnikov's face darkened. 'What about them?'

'What shall I tell them?'

'Tell them what you like, Chadwick. Give them all the money if it makes you feel better. They never gave a damn about her while she was alive but give them the money anyway.'

'Why did you kill her?'

Melnikov stiffened, unsure how to reply. Finally, he said, 'We had an agreement.'

'What sort of agreement?'

For once, Melnikov's face betrayed him. 'A private one,' he said. 'One I don't have to discuss with *you*.'

'You thought she broke your agreement, didn't you?'

'She did.'

'No, she didn't. She never broke whatever agreement you had. If you had understood her better, you would know that. You were wrong about her. Completely wrong.'

'Chadwick, I may be getting old, but I am not a fool. She was with you. It was obvious. I knew it.'

'You knew what?' asked Chadwick.

Melnikov hesitated. It was clear that he couldn't allow himself to say what he really thought. Instead, he repeated, 'She was with you. That she was not with me anymore.'

'Did she say that?'

'Of course not. But she didn't need to. It was so clear. To me and to everybody else. You were the only one who didn't know it.'

'Others? What others?' asked Chadwick. Then he realised. 'So, it was Julija who said it?'

Melnikov ignored the question. His face was flushed. Chadwick had never seen him discomfited.

'It was Julija, wasn't it? And when I sent her to Silje's house, that just confirmed your suspicions, didn't it? So, you had Kataev kill her. I'll bet the two of them had a good laugh about it. About how they made you so jealous that you ordered her dead. You see, there was *nothing* between us. Nothing at all. Not because I didn't want it. Because she wouldn't have it. *She* wouldn't have it. Don't you understand, Melnikov? She was the only one who stayed loyal to you. The only one. And you killed her.'

Melnikov's face had turned to stone. He tried to speak but no words emerged. Sasha came to the entrance of the panic room. 'Did you kill Silje?' he said quietly. Melnikov didn't reply. Sasha repeated the question. Melnikov ignored him, lost in his own thoughts. Sasha stepped out of the panic room and grabbed the lapels of his father's dressing gown. He thrust his face into his. 'Did you kill her?' he shouted. At first, Melnikov continued to stare into the distance, before he slowly focused on Sasha's face, centimetres from his own. 'It's all right,' he said. 'It's all right, Sasha. Silje is fine.'

'You are lying. You are *lying*.' Sasha started to hit his father, first on the chest, and then in the face. Melnikov made no effort to defend himself. Chadwick grabbed Sasha and pulled him towards him. The boy looked down at Chadwick's hand on his arm but said nothing. 'Get in,' Chadwick told Melnikov. 'I'm finished with you. I don't want your dirty money. I never wanted it. What I do want is some justice for the crew of the *Highland Laddie,* for Maclean, for Andreyev, for Silje. And you are going to face justice.'

Melnikov turned towards Chadwick. He had recovered his composure. 'Justice? You want justice? You are a bigger fool than ever I imagined. What justice? Where will you find this justice? In a French court? Don't make me laugh. They couldn't hold me for ten minutes.' He went into the panic room and sat down. He stretched out his hand towards Sasha. 'Come here, Sasha. Come and be with Papa.'

Sasha pulled back and hid behind Chadwick.

'Come, Sasha,' said Melnikov. 'Come to Papa.'

'He's not coming,' said Chadwick. 'I'm leaving and he's coming with me. You seem to have forgotten about the fire.'

'I haven't forgotten anything. It's you who have forgotten. You've forgotten what I told you when I first showed you the panic room. The boat is designed so that the hull will survive any fire. The boat won't sink. The panic room is fireproof and has enough of an oxygen supply to last six hours. More than enough time for the fire to burn itself out. Get in, Chadwick, we'll be perfectly safe.'

Chadwick turned to Sasha. He whispered in his ear, 'Why don't you close the door of the secret room? Your father wants to be alone.' Sasha walked to the front of the dressing room. Melnikov, unsure about what Chadwick had whispered, watched to see where Sasha was going.

'You're wrong, Melnikov. I remembered your explanation very well. That's why I disconnected one of the sea chests. The *Lara* is sinking.'

Melnikov, realising the danger, stood up. Chadwick pointed the automatic at him. 'Sit down,' he said. 'You are not going anywhere. You are right. There is no hope of justice for you. This is the best I can do. Enjoy your six hours on the seabed. Maybe you'll remember what you did to the crew of the *Highland Laddie* and what you did to Silje.' Chadwick leaned into the panic room and put a bullet in the radio and the control panel. The noise of the automatic in the confined space was deafening.

There was a hum as the steel door started to close. Melnikov got up and started walking. Chadwick aimed the automatic at the centre of Melnikov's chest and he stopped just short of the door.

'Chadwick, leave Sasha here, with me. I don't ask this for myself. I ask it for him. He can't survive without me. Don't leave him alone in the world with nobody to care for him.'

'It's his life,' said Chadwick. 'It's not mine to take.'

Melnikov, his face pale, pleaded, 'Don't do this. Please don't do this. What sort of life can he have without me?'

Melnikov tried to hold back the closing door with his fingers, but the mechanism was too powerful. He twisted his body so that he could still see through the rapidly narrowing gap between the door and the wall. 'Please, Chadwick, don't do this. I'm begging you. Please.' At the last second, Melnikov withdrew his fingers, and the dressing room went quiet.

Chadwick stared at the metal door for a second or two, wondering what he had done. Silje had been right. Even at the end, Melnikov had remained true to himself, begging mercy not for himself, but for his son.

Chadwick threw away the pistol and turned to Sasha. 'We have to go now,' he said. Sasha watched him closely, his dark eyes examining Chadwick's face with great care. Chadwick waited for him to make his decision. He felt Sasha's hand reaching for his. Grasping it tightly, they walked out of the dressing room and over to where the nurse lay dead.

Chadwick knelt beside the corpse and reached into the nurse's pocket. He turned his head and saw Sasha watching him anxiously. He pulled out another automatic, which he slipped into his belt. They moved to the door. Smoke was coming in all around the door frame. Sasha went to turn the handle, but Chadwick stopped him. He felt the door. It was hot to the touch. He put his hand next the handle - it was giving off heat. He knew immediately that they couldn't escape by the stairs. If he opened the door, the fire, craving oxygen, would flood in. 'We can't go out that way,' he said. 'There is a fire on the other side of the door and it's dangerous.'

Sasha nodded. 'Dangerous,' he repeated.

Chadwick led him towards one of the windows and made him stand to one side. 'I am going to fire the gun to break the window. It will be a loud noise. Okay?' Sasha nodded. Chadwick indicated that he should cover his ears and when he did so, fired a test shot. It went straight through, making a small hole with cracks radiating from the centre. He tapped the hole with the butt of the pistol and a few pieces of glass dislodged. He turned to warn Sasha that he was about to fire again, but, before he could speak, the door blew in.

A wall of flame ignited the carpet and the curtains. Sasha started to scream, his arms wrapped around his head. Chadwick grabbed him and dragged him away from the door. Holding Sasha with one arm, he held the pistol in the other and emptied the magazine at the nearest window, cutting a circle in the glass. He half-dragged, half-cajoled Sasha towards the window. He kicked the glass, which gave way immediately. The heat from the flames was intense. Sasha started to scream again. Chadwick pulled him towards the window where the air was cleaner, and it was easier to breathe. 'Sasha,' he shouted, 'we have to swim now. We need to go. Do you understand?' Sasha tried to pull away from him, but Chadwick persisted. Finally, Sasha started nodding. Chadwick looked out the window. The *Lara* was sinking fast. What should have been a drop of several metres was now less than a metre. 'Look, Sasha,' he said, pulling him to the window so that he could see the water just below them. 'When we start swimming, swim away from the boat. That's very important. Away from the boat, do you understand? When the boat sinks, we need to be far away.'

'*Far away.*'

He helped Sasha climb through the window. As he reached the point of no return, the boy panicked and tried to climb back in. Chadwick held him back gently and said, 'No, Sasha, we need to go, or we will die.' It was hard to tell if Sasha understood. He stopped trying to climb back in but didn't jump. Chadwick looked around. Melnikov's cabin was completely ablaze. He could feel the heat of the burning his back. Their time was up. He shoved Sasha out of the window and went out after him.

After the heat of the fire, the cold of the sea took his breath away. He emerged a metre or two from Sasha, who was screaming his name, but swimming strongly. He called for him to follow and started swimming away from the *Lara*. He didn't look back. He didn't want Sasha to think that he would swim back for him. If he didn't follow Chadwick now, he would lose him once he swam beyond the ring of light that surrounded the burning vessel. Once he reached the edge of the ring, he turned. Sasha was swimming towards him. He waited until he was within a few metres and resumed swimming.

After a few minutes, the light started to fade. Chadwick turned his head. The end of the *Lara* came quickly. One moment, the fire was burning fiercely, the flames leaping high above the sinking craft's superstructure. The next, it was gone, the flames snuffed out like an errant candle. 'Watch out, Sasha,' he called. 'There will be a big wave.' He waited for the rise and fall of the sea, but it never came. The *Lara* chose to go quietly, disappearing with barely a ripple.

The sea was cold but calm. It stretched in front of them like a sheet of black glass. The cape lay directly ahead, its silhouette sharp against the night sky. To their right, in the far distance, was the orange neon glow of Nice. Chadwick noted that Sasha was swimming strongly. If he could maintain this pace, they should reach the cape in twenty minutes. They swam side by side, too tired to speak, each lost in his own thoughts.

Chadwick thought of Melnikov, as critical of himself as he was of others, adhering to his philosophy to the end, suffocating to death in his metal tomb. He thought of Silje, and her dreams of being an artist. Of Maclean, who never saw his family again. Of Andreyev, a man he had searched for and never really known, who had given up everything to solve the mystery of the *Highland Laddie*. Of Arcier, who, like Calvet, had decided to play out of his league, and had paid the price. Of the innocent crew of the *Laddie*, who had signed on to the wrong ship.

It was over. Once they reached land, he would go straight to the authorities and the operation, that had started so long ago in the South China Sea, would be at an end. Had it really been worth it? *Is this success?*, he wondered. Melnikov would be replaced. This cargo would be confiscated but another would get through. *If this is success*, he thought, *it is a poor kind of success*. He remembered what Farquharson had said on the beach. *'Ours is a business of failures.*

A stream of defeats punctuated by the occasional success so that we can pretend to ourselves - and to our betters - and to a fickle public - that what we're doing is worth the candle.' Was that all he was doing? Pretending?

He looked to his left and realised that Sasha had fallen behind. He slowed and waited for Sasha to catch up. But Sasha didn't catch up. His swimming grew slower and slower until he was scarcely moving. He was in trouble. Chadwick couldn't tell whether it was from fatigue or cold but it scarcely mattered. He tried to encourage him, but Sasha seemed not to hear. The boy had stopped swimming and was beginning to sink. Chadwick moved towards him but stayed out of reach. He knew that if he went too close, Sasha would grab hold of him and not let go. 'We are almost there, Sasha,' he said. 'Keep swimming.'

Sasha turned to look at him and began to speak. But before he could say anything, his head sank below the water.

Chadwick swam behind him and grabbed the collar of his pyjamas. Kicking as strongly as he could, he pulled Sasha forward. 'Keep swimming. Keep swimming.' Sasha seemed at first not to understand and then began to kick his legs. They were feeble kicks but without them, Chadwick had no hope of making the shore. He began to count Sasha's strokes. After forty, Sasha started to fade again. Chadwick checked the distance to land. It was as far away as ever. He whispered encouragement to Sasha, but the boy was spent.

He released his grip on Sasha's collar and moved his hand under his chin so that he could keep his head above water. 'Sasha?' he said, '*Sasha, wake up.*' But there was no reply. He prodded him but there was no response. The boy seemed to have lost consciousness.

Chadwick took stock. The cape was looming above him. It would probably take no more than ten minutes to swim. He might make it alone, but he wasn't strong enough to make it with an unconscious Sasha. He looked around him for anything that might help keep them afloat. There was nothing. Only the dark, shifting waters of the gulf, rising and falling to a rhythm longer than time.

He knew then that it was over. Sasha would never make it to the shore alone and he wasn't strong enough to get him there. Why had he taken him from his father? Was it simply misplaced altruism or just another way of punishing Melnikov? The pretending was over. It was time to accept responsibility for what he had done, for everything that he had done. He couldn't leave Sasha. Too many people were dead for him to let this boy die alone. Who was he to think that his life was worth any more than the ones already lost? If it was to end, it was better that it was here, in these dark waters, drifting downwards into the oily black, numbed by the cold.

It had been a long road from the desert to the sea. The hotel had been a staging post, a refuge on the road. There had never been a way back from the hotel. He could see that now. The events that had led him to the hotel, had led him here. There had never been any hope of redemption.

There were debts he had avoided paying that had long since come due. Farquharson knew it and banished him. Silje sensed it and would have nothing to do with him. They were both right. He had been damaged in North Africa in a way he couldn't admit to himself. He had broken the rules. Not the Office's rules but the rules that he had lain down for himself. The rules that made him who he was.

He had crossed the line with Samira. He had seduced her. He had promised escape. She had trusted him, and he had let her down. And the worse part was that she knew it. She knew that there would be no rendezvous. She went back to the apartment, not to collect her two children, but to protect them in the only way she could. When she appeared on the balcony with them, he knew what she intended but could do nothing to stop her. He could only watch as she hugged each in turn, before taking each child by the hand and climbing onto the balcony wall. He remembered how quickly they fell; how the market crowd went quiet before it surged towards the broken bodies; how the children had clung to their mother, condemned by a man they never knew and would never meet.

He was hardly swimming, just enough to keep them afloat. The cold was no longer external. It was inside him, a drifting fatigue that was slowly extinguishing whatever heat was left. It wouldn't be long, he thought, and wondered if he would be conscious of the waters closing over him. He looked for a last time at the nearby land. They were so close. He could see the branches of the trees at the top of the cape, silhouetted against the lightening sky. He could see the villas bleached white in the moonlight. He could see the lights of Nice in the distance and envied those lucky enough to be asleep in their beds.

He thought of Leclerc, arriving at the café; of Augustin, sitting alone at his desk in the evening sunlight; of Verlaine, who had disappeared. But mostly, he thought of Silje, and how he had betrayed her. She had been right. It was better to see the world as it is rather than how you would like it to be. There had never been any chance of his returning home. He could see that now. It was no coincidence that he had come here and chosen a hotel surrounded by the sea. The sea had been waiting. Waiting to claim him, just as it had claimed Silje, Melnikov and all the others.

He couldn't feel his hands or feet. The cold had been replaced by numbness. It was difficult to move his legs and he knew that he and Sasha were slipping lower in the water. The end was close now. He thought of how little time he had been given with Silje, and whether it could ever have been different. He saw the two of them, as an elderly couple, waiting on a bench, with no further need for talk, grown suddenly old, like leaves that have turned too soon. Better to see the world as it is …

At first, he thought he imagined it, that it was only a movement of the sea. But when it happened a third time, he realised that it was Sasha, that some instinct buried deep inside him had at last decided to fight. The kicks were feeble, but they were kicks. Chadwick kicked too. It was hopeless, but it was better than giving up; anything was better than giving up. He kicked again and again. He shouted at Sasha to keep kicking, to keep kicking. They were moving slowly but they were moving.

He couldn't think what it was, but it didn't matter. It was floating and if they could only climb onto it, they would be safe. It was only when he swam around it that he realised that it was a platform for bathers from the Grand Hotel. He found the steps and pulled Sasha towards them. He spoke to him, but Sasha didn't respond. He pulled Sasha's arm towards the steps and tried to fasten his hand to the hand-rail of the ladder. Initially, Sasha didn't react, but then slowly, he could see his grip close and tighten. 'It's going to be okay, Sasha. We are safe now.' When he was sure that Sasha was secure, he swam around him and pushed his feet onto the bottom rung of the ladder. Sasha was conscious again. He looked around at Chadwick. 'Climb up,' said Chadwick. Sasha slowly began to pull himself up the ladder using the handrail. As soon as he was halfway up, Chadwick put his own feet on the bottom rung and levered himself up, preventing Sasha from falling backwards. Sasha moved slowly upwards. When he reached the deck of the platform, he fell on it, too exhausted to move further. Chadwick sat beside him and began to massage his arms and legs.

After a few minutes, Sasha began to recover and sat up. 'Where are we?' he said. 'Where is the *Lara*?'

'The *Lara* is gone, Sasha. It sank.'

Sasha looked at him in horror, his wet hair obscuring his face. 'Where is my father? What have you done to my father?'

Chadwick ignored the question. He said, 'Sasha, you need to be brave. If you wait here, on this float, and don't move, you will be safe. Somebody will come in a boat to pick you up. Do you understand?'

Sasha seemed not to have heard. 'Where is my father?' he asked. '*I need my father. I need my father.*' He tried to get up but was too exhausted to stand, ending on his hands and knees.

'Stay here, Sasha. They will come and pick you up and you'll be safe.'

Sasha stared at him, as if trying to make sense of what he was being told. Chadwick started down the ladder towards the sea. He was over halfway down before Sasha realised that he was leaving. He started to shout:

'Don't go! Don't go! Don't go! Don't go!'

When he saw that Chadwick was paying no attention, he began to scream. It was a scream of pain, a primal scream, that carried through the fading night and seemed never to end. Chadwick looked towards the Grand Hotel. He could see the lights of torches moving through the gardens to the sea. They would be on the float in minutes. He pushed his head under the water to block the sound of Sasha's screaming and started swimming.

CHAPTER FORTY-TWO

'I am sorry you are leaving,' said Leclerc. 'It won't be the same without you.'

'The season is starting soon,' said Chadwick. 'You will be busy. Besides, I see you have a new waitress to train.'

Leclerc turned to look at the latest addition to the café's staff. 'She has promise, this one.'

'I can see that. If she bends any further over that table, there is going to be an accident in the square.'

Leclerc laughed and clapped Chadwick on the back. 'You know you have quite a reputation around here after everything that happened.'

'A reputation?'

Leclerc leaned closer. 'They say you that you are a British government agent. That you were sent here and that you were involved in the sinking of the *Lara*.'

Chadwick smiled. 'Do they? It's probably better I'm leaving then. If I stayed, I would only disappoint them.'

Leclerc sat back with a satisfied look on his face. 'But you would hardly tell us if you were, would you?'

Chadwick decided against replying. There was no point. If Leclerc wanted to tell everybody that he was a secret agent, he would do it anyway, and the more Chadwick protested, the more convinced Leclerc would be that he was right.

'And Verlaine?' he asked.

Leclerc shook his head. 'Gone. Disappeared. No explanation. No goodbyes.' He shrugged. 'It happens. He was an unusual man, but I liked him.'

'I liked him too. At least, I liked the part I knew.'

'You haven't heard from him?' asked Leclerc.

Chadwick shook his head. 'No,' he said. *I haven't heard from him,* he thought, *but I have seen him.*

McGhee had been waiting for him. He had been waiting all night, sitting in a chair at the end of the dock, his arms folded, his shoulders hunched against the cold. Chadwick saw him first, but he was too far gone to cry out. It was all he could do to reach the end of the small pier. Chadwick was spent. Without McGhee's strength, he might never have made it out of the water. McGhee said nothing but he could tell from the look on his face that he was concerned. There were no jokes. He put Chadwick's arm over his shoulder and half-dragged, half-carried him to the car. The engine was running and the heater on high. He strapped Chadwick in and let his head loll against the window. He didn't try to talk. He knew there was no point.

McGhee drove out of the restaurant car park and towards the main road that ran the length of the cape. The roads were empty. As they approached the crossroads, McGhee slowed, intending to turn. He nudged Chadwick. There was a convoy of black cars approaching from their right. They had blue flashing lights and were racing towards the Grand Hotel du Cap. When they saw McGhee's car at the crossroads, they slowed, keen to see who was out on the cape in the grey light of dawn.

Verlaine was in the passenger seat of the lead car, talking on a mobile phone. He was the last of the occupants to turn, as if he already knew who it was. He smiled, and made a motion with his hand, neither a wave nor a salute, but something in between. Then, he told the driver to speed up and was gone.

'No, I'm afraid you're right about him,' said Chadwick. 'I don't think we'll see him again.'

There was another reason why Chadwick suspected he would never see Verlaine again. Julija Kataev was dead.

She had been pulled from the sea the day after the *Lara* sank. There was no note, but it didn't seem to trouble the authorities. It was ruled a suicide almost immediately. The coroner attributed it to grief, following the death of her husband in the tragic fire that sank the *Lara*. Chadwick couldn't have told you why he thought Verlaine was involved in Julija's death. It was just a feeling that he had, a sense that Verlaine's tidy mind wouldn't accept any loose ends. But none of it mattered. He had never been questioned about her, the murders or about anything else, just as the Chairman had predicted in the morning after the sinking.

When Chadwick woke, it was already lunchtime. Sunlight streamed through the light curtains. The Chairman was there and a man he didn't introduce. It took an hour to tell the story from beginning to end. The Chairman asked some questions, but the other man said nothing. Neither took notes, which only made Chadwick think that the conversation was being recorded. When they finished, he fell back to sleep.

That evening, he had dinner with the Chairman, who didn't ask him any more questions. It was as if he had heard enough. Nor did he mention the man who had been with him earlier.

'You know that you can stay here as long as you like. I'm sure you don't relish returning to the hotel.'

'No, I would like to go back to the hotel.'

The Chairman was surprised. 'Really? I would have thought you would be pleased to see the back of it.'

'It's a bit stark but I've grown used to it. Perhaps, it's because there were times when I thought I would never see it again. When I leave, I want to leave from there. I can't really explain why. It's just something that's important to me.'

Spencer, conditioned by a lifetime of soldiers' superstitions, knew better than to press the point. 'Well, if you need anything there, or you want McGhee to stay with you, just let me know.'

Chadwick, keen to shift the conversation, asked, 'What do you think will happen to the *Highland Laddie* and *Lassie?*'

'Difficult to know. It depends on what cargo Melnikov and his friends are trying to smuggle and who their backers are inside Russia. If it is military, then it comes down to whether it is an "official" operation sanctioned at a high level, or something rather more entrepreneurial. Even if it is the former, the Russians might be quite brutal in how they shut it down. If it's the latter, and likely to embarrass the Russian government, then God help them.'

'And what do you think it is?'

'I don't know. Probably somewhere in between, like most of these things. We'll probably never know. These things always end up being shrouded in mystery.'

'And the ships?'

'Again, it depends on the cargo. If it is very sensitive, it won't just be the Russians who will want to close it down. If it's military and heading to the Middle East, the Israelis will go after it. I suspect the most likely scenario is that the Russians will intercept and board one or both ships. Then, they'll sail them to some secure location, where the cargo will be unloaded, and both cargo and crew flown back to Russia. *Highland Lassie* is significantly less at risk than *Highland Laddie*. It's not carrying anything sensitive. It's probably safe. It is more difficult to know what they will do with the *Highland Laddie*. If the crew are lucky, they'll be boarded and arrested.'

'And if they are unlucky?'

The Chairman frowned. 'Remember, the *Highland Laddie* is now a ghost ship. It doesn't officially exist. If it were to disappear one dark night, nobody is going to miss it, except its current owners, and they will hardly be able to complain. There are few easier targets for a submarine or a fighter bomber than an undefended, unsuspecting merchant vessel. If it gets attacked at night, nobody will get out - it will go down too fast. No, if I had to choose, I would rather be on the *Highland Lassie* than the *Laddie*.'

'Who do you think Verlaine was working for?'

Spencer wiped his chin with his napkin and refilled their glasses. 'Almost certainly a French government intelligence agency. Probably the DGSE. But given his age, he must be either very senior or an exceptional field agent. Again, you'll probably never know. Men like him never leave any traces. From what you've told me, I would guess that it was Verlaine who got the local police to let you go. I can't think who else it might have been. In any case, I'm almost certain the French authorities will leave you alone. Now that it is over, they'll cover their tracks. I very much doubt they'll even interview you and whatever records they have on you will be destroyed. Verlaine will see to that. They won't want to advertise the fact that a major arms smuggling operation was being run by Russians from France.'

'What will they do to Augustin?'

'Nothing, probably. As far as I can see, he's done nothing wrong – at least as far as this operation is concerned. I am sure that he's not squeaky clean but as regards the smuggling, he is more sinned against than sinning. The fact that Melnikov took out a contract on him is in his favour. And in any case, if they move against Augustin, the whole story will come out. No, I think he's pretty safe - provided the contract hasn't been accepted.'

Several days later, Leclerc walked him to the door of the Sebastopol. Chadwick had never seen him do it before for any of his customers and could see the interest it stirred in the café. Leclerc put his left hand on Chadwick's shoulder and shook his hand. He held the grip for some time. 'Goodbye, my friend. Come back and see us some time.'

'I will,' said Chadwick. 'You can be sure of it.'

'Are you going to the station?' asked Leclerc.

'Not quite yet. I have a visit to make first.'

Leclerc nodded. He stood in the doorway of the café, watching Chadwick until he disappeared.

Chadwick walked past the casino but didn't go in. He had seen Augustin the previous evening. The extra security had gone, the casino was filling with tourists, and Augustin had been in a relaxed mood. He was sitting on one of the sofas, smoking a cigar and drinking brandy as he said, 'You still owe me.'

'For what?'

'For the damage to the door of my shipping office.'

'That wasn't me - that was Soldane - or Andreyev as I suppose we should call him. You forget - I had help for my break in - somebody arranged for me to case the joint.'

Augustin pretended to look appalled. 'You mean it was an inside job? That's terrible. There is corruption everywhere.'

'It goes right to the top.'

'I'm sure. I have heard the owner is a crook.'

'But at least he's alive.'

'Yes. And for that, he is grateful.'

'What happened with the contract?'

'Nothing. It was never taken up. And nobody will take it up now because there is nobody to pay them. They are very commercially minded, these hitmen.' He paused. 'Before I forget, I must give you these.'

He levered himself off the sofa and padded over to far end of the office, to a pile of canvasses, each wrapped in brown paper and tied with a string. He selected two and carried them back. He left them leaning against the side of Chadwick's sofa. He returned to his sofa and sat down with a sigh. 'I cleaned out the house and the studio,' he said. 'She would have wanted you to have something. So, I picked out a couple. I think they are among the better ones, but I am not much of a judge. She had talent, I think. She could have done well, if she had focused on it a bit more. But it's hard to focus when you are born so beautiful. You realise very quickly that you will never need to pay a bill.'

Silje's farmhouse belonged to Augustin. Chadwick was struck by how little he knew of their relationship and how he had overlooked it. Augustin had taken charge of everything. He informed whatever family there was in Norway. He emptied the house and paid her bills. He arranged a memorial service in a private chapel overlooking the end of Cap-Ferrat.

It was a lavish affair – sparsely attended. There was an older couple, who he assumed were the caretakers for the farmhouse, the manager from the dress shop in Nice and one or two others he couldn't place. It hardly mattered. The chapel was so filled with flowers that there was scarcely room for mourners. Sunlight streamed through the side windows, cutting the interior into broad swathes of light and shadow. Music filled every corner, spilling through the open door, into the cemetery and gardens beyond, drifting over the cliff and falling like gentle rain on the beach below.

'I must go,' said Chadwick, getting to his feet.

Augustin stood up. He said, 'You'll forgive me if I don't say goodbye. As I get older, I dislike goodbyes. I would prefer to think that you had never left and that we will see each other soon.'

'I understand,' said Chadwick. 'Thanks for everything. Especially these. They mean a lot to me.'

Augustin dismissed it with a wave of his hand. 'My pleasure,' he said. 'And now, if you don't mind, I must go back to taking money from tourists. It's not good for them. It will only lead them into temptation.'

'You're all heart,' said Chadwick.

Augustin laughed, sat down at his desk, and picked up the phone.

Chadwick made his way down the main stairs and went into the Grand Salon. She was standing by the bar. He walked over to her, the canvasses under his arm. She watched him, an amused look on her face. When he reached her, she said, 'Side entrance?'

'Not today. Today is a front-entrance day.'

'Really? What's special about today?' she asked.

'I'm leaving. I came to say goodbye.'

'That's good. I might be able to hold onto my job now.'

'I thought you would be sorry to see me go.'

'I am, but I have to think of my starving children.'

'Do *they* have names?'

'Only numbers,' she said and laughed.

'I'll miss you,' he said.

She stopped laughing and looked at him. 'I'll miss you too,' she said.

'Will I ever know your name?' he asked.

'No. If I give you my name, you'll remember me in a different way. I don't want that.'

'I understand. I hope we meet again.' He leaned towards her and kissed her on both cheeks. She had the same clean fresh smell that he remembered.

'Goodbye,' she said, and pointing to the canvasses, added: 'And try not to cut off your ear.'

'It'll be hard,' he said and left.

He walked across the seafront. The flowers were blooming, and there was real heat in the sun at last. He took the coast path that he knew so well. They were preparing the pink house for summer. There was a mobile scaffold with two men working from it. The air was thick with the smell of paint and the heavy fragrance of the late-spring blossoms. Everywhere there was the same sense of renewal. He walked into and through St Jean. The harbour was bathed in sunlight. Boats were being opened for the season or were heading out to sea, their white hulls and masts reflected in the blue water. It could not have looked more different than the last time he had seen it, but he gave it barely a glance.

He kept walking, turning left out of town and heading up the hill. The high walls built into the hillside on either side of the steepening road, and the trees that overhung them, blocked the sunlight and it was chilly. When he emerged from the canopy, the sun seemed stronger than ever. To his left, a fence and a set of wooden steps led to the beach where he had first met Verlaine. He turned right, through an ornate metal gate, and up some stone steps. He saw it immediately. The others were tarnished. This shone in the mid-morning sun. He walked towards it. It was a simple brass plate set into the wall. It said:

Silje
The sunlight on the garden
Hardens and grows cold,
We cannot cage the minute
Within its nets of gold;
When all is told
We cannot beg for pardon.

...

And not expecting pardon,
Hardened in heart anew,
But glad to have sat under
Thunder and rain with you,
And grateful too
For sunlight on the garden.

Louis MacNeice

Augustin was full of surprises.

ABOUT THE AUTHORS

 Working initially as a model, **Luna de Casanova** is a recognised commentator on both fashion and style. Born in Spain and educated in Madrid and Paris, she has travelled extensively, and has lived in France, Hong Kong, the UK and the US.

 **Robin Mackie** advises both financial and non-financial companies on strategy and corporate finance. Born in Ayrshire, Scotland, he has a degree in English from Trinity College, Cambridge and lives in London.

Printed in Dunstable, United Kingdom